REKHA AND THE INEVITABILITY OF LIFE

AARON RANDOLPH

ISBN: 979-8-9889423-4-4
ISBN-13: 979-8-9889423-4-4

This book is for every little girl
who never got to see herself as the hero in a story.

Acknowledgement

This book wouldn't exist without David and Leigh Eddings, whose fantasy novels were formative to me as a kid, and that means I have to thank my father Charles Randolph for introducing me to them. I also have to thank Rekha Shankar for inspiring the name of my protagonist, Meryn Holtslander for inspiring another name, and thanks to both women for being absolute legends. Erin Scabareti and Kristin Farley have cheered me on every step of the way and volunteered themselves to be my unpaid publicists. Beta readers Caroline Orejuela, author Aaron Conners, author-in-training Madi Sarlo, and hopefully-soon-to-be-published author Mat Van Rhoon gave me absolutely invaluable advice and ideas that enriched this story beyond measure. My BFYTW brothers Stevie and Augie for cheering me on and keeping me sane (mostly by driving me crazy). And, of course, my mother, Linda Randolph-Dunbar, who has consistently made me feel like I can do anything.

Chapter 1

Jamie stared down at the knife in his shaking hands. Despite everyone's assurances, it was impossible to mentally prepare himself to kill everyone he loved.

"Respawn timers have been set and double-checked. Same for respawn coordinates." The voice behind him filled his heart, though for the first time in millenia, it did not bring him peace. "Hey. You okay?"

Jamie turned and fully took in the love of his life. She was beautiful, a mahogany-skinned goddess with carefully-braided black hair still wearing the same blue scrubs she'd worn on the day they met, her brown eyes as warm and comforting as ever. He hated admitting weakness to her, though if he'd learned anything in the last seven thousand years, it was that she wouldn't judge him for it. "I don't think I can do this, Meryn."

She wordlessly hugged him, and in an almost ritualistic manner, planted kiss after kiss on his bald head before kissing him gently on the lips. "I know. It's kind of horrific. But we've all done worse things over the past couple of weeks. And this is the only way to make any of it worth it." She lifted his chin up with her hand, forcing him to look into her eyes again. "You can do this. I believe in you."

Not trusting himself to speak, Jamie grimly nodded. Meryn flashed him a smile and took his free hand, leading him back to the cave's main chamber. Inside were seven stone slabs, all large enough for a person to lay on, six arranged in a semi-circle, all pointing at the seventh, which ran lengthwise and sat just opposite the cave's entrance. Four of the six slabs were already occupied, as Mai, Ethan, Victoria, and Cris lay patiently waiting.

Alera stood by the fifth slab, her ice-blue left eye and warm green right eye both twinkling as she looked up at Meryn and Jamie. "Just triple-checked everything. Respawn is in less than an hour. I'd say it's now or never." She looked up at Jamie in particular. "You've got the commands memorized, right?"

This was the only thing he felt certain about, so he nodded and said, "Been drillin' 'em for three days straight."

"Good. We're in uncharted territory here. We have no idea what's going to appear when we respawn. It could fail, in which case all six of us will just come right back. It could just be one of us. It could be some weird hybrid homunculus thing."

Victoria complained, "Please stop with the homunculus theory, we are not going to become some human-octopus thing."

Cris, Mai, and Ethan chuckled as Alera stammered, "Y-you don't know! It could happen!" She turned back to Jamie. "Whoever or whatever it is, it's likely that they'll be very confused about what's happening. All you have to do is guide them to the endgame and instruct them to put the commands into the terminal. Should take no more than a week or two."

Jamie tried to force a confidence he didn't really feel into his voice. "I got it."

She winked at him. "Let's do this!"

As Alera lay herself down on the fifth slab, Meryn led Jamie, still trembling, over to the first slab where Mai lay watching them curiously. "Jamie, you sure about this? You look like a turkey on the day before Thanksgiving, doll."

Jamie swallowed heavily and lied, "I'm ready."

Mai took his free hand with her left even as Meryn moved to the opposite side of the slab to take Mai's right hand in hers. "It's alright. It's just a simulation. I'll see y'all in a few minutes." As Meryn gazed at him and nodded, Mai added, "I'm ready."

He slowly, hesitantly raised the knife and placed it against her neck. Tears immediately filled his eyes. "I love you, Mai."

She squeezed his hand. "I love you, too. Go ahead. Do it."

Jamie looked at Meryn, steeled himself, and quickly slit Mai's throat.

He cried and firmly squeezed her hand as she gurgled and choked, her lifeblood spilling freely. Meryn gently stroked Mai's hair and quietly whispered, "It's okay, sweetheart. It'll be over soon."

Jamie's tears fell and mingled with Mai's blood as he whispered, "I'm so sorry!"

After a moment, her gurgling ceased and she fell quiet. After a few seconds longer, her hand went limp. Meryn reached across to cradle Jamie's face, then took Mai's other hand from him and folded them over their dead friend's chest.

One by one, Meryn and Jamie went to each slab, took their friends' hands, told them they loved them, slit their throats, and tried to comfort them as they died. Jamie cried the entire time, no matter how much his friends insisted that it was okay and that they'd be together again soon. He'd hoped it would get easier, that he would become numb to the grisly business. But the reality was that it got harder and harder to watch his loves slip away at his hands — and he knew the hardest of all was still coming.

As he watched the light drain from Alera's beautiful mismatched eyes, and Meryn gently closed them for her, the two of them were alone, and the silence was cacophanous.

Jamie begged, "Stay with me. Please."

Her tone reflected understanding tinged with sadness. "I can't."

"If it'll work with six, then it should work with five!"

"We made a promise."

Jamie broke down, sobbing, as he collapsed against the last slab in the semi-circle. "Please...I can't stay here all by myself."

Meryn gingerly knelt down next to him and took him into her arms, cradling his head against her chest as his tears turned the front of her scrubs a slightly darker blue. "My love, my whole world, you won't be alone. Even if I don't come back...you know I'll always be with you."

He gazed at her through the tears. "'Til the end of time."

"Exactly." She helped him stand, and kissed him for a long moment. She touched his face as tears began to well in her eyes. "My beautiful boy. I know we've asked a lot of you, but I wouldn't ask if I thought you weren't strong enough."

She sat on the slab, and lay herself down on it, her eyes never leaving Jamie's face. He knelt at her side, the bloody knife in his right hand burning a hole in his soul.

Meryn took his free hand in both of hers and she just looked at him for a moment. "Oh, what the hell, one more for the road?" And she grabbed his head and pulled him in close, kissing him intensely. When she at long last broke off the kiss, Jamie felt nothing but bitter regret. She reclaimed his free hand.

"I'm ready."

He stared at her for what felt like ages.

"I'm not."

She smiled gently at him. "I know. But we're running out of time. It's easy, love, here —"

She removed her right hand from Jamie's free hand, and softly clasped his knife hand, guiding the blade gently to the edge of her neck.

Jamie's dread manifested as a lump in his throat so big, he was barely able to eke out the words, "Meryn, I—"

Her eyes radiated sorrow. "And then you just—"

She sharply pulled the knife across her throat, cutting deep.

"NO!" Jamie yelled as the blood started to flow. "OH, GOD!"

He struggled to free himself so he could help her, but Meryn's grip was like iron even as she was asphyxiating, though her eyes carried nothing but love and sadness.

"Meryn don't leave me please please please — "

He froze as she started to mouth something.

"My...beautiful..."

She lost her grip, and her arms fell uselessly to her sides. But even in death, her eyes did not leave his face.

Jamie wailed in absolute despair, and threw the knife as hard as he could to the other side of the chamber, where it hit the stone wall and floor with a clatter. He clutched her body, howling, and cried. He climbed onto the slab with her and lay next to her dead body, murmuring the word "no" over and over again.

He was truly and awfully alone.

Time lost all meaning. Every second felt like years. Ice ran through his veins, collected in his stomach until finally he couldn't bear it any longer, turned away from Meryn's corpse and violently retched and heaved, emptying his stomach contents onto the stone floor of the cavern.

He stared at the pile of vomit for a long time. He wasn't thinking, thought was impossible. He was a shell, providing empty reactions to empty actions, and the only certainty now was that he would never be full again.

Jamie stood, bleary-eyed and shaky as he looked across the chamber at the bodies of the only people he'd spent time with for millenia, and he quickly turned, unable to handle even an iota of incoming emotion. He stumbled away from the slabs and towards one of the back chambers, away from anything resembling feelings.

In the empty chamber, Jamie's legs gave out, and he went down hard on his hands and knees. He registered the pain but ignored it, turning his body over to sit on the cold stone floor. He sat, stock-still, and stared at the blank wall. How much time passed, he would never be able to discern. It was just him, the empty cave, and brutal silence.

Until the most unexpected noise broke that silence - a baby's cry.

Jamie didn't react to it at first. The baby's cries continued to echo through the cavern for a while before he could summon the cognitive power to recognize what it was he was hearing. And he allowed himself to feel confusion.

He stood up, and walked on unsteady legs towards the sound, entering the main chamber. His friends' corpses were gone, vanished. Even the blood had disappeared, leaving the six stone slabs as clean as they had ever been. Atop the seventh slab rested the source of the new noises.

A baby with rich copper skin and just a single wisp of jet black hair lay swaddled in a pink blanket, squalling away.

As Jamie tried to grasp what had just happened, she looked at him with eyes like little black marbles, and she quieted as she took him in. And the horror of what he would now be forced to do hit him.

They both screamed, their voices raised in fear and anguish echoing throughout the cave.

Chapter 2

Her first memories were of Lucky.

He was a large, oafish man with flaming red hair and a matching mustache and goatee that he made an effort to keep trimmed. He had bright blue eyes and a big hooked beak of a nose, and while Rekha found him quite scary as a child, he was also very protective of her, and his hugs and smiles were always warm.

The homestead she shared with Lucky was small but cozy, consisting of two small bedrooms and the main room, which included a fireplace and chimney made of stone, a simple table with two chairs, a standing pantry, a hatch in the corner leading down to the larder, and the front door. Lucky had built the house himself in his younger years, and he was inordinately proud of it.

When she was very young, Lucky gave her a stuffed animal for a birthday present. It was kind of a misshapen lump with a silly grin, but she had loved it ceaselessly, carrying it everywhere she went. Unfortunately, there were a number of arguments as he insisted it was a bunny rabbit, when to her eyes it very clearly resembled an emaciated bear. She was an obedient child, though, so she deferred to his judgment and named the toy Bunyo.

Rekha was ever curious, always sticking her nose where it didn't belong and taking apart Lucky's things to see how they worked, but fortunately for Lucky, she was also smart and capable, and she usually successfully put his things back together again. Bunyo was the lone exception to this rule - she would never harm him. Though her love was enough to change his shape ever so slightly that as she got older, Bunyo took on a more worried look, and she, in response, would be even more protective of him.

She was always spending her time with three other children, Varian, a slight blonde boy, Dargen, a tall boy with ginger hair, and Dargen's sister Irynn, who frequently wore her red hair in braids. The four of them were inseparable, and got into trouble as often as not - but their bond was solidified one sunny afternoon when they'd all climbed the tree in Lucky's backyard.

They were sitting together on a thick branch, telling stories and making each other laugh. One of Varian's stories tickled Irynn so much that she lost her balance and started to fall backwards out of the tree. Rekha reacted instantly, locking her legs around the branch even as she threw herself backwards, shooting her hand out to catch Irynn by the foot in the nick of time. Irynn's cries alerted Lucky, who emerged from the house and started running for the tree, even as Varian grabbed Irynn's other foot, and Dargen jumped down from the tree. Dargen caught Irynn's torso and held her up until Lucky arrived to get everyone down safely. Lucky admonished the older children and brought the shaken Irynn inside, giving her milk and sweetmeats until her crying subsided while her friends looked on anxiously.

From that point on, Rekha appeared to have learned a lesson. She practiced good common sense, staying away from dangerous things and places, and often keeping her friends out of trouble besides. Still, no child is immune to accidents, and Lucky occasionally had to whip up a poultice for scrapes and bruises, taking her to the town midwife for the occasional illness, and on one occasion when she'd tripped over a tree root while running, took her on a two-day trip by wagon to Cloydun to see the closest healer who could mend her arm.

One night, when she was eight or nine years old, as she was drowsing in her chair by the fire, Rekha looked up at Lucky and asked a question that was increasingly necessary. "Uncle Lucky, are you really my uncle?"

He kept stoking the fire. "Somebody been carryin' tales or summat?"

"Varian says he's never seen a family with different color skin."

He snorted. "Varian needs tae get out more." Lucky set the poker back in its stand and took a long look at her. "Maybe yer old enough after all. Gimme yer hand."

Rekha went from drowsy to fully alert instantly as she sat up and extended her hand. As Lucky knelt down in front of Rekha, her slender brown fingers were quickly engulfed by his massive pink hand's grip, squeezing her hand gently, before uncharacteristically raising her hand to his lips and kissing it.

"Rekha, love, I'm so sorry. I've got nae idea who yer parents are."

She slumped a little in her seat and her eyes started to water. *My parents didn't want me?*

"An old man I've nae seen before or since came to me door with a basket and said I had tae take care of ye. An' I argued with 'im, and he just said I was made fer this." Lucky's eyes welled up. "An' then he pulled back the blanket, an' I saw yer face. An' I knew. I knew he was right."

Rekha looked into Lucky's loving gaze, at a total loss for words.

"So ye see, it dinnae matter whether you're me blood. I wanted ye to be me own. So ye can call me 'Papa' or 'Uncle' or 'Lucky', an' I'm still gonna love ye and protect ye like me own daughter, lass."

Rekha impulsively hugged Lucky and cried. He swept her up into his arms and carried the little girl into her bedroom as the weeping subsided. He lay her down on her bed, pulling the covers up and tucking her in.

"You go to sleep now, girly. An' take nae heed of Varian or anyone else - family's who cares fer ye, and that's that." He turned to go.

"Uncle Lucky! Could you sing me a lullaby, like you used to?"

Lucky turned around with a smile, and got down on one knee next to her bed.

The moon is high now
The day is ending
Better count up
The sheep you're tending
Close your eyes, love
As you're yawning
I will be here
'Til the morning

"Good night, love." He whispered as he turned and left the room.

All thoughts of her parents banished, Rekha fell asleep easily.

Shortly after that night, she started having sleepovers at her friends' homes. She asked Lucky repeatedly to let her invite her friends to their house for a sleepover. "There's nae enough room for two of us - dispel the thought of five!" was Lucky's standard answer.

One day, while eating breakfast together, Rekha did not accept that. "Come on, Uncle Lucky, they can sleep on the floor. And I'll help with the cooking and the cleaning. Please? I don't ask for much, and I really want this."

"'At's true, ye don't." Lucky sighed. "Ye'll take full responsibility fer 'em?"

Her eyes widened with excitement. "Absolutely!"

He stared at her for a moment from across the table. "Very well. Let yer friends know they can stay with us tomorrow night. I'll even whip up a batch o' me famous cookies, what do ye say to that?"

She squealed with delight and ran around the table, giving Lucky a slightly-awkward hug from the side. "Yes! Thank you, Uncle Lucky!"

"Yer welcome, girly - now finish yer breakfast and get tae school."

Rekha's smile was beaming all the way through the walk to the little red house that served as the town's school. It was the only house in town that was painted, and even then Mr. Abersham had had to travel to Cloydun to buy the paint.

Miss Abersham, an austere but kind woman in her thirties, taught all of the town's younger children reading, writing, and arithmetic during the morning sessions, and the older kids learned history, science, and more advanced mathematics during afternoon sessions. Rekha and her friends were all still in the younger class together, but starting next year, Dargen, being one year older, would start attending the afternoon classes instead.

"Alright, class, settle down, please," Miss Abersham commanded as Rekha was taking her seat. Varian looked over at her, and she just grinned and winked at him.

The teacher smiled at the eight students sat neatly at their desks. "We're going to start today with some social studies. For Nedra, Marth, Soren, and Kavi, this is all brand new, but for Dargen, Rekha, Varian, and Irynn, this is more in the nature of a review, so please let the younger children answer first. I'm still going to need you to pay attention, though, and there will be a presentation at the end from both groups."

Dargen audibly groaned, prompting a sharp look from Miss Abersham. He sighed and lay his head on his hands. "Yes, Miss Abersham."

"Good. Now, who among the younger children can tell me - what's the name of our planet?"

Little Nedra, Varian's four-year-old sister, raised her hand. "Primordia?"

"That's correct! And who can tell me the name of the Kingdom we live in?"

Soren, a brown-haired boy with a perpetually congested nose, raised his hand, and Miss Abersham pointed at him. "Da Kingdom of Vaker."

She raised a finger. "That's 'Vakar', but otherwise exactly right. Who is our current king?" She waited a moment, but none of the younger children raised their hands. She looked expectantly at the older children and said, "How about you, Varian?"

Varian answered, "King Vakar VII."

She nodded. "Long live the King."

The children all faithfully repeated, "Long live the King."

"Now, I'm going to split you into two groups, Dargen and the older kids, I want you to put together a short presentation on how our kingdom was founded. I'll work with the younger kids on a presentation on the benefits we've enjoyed since becoming a kingdom. Alright? Okay, class, huddle up, and let's get to work."

As they pushed their desks together, Rekha prepared to give her friends the good news, but Irynn beat her to it. "Alright, Rekha, spill it."

"What?"

"You've been grinning like a fool since you walked in. What happened?"

Rekha's grin grew even wider. "Sleepover at my house tomorrow!"

Irynn squealed with joy even as Dargen raised an eyebrow. "Didn't Lucky say there wasn't enough room?"

"We'll fit. Promise."

"Hey." Mrs. Abersham leered at them from the younger kids' desks. "Work on your presentation, please - you can gab on your own time. You don't want to make King Vakar mad, do you?"

Varian sarcastically drawled, "Wouldn't want that."

It was pretty much unanimous: Rekha's sleepover was a success.

Lucky had prepared a couple of bedrolls, and Rekha, true to her word, had assisted with cleaning the house and helping Lucky prepare dinner for all of them. After they'd eaten, he treated the group to a groaning plate of cookies that the gang practically devoured in minutes.

He put a deck of cards on the table and asked, "Who here knows how to play 'Go Fetch'?"

Everyone except Varian raised their hand. "We don't have a deck of cards at my house."

"It's nae a problem, lad, I'll teach ya." Lucky's head came up suddenly.

"Something wrong, Uncle Lucky?" Rekha asked with concern.

"I think I mighta left me tools outside. Ya know what—" Lucky handed the cards to Rekha, "—teach Varian the game, I'll go an' make sure everythin's squared away." He got up and went to the front door. "Won't be two shakes."

She lazily shuffled the deck as Lucky left the house. "It's a pretty simple game, Varian. Everybody starts with six cards." She started dealing to the four of them. "The goal is to get rid of all your cards."

Irynn had a slight scowl on her face. "Card games again? This is stupid."

Varian reared back comically. "Whoa there - you're usually the first to suggest a game - where'd this come from?"

"I don't know...I just...I'm not in the mood."

Dargen piped up. "Fulgin got into a huge fight with our parents today. Irynn might be reacting to that."

"I guess that might be it. I don't know."

Rekha stopped dealing the cards. "We don't have to play if you don't want."

The front door flew open, hitting the nearby stove with a bang, causing Rekha to spill the cards on the table. Lucky filled the doorway, his face urgent and intense, and there was a strange orange glow behind him.

"Dargen, is anyone in your house?"

"What?"

Lucky practically shouted, "Is anyone home?!"

Dargen shrank back, confused and afraid. "F-Fulgin said he would be out with friends tonight, b-but Mom and Dad should be home."

Lucky grabbed the front door knob. "Stay in the house!" He headed back out, and shut the door behind him.

Irynn asked with a quiver in her voice, "What's happening?"

Varian went to the window and pushed open the heavy shutter, peeking out. Rekha once again spotted that orange glow reflecting off of his face as his eyes grew wide and he shouted, "Holy Esyu! Guys, your house is on fire!"

Dargen stood and ran to the front door, and the rest quickly followed as they all rushed outside. Once Rekha cleared the doorway, her quick pace started to slow as her brain tried to take in what she was seeing.

The entire house was ablaze. Several people were gathered outside, watching helplessly, as several others with buckets, Lucky included, formed a line reaching to the town well.

Next to her, quietly, Irynn said, "Mom? Dad!"

Even as Rekha turned to look, Irynn burst into a sprint, making a beeline for the blaze right behind her older, faster brother. Rekha and Varian quickly followed.

Irynn screamed, "MOM! DAD!" even as some of the nearby adults caught her and her brother and stopped them from running into the house.

Dargen struggled momentarily and shouted for his parents only once before collapsing in tears.

Rekha and Varian could only stare in shock, but Rekha's attention sharply focused on Irynn, whose wails stopped forming words altogether.

The sound of Irynn screaming in horror again and again would haunt Rekha's nightmares for years.

Chapter 3

The funeral was a quiet affair. Rekha had never been to a funeral before and did not care for the experience. Lucky had insisted they wear their finest clothes, and in Rekha's case, that meant donning a brown woolen dress that she'd always found itchy and uncomfortable.

All thoughts of her own comfort vanished when they arrived and she saw the crowd that had gathered, with more still arriving. *The whole town must be coming.*

The grieving youngsters stood next to the caskets. Fulgin, the eldest, was fourteen, but he already had thick red sideburns and a fair amount of stubble. He was only slightly taller than Dargen but not as big, instead he was thin as a rail. He stood cold and stoic, with only a melancholy gleam in his eye as a hint to his real feelings. Dargen was still in the same clothes he'd worn the night prior, but there was an empty, haunted look on his face.

Irynn was destroyed. She was weeping and clinging to the casket. Rekha's heart shattered, seeing the pain of this gentle girl displayed so openly.

The town Elder was a severe-looking man wearing a long robe that probably used to be white, held closed with a simple rope belt, and wore his long graying hair and beard in beaded braids. He spoke of lives built around love, the love they had for each other as well as the love of their children. He spoke of Esyu taking care of them in the afterlife, words meant to be comforting, but Rekha saw no comfort on Irynn's face, she simply cried harder.

Dargen had to gently pry Irynn's hands from the casket before they could be laid to rest, and he gathered her up in a massive bear hug. She clung to him and wept as her parents were lowered into their graves.

Life slowly mutated into a new normal. The townsfolk made sure that Fulgin,

Dargen, and Irynn always had food and a place to sleep while the town carpenter and the lumberjack worked to rebuild their home as quickly as possible. Fulgin helped out where he could, and seeing his capabilities, the carpenter and lumberjack both took him on as an apprentice.

Rekha had unofficially appointed herself Irynn's caretaker. She was endlessly solicitous of Irynn's comfort, always keeping her company and trying to put a smile on her face. Dargen and Varian also deferred to Irynn's wishes to some degree, and when the little girl realized the power she now wielded, she took advantage outrageously. Irynn learned how to cry at the drop of a hat to get her own way, and Rekha bent over backwards to please her.

Despite being the youngest, Irynn became their de facto leader. As the others began to realize they were being manipulated and crying became less effective, her tactics changed. She wheedled, she cajoled, she negotiated, and when all else failed, she withheld her love.

One day, when the two of them were alone together in Irynn's house, she was feeling particularly peckish, and she preyed on Rekha's helpful nature to steal some cookies from Lucky's pantry. "Come on. Please?"

"No, Irynn, you're gonna get me in trouble!"

"Rekha, when have you ever been in trouble? You're such a goody-good all the time."

She instinctively disliked being called that, and a note of uncertainty entered her voice. "No, I'm not..."

"Look, he probably won't even notice. Just run in, grab a bunch of cookies, and bring them over! Then we'll split them and play some games."

"I don't know, Irynn."

She huffed angrily. "Fine. Just go home and be a goody-good then." She crossed her arms and turned her back.

Rekha squirmed uncomfortably. "Alright. Alright."

Irynn turned back around with a wide grin. "Yes! You'll be fine. I'll be here when you get back, okay? We'll eat cookies and tell each other fortunes with my crystal!"

Rekha slunk back home, hoping Lucky would be in the back or out somewhere, but luck was not with her, as he was watering the potted plants out front, and spotted her right away. "Rekha?"

She started guiltily. "Yes?"

"Irynn send ye home early or summat?"

Her mind raced. "No...I just...forgot something."

He looked at her peculiarly, then shrugged. "Well, go on, get it then. It's only a few hours 'til supper."

She quickly ran inside. With her heart pounding, she spied the hatch in the floor leading to the larder, looking up with a touch of panic at all the open shutters on the windows, letting anyone who happened to walk by see what she was doing. *Okay. Breathe. I can do this.*

Rekha ducked down, lifted the hatch, and slipped inside, letting the hatch close behind her. It was dark, but she knew exactly where Lucky kept the cookies - they were in a large can made out of beaten metal that sat on a shelf right next to the hatch. She reached in and grabbed several cookies, putting them in her pocket.

As she exited the larder and glanced at the windows to make sure she was not seen, Rekha stood up and froze. *Wait. I said I forgot something.*

She went to her room and looked around until she spotted what she was looking for. She grabbed Bunyo and tried to figure out a natural way to hold him such that he would cover the bulge in her pocket. She settled on loosely holding him by the neck at her side, and confidently strode back outside.

As she started to head back to Irynn's, Lucky shouted, "Hey!"

Rekha froze and slowly turned to face him, carefully keeping Bunyo in front of her pocket.

"Yer taking Bunyo with you?"

She nodded rapidly. "Irynn wanted to play dolls. Bunyo's the closest thing I have."

He mulled that over, then nodded. "Just make sure ye remember to bring 'im back. I'll be bringin' a load of vegetables to old man Garnswyth's, and then I'll get dinner started. Don't be late, lass."

Rekha nodded gratefully and quickly headed back to Irynn's house.

Irynn squealed and hugged Rekha when she revealed her ill-gotten gains, and they spent the afternoon eating cookies and telling each other made-up fortunes using Irynn's favorite dark blue crystal. *Maybe she was right. Maybe this wasn't worth worrying about after all.*

She learned how wrong she was when she returned home.

The table had been set, and there sat a bowl of soup lightly steaming in front of Rekha's chair, but Lucky was oddly silent as she closed the front door.

"Thanks for letting me take Bunyo," she said as she deposited him on the bed in her room, "we had a lot of fun today."

Lucky raised another spoonful of soup to his lips, but still said nothing.

She missed that danger signal, and returned to the table to sit in her accustomed chair and grabbed her spoon. "I told her, next time, we'll just use her dolls. She's got plenty."

Lucky dropped his spoon into his half-empty bowl. "Stupid."

Rekha stopped. "Sorry?"

"Ye must think me so very stupid."

"What?"

"Was it yer idea, or did she put ye up to it?"

Uh-oh.

Noting her guilty look, Lucky nodded. "Well, I hope ye enjoyed the cookies ye stole, because I won't be makin' 'em again."

"I'm sorry."

He yelled, "SORRY DON'T CUT IT, LASS!"

Rekha froze. Lucky had never raised his voice to her before.

He breathed heavily for a long moment before quietly speaking, "I didnae know how to sew."

Rekha's eyes were glued to Lucky's face.

"For three weeks, I went to see Lady Abersham, so she could teach me to sew. An hour, every day, for three weeks. I wanted ye to have somethin' special, somethin' that belonged to only you. An' I cannae tell ye what it meant that ye loved him."

Rekha wanted to look at Bunyo, but could not tear her eyes away from Lucky.

"Ye lied to me, ye stole from me, and ye covered it up with a gift I worked so hard to give ye. I thought I raised ye to be better than that, but I'm so disappointed, I haven't the words."

Her eyes welling with tears, she struggled to speak. "I...I..."

Lucky got up from the table. "I'm going to bed." And he went to his room and closed the door as Rekha sobbed behind him.

Rekha's teenage years were more difficult. Puberty's not easy on anyone, but Rekha arguably had it worse than most, as Lucky's first reaction to her bloodstained bedsheets was to go running to the town midwife. She was kind enough to explain to both of them what was happening, but she was also unkind enough to gossip about Rekha's 'becoming' to half the town after they'd left. The boundaries of Rekha's mortification were stretched quite a bit for a few weeks, and she found herself reluctant to leave the house.

Lucky took the opportunity to teach her some self-defense he'd picked up in his army days, and Rekha took to it like a duck to water. She relished the feeling of power and self-confidence that washed over her whenever she managed to best Lucky while sparring.

One particularly sunny afternoon, Rekha was practicing sword-fighting with Lucky with wooden sticks, but Lucky's defense was so quick and masterful, she could not land a single hit. In frustration, she threw her stick at a nearby tree.

Lucky raised an eyebrow. "What's the tree done to ya, lass?"

"It's pointless! I can't hit you!"

"Then ya hafta change it up. Come at me in a way I cannae expect. If ya dinnae like the game, dinnae play — it's that simple, lass."

She thought about this for a moment, then retrieved her stick, returned to her position in front of Lucky and assumed a fighting pose. She struck at his right arm, which he blocked with his stick, pushing hers away. He then launched his own overhand strike, aiming for Rekha's head, but she got her own stick up, blocked it, stepped forward and kicked Lucky in the shin. He yelped and dropped his own stick, hopping on one foot and attempting to massage his shin with both hands.

He laughed ruefully as he sat down on a nearby tree trunk. "Well, that's one way to do it."

Rekha nervously held her stick in both hands. "I'm sorry."

"Don't be sorry, lass. You used another weapon at yer disposal - an' resourcefulness could mean the difference between a great fighter an' a dead one."

Winning was a rare occurrence at first for Rekha, but after a few years of regular training and practicing, she'd matched Lucky's skills, and their practice sessions became less and less needful.

It was also around this time that Rekha started paying more attention to Irynn on a physical level. Her body had started changing about the same time that Rekha's had, and Rekha found those changes *fascinating*. Even when all four friends were together, Rekha found her eyes drawn to Irynn's perfectly rounded arms, the gentle swell of her breasts, or her endlessly pretty green eyes.

On another of a long series of sunny afternoons, the group were hanging out in a clearing they'd found in the woods just outside of town. Varian hadn't arrived yet, but Rekha and Irynn were casually chatting while Dargen appeared to be intently inspecting a tree.

Rekha asked, "What are you doing over there, Dargen?"

Irynn added, "Yeah, what are you up to?"

He replied, "Can't I just admire nature? Why do I have to be 'up to' anything?"

Rekha smiled. "Because we *know* you."

Irynn laughed. "Yeah, since when have you ever enjoyed 'admiring nature'?"

Dargen stood up straight. "Sheesh, I feel like I'm in front of a town tribunal. Not that it's any of your business," he turned and grinned evilly, "but I'm looking for spiders."

"What, so you can torture Varian again? Esyu, what IS it with boys being mean for no reason?"

"It's not for no reason...it makes me laugh."

Rekha raised an eyebrow. "Sorry, she meant 'what is it with boys being psychotic'?"

Dargen scoffed. "Come on. It's all in good fun. You know I'd never hurt him."

"Did it never occur to you that scaring him IS hurting him?"

Irynn's tone took on a note of command. "Dargen, stop it."

He sighed. "You girls are no fun at all."

Just then, Rekha heard the sound of someone running and breathing hard. As she turned towards the sound, Varian burst into the clearing.

Breathlessly, he said, "Armored soldiers...in town square...Elder said...get everyone there, quick!"

Rekha looked at the others, their mouths open in astonishment. "We'd better go."

The four of them covered the distance back to town fairly quickly, though they didn't go at a full sprint, sparing Varian from exhaustion. When they arrived in the square, it was lined with townsfolk. The others split off to go join their families, but Rekha couldn't see Lucky in the crowd, and instead kept her eyes on the center of the square, where four men in full armor were having a conversation with the town Elder.

The soldiers' armor was pristine and burnished to a fine shine. Emblazoned dead center of their chestpieces, in blood-red stone that had been polished until it gleamed was a symbol of an eye with a sharp, jagged outline and a pitch black pupil. The same symbol could be seen on the back of their cloaks.

Rekha couldn't hear what the soldiers were saying to the Elder over the sound of the surrounding townsfolk murmuring to each other, but one word kept popping up in the gossip: "Legion."

One soldier's voice did eventually get loud enough for Rekha to hear over the crowd, as he asked the Elder, "Is this everybody?"

The Elder took one last look around the town square and simply nodded.

The soldier took off his helmet, and removed his chainmail coif, revealing greasy-looking black hair, icy blue eyes, a small upturned nose, and thin lips. He shouted, "Ladies and gentlemen!"

The crowd quieted.

He stalked towards the center of the town square. "Ladies and gentlemen of Bromsford, My name is Captain Malvus of the Legion, and I am here today on a matter of utmost importance. There's been a report of a dangerous criminal in the region, and I intend to find him."

He glanced around the town square. "Has anyone here seen or been in contact with Belgam the Mageblade?"

Rekha's eyes popped open as the nearby townsfolk's jaws dropped in astonishment and the buzz of the crowd rose to new heights. Belgam the Mageblade was a legend. Many of the stories she'd heard as a child from her friends and the occasional traveling storyteller delved into his exploits, but they'd all cast him as a hero - a former master of the Magic Academy who'd retired early in order to hunt down the dangerous yai, mages whose magic had spiraled out of control and threatened reality itself.

And while the buzz from the crowd was most astonished that Belgam would be seen anywhere near Bromsford ("Here?!" being the most-oft repeated refrain), Rekha couldn't wrap her brain around something else Captain Malvus had said.

"He's not a criminal!" She'd said without thinking.

Instantly, Captain Malvus's head spun around, and he locked eyes with Rekha. His mouth twisted in a slight smile, but his eyes burned with a dreadful intensity as he approached the teenage girl.

"Well, I suppose you've heard the stories. We all have." He turned to include the town in that statement, before turning back to pierce Rekha with an unsettling gaze yet again. "But you shouldn't believe everything you hear in stories, little girl."

Rekha didn't respond, choosing instead to cross her arms, though she noted with some concern the nearest townsfolk stepping back to distance themselves from her.

Malvus' grin grew wider. "Unless, of course, you have information you'd like to share? The cells in our Citadel are actually quite comfortable, though I'm afraid you'd find interrogation less than pleasant."

To the right, Lucky emerged from the crowd. "No! Ye get away from—"

Before he could take two steps, one of the other soldiers drew their sword and placed it at Lucky's neck. Lucky froze in place as a gasp went up from the crowd.

With a look of dismay, the Elder shouted over the murmur of the townsfolk, "Captain, there's no need for this!"

Captain Malvus turned. "Now, everybody calm down. We're not interested in hurting people, but any information leading to Belgam's arrest will be well rewarded." He looked back at Rekha. "And anyone found to be assisting him in any way will share his guilt - and his sentence."

Just then, a thunderous detonation elicited a gasp from everyone in the square. Everyone looked around for the source, and Rekha couldn't see anything at first, but after a moment, a column of smoke arose from a long way off to the south, in the direction of Cloydun.

The soldier with his sword at Lucky's throat lowered it and shouted, "Captain! The Citadel!"

Malvus grimaced and turned back to Rekha. "Shame. I think I rather like you, you're a rather unusual little girl."

Rekha's eyes hardened. "You're just another bully."

He gave her a quick grin before turning back to the other soldiers. "Get the horses! We ride to the Citadel, double-time!"

As the other soldiers raced off, he turned back to Rekha, walking backwards as he did so. "Next time we meet, I think you'll find it was a mistake to get my attention." And with that, he turned and ran off.

As Lucky rushed in to hug Rekha in relief, and the other townsfolk began to crowd back in around them, Rekha thought that Malvus' last statement was probably the only thing he'd said that was true.

Chapter 4

Life settled back down after the Legion visitation, though interest in the old stories was renewed, and the gang started having imaginary adventures like they did when they were kids, pretending to be Belgam and a team of mages hunting down yai. More than once, Rekha imagined fighting Captain Malvus, in between bouts of thinking about or staring at Irynn.

While Irynn didn't seem to mind Rekha's attention, it was clear that Irynn was more interested in the changes the boys were going through, and that soured Rekha on the boys just a bit, sometimes preferring to stay home rather than listen to Irynn go on about Varian's hair and cheekbones. Though to Rekha's delight, Varian seemed uninterested in Irynn's attention, and Rekha and Varian grew closer as a result.

It was one of those days she'd stayed in that her hand started tingling and wouldn't stop. Rekha massaged it and her arm, but it just kept tingling. Lucky was no help, he just said, "Ye probably slept on it wrong, lass, it'll work itself out," and went back to tending the chickens. *Yes, and by then I'll have been driven mad.*

After an hour or so, Rekha had had enough. She grabbed her wrist with her left hand, and opened her right hand palm upwards. She imagined the tingling as energy leaving her hand and was surprised to feel a jolt in her mind.

A small candle-sized flame appeared, hovering just above her hand.

Rekha gasped and fell backwards, the flame disappearing even before her butt hit the floor. She looked at her hand, but there were no marks. Her hand was weirdly cold, and it still tingled, but Rekha was less concerned with that at the moment.

She stood up, and held out her arm and opened her hand. She concentrated, once again imagining the energy coming out of her hand, and again she felt that peculiar jolt.

A small flame danced merrily in the air above her hand.

Rekha stared at the flame in awe. *Is this what I think it is?!*

The back door creaked open and Lucky walked in. "Damned foxes got in tae the coop again, I'm gonna have a talk with—" He stopped dead as he spotted the flame above Rekha's hand. "What are ye—yer gonna burn yerself, lass!" He swatted the flame, and it vanished.

"No, Uncle!" Rekha searched for the words but simply said, "Look."

For a third time, she summoned a small flame that danced and bobbled in the space above her hand.

Lucky's jaw dropped. "Esyu have mercy." He looked into Rekha's eyes. "Put it away, girly."

Am I in trouble? Rekha closed her hand and the flame disappeared.

Lucky clasped the girl by her arms. "Do ye know what this means?"

She shook her head.

"Yer a mage, Rekha!" Lucky gave her a great big smile and picked her up, laughing, into a big bear hug. He swung her around with glee before putting her down on her floor again and staring off into the distance above her head. "Bromsford's never had a mage before." Lucky looked back into Rekha's eyes. "I'm gonna speak tae Lady Abersham about yer schoolin', see if there's anythin' to be done. An' then I'm gonna tell the Elder, he's just gonna burst!"

Oh, Esyu, not again. "I'm sorry, maybe we don't tell the whole town weird things are happening to Rekha?"

"Make no mistake, lass, we're nae tellin' anyone but them. Last thing ye need's that damn Legion comin' back."

Why would they come back? I thought they were here for Belgam...

Lucky took in the confusion on her face. "Do ye not understand, girly? This is great news! Once ye graduate from the Magic Academy, yer gonna be a higher-class citizen! You'll be able to go anywhere, do anything ye want!"

Her eyes widened.

Lucky put a hand on her shoulder. "An' knowin' ye as I do, yer gonna do great things."

Great things, my ass.

Rekha pulled the bucket through the effluvium at the bottom of the pit under the outhouse, and with an exhalation of disgust, dumped it in the wheelbarrow. It had been six years since Rekha had learned she was a mage, and between that and being two months from her eighteenth birthday, Rekha had hoped she would no longer be expected to handle certain unpleasant chores, but Lucky disabused her of that notion swiftly.

Taking care not to inhale through her nose or touch any part of her face or clothes, Rekha tossed the wooden bucket into the wheelbarrow and grabbed the handles.

A familiar voice shouted from behind her. "Hey, Rey!"

Rekha grinned as she spun around. While puberty had indeed been kind to Varian, he was still a slight boy for his age, with undeniably pretty, almost feminine features, and he was wearing his usual white shirt open to the chest and tight, form-fitting leather trousers. He also wore a smile from ear to ear.

A passing breeze blew a whiff of fecal matter between them and both smiles dissolved.

"Oh, Esyu!" Varian waved his hand in front of his face. "Wash day, huh?"

Rekha nodded. "Yeah, sorry. It's my turn. I—"

She quickly picked up the wheelbarrow and rolled it a few more steps away before returning to her friend.

Varian said witheringly, "I cannot believe your uncle makes you muck out the outhouse."

"I can't believe you suckered your mom into doing it for you."

Varian's eyes flashed. "Suckered is a strong term. We have an arrangement, I clean and put away the dishes for every meal, and literally anyone else takes care of the outhouse. I'm not a muck boy."

Rekha went to wipe her brow, but caught herself in the nick of time, carefully keeping her hands away from her face. "Yeah, it's not fun. So, did you just come by to rub it in, or is something going on?"

"We're getting together at the clearing later. Dargen says he's gonna try to swipe some honey wine."

Rekha laughed. "Hasn't he learned from the last time?"

"Apparently not. The scars still haven't healed from the thrashing his brother gave him."

"Well, as soon as I'm finished - and bathed - I'll head over."

Varian smiled. "Great, see you there!" He turned to leave, and was a few steps away when he suddenly stopped and turned back around. "Oh, and Rekha?"

She wiped her brow, and cursed when the putrescence assaulted her nostrils. "Yeah?"

"You might want to sprinkle some crushed rose petals in the bathwater. Just sayin'." He waved his hand in front of his nose and strolled away.

After Rekha had returned the wheelbarrow and the shovel to the shed, she heated up some water over the fireplace, filled the shallow washbasin behind the house, took Varian's advice and added quite a few crushed rose petals, and luxuriated in her bath for quite some time. *Always feel like I could spend a week in here after cleaning the outhouse.*

When she finally finished, Rekha got dressed in her favorite outfit, a tight-fitting leather vest that left her arms bare, brown cotton pants tightened around her waist via drawstring, and soft leather boots. She pulled a comb through her hair and checked herself in the mirror before heading out.

As per usual, she could hear her friends before reaching the clearing. They seemed to be engaging in something causing raucous laughter. She heard Dargen say, "Wait, wait, let me try again!" Curious, Rekha ran to the clearing.

She cleared the tree line to see Varian leaning against a tree with a smile on his face, and Dargen standing in the center in a simple green tunic and plain trousers, red-faced, holding one hand out, palm forward. Irynn was standing a few feet behind him in a green peasant dress with her arms folded and a smirk on her face.

Rekha said, "What is—"

Varian and Irynn both waved her off, with Varian adding, "Wait for it."

Bemused, Rekha watched as Dargen strained with effort.

"HeeeeyyyyYYYYAAARGH!"

The moment his shout ended, all of them heard a tiny, squeaky fart.

Laughter immediately burst out of the group, even as Irynn judiciously took a few more steps backwards and Dargen attempted to catch his breath. He was now the tallest boy in town, and was frequently seen "walking out" with this girl or that, given his rugged good looks and muscular physique. Irynn was frequently in braids or pigtails, and today she'd opted for both, with her ginger locks setting off what Rekha thought of as the prettiest green eyes.

As his laughter wound down, Varian opined, "Sorry, Darg, I don't think you'll ever be a mage."

Irynn laughed, "Pretty sure they don't cast their spells from their backside."

Rekha scoffed. "Might as well do."

Varian stood up straight. "What do you mean?"

"It's been six years. I'm turning eighteen in two days, I'll be heading to the Magic Academy in three months, and all I've ever figured out how to do is this."

Rekha held her palm up and summoned a small, hovering flame, like she'd done a thousand times before. *Although I still don't understand why it makes my hand cold instead of hot.*

While Irynn looked on with awe, Varian shrugged. "It's still more than I can do, Rey. And even Belgam had to go to the Magic Academy."

Dargen had gotten his breath back. "I just want to know why you can do it and I can't."

Rekha closed her hand around the flame, and when she opened it again, the flame had vanished. "If I could give it to you, I would. About all it's good for is lighting candles and toasting bread. Speaking of toasting, I seem to recall hearing somebody was gonna swipe some honey wine."

Dargen slyly smiled and pulled a flask from inside his shirt. "You want a toast?" He held up the flask like a wine glass as a serious expression crossed his face. "Here's to Rekha, a great friend who's gonna save the world someday."

As Dargen drank, Varian said, "Hear, hear!"

Rekha abashedly replied, "Come on, you guys..."

"No, I was saying give it here, here, so I can have a drink."

The gang laughed as Dargen handed the flask to Varian.

"You could do it, though..." Irynn mused.

Rekha raised an eyebrow. "Do what?"

"Save the world."

"I appreciate your confidence in me, girly, but my powers aren't strong enough to save myself, let alone the world."

Irynn's eyes widened. "Then all we have to do is strengthen your powers."

"Irynn, what do you think I've been trying to do for six years?"

"Yeah, but have you tried it with the Irynn method?"

Varian held up a finger. "I wouldn't, the last Irynn method attempt produced a fart, and you've been around enough of that smell for one day, Rey."

Rekha smirked at him. "Oh, ha, ha."

Irynn was insistent. "You described it as feeling tingly and pushing that tingly energy out, right? Well, try building up that tingly feeling until you're tingling all over your body, and when you can't stand it anymore, push it all out at once!" She took a couple of steps closer to Rekha. "Come on. Try it. Please?"

Rekha realized all eyes were upon her, and caught between that and her difficulty saying no to Irynn, she gave up and sighed. "Alright, but prepare yourselves for disappointment."

She spotted a tree at the other end of the clearing and held a hand up to face it. *It's not going to work. This never works.*

Rekha seized on that frustration, and the emotion added fuel to her resolve. She imagined pulling every ounce of heat she could muster from every nearby source and concentrated harder than she ever had in her life. She felt her own body go cold, and Irynn's jaw dropped even as Dargen's smirk faded from his face.

When the feeling started to overwhelm her, Rekha pointed a single finger square at the middle of the tree and screamed, "BURN!"

A tiny flame appeared at the end of Rekha's finger and slowly started floating towards the tree, dancing happily as it went.

Rekha collapsed to the ground even as the others started laughing. She stared at the flame in disbelief. *I could swear for a moment there it was going to be different this time.*

Dargen scoffed. "So much for the Irynn method." His sister responded by sticking her tongue out at him.

Varian walked over and extended a hand to Rekha. "Well, I'd say that beats a fart."

As he picked her up off the ground, Rekha shivered. *I'm still cold all over, what is this?*

"You're trembling." Varian's face had taken on a concerned cast. "Are you alright? Do you need anything? My house isn't far."

"I...I don't know. I feel...weird. And cold."

"You might have caught something. Well, listen, I'm gonna run to grab my guitar anyway, maybe I should grab you a blanket while I'm at it. Do you need anything else?"

Rekha smiled at him. "No, no need, I'll be fine in a minute, I think."

Varian added, "I'll be right back, okay?"

As Varian jogged off, Dargen walked towards her. "Hey, Rekha, don't sweat it. I know how much it bothers you, but I'm sure you'll start getting stronger once you start going to the Academy."

Irynn pointed at the flame, still merrily bobbling towards the tree. "Hey, guys? What should we do about that?"

Dargen shrugged. "I doubt it's big enough to cause a forest fire, but we probably shouldn't take any chances. Snuff it."

As Irynn reached out to the flame, Rekha was consumed by a horrible dread.

She rushed towards Irynn and screamed, "IRYNN DON'T—"

Irynn's hand closed around the flame.

The resulting explosion blew Rekha several feet backwards through the air. Her back and head slammed against a tree, and she slumped to the ground.

Woozy, Rekha looked up to see Irynn across the clearing. Most of her right arm was gone, and the rest of her was engulfed in flame, screaming.

Dargen, also having been knocked off his feet in the explosion, sat up in horror and screamed. He got up and disappeared into the woods, screaming the whole way.

Rekha stared uncomprehending as Irynn cast this way and that before slowly collapsing in the middle of the clearing. She stopped screaming, but she continued to burn.

Rekha knew she should do something but she just couldn't think properly for some reason. After a few seconds, her eyes rolled back and she blacked out.

Chapter 5

There was only black, inky nothing. She could hear voices that seemed so far away as to be little more than whispers. Rekha floated, calmly curious.

A tiny mote of light appeared, far in the distance, and Rekha focused on it for a moment, and then it vanished.

The voices sounded a little louder, and she could tell that they weren't whispering, but Rekha still couldn't make them out.

The light returned, and looking at it, Rekha noticed it was more of a line than a dot before it disappeared again.

Again the voices loudened, and again, Rekha could not discern individual words.

The white pillar of light reappeared, much closer this time, and Rekha realized it was moving towards her incredibly quickly between appearances.

The voices clashed loudly, and Rekha thought she recognized some of the words. She shouted, "I can't understand you!" The voices continued to overlap, but she could only just make out one of them, a feminine voice, saying, "Be calm."

Suddenly, bright white light was all she could see.

Rekha awoke with a terrified gasp, and instantly sat up, breathing quickly in near-panic.

Immediately, Lucky was there at her side, putting his arm around her. "I'm here, girly."

She looked at him with horror in her eyes. "I..I saw..."

As she reached for the words, Lucky held up a finger to her lips. "Shhh. Be calm, lass."

Those words again!

She threw him a confused look before seeing an unfamiliar wall behind Lucky. She quickly looked around at the sparse wooden walls, and the small, plain bed she'd been sleeping in. "Where am I?"

"Elder's house."

Everything came rushing back. "Oh, Esyu — Irynn!"

Lucky's voice wobbled. "I'm sorry, love. Irynn's dead."

Rekha shuddered, tears running down her cheeks. She hadn't wanted to think of Irynn, didn't want to remember. But now the memories came flooding back like a tidal wave—memories of playing together in the village square, of sipping tea at Elder's house and stealing cookies from Lucky's stash in the larder. Most of all, Rekha could see Irynn's smiling face throughout it all—but that was violently torn asunder by the memory of Irynn consumed by fire.

A fire Rekha had created.

The horror and enormity of it hit her like a great hammer and she doubled over in grief, sobbing uncontrollably. "I...I killed Irynn..." she gasped between sobs, clinging desperately to Lucky for comfort as he held her tightly.

And as Rekha sobbed and wailed, he did not let go.

Rain had begun to pelt the wooden shutters covering the nearby window by the time Rekha's personal storm of weeping had subsided.

"Are...are the others okay?"

Lucky shrugged. "After the explosion, I gather Dargen bolted straight back tae town tae git help. Varian ran back tae the clearing, found ye, an' carried ye here."

Rekha's eyes widened. "He ran *towards* the explosion?"

"Aye. Varian an' I've not always seen eye-to-eye, but he's a ruddy hero in my eyes."

Rekha struggled to reconcile Varian's newfound bravery with the image she had in her head of the slight boy who was always afraid of spiders.

The two sat in silence for a moment, as the rain continued to hammer the window shutters, until there was a soft knock at the room's only door.

Lucky half-turned in his seat by the bed. "She's awake, Elder, come in."

The door opened with a sustained creak, and the Elder swept into the room. He was wearing his usual robe and braids and his eyes were as kind as ever.

"Esyu be praised. How is little Rekha?" asked the Elder.

"You could try asking me yourself." Rekha was mildly irritated that the Elder STILL referred to her as 'Little Rekha.' *He'll probably still be calling me that when I'm old and grey.*

The Elder bowed slightly. "That was a little condescending, wasn't it? I apologize. To say today's events have flustered me somewhat is an understatement, but I shouldn't forget my manners."

"Did the fire get put out?" Lucky asked.

"We put together a bucket brigade, but it was just a small grass fire. And Mr. Abersham kindly volunteered to bring Irynn back to her family for proper burial."

Rekha closed her eyes as they threatened to moisten again. "So it's true, then. Irynn really is dead."

The Elder's face darkened. "Yes, child. Which brings us to another problem: what to do with you."

"There's plenty of rope around."

Everyone turned to the doorway to see a tall man with a lean, whip-like figure, wearing a simple rain-slicked leather vest and trousers, and even though she'd only seen him a few times before, Rekha instantly recognized Dargen and Irynn's older brother, Fulgin. He now wore his red hair quite different from his younger sibling, trimmed short with mutton chops.

He continued, "Let's string her up. That's the punishment for murder, ain't it?"

As Rekha's jaw dropped, Lucky said, "Ye cannae be serious!"

Fulgin gave Lucky a hate-filled look. "My sister burned to death today, I think you'll find I'm incapable of joking right now."

The Elder held up a hand. "I'm afraid it's not so simple. Your own brother said it was an accident."

"Dargen doesn't speak for this family, I do, and I want that *yai* charged for murder."

Rekha reeled back. According to the stories, yai were mages whose powers were out of control, causing great calamities and bending reality itself, and they were typically killed as soon as they were discovered. In fact, Belgam the Mageblade had become famous through his astonishing success at hunting down and eliminating escaped yai.

Fulgin continued, "Don't look so surprised. You know what she is. And you know what she's capable of. We could all be next if you don't have her swinging from the gallows by midnight."

Rekha found her voice. "I didn't mean to hurt—I tried to save her!"

His eyes blazed as he shouted, "WITH FIRE?!? I'LL—"

Lightning-fast, Fulgin lunged at Rekha, hands outstretched, but the Elder and Lucky caught him and pushed him back towards the door. The three men struggled for a moment, but Lucky and the Elder were too strong for Fulgin, and they shoved him back through the doorway.

As Fulgin regained his balance, the Elder straightened authoritatively. "The town will decide her fate, not you, Fulgin."

He showed no sign he'd even heard. Fulgin's baleful eyes had never left Rekha's face. "I *will* see you hang. I promise you that." He stepped back, turned, and left.

As the shock of the moment passed and the Elder and Lucky stared at each other, Rekha's eyes filled with tears again. "It WAS an accident — I swear it! I never wanted any of this to happen."

Lucky sat back down and put his arm around her as the Elder held a hand up. "I believe you. Dargen and Varian have both said that they all goaded you into trying to do something powerful and that it was even Irynn's idea, but unfortunately, it's out of my hands."

She turned her tear-stained face to meet Lucky's concerned gaze. "Uncle Lucky, what if I AM a yai?"

"Then we'll deal with it, love." He put a huge hand on the side of her face, gently cradling her head. "Like we always have."

She leaned forward and hugged Lucky once more before sitting back on the bed. As she wiped her tears from her eyes and sniffed, she asked quietly, "So, uh, what happens now?"

The Elder sighed. "Well, for tonight, you might want to stay somewhere safe. I've never seen Fulgin like this, so I don't know what he might do."

Lucky nodded his head. "He'd be making a mistake if he did — but Varian's folks, Arden and Shilo, they've already shored tae put us up." He looked at Rekha. "We can stay there if ya want."

Rekha nodded as the Elder continued, "And tomorrow, at noon, we'll be holding a town tribunal, and once we've heard all the testimony, the town will vote on exile, some other punishment, or the gallows."

"Uh, sorry. I'm afraid none of that will be happening."

As everyone turned to look, a barefoot short-statured old man wearing soft blue robes and utilizing a fancy carved walking stick reached and stood in the doorway. He was bald, thin as a rail, and he had a long, white, unkempt-looking beard and mirthful eyes.

Lucky stood up as his jaw dropped in amazement, and he pointed at the newcomer. "That's him!" He turned back to Rekha. "He's the man who brought ye to mah doorstep as a baby in a wee basket!"

The man bowed extravagantly. "Hiya. My name's Belgam, you might know me better as the Mageblade. And that young woman will be coming with me."

Chapter 6

Rekha was dumbfounded. *This tiny old man is the greatest mage on life? He looks like a solid sneeze would knock him over.*

The Elder appeared to have similar doubts. "Uh, Mr. Belgam, I—"

"Just Belgam, please. Mr. Belgam is my father." The old man smiled with a hint of mischief.

If anything, that response put starch in the Elder's spine. "Sorry, Belgam, but I cannot permit Rekha to leave the village until the town trial is concluded."

The old man's jaw set. "You're a reasonable man. I'm sure you can come up with something."

Suddenly, Rekha felt something very much like the familiar jolt in her mind whenever she summoned a flame, but this felt distant, and it reverberated like it was underwater.

The Elder's frown softened. "Well, there are two witness accounts corroborating the incident to be accidental in nature, so even if the town were to rule against her, the punishment would be exile. If she chooses to leave of her own accord, I suppose that would be amenable."

Belgam smiled. "Great!" He turned to Rekha. "Pack your things."

This is all moving way too fast!

Lucky stood up, "Now just hang on a moment—"

The old man turned to Lucky and smiled. "Yo, Lucky, wasn't it?" He reached inside his robe, and as he did so, Rekha felt another reverberation. Belgam pulled out a sack, shook it lightly, and the contents made a jingling sound. "You've done an excellent job, and I believe this is fair pay for your trouble, sir."

Lucky reached out and took the sack with a suspicious glower, but upon looking inside, his eyes popped and his face turned incredulous. "Holy Esyu! This is more money than ah'd see in fifty years of farming!"

"I'm very appreciative, really." Belgam placed a hand on Lucky's shoulder, and Rekha again felt that distant jolt. "But your services are no longer required."

Lucky grinned. "Nae a problem." He turned to Rekha. "Ye heard the man — pack yer things!"

"What?!" Rekha felt her whole world slipping away from her. "Uncle Lucky, think about this, this is insane—"

"Hold on now, missy." Lucky interrupted. "I'm nae yer uncle, I'm yer lodger, that's all. And I'd take it as a kindness if ye'd be out by midnight. Thanks, lass."

And with that, Lucky turned and walked out of the small bedroom, leaving Rekha speechless as the one person she could always count on completely abandoned her.

Rekha numbly stuffed her clothes into a sack Lucky had given her 'free of charge'. Belgam leaned against the doorway of what used to be her bedroom silently watching while Lucky appeared to be sitting at the dinner table counting his money.

"Yo, I wouldn't be too hard on him, if I were you."

Rekha lashed out with an acidic tone. "I'm not in the habit of taking advice from people who completely destroy my life."

"It's a bit hard to take advice from yourself, don't you think?"

She scoffed. "Esyu. This morning, I was happy and everything made sense, and tonight I've killed Irynn, my only family has turned his back on me, and I'm being kidnapped by the creepiest old man I've ever met."

Belgam stood up straight and faced Rekha directly with a quizzical look. "I'd have a retort, but nothing you've said is technically incorrect." He shook his head. "Regardless, I'm just pointing out that strictly speaking, none of what's happened here is my fault."

Rekha scoffed again, angrily throwing an old toy in the sack.

"In fact, I'd say I'm showing you extreme kindness."

Rekha spun to face him, her eyes blazing. "KINDNESS?!"

Belgam's face had always appeared mischievous and playful until that very moment, as he dropped it for an intensely serious look and crossed to her in two steps. "Yes. Kindness. Have you already forgotten that you are a yai?"

Rekha's fury gave way to deep sorrow as the image of Irynn burning flashed up from her memory.

Belgam's voice plummeted to a harsh whisper so that Lucky wouldn't hear him, "We both know how much he cared for you and would never let you go.

Even now your guilt over your friend overwhelms you, but try to consider what might happen if your powers escape from your grasp and you end up taking the life of the person who loves you the most."

Rekha's mind shuddered away from the thought.

The old man's voice softened. "I changed his memories of you, so as far as he knows, you've only been here a day, and he barely knows you. He will not know the pain of being separated from you and I paid him enough money to retire, if he wants. I think I've been extremely kind."

The despair that enveloped Rekha was threatening to swallow her whole. *I don't have anyone now.*

The voice that emerged from her lips was guttural and small. "You should've just let them hang me."

Belgam tilted his head in confusion. "Why on Primordia would I do that?"

"Because that's what you do to yai — you kill them. You, specifically." She raised her face to look up at the ceiling, displaying her neck as her voice cracked. "I'll make it easy, just do it quickly."

The old man seemed to shudder for a moment before turning away from her, running a hand over his bald scalp with a sorrowful sigh. His voice was quiet when he spoke again, like the whisper of the wind picking up outside the window. "You shouldn't expose your throat like that."

"But I—"

Belgam turned back to face Rekha with surprising intensity in his eyes. "And I'm not going to kill you. Far from it."

She sighed with defeat. "What do you want from me, then? What could I possibly do for you?!"

Belgam smiled and his eyes twinkled as his face filled with mischief once more. "Well, personally, I was hoping you might save the world." He beamed. "Finish up, I'll be outside." And he turned and swept from the room.

Rekha stared after him in utter disbelief.

Rekha had packed her entire life into the sack, and had decided to take one last look around the room before leaving when it occurred to her to check under the bed. She got down on her knees, and leaned over, pulling up the skirt as her eyes scanned the darkness.

In the back corner, she spotted a misshapen lump, and her heart skipped a beat.

Bunyo!

She reached as far back as her arm would go, managing to clip a small piece of the object between her fingertips, pulling it a few inches closer so she could pick it up and pull it out with her whole hand. It was a little dusty, but she blew as much dust off as she could, and brushed even more off with her hands, and her eyes got misty as she looked at its face.

Rekha laughed softly to herself, and hugged Bunyo to her chest as the tears crossed her cheeks. *I may not have Lucky anymore, but I still have his love.*

She packed Bunyo into her sack, tied it shut, and threw it over her shoulder. As she passed Lucky still counting his money in the main room, she raised a hand to him as if to caress his cheek, but thought better of it and put her hand back down.

"Goodbye, Lucky."

He finally raised his head. "Yes, goodbye, lass. Thanks fer stayin'!"

She turned away and kept her voice steady. "No, thank you."

She opened the front door and quietly left the only home she'd ever known.

Chapter 7

"So," Rekha said, stepping off the stoop and putting an edge in her voice, "how am I going to save the world, exactly, old man?"

Belgam smiled. "Oh, there'll be thrilling adventures, heroic feats, you know, the usual stuff." He turned and started walking towards the trees.

"No, I meant...wait, where are we going?"

"My cave."

Rekha dropped her sack to the ground. "I am NOT going to some cave with a creepy old man!"

Belgam kept walking, though he did start speaking more loudly. "I think you'll find you are, actually, and if we move right along, we can get you settled in before midnight. It's just a short way through the Wanderer's Forest."

Rekha folded her arms. "I said, I'm not going."

Belgam was almost at the tree line. "Personally, I'm amazed that it's been over an hour since you learned I dropped you off with Lucky as a baby, and you haven't asked me a single question about your parents." And with that, he vanished into the shadows.

Rekha's mouth dropped open for a moment before she hurriedly picked up her sack, slung it over her shoulder, and jogged into the trees to catch up.

She found Belgam leaning against a tree, wearing a huge, knowing grin. "Yeeeesssss?" He asked.

Rekha glared at him. "My Esyu, I think I hate you."

"Well, in that case, I've got a great idea. I'll answer one question about your parents for every time you hit me." He punctuated this statement by leaning his walking stick against the tree, and stepping into the dead center of the trail.

Rekha instantly reacted, lashing out with her left foot, but he nimbly sidestepped it to her right. Dropping her sack to the forest floor, she threw a right straight punch at his face, but he smoothly spun further to her right. *He certainly doesn't MOVE like an old man. What in the Abyss is going on here?*

He smiled at her. "Surely you can hit a decrepit old—"

Rekha feinted with her left fist and tried to spin kick his lead leg in the knee, but he merely lifted his leg off the ground, holding it straight out, parallel to the ground. She reversed the spin and followed with a right roundhouse punch to the face, but Belgam bent backwards under it, keeping his lead leg elevated and balancing precariously on his rear leg. Laughing with triumph, Rekha spun a third time and attempted to sweep the back leg, but the old man flexed and jumped off his back leg over the sweep and into a handstand.

Rekha looked at the old man with dismay. Belgam merely winked at her — and then his long beard fell in front of his eyes.

She took the opportunity to launch a right front kick at his midsection, but he simply let himself fall backwards to the forest floor. With her right leg still in the air, she extended the front kick into a stomp aimed at his head, but he was already rolling to her left. Once clear of her stomp, Belgam smoothly got to his feet, and ignoring her furious glare, extended a single hand and beckoned her to come at him.

Rekha screeched and launched a furious all-out assault on the old man, but no matter what she tried or what part of him she tried to hit, he simply wasn't there anymore. Her attacks eventually devolved into screaming obscenities and throwing simple, repeated slaps and jabs, and Belgam no longer bothered to get out of the way, choosing instead to gently deflect her increasingly weaker blows with his hands.

She whimpered with tears in her eyes, still clawing at him, "Just....just do it. Just...kill me."

At this, Belgam grabbed her wrists with both hands. "That's not going to happen."

"I'm a monster! I killed Irynn!"

"And if you truly loved her, don't you owe it to her to keep going, despite the pain? And maybe even prove her right about you?"

Rekha's eyes snapped open.

"What happened to Irynn was a tragedy. Your death would just compound that tragedy, causing more pain and misery. If you really want to make things better, that means taking responsibility, not running away from it." Belgam released her arms and strolled over to grab his walking stick.

Rekha seethed. "How do you know what she said about me?"

He turned back to face her. "Because I've been watching over you your whole life, yo. As I promised your parents I would."

As he turned to leave, Rekha looked down at the forest floor, searching for the words, but she found only one. "Please."

Belgam stopped. "What?"

She looked at him with pleading eyes. "Please?"

He sighed, looked at Rekha for a long moment, and then set his shoulders. "Fine. If it'll help, and get us back on the road, so to speak," Belgam set his walking stick down, "then I'll let you hit me. Just once, mind."

Rekha scoffed, "That's not what I—"

"Ah-ah-ah! Remember our deal? Go ahead and hit me, and I'll tell you something about your parents."

"And you won't cheat this time?"

Belgam became indignant. "How dare you? I was teaching you a lesson."

"Was that lesson that dirty old men are cheaters, by any chance?"

His eyes flared. "I was teaching you that no one can ever hurt you unless you let them."

Rekha was confused. "Do you mean...are you going to teach me how to move like that?"

"Among other things, yes. Now, give me your best shot. I've earned this." Belgam steeled his jaw and tensed his muscles.

Rekha thought a moment, then wound up and kicked Belgam hard in the groin.

"OOF!" He collapsed to the dirt and spoke in a high-pitched squeal. "I'm an old man, why would you do that?!"

She tilted her head and smiled. "And my parents?"

The old man got to his feet and threw Rekha a bitter look. "Wouldn't be particularly proud of that move." He sighed. "Your parents were some of the finest people I've ever known. And my absolute best friends." Belgam looked away and raised a bemused eyebrow. "Technically, they were my *only* friends."

Rekha spread her arms to indicate the empty space around her. "Here I stand, with all of my surprise."

"They were courageous, loving, and super smart. I loved them ferociously."

Her throat felt thick. "And you keep using the past tense because...?"

Belgam seemed momentarily distracted by a nearby squirrel chittering at him. "Sorry, yes." He turned to face her with sorrow all over his face. "They were killed."

Rekha started to tear up. "By who?"

"That's a longer story, and we're already late. I'll tell you what - I'll fill you in on the way. You're going to want some time to prepare your room before bed, I suspect, and it's already dark."

Rekha sighed. "Fine. But I want everything." She headed back to grab her sack.

Belgam turned and started walking up the path. "Have you forgotten? The deal was one hit for one detail."

Rekha shouldered the sack. "Then I want a NEW deal!" She stormed up the path after him.

The walk was mostly uphill, but their conversation immediately went in the other direction. After they'd argued pointlessly for perhaps a quarter of an hour, the old man finally changed the subject. "Yo, have you heard of the Legion?"

"Why do you keep saying 'yo'? What does that mean?"

He looked confused. "What? Oh, sorry, it's just like a word to get your attention, like 'hey'."

"Well, it sounds dumb." Rekha ignored his grimace as she wiped her brow. "The Legion came to the village when I was younger. They said you were a dangerous criminal."

Belgam snorted. "To them, I suppose I am. They're cold-blooded murderers barely bothering to masquerade as a political force for change. They've practically declared war against the Magic Academy, and their ultimate goal is to stamp out all magic-kind in Primordia." He cleared his throat. "The Legion began when certain Vakar nobles (who wouldn't know actual nobility if it walked up and introduced itself) took umbrage at the idea that commoners could be born with magic powers instead of them."

Rekha dryly replied, "How dare they."

"For years, they looked for a way to give themselves magic powers. When they failed, they successfully lobbied the king to create an armed militia with wide-ranging powers to quote 'investigate the magic conspiracy'. And ever since then, mages and other magic-kind have been disappearing at an alarming rate."

"Disappearing? How?"

"Violently, is my guess. I've personally found destroyed furniture and traces of blood in the homes of those who've disappeared, and the one time I caught Legion soldiers entertaining themselves, the mage whom they'd dismembered lived just long enough to tell me they laughed as they cut off his arms."

Rekha shivered in horror as she walked, carefully avoiding a large tree root.

"It wasn't always like this, you know? Mages used to be a welcome sight in any city. We'd travel the world and perform good deeds, helping the less fortunate with whatever they needed." Belgam sighed wistfully. "Now the only place we can safely perform our art is at the Magic Academy. And it's just a matter of time before the Legion puts an end to that as well." The old man stopped in his tracks and looked at Rekha until she stopped and looked back at him. "That's why I need your help. I'm hoping you can do what I can't: stop the Legion once and for all, and save the last remnants of a dying people."

The weight of that responsibility was a bit much for Rekha to parse in that instant, so instead she turned away and changed the subject. "And my parents were mages?"

"They were. Powerful mages."

"As powerful as you?"

He sighed again. "They would have been, had they lived. Instead, only I survived, and made my mark on Primordian history..." He broke off, looking over at Rekha. "...though now that I think of it, maybe they have, too."

Rekha frowned. "I doubt it. So far I'm the girl who lit candles and killed her best friend."

"I know it's still fresh in your mind, as it happened just earlier today, but I wouldn't dwell on that."

A squirrel rushed down a nearby tree and chittered at Belgam. To Rekha's surprise, the old man made similar chittering noises back to the creature, who bounded around in a circle before scampering back up the tree.

Before she could react, Belgam pointed up the hill. "The cave's just there. Let's get you settled in, it's nearly midnight."

"Hold on, you can talk to squirrels?"

He wore a befuddled look. "Are you telling me you can't?"

Rekha's eyes narrowed. "You *know* that I can't."

Belgam grinned. "Guilty. I was just having a little fun. Squirrels are surprisingly easy to get along with, and they can be pretty useful besides."

"What, like, telling you where to find walnuts?"

The old man turned around. "Well, for example, they told me that your friend Varian has been following us since I told you about your parents, and —" He pointed a finger. "—he's currently in that bush."

The bush he was pointing at nervously laughed.

Chapter 8

Varian stood up from the bush he'd been hiding in, and one of the branches scratched his hand. "Yowch!" He grasped his hand, making sure it wasn't bleeding. "That's gonna leave a mark."

Rekha dropped her sack and ran full tilt at Varian, ignoring the surprise in his eyes and clasping him firmly in a hug, even as she started to cry.

"Varian, I'm so sorry."

He embraced her. "I know, love. I know."

Belgam cleared his throat. "Hey, Varian! Nice to see you, too, but you could've just walked up and said hello."

Varian just raised an eyebrow at him.

Rekha finally released the hug, and clasped Varian's arms. "Not that I'm not happy to see you, but what are you doing?"

"Well, we were expecting you to stay with us, and when you didn't show, I wanted to check that you were alright. When I saw you wandering into the woods — at night — with a creepy old man — I thought, yeah, better make sure this is legit."

Belgam sighed. "I really need to do something about my image. I try so hard to come across as friendly and whimsical, but you're the second person tonight to call me creepy. But then, creepy is traditionally used to describe people who aren't physically attractive, so maybe you're the bad person for only caring about my looks."

Rekha deadpanned, "No, your behavior's creepy, too."

Varian turned back to her. "Rekha, who is this weirdo, and where are you going with him? And where in the Abyss is Lucky?"

The mention of Lucky brought her spirits crashing down. "Lucky...isn't my uncle...anymore."

"What? How in the Abyss is that possible?"

She looked over at the old man. "Varian, I have the extremely dubious honor of introducing you to Belgam the Mageblade."

Varian's stared with his mouth agape as Belgam beamed.

Rekha turned back to Varian. "Disappointing, isn't it?"

"So, if I'm understanding everything correctly," Varian summed up with a look of slight consternation, "to avoid the lawful prosecution for the death of Irynn, Belgam the Mageblade erased Lucky's memories and is taking you to a cave to train you to control your powers so that you can save the world?"

Belgam mulled it over. "When you put it like that, it sounds crazy, but I can't come up with another way to put it."

Rekha said, "This...is apparently my life now."

The old man leaned in towards Varian and added, "She left out the part where she's asked me to kill her twice tonight. I'd appreciate if you'd help dispel that notion, yo."

"WHAT?!"

Rekha sighed. "You didn't have to tell him that."

Varian was outraged. "Are you OUT of your MIND?!"

"YES! I thought that was obvious!" Rekha shuddered as she faced her best friend. "I killed Irynn. And nothing I can ever do will ever make up for that! And on top of it all, I lost my only family and I'm shackled to this lunatic." She glanced over at Belgam and added sarcastically, "No offense."

"None taken."

Varian put his hands on her shoulders. "Rekha, I can forgive you for taking Irynn away from me, from us." His voice wavered. "If you take my best friend away from me too? I will NEVER forgive you."

She hugged him tightly. "I couldn't bear losing you, either."

Belgam smiled. "Aww."

Rekha scoffed with disgust, released Varian and spun to face the old man. "Dear Esyu, is there ANYTHING you don't know how to ruin?"

A retort died on Belgam's lips as profound sadness seemed to wash over his entire body. He morosely mumbled, "I guess not," before turning and continuing to walk up the hill.

After watching him go for a moment, Varian turned to Rekha. "What is the deal with that guy? He's nothing like the stories."

"I know! He's like a big obnoxious kid in an old man's body until he gets upset or serious and then he becomes incredibly maudlin. And I thought Belgam hunted and killed yais, now all of a sudden, he's training one? I don't get any of it."

"Are you really going to stay with him?"

Rekha suddenly had an unwanted vision of Varian being caught in an explosion of fire. "I don't want to, but he's right. If my powers go berserk again, I'd rather it be him who suffers for it than anybody else."

Varian nodded. "Alright. Well, I know where you'll be, I think, he said the cave's just up this hill?"

Rekha nodded in return. "But don't let Fulgin find out. He was pretty out-of-control in the Elder's house."

"I heard. I'll head back and let people know you've left the village. Hopefully, Fulgin will calm down, but from what I've seen, he's beside himself with grief. Dargen's not much better."

Memories of Dargen's disbelieving face upon seeing Irynn ablaze intruded upon Rekha's thoughts. "Dargen...oh, Esyu, how am I ever going to make this up to him?"

Varian shook his head. "I don't know, but I don't think he blames you for it. I know I don't."

Rekha embraced her friend one more time. "You'd better get back. It's gotta be close to midnight. Hug your parents for me, tell them thanks for everything, and I hope this isn't goodbye."

Varian stroked her back with his right hand. "It damn well better not be goodbye." He released the hug and took a step backwards. "I know he seems weird, but Belgam might be the only person who can teach you how to control your powers. If I were you, I'd learn all you can from him - the faster you learn, the faster you can come home." And with that, Varian turned and walked back into the trees.

Rekha arrived at the cave entrance to find Belgam leaning against the rock wall. He gruffly cleared his throat and said, "I thought you were going to chat all night." He gestured towards the entrance. "Shall we?"

Rekha was too tired for a sarcastic retort, so she merely nodded and followed him through the entrance into a large chamber with mostly porous limestone walls, though one wall was of smooth granite that looked practically polished to a mirror sheen. There wasn't much furniture, just a crude wooden table and a stool, with a candle sitting in the brass candlestick holder in the center of the table providing the room's dim light. Aside from the entrance, there were three passageways leading out of the chamber, all semi-covered by multi-colored curtains of beaded strings.

Belgam turned back towards the cave mouth and Rekha could again feel that muffled jolt, and the sounds of crickets serenading each other suddenly cut off to silence. She quickly spun to look back at the entrance, but couldn't see anything unusual in the dim light.

He turned back to face her. "I've just put up a barrier, nothing will be able to get in until I take it down."

So that's what that was. I can feel *when he casts magic.*

Rekha arched an eyebrow at her host. "Or out, I take it?"

Belgam arched an eyebrow right back. "I'm afraid not, but if you need to go outside, let me know, and I can take it down again."

"That's going to make going to the outhouse awkward."

"Oh, there's no outhouse."

Rekha's jaw dropped. "What?! Where in the Abyss am I supposed to relieve myself?"

Belgam raised a finger and walked towards the middle passageway, pushing past the beads. Rekha followed with some reluctance. *Dear Esyu, does he poop in a box or something?*

At the end of the short passage was a room half the size of the main chamber, and to Rekha's relief, it actually smelled like pine trees, though looking around, she couldn't determine why. The room contained three odd fixtures, all apparently made from a glossy white stone Rekha didn't recognize. One appeared to be a very large washbasin, if quite a bit shorter and a lot wider than she was used to. The second appeared to be some kind of standing washbowl with a lit candle resting behind some metal appendages on top of it, and the third was a squat bowl with some sort of box attached to the back of it, and unlike the other two, this bowl had water standing in it.

Rekha's eyes were as wide as they could be as Belgam explained how to use the sink, the tub, and finally, the toilet. Weirdly, all of these things felt familiar to her as he explained them. "It's...it's like a self-cleaning outhouse? Where does it go? Is it magic?"

Belgam wrinkled his brow. "In the order you asked, yes, out into the river behind the cave, and sort of. I installed it using magic, but the principles behind it are just engineering."

As Rekha wondered at that, Belgam walked back out to the main chamber and when she didn't follow straight away, he whistled shrilly, and Rekha quickly left the bathroom.

As she re-entered the main chamber, Belgam apologized, "Sorry to rush you. It's just very late, you can look at anything you want tomorrow." He gestured to the beaded passageway to their left. "That leads to your bedroom - you should find everything you need, but if you need something, my room's directly opposite. We'll start your training after breakfast tomorrow. Sleep well, Rekha."

As the old man toddled off in the other direction, Rekha pushed past the beads to find a bedroom bigger than she'd ever seen in Bromsford. The bed was absolutely massive, it had four columns holding up a roof of some kind, and Rekha had never seen a bed with a roof before. The white pillows looked super-soft and the covers looked extremely comfortable, and she had to stop herself from dropping everything and climbing in.

The room also contained a massive wooden dresser with six drawers, though Rekha dismissed the thought of unpacking tonight. Next to the bed was a small table with a tall, lit candlestick in a brass holder. The cave floor was mostly covered by a collection of woven rugs. To all appearances, Belgam had gone to quite some length to make her room comfortable and cozy, but all Rekha really wanted was to be back home in her tiny bedroom with Lucky's loud snoring serenading her.

Rekha opened up her sack and pulled out Bunyo, laying him on the bed. She quietly disrobed and got under the covers, clutching Bunyo to her. She licked her fingers and reached over to snuff the candle's flame, and as she closed her eyes and lay there in the dark and silence, she quietly prayed to Esyu that there would be no dreams tonight.

Chapter 9

The scents wafting into Rekha's bedroom roused her from her slumber, and her stomach immediately started growling, having been bereft of dinner the previous day. Rekha languorously stretched and reluctantly slunk out of bed. She quickly pawed through her sack, put on some fresh clothes, and headed for the source of those delicious smells. *Though I don't recall seeing any stove... unless his kitchen is in his bedroom?*

Rekha emerged into the main chamber to see the table groaning under the weight of an absurd amount of breakfast foods. In addition to the bacon and eggs that Lucky was fond of having for breakfast, there were various fruit bowls, breads that had been dipped in some kind of batter, and other dishes she didn't recognize.

Belgam's bald head popped up from behind the dishes at the other side of the table. "There you are! I thought you were going to sleep all morning. Dig in!"

A retort died on her lips as Rekha's stomach audibly growled.

"Oh, my," Belgam said, "eat all you want, I can always make more."

She quickly sat down and started piling her plate with food. As she started stuffing her face, Belgam walked around and placed a mug of orange juice beside her plate, which she eagerly drank from.

As she wolfed down her food, she saw Belgam put some of the battered bread on his plate, which he then slathered in a brown liquid from an oblong bowl of some sort.

"What's that?"

Belgam looked up and smiled. "French toast! With maple syrup. Want some?"

Rekha was surprised to realize the term felt familiar to her, even though she could swear she'd never heard of it. To cover her confusion, she asked, "What does French mean?"

His eyes widened. "Oh! Um...that's probably the name of the person who invented it."

"Oh." *I feel like something's not quite right about that, but why would he bother lying about it? Esyu, I'm looking for faults in everything he says or does.* "I just felt like I'd heard that term somewhere before, but I can't put my finger on it."

"Really?" Belgam dropped his still-loaded fork on his plate. "Does anything else feel oddly familiar? Like this room, perhaps?"

She looked around, but the chamber didn't elicit that same feeling. "Not really. Why?"

"You were born here."

Now it was Rekha's turn to drop her utensils. "Wait, what?"

There was a mournful tone in his voice as Belgam sighed and his shoulders seemed to slump somewhat. "It's true. On a stone slab not six feet from where you sit right now."

Rekha followed his eyes to a spot in front of the cave's entrance. "My mother gave birth to me on a big rock?" When Belgam didn't respond, she looked back to see he had shut his eyes, and was wincing like he was in physical pain. "Are you alright?"

He shook his head and held up a hand, still grimacing. "Please...I can't...I can't talk about it. Not right now."

Moving past it, she asked, "Do you have a kitchen back there?" indicating the one room she hadn't been in with one hand as she lifted another forkful of egg to her lips with the other.

His face relaxed somewhat as Belgam raised one eyebrow. "Do you remember what I brought you here to learn?"

"You created all this with magic?" *Wait.* "Can you just create anything you want?"

He nodded. "There are some limitations. I don't create anything living, and I recommend against improvisation, especially with anything large, sharp, or —" He suddenly froze, staring at Rekha.

She dropped her fork and crossed her arms coolly. "Were you going to say fire?"

His eyes softened. "I was going to say the elements, but same diff."

Rekha nodded and tears came to her eyes. "I've lost my appetite. I'm going to go unpack."

She stood up and walked away, not seeing Belgam's mournful look behind her.

Rekha was pulling her clothes from her sack and folding them, trying her best not to think, when there was a faint cough behind her. She spun to see Belgam's silhouette standing behind the beads at the end of the passage leading to her room.

"I don't mean to intrude on your self-flagellation or whatever—"

Rekha interrupted him with a sigh. "I think we're just doomed to never understand each other, and the faster I learn to live with that, the faster this will all be over."

"—but you have a visitor." Belgam turned and walked away.

"Varian?" Rekha dropped the shirt she'd been folding and quickly headed to the main room.

As she entered, she saw Belgam standing to one side of the cave entrance, and just beyond the entrance stood someone she recognized.

"Dargen!" She started to run towards him before realizing that Dargen was banging his fists on empty air, and although she could tell he was yelling her name, she couldn't hear a thing.

Belgam held up a hand. "I can remove the barrier if you're sure he's not here to hurt you—"

"He's not! Let him in!"

"And I'll need you to remind me to put it back up after he's gone, because I'll forget—"

Rekha angrily turned on him. "Will you shut up and let him in?!"

Belgam lowered his hand, causing Dargen to stumble forward. Rekha caught him in an embrace and held the big man up as best she could, whispering as she cried, "Dargen, I'm so sorry!"

Dargen's eyes filled as he gained his balance and held her in his strong arms. "It wasn't your fault, Rekha. It wasn't your fault."

Belgam said, "I'll let you two have your privacy. I'll be in the other room if you need anything." And he swept away.

Rekha released the hug and looked at Dargen's face. "Varian told you where to find me - does Fulgin know?"

He shook his head. "Varian got me alone, Fulgin's got no idea."

Rekha looked behind her. "Here, let me—" She pulled two chairs from the table and set them facing each other. "Let's sit down."

As they sat, she continued, "This is probably a stupid question but how are you holding up?"

Dargen rubbed a hand on the back of his neck. "Not great. Fulgin and I got in a huge fight last night and again this morning before the town tribunal —" He suddenly looked up to Rekha's face. "—you know the Elder's declared you exiled, right?"

She nodded. "It was part of the deal that landed me here in a dank cave with a weird old man."

"That's the thing that gets me - Belgam's been living a short walk from our town, what, your whole life? Bizarre."

"You don't know the half of it." She sighed. "I wish to Esyu I could just take everything back. Especially with Fulgin. I know he's been rough with you a time or two, and I'd never call him friendly, but he was ready to strangle me back at the Elder's House."

Dargen leaned back. "You really don't remember, do you?"

"Remember what? Fulgin and—your parents?" She gasped as the memory of that awful night hit her like a runaway horse. "Your parents!"

Dargen looked down at the stone floor and said quietly, "At their funeral, Fulgin swore to them he'd protect us no matter what." He shuddered. "And not only has he failed to protect Irynn, but she died the same way our parents did."

The image of Irynn burning flashed in front of her eyes unbidden, and Rekha gave off a strangled cry as she started sobbing. "I just...keep seeing her..." she weakly cried.

Dargen was crying as well. "Me, too. And I just...I just ran. Like a coward."

That jerked Rekha up short. "What? No, the Elder said you ran to get help."

"And I wish to Esyu that was true, but I just panicked. I could've put her out. I could've done something - what kind of person runs away when their sister needs help?"

"A normal person, Dargen. I probably would've run away, too, if I hadn't passed out. You can't blame yourself."

Dargen wiped the tears from his face. "Well, I refuse to blame you. I know you tried to stop her, and I know what she meant to you, and what you meant to her, which reminds me—" Dargen reached into his pocket. "—Irynn was making this for you, for your birthday. I know she'd want you to have it."

He held up a necklace made out of a leather string tied to a thong which was wrapped tightly around a beautiful dark blue crystal.

She let out a low cry. "Her favorite crystal...she found it when we were kids, I can't take that!"

Dargen took her hand and placed the pendant into it, folding her fingers carefully over the crystal. "She said she didn't want you to go off to Magic Academy without something to protect you. I think she'd be upset if you didn't take it." He gave Rekha a sad smile. "And I wouldn't fight with her, you know how that ends."

Rekha matched his smile. "I do."

Dargen stood up. "I'd better go. If I'm away for too long, Fulgin might start looking for me, and you DON'T want him finding this place."

"Agreed." Rekha stood up and tied Irynn's pendant around her neck, but no matter what she did, she couldn't get the crystal to sit perfectly straight.

Dargen laughed. "She was still working on it, remember. But it looks good on you." He hugged her again, and headed for the cave entrance before turning back to face her. "One more thing. We're setting up the funeral for tomorrow. I know you'd want to be there, but between the exile order and Fulgin, it's a really bad idea. But I want you to know that you'll be there in my heart."

He took a deep breath. "Irynn believed in you, believed in your strength. And she wasn't alone. Do what you have to do, Rekha. We'll be here when you're done. And hopefully I can get Fulgin to see reason by then."

With that, Dargen spun on his heel and marched straight out of the cave. Rekha touched the crystal resting against her chest as she watched him leave.

Belgam said, "Your training will be fairly simple. I'm going to show you how to do something, and then you'll practice it until I'm convinced you've got it cold. Understood?"

Rekha nodded.

"But first, I need to see what you can do, and possibly more importantly, I need to see how you're doing it."

"Well, up until yesterday, I could only do one thing." She took a deep breath, grabbed Irynn's crystal with her left hand, and willed herself not to think about Irynn's death.

She calmly held up her right hand, and summoned the small dancing flame in the air.

Belgam's eyes widened a little. "Interesting - you didn't create that flame, it looked like you pulled all the heat from your hand and merged it into a single point."

Rekha was startled. "Wait - is that why my hand gets cold?!"

"Yes, it would actually be much easier to simply create the flame, and it won't make your hand cold. If you do it right, it'll have the opposite effect. Watch, and use all of your senses."

Belgam held out a hand, and Rekha noticed that there was no build-up before she felt the now-familiar subdued jolt, and a noticeably larger flame appeared in the air above Belgam's hand. As Rekha took a step closer to it, she could feel the warmth emanating from it. When Belgam closed his hand, the flame vanished.

"How did you do that?"

"So, creating just requires you to concentrate on what you want to spawn.

When you start out, you might want to make sure you include every property of the object, but later on, we can tinker with leaving certain properties out."

"Wait, spawn? Doesn't that mean giving birth to something?"

Belgam looked confused. "...um, well, I've always used the word to mean creating something. You might be right. In any event, you should try spawning something yourself." Belgam stepped back and watched Rekha intently.

She held her hand out and tried to imagine a flame appearing in her hand, and she imagined her hand tingling.

"STOP!"

Rekha dropped her hand and stopped focusing on the flame, looking at Belgam in confusion.

He questioned, "What are you doing with your hand?"

"I need to do the tingle and push it out to cast the flame." *That's the dumbest sentence I've ever spoken aloud.*

"No, you don't. This is what I'm talking about with properties - you're transferring energy from your own body that you don't need to. Drop your hand, no tingling, just concentrate on the flame and the heat, and spawn it right on the floor."

Rekha furrowed her brow. She imagined a hot flame burning on the floor for several seconds.

"You have to release it."

Through gritted teeth, she growled, "I don't know how to release it without the tingle."

"Relax."

She dropped her focus again, this time with a sigh of vexation.

Belgam gave her an empathetic look. "Releasing the spell requires an action - it can be a word, or pointing a finger, or snapping your fingers. When you get good and practiced at it, you'll be able to release it with a thought. Try concentrating again, and when you're ready, snap your fingers."

Rekha turned her frustrated face back to the floor and imagined the flame, imagined she could feel the heat coming off it, and snapped her fingers.

A fist-sized flame appeared on the floor. Rekha reached out a hand towards it and could feel the heat coming off it.

"Very good. Now, get rid of the flame."

She moved as if to squash the flame with her foot, but she saw Belgam frowning. *Oh. Right.* Rekha imagined the flame was gone, concentrated, and snapped her fingers.

The flame vanished, but there was a new black mark on the floor.

"Oh, I'm sorry!"

Belgam waved that off. "I wanted you to see that. It's important that you know that the things you create this way are *real*, and they have real consequences just by existing in this world. So just because you can make something, doesn't mean you should."

"Yeah, I'm all too familiar with the damage fire can do."

Belgam sighed. "You really have to get over that."

"It's been less than a day, do you REALLY think you'd get over killing your best friend that fast?"

Belgam froze and Rekha instantly knew she'd struck a nerve. Almost apologetically, she added, "Maybe I should practice some more."

Belgam nodded gratefully. "There's just a few things you need to know. First, you can't create living things, they're simply too complicated to get right. If you leave out a single important thing, you've got a grisly mess on your hands."

Rekha looked at him in horror.

"Second thing, and this is extremely important - never, ever, EVER un-create a living thing. EVER. If you want somebody dead - then kill them. Stab them, fill them full of arrows, drown them, set them on—uh, a high tower and push them off, but what you can NOT do is delete them."

"Why?"

"Because deleting a living thing removes them from all of existence. Everything they ever did is undone, and no one apart from magic users will remember they ever existed. This has wide-ranging consequences that are impossible to predict."

Rekha stared at him uncomprehendingly. "Like what?"

"I hunted a yai who deleted the Elder of a mining town far away from here. He was the head of a large family, and most of them also vanished. Since almost all of them performed important jobs, the whole town fell into disarray and basically collapsed within weeks. And since they provided most of the iron for the region, the entire region's economy fell into a deep depression. Thousands of people suffered for years."

Rekha could only stare in astonishment.

"So trust me. Just. Don't. Do it."

Rekha practiced creating and deleting objects for the rest of the day. Dinner passed without event, and she continued practicing until Belgam called a halt. Rekha had to admit she was getting sleepy, so she drew herself a bath in the tub. Although she'd be loathe to admit it, Belgam's bathroom was a million steps up from the washbasin and the outhouse at Lucky's. *Never having to muck out the outhouse ever again makes this almost worth it...almost.*

Belgam shouted from outside the bathroom, "I left you a little something on your bed. A little reward for your hard work today."

"What is it?" She shouted back, but she could no longer sense his presence.

When her bath was complete, she returned to her bedroom to find a small, flat wooden object lay on her bed. She sat down and picked the object up, and when she turned it over, she very nearly dropped it in shock.

The object appeared to be a wooden frame in which had been set an incredibly detailed portrait of Rekha and Irynn, laughing together in Lucky's house. It was so lifelike, Rekha could almost hear the laughter.

Rekha teared up and touched Irynn's face on the portrait. *I miss you so much.*

She looked out towards the passageway to the main room. *And thank you, Belgam.*

Rekha set the portrait up on the dresser so it would stand up facing the bed. And as she disrobed and climbed into bed, she stared at the portrait and could almost imagine her friend singing gently to her, mixing with the distant serenade of crickets and other nocturnal creatures, and eventually carrying her off to sleep.

A tiny mote of light appeared, far in the distance.

As the light vanished, Rekha floated in the black, inky nothing. She could hear the voices once more, though they were very distant. Rekha remembered this place.

The light returned, more of a line than a dot, before vanishing yet again.

Rekha didn't wait for the voices to get louder. She shouted, "Hey! I'm here!"

The voices held a quick whispered consultation that stopped suddenly.

The white line reappeared, a bright capsule against the black. And then it was gone.

A familiar feminine voice came out of the space directly in front of her. "We don't have a lot of time, so please listen closely."

Rekha asked curiously, "Who are you?"

The white line reappeared, now as big as Rekha herself, before vanishing once more.

A different, angry, masculine voice could now be heard coming from seemingly all around her. "...got her image...like some damn trophy..."

The female voice ignored Rekha's question and the new voice. "I'm going to show you how to create and manipulate pure force, okay?"

Suddenly, in her mind, Rekha understood how to create energy and wield it as if it were a physical object, even as she felt the sensation of a heavy weight on her chest.

The white line returned, now the size of a giant pillar, before it disappeared.

The female voice continued, "Be calm and remember what I showed you, okay? And try not to be too hard on Belgam."

Rekha stared in confusion even as she felt something brush down the back of her head and hair.

The female voice shouted, "WAKE UP, REKHA!"

Rekha suddenly felt pressure on her throat, causing her to gasp for air, even as everything suddenly flashed bright white.

Her eyes snapped open. Sitting on her chest was Fulgin, his face full of rage, even as he tightened the noose around her neck.

"I keep my promises, murderer."

Chapter 10

Rekha immediately imagined an energy bolt and snapped her fingers.

A bolt of blue energy came out of Irynn's crystal and slammed into Fulgin's chest. He was immediately blown upwards and backwards, letting go of the noose as he crashed into the bed's roof, falling back down at the foot of the bed and collapsing to the floor.

Rekha was still unable to breathe, and she tried to loosen the knot at her throat with her hands as she choked, but it wouldn't budge.

Belgam suddenly appeared out of nowhere wearing a dressing gown. He took one look, and raised a hand.

The noose around Rekha's neck vanished, and she gasped for air, taking in huge lungfuls.

Fulgin crawled back up onto the foot of the bed. "This ain't over!"

Belgam said, "Oh, it most certainly is," and whipped his hand upward.

Fulgin vanished from sight.

Still breathing hard, Rekha looked at Belgam in disbelief. "I thought...you said...we couldn't do that?"

"What? Oh, I didn't delete that wretch, I just teleported him about a thousand feet straight up. Standing on empty air for a day or two might smarten him up. Are you alright?"

Rekha was breathing more easily now. "I'll be fine."

Belgam cleared his throat. "This is why I asked you to remind me to put the barrier back up."

He turned and waved a hand back at the passageway to the main room, and the sounds of crickets suddenly cut off.

"From now on, any visitors, the barrier goes back up behind them, no exceptions."

Rekha rubbed her neck. "Understood."

With that, Belgam grunted, turned, and walked away.

Rekha tried with some difficulty to get back to sleep, but her rest was fitful at best. So it was that she was out of sorts and grumpy when she trudged out into the main room to find a similar breakfast feast as yesterday's waiting on the table and Belgam standing at the cave entrance, peering outside.

"What in the Abyss are you staring at?" Rekha asked.

"Nothing in particular. I'm just thinking."

"Is that a first?" Rekha sat down and was about to grab a carafe of orange juice when she spotted a slice of cake already on her plate and a small, lit candle sticking out the top of it. She looked at the old man with wonder. "How did you know?"

His tone was mildly sardonic. "That it's your birthday? Do you remember that thing I said yesterday about keeping an eye on you for eighteen years?"

"Well, thanks, I guess." She blew out and removed the candle before picking up a fork.

He still hadn't turned away from the entrance. "You might be interested to know that your friends apparently did not give your location up to Fulgin."

She started pouring orange juice into a mug. "How do you know that? And where is he?"

"The squirrels say he followed Dargen yesterday, hid in a bush until Dargen left, and then left shortly after." Belgam folded his arms. "He probably came back late last night right before he attacked you, but even squirrels have to sleep, so they didn't see him return. And right now, he's sleeping in the sky."

Rekha had finished the piece of cake, and she was now piling breakfast food onto her plate. For some reason, she was ravenous this morning. "How can he be sleeping up there?"

Belgam turned. "I put him to sleep. Even that far away, his screaming was seriously setting my teeth on edge."

"What are you going to do with him?" She cast a somewhat fearful look his way. "You can't keep him up there forever." She bit off a piece of bacon.

"Well, at least a few days, until he gets the hint. And then I'll let him down." He grinned. "Eventually." And he walked off toward his bedroom.

Rekha continued to eat in silence, thinking about everything that had happened. She absent-mindedly fiddled with Irynn's crystal as she stared at the oddly polished granite wall.

Stuck in her reverie, her eyes wandered to Belgam's bedroom hallway, danced over the cave entrance and the shadow standing there, and then back down to her plate.

Wait a minute—

Rekha looked back up at the cave entrance to see a dark silhouette of a girl.

She gasped and dropped her fork to the plate with a clatter.

The silhouette merely waved calmly.

Okay, calm down. The barrier's there for a reason, and it'll keep out everything...including, hopefully...ghosts?

Rekha got up and took a step towards the entrance. "Irynn? Is that you?"

The silhouette tilted its head slightly and then shook its head.

Rekha took a few more steps towards the entrance, and as her eyes adjusted to the light, the silhouette revealed itself to be a girl around Rekha's age, maybe slightly younger. She was wearing a simple sleeveless blue dress over a white tunic, gathered at the waist with a brown leather belt, and she also carried a long tube-like canister on her back, held in place by a strap over one shoulder. She wore her long brown hair pulled back into a ponytail with a leather thong, and had big brown doe eyes, a cute button nose, and thin lips upturned in a pretty smile.

The girl waved again.

Rekha stared at her. "Uh...can I help you?"

The girl looked flustered for a moment, then held up a finger. She stepped back a few paces and hunched her back, pretending to walk with a stick, and turned to Rekha with her eyes crossed and a goofy smile.

Rekha burst out laughing. "Brilliant. That made my day. Hold on, I'll go grab him." She turned and headed down the stone hallway leading to Belgam's bedroom.

The hallway was twisting and winding, and seemed to go on forever. After almost a full minute of walking, Rekha shouted, "Belgam?"

His voice immediately came back from just ahead. "Rekha? You need something?"

Rekha walked around a few more bends and turns, but all she found was more hallway. "Ugh! Whatever. You have a visitor this time."

"Oh, I'll be right there!" His voice still appeared to be coming from just ahead.

Rekha shrugged and turned around, expecting to walk for some time to get back, but the main room was just past the first turn. Rekha looked back at the impossible hallway in some confusion just as Belgam emerged.

"Who's here?" He asked, before looking at the main entrance. "Ah! I should have guessed. Who else would it be?" He raised a hand, and Rekha could again hear birds chirping and the faint sound of a light breeze disturbing the leaves in the trees. He beckoned the girl in, and she entered.

She produced some rolled parchment from the canister at her back. "For you, sir." Belgam took the rolls and handed the girl some coins, which she immediately tossed into the canister and secured with the lid.

The girl then turned to Rekha with a bright smile. "Pleased to meet you! I'm Sarli!"

Rekha smiled and clasped her hand warmly. "I'm Rekha, nice to meet you!"

The nature noises cut off abruptly as Rekha felt the subdued jolt of Belgam putting the barrier back up. "Sarli's from Cloydun. She's kind enough to make the trip to deliver the news scrolls from her mother's stand twice a month."

Sarli gave him a hard look. "And he's going to teach me how to do magic."

Belgam rolled his eyes. "And no matter how often I explain that I cannot simply teach someone magic, she does not get the hint."

Her posture straightened. "I am GOING to be a mage. It is you, sir, who is not getting the hint."

Belgam shook his head and sighed.

Sarli turned to Rekha. "I've never seen anyone else in this cave. If you don't mind my asking, what are you doing here?"

Rekha simply could not resist. "Oh, Belgam's teaching me how to do magic."

Sarli's eyes widened and she slowly turned to give Belgam a look that would have withered a normal person. "WHAT?!"

Belgam gave Rekha a disapproving look. "Oh, very funny. Rekha here is a yai - I am teaching her to *control* her magic. I did not give her magic powers, and I cannot do the same for you."

Sarli's mouth wrinkled and puckered up as she tried to find something wrong with that. "Well, can I at least sit in? I promise I won't be a bother!"

Belgam rolled his eyes. "Do whatever you please. But don't get in the way." He started moving the furniture to the walls, clearing space in the middle of the main room.

Rekha looked askance at Sarli. "Why do you want to be a mage so badly?"

Her eyes widened and she grinned. "Are you telling me you don't? I've wanted to harness the powers of magic since I was a kid!"

"The first major thing I did with magic was kill my best friend."

Sarli's exuberance faded significantly. "That would give one a different perspective. Sorry."

Belgam approached the girls. "Sarli, if you wouldn't mind sitting against the wall, please?"

"Of course! I won't say a word."

As Sarli turned and headed for the wall by the entrance, Rekha caught a glimpse of her backside and was thunderstruck. Even through the dress, Sarli's rear end was physically shapely and moved in a way Rekha found extremely attractive. Sarli sat down against the wall, crossing her legs and smiling as Rekha stared at her, and Rekha, startled and embarrassed, reddened and shook her head to try and free her mind of it. *I also feel a bit guilty, like I'm betraying Irynn somehow by looking at another girl.*

Belgam cleared his throat. "Let's begin, shall we? Let's talk about limits. Technically, a mage doesn't have any. You can cast magic all day and all night as long as the spells you're casting don't require any energy or resources from yourself. For example, spawning or deleting objects all day yesterday didn't tire you out especially, correct?" Rekha nodded. "But if I asked you to repeatedly generate a flame the same way you used to?"

"I'd be tired and maybe even a little sick by the fifth or sixth flame."

"Exactly. Now, just because there isn't a *personal* cost to spawning things doesn't mean there's no cost at all. Too much magic in one place at the same time can cause reality itself to bend or even break, and some mages go completely out of control. This is how yai are created."

Sarli raised a hand.

Belgam sighed. "Yes, Sarli?"

She lowered her hand. "Sorry, didn't you say that Rekha was a yai?" He nodded. "Then, I don't mean to pry, and I apologize if this involves your friend at all, but what was it like when reality bent?"

Rekha furrowed her brow. "It didn't, really. I just created a flame and it...it exploded when Irynn grabbed it."

Belgam waved Sarli off. "The reality bending could have been the explosion itself - or it could have happened in a different way or location entirely."

Sarli persisted. "Is there no test to determine whether or not a person actually is a yai?"

He sighed deeply. "No."

"So it's basically just a social construct and effectively meaningless."

Belgam shrugged. "Maybe so, but it's a part of our world and has been since its creation. Take it up with Esyu if you've got complaints, but do you mind if I continue the lesson?"

Sarli remained silent, but she once again puckered her lips and squinted at Belgam, pointing two fingers at her eyes before swiveling her hand to point at him, causing Rekha to laugh. Sarli laughed along with her and winked at Rekha.

Belgam cleared his throat. "Now, today you're going to learn how to change properties of things." He held out a hand, and an empty wooden box appeared on the floor between himself and Rekha. "How would you describe this object?"

Rekha shrugged. "It's a box. It's brown, it's made of wood. And there's nothing in it."

Belgam asked, "How tall is it?"

"I don't know, a foot?"

"How wide is it? How long is it? How old is it?"

Rekha raised an eyebrow.

"Is it breakable? How does it react to the elements? Who built it?"

"How would I know that?"

Belgam smiled. "Well, you can easily find out. All of these things are properties, and they can be seen or even changed on the fly. You can change how it's affected by gravity, whether it absorbs certain elements or not - you can even move it forward or back in time, but I don't recommend messing with that. Making or even just thinking about a box that only exists thirty seconds in the future is liable to cook your noodle."

Rekha tried to grasp how such a thing would work and failed. *Does that mean when we get to thirty seconds from now, it would appear? Or would it still be thirty seconds ahead? Wouldn't it be here now if it was thirty seconds ahead thirty seconds ago?*

Belgam laughed at the confusion on Rekha and Sarli's faces. "Didn't I just say not to do that?" He shook his head. "If you get good enough at it, you can even change properties of yourself. For example, keep your eyes on me."

Rekha felt a slow, sustained buzz as Belgam appeared to get younger right in front of her eyes. Slowly, the lines in his face and hands diminished, and his posture straightened as his eyebrows and beard darkened from white to a blonde-tinged ginger color. Weirdly, his hair did not grow back, even as fifty years or so of age simply vanished from his countenance. *Has he just always been bald?*

Even Belgam's voice was now that of a man in his twenties, though there was still a twinge of gravel in it. "That's much better. What do you think?"

Rekha simply said, "Wow."

Sarli stared at Belgam in open wonder. "Are you immortal?"

"I don't know, I haven't died yet. I'll let you know after I die once - or twice."

Sarli just stared at him open-mouthed.

Belgam tossed his walking stick away and it vanished in mid-air. "Well, Rekha, let's see if you can change a property of this box."

Rekha asked, "How does it work?"

"Focus on the object you wish to change and think about the word 'properties.' Imagine a list appearing in your mind of all the properties of the object."

Rekha stared at the box and concentrated, and in her mind she saw a large, tower-like white panel with black lettering indicating the different properties to choose from. She noticed that as her attention focused on any single property, a portion of the panel rose up slightly as if to greet her, and it fell back into place as her attention moved away. She maintained focus on the box as she asked, "What are X, Y, and Z coordinates?"

Belgam's voice came back to her, "That's the position of the object in space along the three vertices. Why don't we start there? Try adjusting those and watch the box move around."

"How? I just see a really long number next to those properties."

"Imagine grabbing the number and pulling it to the left or right, but go slowly - we don't want the box to go zipping out of the cave."

Rekha didn't really understand, but she imagined reaching her hand out and slowly pulling the X coordinate number to the right, and she was astonished to see the number change in her mind's eye while simultaneously seeing the box move to the right silently in the cave. She tried moving the Y coordinate and saw the box move forward and backward. She then tried shifting the Z coordinate and watched in astonishment as the box submerged into the cave floor, and then hovered in mid-air.

Sarli whispered, "Whoa." She raised a hand again.

Belgam shut his eyes. "Yes, Sarli?"

"What happens if you change the properties of a living person?"

He grinned. "What an excellent question." And he turned to look at Sarli.

In an instant, Sarli went from sitting against the cave wall with a curious look on her face to standing stock-still, with her arms and hands extended straight out from her shoulders to her left and right, staring straight ahead with a blank expression.

Rekha was horrified. "What did...you put her back the way she was, right now!"

Belgam looked back at Rekha, and instantly, Sarli was sitting back in the position she was in before, although she looked at the other two with some alarm. "How did you guys move so fast?"

Rekha said, "He tried messing with you, and you suddenly appeared standing up, still as death."

Sarli furrowed her brow. "I've been sitting here the whole time."

Belgam gestured to Sarli but kept his eyes on Rekha. "She doesn't remember a thing. Non-magical people cannot tell when you're accessing their properties, and they don't even know that they've been paused, so to speak. Magic users can't be paused, but they also can't tell when you're changing their properties: look at your fingernails."

Rekha lifted her hands to see her fingernails now had a vibrant orange glossy coating on them of some kind. She sniffed her fingers. *I don't know what this stuff is, but it even smells like oranges.*

Sarli cooed, "Ooh, cute!"

"I didn't feel a thing. Is there a way to stop someone from changing my properties?"

Belgam nodded. "Sure. Try to change something about me."

Rekha concentrated, and once again saw that long white panel and a list of options on it, but now there was a symbol of a box with a U-shaped handle next to every option, and no matter what she did, she couldn't change a thing.

He continued, "As you can see, I locked my properties while you were looking at your fingernails."

"So, wait, you can access your own properties?"

"Yeah. Just focus on yourself for a moment."

Rekha concentrated and looked through the list until she found 'Fingernail Color'. She practiced changing her own fingernail colors a few times before finally settling on purple, and Sarli volunteered to have her own fingernails colored blue. Belgam flatly refused to join in, so instead, Rekha practiced on the box for a while.

After some time had passed, the box was now three times as large on the inside than it appeared on the outside, smelled like a weird mix of lemons and roses, and was decorated with a riot of conflicting colors and shapes.

Belgam held up a hand. "That's enough for today. Congratulations. You've now learned how to control magic."

Rekha was confused. "Wait, what? Are you saying I'm done? It's been two days!"

Belgam grinned. "Yeah. That's it. Pretty much all magic is either creating something or changing it. You know how to do both now. Sorry I don't have a certificate or a diploma to give you."

Sarli looked angry. "People go to the Magic Academy for four years! There's no way anyone could learn everything about magic in two days!"

Belgam gave her an even wider smile that carried up to his eyes. "And yet!"

Sarli scoffed. "You've gotta be kidding!"

Rekha crossed her arms. "I think he means that's all he knows how to teach."

Belgam cleared his throat. "That's all the lessons for today. Sarli, you should probably get moving. It's a two-day trip home for you, and you'll want to get home before dark tomorrow."

Sarli's mouth puckered up and her eyes narrowed in an expression of both doubt and disappointment. "Very well," she said slowly.

Rekha quickly walked over to Sarli's side. "Can I help with your stuff?"

"Oh, it's no big deal, just a tube," Sarli said, threading her arm and head through the strap, "I appreciate the gesture, though!"

"Yeah, it was just really nice to meet you. And," Rekha's expression soured a little, "thanks to all this, I can't go back to where my friends are."

Sarli's smile faded. "Well, I'm sure they'd come to you - and hey, if you're ever in Cloydun, you're welcome to look me up. Shouldn't be hard to find, you can probably hear my mom from here, just head towards the sound."

Rekha gave her a quizzical look, but Belgam added, "Sarli's mother's probably the most enthusiastic salesperson I've ever seen. She gets LOUD. As a matter of fact, I only agreed to have Sarli deliver my news scrolls to stop her yelling at me." He smiled at Sarli. "Just in case she complains about your blue fingernail coloring, tell her it'll wash off after a day or so. I'll drop the barrier for you." He raised a hand, and Rekha could once again smell fresh air.

"Great. Thanks for letting me sit in, this has really been illuminating."

"And I hope it's convinced you to drop this nonsense about becoming a mage."

Sarli grinned. "Are you kidding? This was awesome! I'm even more certain that's what I want to do!"

Belgam rolled his eyes.

Rekha impulsively grabbed Sarli's hand. "I can't wait to see you again. Safe travels!"

Sarli smiled wider and said, "Yeah, hope to see you again soon! Farewell!"

And she turned and walked through the entrance, and as much as Rekha tried to resist it, she could not help but think about Sarli as Belgam put the barrier back up. *Esyu, she's brilliant, funny, beautiful...really hope I get to see her again.*

As she forced herself to turn away, she realized she had seen a bit of an orange glow, but was so focused on other things that she had paid it little attention. *Odd, I didn't think it was that late in the day.*

Belgam had deleted the box and was putting the table and chairs back where they belonged. "She's a remarkable young girl."

Rekha murmured, "Yes. She's amazing. And...kinda...hot."

Belgam stopped short. "Pardon?"

"Oh, come on. I know you're eight million years old or whatever-"

"I am seven-thousand one hundred and thirty-seven, thank you very much."

"-but even YOU have to have been attracted to someone at some point. Though, now that I think about it, I've never heard stories of Belgam dating or being married."

Belgam set down the last chair with a deep, sorrowful sigh. "Rekha, the only woman I ever loved and will ever love is dead. I have no need to notice anyone else." With that, he turned and headed to the bathroom.

Rekha shook her head. *That was morose, even for him. What happened to him and the woman he loved?*

Just then, she saw something moving quickly out of the corner of her eye. Rekha turned to see a shadow waving frantically on the cave floor, and she looked up to the cave entrance to see Sarli, eyes wide with panic, waving and pounding on the barrier.

Oh, Esyu, what if she's in danger? Rekha turned to the bathroom and yelled, "Belgam, quick, drop the barrier!"

She heard back, "What? I'll be right there."

She looked back at Sarli still urgently waving at her. "Oh, never mind, I'll do it myself!"

Rekha imagined the barrier vanished and snapped her fingers, and Sarli nearly fell through the space where the barrier had been.

Rekha caught her and helped her up. "What is it? Are you okay?"

As Belgam came rushing back in the room, Sarli said, "No, I'm fine, but look!" And she pointed out the entrance.

As Rekha looked, she realized that orange glow she'd seen was fire, and that fire was coming from the rooftops of Bromsford. *It can't be!*

Rekha sprinted out of the cave, ignoring Belgam's quick shout of "Rekha, wait!" And she darted into the trees.

Chapter 11

All thought had vanished from her mind, she was operating on pure instinct. She sprinted at top speed into the Wanderer's Forest, and she took care to ensure her steps safely cleared the tree roots and other dangers, but was otherwise only focused on speed and direction.

Even in her rush, she noticed when the weather changed from being a sunny cloudless day into a torrential downpour. The rain was another threat, creating mud or slick patches that were just as capable of taking her down as errant tree roots and underbrush. Though in the back of her mind, she recognized that it might help put out the fires. *And it will conceal me from possible threats.*

The trip down still took several minutes, even at Rekha's speed. It was only when she was nearing the outskirts of town and the first few houses that she began to slow down, as she began to encounter signs that this was much worse than a simple fire.

The first few bodies she found had been shot with arrows. The next was the woman who ran the local cobbler's shop. She had horrible gashes in her torso, and her husband was missing most of his head. The worst were the children. The hard rain thankfully obscured some details, but some images would stay with Rekha for the rest of her days.

She emerged into the town square to find a ghastly scene. The town elder's severed head, a look of shock forever frozen on his face, had been impaled on a post dead-center of the square. The post was surrounded by the mutilated bodies of men, women, and children.

As horrible as it all was, Rekha forced herself to check each and every one of their faces. It was hard to tell through the rain and the tears, but she could not find Dargen, Varian and his family, or Lucky amongst them.

Rekha numbly trudged to Lucky's house, dreading what she would see. She almost collapsed on seeing her childhood home badly burned. The roof had mostly collapsed, leaving the main room and Rekha's former bedroom mostly open to the sky. The rain had reduced the fire to smoldering wreckage, but there was no sign of Lucky anywhere.

She cautiously cleared off the ash and debris, and moved the burned table from atop the larder hatch. She took a breath, and lifted it open.

There was nothing inside but food stores.

"Esyu damn it!" She dropped the hatch with a clatter, and sank down to the floor, wrapping her arms around herself. She gaped with wet eyes and astonishment at the burned-out shell of her old room. *Can't stay here, gotta find Lucky, Dargen, Varian, ANYONE.*

As she scrambled to her feet, she heard a voice behind her. "Careful, Rekha."

She spun, and through the open door, she saw Belgam and Sarli standing just outside.

Belgam continued, "While I'm grateful you made enough noise for us to find you, the people who did all this could still be here somewhere."

Sarli's face was tear-streaked, and Rekha stumbled gratefully into her new friend's arms. "I'm so sorry," was all she said, but it was enough for Rekha.

She regretfully broke off the hug. "I still haven't found Lucky, Dargen, or Varian and his family."

Belgam nodded. "Let's go."

Dargen, Fulgin, and Irynn's house had burned down a second time, but there were no bodies in the wreckage. Another horrific sight awaited them at the burned-out schoolhouse. Mr. Abersham's body, riddled with arrows, lay in the entranceway, while a group of bodies, burned beyond recognition, lay huddled together in the center of what remained of the classroom. As they exited the schoolhouse, Belgam grimly inspected a set of hoofprints mere feet from the entrance. "The bastards penned them in and watched them burn." His voice wavered, whether from anger or sadness, Rekha could not discern.

As she approached Varian's house on the other side of town, she started seeing new bodies wearing armor and an all-too familiar image of a blood-red jagged eye emblazoned on it. "Legion!" she breathed.

"As I suspected. The cruelty here has an all-too-familiar ring. But to slaughter an entire village...even I didn't think they could be so brazen." Belgam harrumphed.

When she finally saw Varian's house, Rekha gave a low cry that nearly became a wail.

He was sitting against the front door, surrounded by bodies of Legion soldiers, some viciously slashed at weak points in their armor, and one with a helmet that had been severely dented on one side. His right hand lay open on the ground, the handle of a blood-covered wood axe still resting in it. His left hand clutched at one of the three arrow shafts sticking out of his torso. His flaming red hair hung wet and lifeless down the sides of his head, his eyes were closed, and his hooked beak of a nose shuddered as he struggled to draw breath.

Rekha threaded her way through the corpses to kneel at Lucky's side. "Lucky! I'm here!"

He coughed up a small amount of blood, then squinted at her. "Rekha?"

"Yeah, Lucky, it's me. You're gonna be okay!"

"Look out, girly!"

A shadow fell on Rekha from behind, and she spun to see Belgam and Sarli quickly approaching. "It's okay, Lucky, they're friends! Belgam, please, we have to save him!"

A mournful look crossed Belgam's face. "We can't."

"WHAT?! BUT YOU'RE—"

"Magic doesn't heal. It creates, it changes, it destroys...but it cannot cure."

Rekha scoffed in disbelief and looked at the arrow shafts protruding from Lucky's chest. She raised a hand—

An invisible force knocked her hand away before she could snap her fingers. Belgam shouted, "NO! Those arrows are the only thing keeping his blood in his body, if you remove them, he'll bleed out in seconds!"

Lucky sighed. "He's right, love. I'm done."

"NO!" Rekha focused on Lucky's properties, and ignored the fact that he was suddenly standing straight up, holding his arms out, stock-still. She desperately searched the list for anything that indicated physical health or condition.

There was nothing.

"No...please..." Rekha let go and collapsed next to Lucky, who was once again sitting against the front door, wheezing.

"Lucky, we didn't find any sign of Varian or his family," Belgam asked, pointing at the door the big man rested against, "are they in there?"

Lucky shook his head. "Got away. Dargen, too. Held off the Legion...while they ran. Told them...tae go through the woods...tae Cloydun."

Belgam sighed with relief. "You may have saved all their lives."

Not knowing what else to do, Rekha looked at the man who'd been her only family for eighteen years. "Please, Lucky. You can't die."

He looked up at her. "Dry yer eyes, lass. I'm just goin' tae sleep." He sighed and coughed some more.

Rekha, her heart breaking, sang to him.

The moon is high now

The day is ending
Better count up
The sheep you're tending
Close your eyes, love
As you're yawning
I will be here
'Til the morning

Lucky looked at her in wonder and confusion, and as the lullaby came to an end, his eyes widened in astonishment.

"Rekha?"

She turned to him with her shattered heart in her eyes. "Yes, Lucky?"

"Get inside. It's rainin'. Yer gonnae catch cold."

Lucky shuddered one final time and went limp.

Chapter 12

Burying the dead villagers took a surprisingly short amount of time, as with Belgam's powers, digging graves took seconds. Sarli even helped as much as she could, grimly piling bodies into a wheelbarrow and transporting them to their new homes. Rekha did her best to mark each grave, but there were a few people whose names she did not know. This led to tears a couple of times until Belgam informed her that you could look up a person's name in their properties, even if they were dead.

Once they were done with the villagers, Sarli pointed at the Legion bodies. "What should we do with them?"

Rekha answered, "Let them rot."

Sarli looked at Belgam, who simply nodded. She shrugged her shoulders and returned the wheelbarrow where she'd found it.

The sky had now turned orange for real, with bright purple clouds signaling night's coming. As Rekha said her final goodbyes at Lucky's grave, Belgam announced, "It's no longer safe here. And as it'll be dark soon, it's not safe for Sarli to travel alone in the forest. I recommend we all head to Cloydun, get Sarli home safe, and then Rekha and I will try and link up with any survivors there." Sarli nodded in agreement.

Rekha stood up. "Can we stop by the cave so I can pick up some of my things?"

Sarli held a hand up. "We have to, my horse is tied up just past the cave. Besides, it's on the way."

It was a short trip to the cave, but even in those few minutes, the sky had turned from orange to a darkening blue. As the cave entrance came into view, Rekha spotted a brown-and-white spotted roan horse tied to a tree to one side.

"Is that your horse, Sarli?"

Sarli beamed. "Yup. Her name is Phi, and she's far and away the smartest horse I've ever met."

As if in response, Phi impatiently began to paw at the ground with her left forehoof.

"I know, I know, sweetheart," Sarli cooed as she pulled a handful of oats from one of Phi's saddlebags and held them up to her mouth, "we'll be leaving soon. Okay?"

Rekha asked, "Can all three of us ride her?"

Belgam shook his head. "Phi could probably handle that, but it's unwise. Don't worry, I've got it covered. Go get your things, we'll be ready to go by the time you come back out."

Rekha nodded and headed into the cave alone. Entering her bedroom, she quickly put Bunyo and Irynn's picture into the sack with her clothes, and headed back out to where Belgam and Sarli should have been waiting with her horse.

Instead, she found Sarli and two horses.

Rekha looked at the second horse, a mottled grey, and looked back at Sarli, who sat atop her roan horse, both her and Phi's wide eyes communicating amusement and horror respectively.

Rekha asked Sarli, "I'm just gonna ride with you if that's okay?"

The mottled grey vanished, and Belgam instantly reappeared in its place. "Aw, what's wrong with riding me? As a horse, I mean."

"You mean besides *everything?*"

Belgam absolutely terrorized Phi for the first few miles, transforming into a new animal every few minutes. The wolf made Phi shriek in terror and gallop away. It took all of Sarli's control to calm Phi down and find their way back to the group. She snapped at him upon seeing him back in human form, "Could you please try transforming into something a little less predatory? This is going to be a long trip if you keep changing into things that kill horses."

Belgam transformed into a shaggy grey wolfhound and sat back on his haunches.

Phi sniffed curiously at Belgam for a moment but otherwise did not react.

Sarli smiled. "That will do nicely, thank you."

For her part, Rekha numbly clung to Sarli as they rode, her arms around Sarli's stomach and resting her head on Sarli's back. She wanted to cry, felt like she should cry, but no tears were forthcoming. *Irynn, Lucky, the Elder... everyone in town...even the few who survived lost their homes. And for what? Am I just a harbinger of suffering and death?*

They rode in blessed silence for several hours through the forest, staying off the commonly used and worn tracks in case the Legion were patrolling them. Lucky had always warned Rekha to stick to the woods she was used to, so every noise she didn't recognize made her jump. Sarli was quick to calm her down, pointing out what had actually made the noise was just a mouse or an owl.

Rekha took a great deal of comfort in Sarli's presence just then, and she was honest enough with herself to recognize that there was more to it than friendship. She got the same butterflies-in-her-stomach feeling that she used to get when talking to Irynn, and there were zero misconceptions of how she'd felt about Irynn. *Burying a village together would create a strong bond, I suppose. But it's more than that. She's super smart, she's beautiful...* Rekha let the thought trail off as the image of Irynn burning forced its way front and center in her mind yet again.

Belgam suddenly loped out of the trees directly ahead of them, and changed back into himself again. "There's a lean-to somebody left set up just off that way, it'd be a solid place to camp for the night."

Sarli nodded. "Yeah, let's do that, I'm bone-tired."

Phi followed Belgam until they found three trees grown close enough together to form something of a wall, and a large canvas tarpaulin tied to one of its lower branches and staked to the ground just a few feet away.

Sarli took in the remarkably clean, brand-new-looking tarpaulin with surprise as she dismounted and extended a hand to Rekha. "Somebody just left this here?"

As she took Sarli's hand and awkwardly jumped down, Rekha glared at Belgam and drawled, "I have my suspicions about that."

"Well, I couldn't exactly spawn a hotel, now, could I?"

Once again, Rekha felt like that was a term she knew, even though she'd never heard it before.

Sarli asked, "What's a hotel?"

Belgam looked at her with surprise for a moment, then shook his head. "Anything larger or more obvious risks being found by the Legion. This is small and hidden away, not likely to be noticed, it's perfect."

Rekha flushed with anger. "Why are we hiding from them?"

Sarli reached a hand to Rekha's shoulder. "Rekha..."

Rekha stepped out of range of Sarli's hand. "No, I'm serious. Between you and me, Belgam, we've got more than enough power to wipe them out."

Belgam raised an eyebrow. "Oh, we do, do we?"

Rekha felt a little less sure of herself. "Well, you're extremely powerful, couldn't you—"

"Apotropaicite."

"...apotrowhat now?"

Belgam sat down on a particularly large tree root and clasped his hands together. "Surely you've seen their logo, and the red stone it's made out of."

"What about it?"

"Apotropaicite has anti-magic properties. While standing next to a Legion soldier, you and I are no different from any other person. I could not so much as spawn a single piece of string in their presence."

Rekha furrowed her brow. "Okay, so we fight them from a distance, then. We should still be able to take them out if we don't let them get close, right?"

He sighed. "It's not that simple."

"What's not simple about it? They murdered everyone in Bromsford, and they need to pay for that!"

"That's not what I'm saying."

She let her scorn come into full bloom. "What ARE you saying? Why is the GREAT and POWERFUL Belgam the Mageblade afraid of the Legion?"

Belgam stood and faced her with a dangerous look on his face. "I'm not afraid of them."

"Then let's fight them, damn it! Didn't they kill your best friends - and my parents?!"

Belgam's head sank low. "No, actually, the Legion didn't kill them."

She sat back, confused. "Well, who did, then?"

"I did."

Her eyes popped wide open.

"I killed them."

Before she could think, she was moving, her fist darting for Belgam's face as fast as she could muster, but Belgam was already rearing back, and she missed by mere inches.

"I'm sorry, Rekha."

She slid forward along the ground and raised her right foot up, intending to kick him in the stomach, however, yet again, Belgam merely sidestepped the blow to her left. She instead planted that foot, stood fast, and shot her left fist out in a lightning-quick jab at his face, which Belgam brushed aside with his equally-fast cane.

Sarli was anxiously clasping both hands together, staying out of what was technically none of her business, but she kept opening and closing her mouth like she wanted to interject and kept thinking better of it.

Rekha spun on her planted heel and kicked her left foot upwards, hoping to catch Belgam on the jaw, but Belgam pushed her leg aside with one hand, and while she was off-balance, placed a hand firmly on her stomach and pushed. Rekha fell backwards to the ground, unhurt but seething.

She pushed herself up with both elbows to face him. "WHY?! WHY

WOULD YOU KILL THEM?!"

"BECAUSE THEY BEGGED ME TO DO IT, DAMN IT!"

Rekha stared uncomprehendingly at her parents' murderer.

"They begged over and over again, and no matter how many times I said no, they insisted." There were tears in Belgam's eyes now. "They were my best friends. And I loved them more than life itself."

Her eyes blazed. "Horseshit."

His shoulders relaxed as if all the fight had gone out of him. "It's the truth."

"Tell me why, then. Why did my parents want to die?"

The sorrow in his face gave way to bitterness as Belgam threw Rekha an accusatory look. "Like everything else in this world, it was for you."

"What?!"

"Your parents needed to die so that you could exist."

Rekha pushed herself to a sitting position as her mouth fell open and she stared unblinking at him.

"Killing my loves, living in pain and anguish and absolute torment for the past eighteen years, ALL OF IT —" Belgam leaned forward suddenly and Rekha involuntarily flinched, "— HAS BEEN FOR YOU!!" His anger left him vibrating and he took a shaky inhalation. "And all I get from you is endless disgust and derision. It's a real shame I don't meet with your approval, but check this headline — nobody gives a SHIT what you think! And I'm super sorry you killed one of your friends, by the way, it's been a real treat watching your non-stop woe-is-me bullshit. I GAVE UP EVERYTHING!!" Belgam's shout echoed through the suddenly silent forest.

He turned his back to her. "I'm starting to think it wasn't worth it." And he walked out of the small clearing and vanished into the trees.

By the time Rekha had recovered, Sarli had already dug a small firepit and was laying in some wood.

Rekha sheepishly asked, "Need a hand?"

"No, I got it." Sarli dropped an armful of sticks into the pit. "That should be enough. I'm fairly certain it's just going to be the two of us."

Rekha's right eyebrow rose and she sarcastically muttered, "Whatever gave you that idea?"

Sarli snickered. "Sorry. He's always been kinda moody. I guess now we know why."

"Has he said anything about any of this to you?"

"No. I just knew he hunted yai from the stories. I don't remember anything from the stories about him having friends."

Rekha put her hands on her hips. "And every time he mentions my parents, I'm left with more questions than answers — now that I think about it, I don't think he's even told me their names."

Sarli set up the pot stand over the firepit. "Well, good luck getting anything out of him now. And without him, I guess we'll have to start the fire by hand."

Rekha shook her head. "I can handle it." She held out a hand, and imagined a bolt of fire leaping from it, and instantly she remembered Irynn burning. She grimaced with pain for a moment, then clenched her jaw. *I have to get over this if I want to have any chance of being able to fight the Legion.* She firmly pushed the memory of Irynn from her mind, concentrated, and snapped her fingers.

A bolt of fire flew from Irynn's pendant and hit the sticks in the firepit, causing several of them to catch fire.

Sarli nodded encouragingly. "Well, alright. Anyone ever tell you you're a handy person to have around?"

The smile on Sarli's face plus the compliment made Rekha's heart sing. "You're very capable yourself. Do you travel often?"

"Only twice a month to deliver Belgam's news scrolls. But you learn quickly to take care of yourself out here. Do me a favor, carve some slices of bread off that loaf, I'll toast them on the pot lid. I think I've got a bit of butter left, too." She started cutting chunks off a slab of cured beef and tossing them into the pot. "Where did you learn to fight like that?"

Rekha stopped mid-slice. "Oh. My uncle Lucky."

"Was he the one who—"

Rekha didn't think she'd be able to stop herself from crying if she spoke, so she just nodded her head quickly.

"I'm sorry. He seemed like a good man. And he must have been an incredible fighter if he could take out six Legion by himself."

"He was. He was a sergeant in the army, and his lieutenant always said he was the finest hand-to-hand fighter he'd ever seen. He was very proud of that."

Sarli had sort of a hungry look in her eye. "You must be very good then, if he trained you."

Rekha laughed as she handed Sarli four slices of bread. "For all the good it does me. I can't even lay a finger on Belgam unless he lets me."

"Well, he's cheating."

They both laughed.

"Hey, Rekha. Do you think you could teach me how to fight like you?"

"Yeah! Absolutely! If anything, it'd be nice to have a sparring partner I can actually hit. Let's eat, and I'll show you some moves."

The two of them ate together, and they trained and talked by firelight until the need for sleep overtook them. Rekha went to her bedroll with a spring in her step.

An owl hooted in a tree overhead as Rekha slipped into her bedroll. "Good night to you, too, Belgam. And, for what it's worth, I'm sorry."

The owl hooted again, but stayed put and gave no indication he understood. Rekha shrugged and closed her eyes.

"Rekha, wake up. He's back."

Her eyes opened to see the beautiful sight of Sarli smiling down on her while gently shaking her awake. "Mmm. Good morning."

"Good morning. Breakfast is almost ready."

Rekha emerged from her bedroll to see Belgam in quiet conversation with Sarli. As they finished and Sarli turned back to the cookfire, Belgam turned to Rekha. "I was just telling Sarli, I'm going to scout ahead, try to find any pockets of Legion in our path, and also see if I can find any signs of survivors. See that you get on the road quickly - if we make good time, we might reach Cloydun before late tonight."

Rekha nodded. "Do you wanna—"

Belgam interrupted, "No." He transformed into a red-tailed hawk, flapped his wings and flew off.

She sighed. "...talk?"

The two girls ate their bacon and toast quickly before packing up and riding Phi out of the clearing.

Rekha had thought riding a horse was a pleasurable affair, but that opinion changed dramatically when they left the forest paths and reached the dirt road. Sarli pressed Phi into a gallop at that point, and for the first hour Rekha held onto Sarli tightly out of fear. For the remaining four hours Sarli slowed Phi to a canter, but Rekha's butt was already in agony, and she held on tightly in an effort to minimize the juddering and bouncing. When she finally convinced Sarli to stop for a quick lunch, Rekha was positive her legs would never work right again.

"You just need to get used to it," Sarli explained as she cut off a hunk of cheese and handed it to Rekha, "it took me a week before the pain and soreness went away, and it was a month before I'd called myself a proficient rider."

"I don't think I'm going to have a week to practice. Besides, I've got a better idea. If he can do it, why can't I?"

Rekha concentrated on her properties and skimmed the list until she found something promising, 'Species.' She checked the menu and found some options that intrigued her, some that horrified her, but she eventually settled on something that might be safe.

"Here goes nothing."

Rekha changed her 'Species' from 'Primordian' to 'Dog.'

Instantly, everything felt wrong. She could still see, but everything was in hues of blue, yellow, or grey. She was also much lower to the ground. She lifted up her paw to look at it, and she tried to exclaim her amazement, but it came out as a bark, which startled her.

Sarli knelt down. "Look at you!" Her expression radiated joy. Phi just snorted and shook her head.

Rekha loped over and sat down in front of Sarli. She absently noticed that Sarli smelled very nice, something she had noticed in her human form, but the effect was much more powerful and intoxicating now. Indeed, she could smell a lot of things. Phi was particularly fragrant, as was all of their packed food. Rekha noticed she knew, without knowing how she knew, exactly where and how far away everything she smelled was, even if it was behind her.

Sarli cooed, "Who's a pretty girl?" She gently cradled Rekha's furry face.

Why couldn't you say that when I was in my real form? Rekha's slight indignation led her to cheekily swipe her tongue from Sarli's chin to her forehead.

"Ah!" Sarli giggled. "Rekha! You stop that!"

Rekha loped off a ways down the road, then stopped and sat down, pointedly looking back at Sarli.

She grinned. "Let's ride!" Sarli stepped in the stirrup, grabbed the saddle's pommel, and swung her leg over Phi in one smooth motion. She gently shook the reins and Phi cantered back onto the road.

There was an exquisite, euphoric feeling as Rekha ran alongside Phi. Her muscles felt tight and responsive, bunching and flowing as she practically flew along the road. She had always enjoyed running, but it was something entirely different to use your entire body to run, and it took a long time for Rekha to start to feel tired.

They made good time, and the sky was starting to darken with rain clouds overhead as they reached a rise in the road. Rekha, panting hard, pulled off to the grass on the side of the road, and transformed back to her human form even as light rain started to fall. Sarli slowed Phi down and pulled off with her.

Rekha was still panting and covered in sweat in human form. "Now that... that is an exercise."

Sarli grinned down at her. "Regretting not riding with me after all?"

Rekha looked up at Sarli through the rain. "Not...in the least. That was... amazing."

"Well, we're almost there - you'll be able to see the city just past this ridge."

Rekha's tiredness vanished, and she got up and ran to the top of the ridge in excitement, looking out at the valley below.

The road curved around the ridge and down into the valley through some farmlands before entering the city proper. To her disappointment, the cluster of brown stone houses with slate roofs seemed only slightly larger than Bromsford, but it did seem more industrious, with hustle and bustle located primarily along the main road through the city. A grey miasma appeared to hang over the city, but even through that, she could see taller, multicolored buildings further south, and a massive, yet incomplete stone tower at the far end by the bay. At this distance, she couldn't make out the symbols on the banners, but their red coloring left little doubt as to who it belonged to.

Sarli wryly announced, "Welcome to dear old mucky Cloydun."

Rekha nodded towards the tower. "And home of the Legion."

In a nearby tree, a red-tailed hawk let loose a piercing screech.

Chapter 13

After some discussion, the two girls decided to walk the remaining distance to Cloydun. The fact that Phi actually appeared to be steaming in the rain was a major factor in their decision.

They ambled down the road into the valley at a gentle pace. Rekha didn't mind the rain all that much, as it matched her mood. Her boots were well made and handled the mud without difficulty, though as a concession perhaps to Lucky's last words, she did put on a leather hood.

As they began to approach the farmsteads on the outskirts of the city, a red-tailed hawk touched down behind them before instantly transforming back into Belgam, whose countenance was all business. "We're getting close. I figured I had better rejoin you in this form before we get within sight of witnesses. Legion coin can persuade any witness to have seen anything the Legion requires."

Wouldn't that mean it doesn't matter if anyone sees you or not? Rekha was about to voice that thought but Sarli interrupted, "No sign of Legion or survivors from Bromsford, I take it?"

He shook the rain from himself like a wet dog. "None. The Legion appear to have considered the job done. As for the survivors, either they beat us here or they took a more circuitous route."

"I just hope they're okay."

Rekha avoided looking at Belgam, since he seemed to be giving her the same treatment. "There's only one way to find out."

They continued down the road towards the city. Rekha had assumed that travelers would result in some curiosity from the farmers, but if anything, it was the opposite. Doors and windows slammed shut as they drew near. "Skittish bunch."

Belgam continued to stare straight ahead. "The Legion rule here. They typically don't brutalize their subjects, but they can - and do - make life extremely difficult for those who get out of line, and folks would simply prefer to avoid even the appearance of noncompliance. So they avoid all contact with strangers."

Rekha grunted. *One more reason to take them down. As if I needed more.*

The volume of the city grew as they approached. As their surroundings changed from farmsteads and fields to stone roads and homes, even at this hour, when most of Bromsford would've been enjoying a quiet supper in their homes, some few merchants were stridently hawking their wares from small stalls up ahead in the street.

The loudest voice by a country mile was a lady bellowing, "NEWSSHEETS! ALL THE LATEST! MAGIC ACADEMY STRIKES BACK AGAINST THE LEGION! NEWSSHEETS!"

Sarli wore a wide smile. "That's my mom! Come on, I'll introduce you!"

As Sarli took the lead, Rekha asked, "So the Magic Academy is fighting the Legion as well? This may not be as bad an idea as you make it out to be."

Belgam scoffed, "I've already read that newssheet and I wouldn't get too excited if I were you. The Magic Academy has sent an envoy to the King - that's all."

"It's still a step, isn't it?"

"Not a very good one, but I guess it still qualifies."

They approached the news seller's stall, which was positioned at the far end of the market. *Possibly as silent commentary on the power of the woman's voice - not even Lucky could be this loud.* The seller was a short, middle-aged woman with curly black hair portioned off into two bushy buns with leather thongs, piercing dark brown eyes, a button nose, and thin lips, wearing a pitch black apron over a simple brown homespun dress.

When she spotted the group, she stopped shouting immediately and squealed instead. "My baby!" She ran around from behind the stall even as Sarli handed Phi's reins to Belgam, and they collided in a fierce but oddly uneven hug - Sarli was easily a full foot taller than her mother. "Oh, baby girl, I've missed you!" The seller leaned up on tiptoe and kissed Sarli's forehead. "Thank Esyu you're back safe."

Rekha wryly commented, "Oh, you don't know the half of it." She smiled in an effort to appear grateful rather than smug.

The woman disengaged from her hug. "Now, who's this you've brought with you? I don't recognize them."

Sarli brightened. "This is my new friend Rekha, she's from Bromsford."

Rekha shyly smiled again. "Hello, ma'am."

"Oh, where are my manners? Rekha, this is my mom, Elena."

Elena took Rekha's hand in hers. "It's a pleasure to meet you, sweetie!" She pulled Rekha into a hug, who stiffened with surprise. "Oh, my. You're all skin and bones, does nobody feed you back in Bromsford?" Elena held Rekha at arm's length. "And you're so rigid. Is everything alright?" She looked into Rekha's eyes and all joy and light vanished from her face. "Oh, no. Oh, sweetheart, what happened?"

The shock of Elena seeing right through her combined with the woman's genuine motherly concern burst the dam wide open. Rekha sobbed, "They're all gone," before clutching Elena in another hug and crying hard into her shoulder.

Elena held Rekha tightly. "Shh. Who's all gone, precious?"

Belgam spoke up. "I'm afraid the town of Bromsford isn't populated anymore. The Legion killed...murdered...everyone in town."

Elena's eyes were impossibly wide. "You're joking! An entire town?! There's no WAY the King would stand for that!"

Sarli's eyes had filled. "It's true, mom. I saw the bodies, both Legion and townsfolk. It's not a joke, and there's no denying the Legion did it."

Elena's eyes became shrewd, and without letting go of Rekha, she scanned the market. She whispered, "Not here." She looked over at Sarli. "Get Phi to the stables. I'll pack up and get them to the house."

Sarli nodded, remounted Phi, and rode back the way they had come.

Elena turned to Belgam as Rekha began to get control of herself. "And you, sir, you are the girl's caretaker?"

"In a manner of speaking, though neither of us are happy with the situation. She is a yai. No need to be afraid, I've been teaching her to control her powers, and she has proven adept."

"Oh, dear. This sweet little girl doesn't look dangerous to me." She stroked Rekha's back as she peered at Belgam more closely. "You, on the other hand - why do you look familiar to me?"

"Because the last time you saw me, I had loads more wrinkles and a long white beard clear down to here." Belgam indicated his waist as he laughed.

Her eyes widened again. "Belgam?! Wait...you can...you can just become younger any time you want?"

Belgam sheepishly nodded.

As Rekha released her, Elena's tone took on a slightly bitter cast. "Well...... good for you, dear."

Belgam shrugged. "I can make you younger if you really want, but the Legion would probably hang you for crimes like 'cavorting with heathen sorcerers' and whatnot."

Elena raised an eyebrow. "Honey, I'm forty-three years old, my husband passed a long time ago, my daughter's fully grown, and I live in a city that's become a suburb of the Abyss since the Legion moved in. I'll cavort with any heathen sorcerers I please." She wryly chuckled. "But we can talk about that another time. Let's get my stall packed up and get out of the rain, shall we?"

Packing up the stall took a surprisingly small amount of time. Elena packed her remaining news-sheets into a tube that was slightly larger than Sarli's, and the stand folded up neatly. Rekha volunteered to carry it for her, but Elena refused. "I got it, sweetheart, don't you worry about a thing. You just think about what you'd like for supper and I'll make it for you if I can."

Elena led them through to the southwest quadrant of the city as the rain lessened to a light drizzle. As she followed, Rekha's eyes were naturally drawn to the Legion's tower in the southeast. Belgam leaned over and whispered. "If anyone sees you staring at it, they're liable to report you. Ignore it."

Elena added, "Don't pay that eyesore any mind, now, sweetheart. We're almost there."

Once Rekha had torn her attention away from the tower, despite it getting noticeably darker out, she realized that the buildings in this section of town were built differently than over by the market. The first level was still built out of stone, but there were as many as four more levels above that built out of wood. What's more, each building in this part of town was painted vibrant colors, pinks, yellows, and oranges. There was one townhouse near the end of the path they were walking that had been painted a brilliant sky blue. *I don't understand why Sarli would call this place mucky - it's beautiful.*

"Miss Elena?" Rekha asked, "Why are the houses in this part of town such pretty colors?"

"Makes deliveries and directions a lot easier if you can give them the street and a color to find it by, sweetie! Plus, as you said, it's easy on the eyes!"

Belgam cleared his throat. "It'll get even easier when you come up with addresses."

Elena stopped short. "What's an address?" Rekha also looked curiously at him.

"Ah, never mind. This is it here, correct?" *That's not the first time he's said something that felt simultaneously familiar and unfamiliar.*

Elena pointed at the sky blue townhouse Rekha had noticed before, and Rekha's smile grew wider. "That's my favorite one!"

Elena grinned. "You've got good taste, Rekha. This is home sweet home!" She reached into a pocket of her apron, pulled out a metal ring with keys, pushed one into a hole in the door and turned it. The door slid slowly open as Elena stood to one side. "Guests first, come on in!"

"Wow!" Rekha exclaimed as she walked through the door. "Only the richest folks in Bromsford had locks on their doors."

Belgam entered behind her. "They're a little more common in cities than they are in villages and towns."

The townhouse was thinner than Lucky's house had been, but also longer. There was a thin staircase against the right wall that led up, and there appeared to be a similar staircase underneath it leading down. The front of the house had an oddly high-angled table next to the front door, and a heavy string tied from wall to wall at head height just a few feet behind it. Rekha ducked under it and walked further towards the back as Elena stepped through the door and began to close and lock it from inside. Just opposite the stairway was a small table and two comfortable-looking horsehide chairs, and the table's centerpiece was a vase holding a dying flower in it. At the back of the house was a simple stove built into the stone wall with a small wood supply laid nearby, and a rear door, which Rekha assumed led to an outhouse.

Rekha smiled and said, "Your home is lovely, Miss Elena."

Elena put the folded-up stall in the space behind the angled table, and leaned the tube up against it. "Why thank you, sweet thing! Did you decide what you want to have for supper?"

She threw Belgam a look. "Oh, thank you, Miss Elena, but Belgam and I can use magic to create any food we want. We should make you and Sarli something instead."

For the first time since yesterday, Belgam looked at Rekha, but there was no anger in his face. "Sorry, but we'd be risking getting Sarli and Elena in trouble. Do you want to be responsible for them losing their home? Or worse?"

Elena smiled warmly at them both. "Then it's down to me, so what would you both like to eat?"

Belgam held up a hand. "A simple beef stew would be lovely."

Rekha nodded. "Sarli made a very good beef stew for dinner yesterday, you taught her how to make that?"

Elena laughed. "I wouldn't say I taught her so much as she learned. That girl learns like nothing I've ever seen. And once she learns something, it's on to the next thing she wants to learn. My baby has the hungriest brain I've ever seen. Anyway, beef stew, coming right up." Elena took off the pitch black apron and laid it on the angled table, putting on a nearby tan apron instead before bustling downstairs.

Belgam leaned over and gave Rekha an empathetic look while talking quietly. "I get what you're trying to do, and I appreciate it. I, too, would like to show Elena and Sarli my appreciation for their hospitality, but these houses are all built up against each other, and the walls are thin."

As if to emphasize his point, there was a sudden crash from beyond the wall Rekha stood next to, and she jumped. "I concede your point."

"Besides, there are other ways we can be gracious guests without using magic, for example, we can set the table, and we can wash the dishes afterwards. Just don't take no for an answer, Elena can be...forceful."

Rekha looked up at Belgam. "Thanks for the olive branch. And I'm sorry about last night."

Belgam looked down at the floor for a long moment. "Wasn't your fault. You had the misfortune of rubbing a nerve that had been raw for eighteen years." He looked back into Rekha's face with kindness in his eyes. "I know you want more answers about your parents, and I want to give them to you. I just don't know how I'm going to respond whenever the subject comes up."

Rekha let out a short, cynical laugh. "We both killed the ones we loved. Does that qualify as common ground?"

Belgam tried to hold back a laugh, but it came out as a sort of bark instead. This just made him laugh harder, which caused Rekha to laugh along with him. As he wiped his eyes, he got serious and said, "There's one thing I can tell you."

Rekha pulled out a chair for him at the small table, and sat herself in the other, while Elena came back upstairs with a side of beef, a couple of glass containers with some amber liquid inside, and a loaf of bread.

"Their names...their names are - sorry, were...Jamie and...and Meryn."

Rekha committed their names to memory and somberly nodded. "What were they like? If you don't mind?"

Belgam took a long, shuddering breath. "Meryn was...she was a true beauty. One of the most magnificent creatures I've ever laid eyes on. She took care of me, took care of all of us. She was loving, and protective, and she was a fighter...a survivor." He bitterly snorted as a single tear rolled down his cheek. "Until she decided otherwise, I guess."

Rekha reached across the table and clasped his hand, feeling her own eyes well up as she imagined the mother she'd never get to know. "And Jamie?"

Belgam laughed. "Your father was a little shit." They both laughed. "At least at first. He calmed down as he got older, though. What I loved about him was that he always tried to do right by people, no matter who they were. And he kept an open mind, believed in people even if they'd done something suspicious or wrong. And have mercy, he LOVED your mother more than anything. There wasn't a thing Jamie wasn't willing to do for your mother." Belgam's voice hitched. "Including laying down his life."

Rekha squeezed Belgam's hand with both of hers. "Please, I HAVE to know...why? Why did they have to die so that I could live?"

Elena's voice rang out. "Oh, my Esyu..."

Rekha looked up to see Elena standing a few feet behind Belgam. *Forgot we weren't alone.*

"Is that true?" Elena asked. "I'm so sorry for intruding, but I couldn't help but hear - both of your parents died? To save you?"

Rekha released Belgam's hand and nodded.

Elena walked to her side and clasped Rekha's head to her bosom. "Oh, you poor, sweet, darling little thing..."

Rekha was simultaneously comforted and frustrated. "It's okay, Miss Elena, really."

"Any time you need a mom, you just let me know, sweet pea. Okay? I might not be the real thing, but I'll be the best mom I can be, I promise."

Rekha gave up and hugged Elena. "You got it."

As Elena released Rekha, she turned quizzically to Belgam. "But why did both parents have to die? I've heard of the mother dying in childbirth, it happens all the time. It happened to Lartia just last week, and now Mikel's going to have to raise that baby on his own, the poor dears."

She's right. That doesn't make sense. "Yeah, why did my father also have to die again?"

Belgam sighed. "That is a very long and complicated story..." His eyes suddenly widened. "...that I don't think I'm going to have time to tell you." He pointed behind Rekha, and she turned to look.

There were numerous shadows in the small space under the front door, moving back and forth rapidly. After a moment, there was the sound of something metal hitting the lock. Rekha concentrated and imagined a bolt of energy firing towards the door, holding one hand out, ready to snap.

There was a click, and the door suddenly opened. It was dark outside, so she could only see the person's silhouette. *But I've seen that silhouette before.* Rekha relaxed as Sarli walked inside, leading a familiar-looking group of people in after her.

Belgam stood up in surprise. "Arden! Shilo! And Nedra! You all made it!"

Despite Belgam's joy, there was little cheer among the family of refugees. Rekha felt her gut turn to ice. "Where's Varian?!"

Arden's visage twisted mournfully. "They...they took him."

Rekha asked the question, even though she already knew the answer. "The Legion?"

Arden nodded angrily as Shilo and Nedra began to cry.

Chapter 14

Sarli had gone upstairs to get a few more chairs for the new arrivals, and Elena had bustled back downstairs to get more food. Shilo was busily brushing Nedra's long hair in front of a mirror, while Arden had pulled Belgam and Rekha aside. "I never knew my boy had that kind of courage. He saved us all."

Belgam asked, "What happened?"

"We were hiding from a Legion patrol in a thicket a few miles south of Bromsford. They were just about to move on when Nedra sneezed. They looked like they were about to start randomly stabbing their swords into the thicket when my boy said, 'Don't worry about me, just get them to Cloydun!' And before I could stop him, he bolted out of the thicket, screaming bloody murder, and the Legion chased after him. I got the girls clear, and crept back to where we'd been hiding, praying to Esyu the whole time that my boy was alive."

Rekha's jaw had set as she imagined how the story played out.

Arden continued, "I couldn't find his body anywhere, or even any blood, but I did find sets of horse tracks leading south to the main road. I can't even be sure they've taken him." Arden's face became anguished. "Who's to say they didn't kill my boy and bury him somewhere - I could've walked right over him, for all I know."

Belgam shook his head and gently stated, "I don't think so. There are two things that point to Varian still being alive. First, the soldiers in Bromsford didn't bury anybody. They just left the bodies where they lay. If they'd killed him, you probably would have found him. And secondly—"

Rekha interrupted, "Varian knows where Belgam lives."

"Exactly. From even what little I know of Varian, I believe he's smart enough to use that information as a bargaining chip for his life."

Rekha asked, "Where would they take him? That tower?"

"Likely so. That's not the Legion's only holding in the city, I'm sure, but it's definitely their base of operations for this part of the world."

Arden urgently asked, "What'll they do to him? They won't torture a boy... will they?"

Belgam laid a hand on Arden's wrist. "We can't think about that now - right now, we need a plan."

"What you need is to eat." Elena placed an earthenware bowl of beef stew with a hunk of bread in front of Arden. "I'm sure all of you are exhausted from your journey here, and nobody can think properly when they're tired and hungry." Sarli placed a chair on the floor behind Arden as Elena put another bowl in front of Rekha, who was suddenly ravenous as the delicious smell of the stew wafted under her nose.

Arden became agitated. "Ma'am, please don't take this the wrong way — we're very grateful for what you are doing for us, but I can't sit here and eat while my boy is having Esyu-knows-what done to him! I have to...isn't there something that we can..."

"Calm down, Arden. Your boy will not be helped at all if you rush directly into Legion hands or collapse on the way." Belgam threw Rekha a look. "We need information. Ideally, we need to find his exact location, and the more we know about the defenses there, the better. Let's think this over carefully, and maximize our chances of getting Varian out without losing anyone else."

Arden slumped in his chair. "I know...it's just...I feel so helpless."

"Don't worry, Arden. We'll get him back. Belgam..." Rekha hitched a moment. *I can't believe I'm saying this about the man who killed my parents.* "Belgam is the greatest mage alive. And I'm sort of his apprentice now. I'm sure between the two of us we can rescue Varian."

Belgam arched an eyebrow.

"I mean, he can probably do it by himself." Rekha's tone grew sarcastic. "Wouldn't want to get in the way."

The group ate and discussed the situation. They came to the consensus that the people most likely to have seen Varian would've been the market vendors near the entrance to the city. Since the market had closed for the day, the best option would be to go down in the morning and ask around.

As she mopped up the last bits of stew with her bread, Sarli asked, "Wouldn't they just report you for asking questions?"

Belgam answered, "Rekha and I can effectively disguise ourselves as anyone we want, so they can report us all they like, but the Legion will be looking for the wrong people."

"And once we have Varian's location?"

"You, Rekha, and Arden will wait outside as backup, and I'll go in alone and get him out safely."

Arden asked, "Alone, is that wise?"

"Anyone else will just slow me down. I'll go in as a bird or a bug, something small and unlikely to be noticed. I'll find Varian and transport him out." Belgam looked directly at Rekha. "Once he's out, he's likely to be very confused and disorientated, so grab him quickly and get him out of sight. If I need anything, I'll communicate like this."

Belgam glanced at the wall opposite, and black words suddenly appeared on it reading, "I'LL PUT WORDS ON A WALL NEARBY."

Rekha swallowed the last of her bread. "And if something goes wrong?"

He shrugged. "We'll improvise."

Sarli remarked, "It's not much of a plan."

"It'll have to do. We'd have a really hard time getting our hands on the plans for that tower. For all we know, those plans are inside the tower anyway. I don't see any way to get more information that could help us."

Arden sat back. "It chafes something awful waiting all night. But it's a solid plan, and I think it's got a good chance of getting my boy back. Thank you, all of you." He sauntered over to his wife and tousled Nedra's hair as he whispered reassuring words into Shilo's ear.

Sarli put a hand on Rekha's arm, and her heart fluttered involuntarily. *Keep it together, Rekha.*

She said, "We've got a couple of extra beds, but not enough for everybody. Do you want to help me get some bedrolls out of the attic?"

Rekha nodded. "Happy to help."

They walked upstairs, and yet again to the third floor. Sarli grabbed a peculiar rod with a small bit of rope looped at the end, and she used it to reach the knob of a hatch in the ceiling. She pulled, and the hatch swung open, dislodging a bit of dust at the same time. Rekha batted the dust away and tried not to breathe.

"Been a few years since you had visitors, I take it."

"More like 'been a few never'...I mean..." Sarli wore a rare flustered expression. "I don't know what I mean."

Rekha laughed. "How do we get up there?"

"There's a ladder in the closet over there. Mind grabbing it for me?"

Rekha walked to the door Sarli indicated. She found a sturdy-looking ladder almost immediately, but it was on the floor, so she bent over and picked it up, carefully walking it out of the closet.

Sarli smiled and took the ladder from her, placing it against the lip of the open hatchway, and started to climb.

Rekha, finding herself blessed with a magnificent view of Sarli's rear as it swished to and fro up the ladder steps, couldn't help herself and fully took in the sight. *Esyu, have mercy.*

Sarli stopped climbing and looked back over her shoulder. She said something about following her up, but Rekha realized too late that she wasn't paying attention to Sarli's words.

"Uh, sorry. What was that about following you?"

"I said, you don't have to follow me up if you don't want. Wait." Sarli's eyes grew wide, and she turned on the ladder so she could look down at Rekha. "Were you...were you looking at my butt?"

YES. "No!"

Sarli's mouth fell open in a shocked smile. "Yes, you were! You were looking at my butt!"

Rekha stammered, "I-I-I was just tired! And not really paying attention to where I was looking. Also, it's not my fault, because your butt is literally hypnotic." *OH MY ESYU DID I REALLY JUST SAY THAT?!?!*

Sarli burst out laughing. "Wow...hypnotic, you say? Interesting..."

Rekha's face burned. "Never mind. I'll just look over here. Just tell me when you've found the bedrolls."

"No, please, it's okay. It's only fair. Because I...sorta...maybe...snuck a peek while you were picking up the ladder."

The burning intensified. "Wait, what?!"

"I'll be right back with the bedrolls." With that, Sarli scampered up the ladder and disappeared from view.

Oh, my. Sleeping tonight should be fun.

Rekha floated once again in the black, inky nothing. She squinted, peering around until she spotted the tiny mote of light that signified she was in a familiar dream.

"Hello? I'm here again! Are you there?"

There was no multitude of voices this time. A single, familiar, clear feminine voice reached Rekha and seemed to warm her soul.

"Hello, Rekha. As usual, we don't have much time."

The light reappeared as a far off white pillar. After a second or so, it vanished.

Rekha shouted into the void, "Is Fulgin attacking me again?"

"No, Rekha. This time, it's Varian who's in danger."

The white pillar returned, this time three times its previous size. And it disappeared again.

"We're going to try to rescue him in the morning."

"If you do, you'll be too late. You need to go tonight, right now - and you have to go alone."

The pillar reappeared, now as large as Rekha and much closer, before vanishing.

Rekha went white as a sheet. "Wait, what? Why do I have to go alone?"

"Well, maybe not alone, but you have to leave Belgam behind. Or else you will fail. Trust me, I know you can do this."

The white pillar was now enormous, bigger than Elena's townhouse. And then it was gone.

Rekha shook her head. "If I'm going to trust you, I need to know who you are."

The mystery voice paused a moment. "Very well. My name is Meryn."

Rekha froze.

"And I guess, in a way, you could say that I was your mother."

Suddenly, white was all Rekha could see. She knew she was about to wake up, and she didn't have a lot of time, but she could only think of one thing to say.

"Mommy?"

Chapter 15

Rekha awoke in a cold sweat. *I don't know whether I should fully trust that voice, but she* did *save me from Fulgin. And she FEELS like...like warmth and goodness... like she's my mom. But that means I have to go rescue Varian right now. Oh, boy...here goes nothing.*

Rekha dressed as quietly as she could, then considered her options. *I could transform myself into something, but if I can hear Belgam doing magic, then he can probably hear me, and I don't know if that would wake him up. Looks like I'm going to have to do this the old-fashioned way.*

Rekha carefully and slowly walked to the bedroom door, and slowly turned the knob, letting it make no noise. She slowly pushed the door open, and one of the hinges creaked, causing Rekha to freeze, expecting to be caught any moment. After a breath or two and no sound of people running her way, she slipped out into the third floor hallway.

Thankfully, Elena had rugs down on the floors, and Rekha's leather-soled shoes were virtually silent as she crept along, but soon she had another problem. The stairs were plain wood, and Rekha seemed to recall they'd all creaked on the way up. *But the stairs have bannisters, and they don't creak.*

Just to test that theory, Rekha grabbed the bannisters with both hands and lifted her feet off the floor, putting all of her weight on the handrails. No noise was forthcoming, so Rekha lifted her feet up and gently placed them on the bannisters ahead of her hands. Satisfied, Rekha slowly spider-walked down the bannisters to the bottom of the stairs, where a helpful red rug awaited her.

Rekha quietly sneaked around to the next stairs down, where she could hear someone lightly snoring below. Given the risk, she spider-walked especially slowly and carefully down to the ground floor. Arden's family were here, sleeping on the floor in their bedrolls. Arden's mouth was open, and the snoring was his, but it seemed like Shilo was sleeping fitfully. She moaned and reached out for something, but she did not wake.

Rekha breathed a quiet sigh of relief and proceeded to the front door, where she realized she had another problem. *Oh, crap. I don't know where the keys are. I don't think I need one to unlock the door, but that means I'll be leaving the house unlocked and unprotected when I leave.* She considered looking for the key for a moment. *Varian's life is at stake. I'll apologize until I'm blue in the face in the morning - if we survive.*

Rekha painfully slowly turned the lock mechanism, remembering it to be a loud click when it finished turning. She shielded the lock with her body to try and muffle it, but the click that emerged when she finished turning it was infinitesimal.

She slowly pulled the door open, stepped through, and pulled the door shut behind her. She waited a moment, but she didn't hear anything from inside the house. *Phew. Made it. Now for the hard part.*

Rekha trekked back down the street, grateful to see that the rest of the city appeared to be as sleepy as those in the house. She stuck to the shadows whenever possible, expecting to see a town guard or even a Legion patrol any second. None were forthcoming as she crossed the city streets. Thankfully, finding her way was simple - the tower was easily visible from anywhere in town.

As Rekha was nearing the edge of the southwest quadrant, she heard the unmistakable sound of armored footsteps. She ducked into the shadows behind the stairs leading to the front door of a nearby house and waited, peering just over the edge of the top stair.

Two Legion soldiers rounded the street corner, one of them holding a lantern, their armor emblazoned with the now-familiar jagged eye symbol in blood-red stone. *Apotro...something.*

"Man, you've gotta relax, Wilkin."

The soldier holding the lantern turned slightly. "'Kid is gonna get 'imself killed, bruv."

"So what? It's not your problem, man."

"Everybody already hates us, bruv. And I didn't sign on to the Legion to murder children."

As they drew nearer to Rekha's hiding spot, she ducked down and listened. *Are they talking about Varian?!*

"That boy looks nearer to an adult than a child to me, man. Besides, if you're that concerned, tell the kid to stop mouthing off to Keldin, and he'll be fine."

"I dunno, Janim, I sometimes fink we're on the wrong side in all this."

"SHHH!!!" The soldier stopped his partner in the middle of the street, and Rekha realized the lantern was now illuminating her. She held her breath. "Are you TRYING to get reported, man? Because you'll end up in a cell with him if you're not careful!"

"It's not right, Janim."

"Man, people live in these houses. All you need is just one of them to be unable to sleep, and you'll be forever branded a traitor. And you and your entire family will suffer. Is that what you want, man?"

The soldier with the lantern looked down at the cobblestones for a moment before looking back at his partner. "Fine. I won't say nuffin'. You don't mind if I still fink fings?"

The other soldier smiled and put his arm around Wilkin. "Man, I don't care if you mentally swear an oath against the kingdom, just keep it to yourself. I don't want to lose the only good partner I've had since I joined the Legion." He started to walk down the street.

Wilkin stayed put, his lantern still making Rekha visible. *If he turns his head, I'm caught.* Rekha began concentrating, ready to fire energy bolts from Irynn's crooked pendant if needed.

"D'you really mean that?"

Janim turned back around. "Yes, I really mean that. Patrols are actually enjoyable with you. Man, why are you making me say this stuff?"

Wilkin smiled. "Aww. Thanks, bruv. 'At's made my night, that has." He continued to walk down the street, and after a few moments, Rekha was in darkness again, and she released a breath she hadn't realized she was holding. *That was closer than I'd like.*

Rekha waited until they'd traveled some distance away before leaving the safety of the shadows and continuing her journey towards the tower. After crossing a few more streets, Rekha could finally see the tower in its entirety. The tower was easily eight or nine stories tall, with several banners depicting the jagged eye symbol waving in the night breeze. Rekha idly thought about burning every single banner to ash.

There was a wide causeway leading to a walled courtyard. The gate was open, allowing Rekha to see the entrance of the tower, two large, heavy wooden doors. Two soldiers stood at attention outside those doors. *Not getting in that way...*

Rekha scoped out the tower from her hiding spot, looking for alternate ways in.

The voice came from behind her. "Looking for anything specific?"

Rekha froze. *Wait a minute. I know that voice!* Rekha turned to see Sarli crouched down behind her, with a wide grin on her face.

Rekha started. "What are you doing here?"

"What are YOU doing here?"

"SHHH! Keep your voice down!"

Sarli whispered. "Well, I saw you heading downstairs, fully-dressed, so I decided to dress quickly and follow you. Thank Esyu I did, somebody had to lock the front door!"

Rekha whispered back, "I didn't have a choice, I had to leave, and I didn't have a key."

Sarli's breath was warm against Rekha's ear, and her heart beat faster. "I thought the plan was to wait until the morning."

"The plan has changed. I have to rescue Varian right now or he'll die."

"And you know that because...?"

"My dead mom came to me in a dream and told me."

Sarli raised an eyebrow and sarcastically whispered, "Oh, well, in that case, that's ironclad, carry on."

Rekha turned to face Sarli directly. "Look, I know it sounds like ridiculous nonsense, but that's my whole life now, so trust me when I say she knows what she's talking about."

"You've had prophetic dreams before?"

Rekha's shoulders slumped a bit as she gave an exasperated sigh. "I believe Varian's life is in danger. And every second could count. So can you please just trust me, and help me find a way in there?"

Sarli puckered her mouth for a second, but her posture quickly relaxed. "Alright, let's see then..." She scanned the tower. "No windows, naturally. Just arrow slits."

Rekha spotted something up on the east face of the tower. "Looks like there's a parapet up there, but it's about four stories up."

"It'd be hard to get up there unseen."

Something hooted and both girls jumped. Rekha looked up to the roof of the building opposite her and saw a brown tufted owl perched on the edge. It seemed to be looking right at her. She waved at it, trying to get it to go away, but the owl remained, turning its head up to glimpse the night sky.

Sarli furrowed her brow as Rekha tried futilely to banish the bird. "You know what?"

"What?"

"Why don't you steal Belgam's plan, and go in as a bird?" She pointed to the tufted owl. "That one, to be precise."

"I think you might've hit your head on the way out of the house."

Sarli scoffed. "I'm serious. Think about it - you transform into an owl, and you fly up to that parapet."

"And then they shoot me full of arrows."

She indicated the tufted owl watching them. "No, Rekha, owls are a common sight at night here. Nobody'll give you a second glance."

Rekha looked back at Sarli. "Are you sure about this?"

"Nothing simpler. You fly up, and when the coast is clear, hop down to the parapet floor and change back into Rekha. Find Varian, grab him, and get out."

Meryn made it clear time was of the essence. Rekha looked back up at the owl, which was once again staring down at her. "No time to spare. I'm going."

"Okay! What do you want me to do?"

"Keep watch. If they sound the alarm and Varian and I aren't out yet, go get Belgam."

Sarli looked like she was about to argue, but then she nodded. "I know how strong you are, but the Legion are extremely dangerous. Please be careful."

Rekha said, "I promise." She turned to look back at Sarli. "Besides, I'd never hear the end of it from Belgam if I got caught."

Sarli held up a hand. "Wait, just a second." She reached up behind her head and fiddled with something for a moment before shaking her hair loose and offering something in her hand to Rekha.

It was the long leather thong from Sarli's ponytail. Now that it had been unfurled, Rekha could see that it had the words "SARLI AND PHI" as well as a crude image of a horse carved into it with a knife of some kind. She could only stare at Sarli in amazement.

"For luck."

A million responses filled Rekha's mind. "Just for luck?" *STUPID, STUPID.*

Sarli laughed quietly. "Please, just take it. I got it the same day I got Phi, so it's the luckiest thing I own."

"I can't take that."

"Yes, you can." Sarli took Rekha's hand, put the thong into it and then wrapped Rekha's fingers around it. Her face burned as Sarli grinned. "Now go on, get out of here, before I change my mind about not telling Belgam what you're up to."

It felt like Irynn's pendant was burning a hole in Rekha's chest as she quickly tied Sarli's thong around her wrist. "I...I don't know what to say."

"Just come back safe." Sarli playfully pushed Rekha. "Now GO."

Rekha struggled to put aside her now-chaotic feelings long enough to concentrate on her properties, but when the menu came up, she selected 'Species,' and changed from 'Primordian' to 'Owl.'

After her first transformation, Rekha thought she was ready for the changes this time, but she was wrong. She had expected the height difference, and she expected to see things differently. She did not expect the absence of all color, everything was in various shades of grey. But what really threw her was that she could not turn her eyes. They were permanently locked facing forwards. She turned her neck out of panic and turned it too far, too fast, spinning around to nearly see behind her, and the sudden disorientation made her stumble and nearly fall.

Sarli asked, "Rekha, you okay?"

Rekha twisted her neck around a few times, getting used to the extra range of motion. She marveled at her eyesight - even though there was no color, she could see minute details from far away. She looked up at the tower and the parapet, and she judged that the small balcony was indeed empty at the moment. Then she slowly turned her whole body around and looked at Sarli to find that close-up things appeared somewhat blurred. She gently hooted at Sarli.

"Varian's waiting. Go get him!"

Rekha turned, spread her wings and started flapping. After a couple of seconds, she was successfully able to hover a few feet off the ground. She slowly turned and faced the tower, and left the safety of the darkness in the shadow of the house they were hiding behind. She was immediately hit with a breeze blowing her off course, and she briefly panicked, but was able to maintain control, though it felt like she was fighting the air.

The tower was right next to the city docks. Rekha landed on the nearest dockhouse to the tower, gripping the roof edge with her talons. She idly spotted a mouse crawling through the garbage on the ground below and was seized by the urge to swoop down and grab it. Horrified, Rekha pushed that image away from her mind. *Oh, Esyu, why did that make me hungry? Ugh.*

She was about to take off again and did a quick head turn to make sure nothing was looking her way when she spotted three large ships moored to the docks, gently rising and falling with the waves. They all sported Legion banners. *Those ships could carry* hundreds *of men. I gotta find Varian NOW and then I think we need to leave Cloydun - fast.*

Rekha squatted down and launched herself off the roof and flapped her way up to the tower's parapet, and aimed for the near corner of the battlement. She steeled herself, and settled down on the battlement, gripping the stone as tightly as she could with her sharp talons.

The door to the parapet was wide open, and she could see another door directly across from it. But no one was visibly nearby - the coast was clear. *Gonna have to thank Sarli for that luck.*

She was about to jump down when she heard the sound of armored footsteps approaching. Rekha froze in place.

Sure enough, a young soldier walked out onto the parapet, staring straight out into the night, though he did look briefly at the stock-still owl gazing fearfully at him. "Relax, friend, I'm not here for nightfowl. Just doing my patrol. Though why I have to check this balcony every time is beyond me."

He turned to face Rekha. "Who would be crazy enough to try to get in this way? Who, I ask you?"

Rekha, emboldened, hooted at him. "Hoo!"

The young soldier laughed. "Thanks, my friend. If only your opinion could influence Legion policy. Kill a few mice for me, will you? Good hunting." He nodded and left.

Rekha waited for the sound of his footsteps to vanish, then she jumped down to the stone floor, flapping once to slow her descent. She stretched out her wings and shook herself, and then focused on her properties, changing 'Species' back to 'Primordian.'

The transition made her a bit dizzy, but she clung to the stone wall until everything stopped spinning. *Okay. The appearance of my young friend just now has given me an idea of how I can move around without raising alarm.*

She concentrated and tried to spawn a set of Legion armor, snapping her fingers.

Nothing happened.

She tried it again to no avail. *What in the Abyss?*

Rekha peeked her head through the door into the tower and looked around. She was in a hallway that appeared to run along the outside of the tower. Directly opposite the parapet door was the closed door she saw before, set in a curved stone wall that indicated it led to a circular room. Above the door was the Legion symbol, the jagged eye, in blood-red stone. *That's why. Belgam wasn't kidding about that stone. Spawning doesn't work. But it looks like I can still change my properties, at least.*

Rekha stepped out into the hallway and closed the parapet door. She listened at the door opposite, but didn't hear anything. *It's as good a place to start as any.*

She slowly turned the doorknob and quietly opened the door and peeked inside. The circular room was garishly appointed, a large black rug with the jagged eye logo in red preceding a maple wood desk. Papers lay in neat piles across the top, along with an inkpot and quill. Behind the desk was a comfortable-looking high-backed red upholstered chair, which was currently empty. There appeared to be a large map of the region strung up along the wall behind the chair.

Rekha stepped through the doorway, quietly closing the door behind her. She crept up to the desk, hoping to find Varian's location in the pages there.

"Private Angus, is that you?"

Rekha froze. *I know that voice...*

From behind the high-backed chair, a man in full armor appeared carrying a thin hardbound book. His chestpiece bore the Legion insignia in blood-red stone, and his greasy black hair and ice-blue eyes were exactly as

Rekha remembered them. *So much for being lucky.*
She said, "Malvus."

Chapter 16

"Well, as I live and breathe, if it isn't the staunch protector of Belgam's virtue." Malvus smiled as he dropped the book onto his desk. "I'd hoped I'd run into you again, but I never imagined it'd be like this."

Rekha retorted, "Personally, I'd hoped I'd never see you again."

"I'd imagine so, but truthfully, I mean you no harm. You believed in the stories, the heroism attributed to the man, and I admit I did as well, once upon a time. You're just wrong about him, that's all."

"And that's justification for you slaughtering an entire village?"

Malvus looked confused. "I beg your pardon?"

"The Legion came back to Bromsford two days ago. They killed everyone, men, women, and children."

Malvus' eyes widened.

Rekha felt herself seething with rage. "NOW tell me I'm wrong."

He said, "This office hasn't authorized...are you sure Legion was responsible?! They weren't defending the village from attack, but actively doing the attacking?"

She was vibrating. "I have witnesses, refugees in the city right now...and my uncle himself died with Legion arrows in his chest."

His brow furrowed and he turned to the desk, going through the papers nearest him one-by-one, eventually pulling two out of the pile and holding them up. "Here we are. It's true, we received a tip that Belgam was hiding in Bromsford two days ago, in the early hours of the morning. Standard response to a tip like this is to send a small company to investigate. But even if we had responded, it's a full day's ride to Bromsford from here. We couldn't have reached Bromsford that fast."

"Legion lies. They wore your armor, used your equipment. Next, you're going to tell me several soldiers reported their armor and weapons stolen, correct?"

Malvus appeared genuinely baffled. "No, nothing like that. I don't know who these supposed imitators are, but they did not come from the Citadel. And we don't have any troops stationed anywhere near Bromsford, look!" He pulled the chair away, and Rekha could now see the entire map on the wall. Malvus walked to the map and held up a finger to Cloydun. "See these red marks? These are troop stations. And the nearest station aside from Cloydun is the King's castle in Evermire, that's twenty leagues away from Bromsford due north, at least two days' ride."

Rekha studied the map. There were no other red marks within a hundred leagues of Bromsford. *And Malvus couldn't possibly have known I was coming... but he could have suspected someone would come.* "Easy enough to fudge your own map and provide your people an alibi, Malvus."

"It's the truth. We have a reputation for being heavy-handed, I'm aware of that. But we don't slaughter civilians."

"Then why do you have one of Bromsford's few survivors locked up, and being interrogated by a man called Keldin?"

Malvus reared back. "How...how do you know all this?"

Her eyes blazed. "Where is he?"

He looked somewhat irritated, but he peered back down at the piles of paper and rummaged through one of them until he pulled another page out. "Only new prisoner this week was brought in yesterday, claims his name is Varian, and that he knows where Belgam is." He put the paper down in front of Rekha. "I mean, that's reason enough for us to bring him in."

"He only said that because he was afraid your men were going to kill him like they did the rest of the villagers - he hasn't got a clue where Belgam is."

"But you do, don't you?"

Rekha hitched a moment and immediately realized that hitch had betrayed her. "Th-that's not important right now..."

"I beg to differ! How did you get in here? The lower levels are all patrolled, so you must have gotten here by magic means, yes?"

"No...it was-it was a rope, through the parapet."

"If you'd climbed up a rope, you would've been spotted and the alarm would have sounded, and I genuinely thought you were smarter than that." Rekha snarled at him, but he carried on. "Now, I do think I've been very polite, answering your questions and so forth, but we both know there's no non-magical way you could have gotten up to the parapet undetected. So I'm afraid I'm going to have to insist you tell me where Belgam is."

She struck a fighting pose. "Who's going to make me? You?"

His eyes lit up. "Can you seriously fight?"

"Since I was twelve years old."

He smiled, walked around the desk to face her, and put up his fists. "Let's see what you can do, little girl."

He threw a soft left jab at her face, which Rekha swatted away. He followed with a right cross - she ducked it and aimed an uppercut at his jaw, but he just managed to block it with his left hand. She bodily pushed him backwards, and Malvus staggered back a step, but kept his fists up. He grinned. "Not bad."

He launched a huge right front kick for her midsection, Rekha blocked and trapped his foot against her body, leaned back, lifted her left foot, and kicked him in the back of the head. He instantly responded with a right backhand that caught her in the forehead, and she dropped his foot and staggered back. They both shook their heads, clearing the momentary daze.

Rekha glared daggers at him, but if anything, Malvus' smile grew wider, and he laughed. "You're almost as much fun as I'd hoped. Again?"

She aimed a flurry of blows at his head, but he blocked all three. She traditionally followed that combo with a knee to the stomach, but at the last second, she planted her foot on his hip instead, intending to push him backwards, but he caught and trapped her foot with his armored hands. He then twisted her foot downwards, but instead of letting this hurt her, she spun her body in the air so that she was now facing the stone floor. She dropped her body to the floor, holding herself up with her hands, and pulled Malvus close with her right leg, while shooting her left leg out, kicking him square in the face. He released her other foot and fell backwards to the floor, laughing gaily.

Rekha leapt to her feet again. "Had enough?"

Still laughing, Malvus struggled to get to his feet, but when he did, he drew himself up to full height with a wide grin on his face. "Oh, you're good. You're very good."

She nodded, spotting the book on his desk out of the corner of her eye. "You're not half bad yourself."

His face took on a rueful cast. "But we both know how this ends." He took a deep breath as if about to shout.

Rekha grabbed the book and whipped it at his throat. Her aim was true, and as it connected, instead of shouting, Malvus started choking. She leapt at him, smoothly blocking his hastily-thrown left jab with her own left hand, locking his wrist, pulling him forward a step, and sliding her right arm around his neck. As he futilely tried to grasp at her with his right hand, Rekha reared back and tried to look through his properties, but they were all marked with that weird symbol indicating his properties were locked. *Shame. Spending a few days as a pig might improve his social skills.*

Despite choking, Malvus still tried to speak. "How—?"

Rekha increased the pressure. "You work too hard, Malvus. You deserve a nap."

"I knew—" Malvus struggled to speak despite the chokehold. "I knew...you were..." He stopped struggling and went limp.

Rekha released the hold and gently dropped his body to the floor, watching him for a moment to make sure he was still breathing. Satisfied and feeling rather proud of herself, she turned her attention to the papers on his desk, particularly the one detailing Varian's capture. She scanned the page for a location, and didn't find one, but there was a note added to the bottom of the page by someone other than the original author, possibly Malvus himself. It read, "Archprelate's Honor Guard?? - prep fifth level cell." *Not sure what an Archprelate is, or why someone would guard it. But that cell's gotta be for Varian!*

Rekha quietly left Malvus' office and crept along the corridor. *I'd guess I'm on the third or fourth level now. Gotta head up.* Rekha found a set of stone stairs at the end of the hallway leading up. The stairway took up the width of the hallway, so there was nowhere to hide. *And I can't spawn energy bolts. Perfect.* She grit her teeth and held up her arms in a fighting stance as she slowly climbed the stairs.

As she emerged into the next floor, the curved hallway ahead of her seemed clear, but after a moment, she heard a gruff voice. "I gots to thinking, yeah? Why would this kid deliberately push me, goad me? Then it hits me, yeah? This boy WANTS me to kill him."

Rekha's eyes widened and she quickened her pace. The voice got louder as she approached a doorway set in the inner wall. "And I'm a nice guy, yeah? So I'm gonna make your dreams come true, kid."

She quickened her pace until she reached the doorway. The door was opened a crack. Carefully, quietly, she pushed the door open wider until she could see most of the room. Like Malvus' office, the room had stone walls and flooring, but instead of a desk in the center of the room, there was a simple wooden table, upon which sat various metal tools and implements, very few of which Rekha could recognize. A large, hirsute man stripped to the waist and covered in sweat stood facing the back wall. Behind him, Rekha could only see a pair of manacles bolted to the wall, and a pair of delicate, pale hands sat trapped in them. *VARIAN!*

The man continued, "Lucky for you, I enjoy killing. So I take my time."

Rekha abandoned stealth, ran to the desk, grabbed what looked like a heavy pair of tongs and swung for the man's head. He turned just in time to catch the blow full in the face. He spun and collapsed to the floor. "Took too long, Keldin." She dropped the tongs next to his body.

Varian, disheveled, exhausted, bruised all over and bleeding from the nose and right arm, gaped at her. "Rey?!"

She grabbed one of his manacles and found a keyhole. "Where's the key for these?"

"I think he put it on the table. What took you so long?"

Rekha stepped back. "I should just leave you here. I flew up to the parapet, four stories up, and I have taken out two Legion officers to rescue you, and this is the thanks I get?"

"I'm sorry, I can't help it. I've been in full snark mode for a whole day at least."

She turned to the table, searching for the key. "Yeah, trying to get yourself killed. If we'd waited until the morning," she indicated the man on the floor, "your friend Keldin here would have succeeded."

"I'm sorry, but...I realized very quickly, when they started torturing me...I'm weak. I wanted to break. I wanted to tell them everything just so they'd stop hurting me. But that would've meant giving Belgam up, giving you up. I couldn't...I couldn't let that happen."

Rekha moved aside a pair of pliers, and found a small key underneath it. She grabbed it and inserted it into the lock of the manacle holding Varian's right hand. "Well, you don't have to worry anymore, okay? I'm gonna get you out of here."

As the manacle opened and his right hand came free, he said, "My family - where are they?"

She quickly unlocked Varian's other manacle. "They're safe."

Varian surprised Rekha by immediately hugging her tightly. He shuddered as he said in her ear, "Thanks."

She hugged him back. "Any time." She released the hug, but Varian did not let go. "Come on, we have to get out of here."

He let go. "Right, sorry." He straightened his shirt and moaned when he spotted a tear in it. "And I liked this shirt. Ugh. So what's the plan?"

"The plan?"

"You DO have a plan for getting out of here, right?"

She looked at him in consternation. "Uh...no."

"You came in through the parapet, you said? Can we get out the same way?"

"Well, I had to change into an owl, and it took several minutes to figure out how to fly. And you're gonna need to be able to fly - it's a forty-foot drop to the ground."

Varian touched his swollen eyelid tenderly. "I'm in pretty bad shape, but I think I can manage. You CAN turn me back after, right?"

Rekha took a moment to check Varian's properties and immediately saw a familiar symbol. *Shit.*

"That plan won't work. My magic's limited here, the Legion have some sort of stone that blocks me. I think the only way out is down."

Varian picked up the tongs Rekha had discarded and swung them once, nodding with satisfaction. "I'm as ready as I'll ever be."

"Yeah, come on, let's get out of here."

Rekha guided him back to the stairs down, and they were approaching the parapet door when she heard voices approaching quickly. She opened the door to Malvus' office instead and herded Varian inside, whispering, "Go, go!" She jumped in after him and almost fully closed the door, leaving it open a crack.

The voice was male and intense. "...says she's alone, but I doubt it. We caught her watching the Citadel." The voice was getting closer. "Either she's recon for a future intrusion, or we have intruders—"

The knock at the door was strong enough to swing it open. Rekha jumped clear so as not to be hit by the door, but in doing so, revealed her and Varian's presence to the surprised soldier standing in the doorway.

"...right now?!"

Rekha lunged at the man and pushed him back against the outer wall. As he collided with the stones, she saw to her right another soldier holding a chain that was tied around a dejected-looking Sarli's wrists. "Sarli!"

Sarli recovered fastest and hit the guard in the face with her chained fists. As he staggered back, the other guard went for his sword. Rekha lunged again and pinned the soldier's wrist to his chest, leaving half of his sword trapped in the scabbard. At the same time, Varian swung overhand with the tongs and hit the man square on the top of his helmet. The soldier's eyes went unfocused and he released the sword. Rekha punched him across the face, and he collapsed and went limp.

Sarli hurried over to the two of them, "Quick, get me out of this!"

As Varian helpfully unraveled the chain from around Sarli's wrists, Rekha looked around. "Wait, Sarli, where did your guard go?"

A bell started ringing rapidly and urgently from farther down the hall.

Oh, Esyu! "RUN!" Rekha turned and bolted away from the bell.

Varian tried to keep up. "Where are we going?!"

Sarli had no trouble keeping pace. "To the roof?"

Varian asked as they raced up the stairs, "Do we still not have a plan?!"

Rekha slowed to look inside the interrogation room where she'd found Varian. The big man inside was on his hands and knees, shaking his head. When he looked up towards the door, he said, "YOU!!" And then as she ran away he started shouting, "ALARM! ALARM! INTRUDERS!"

She turned back briefly to her friends and said, "Let's keep going up!" She faced forward and ran for the next stairway up.

They reached the next floor, and Rekha saw metal barred doors to what looked like cells.

Varian said, "Keep going, these are the prison cells, there's nothing here!"

The trio raced around the tower to the next staircase up, and emerged into open air. Rekha came to a stop. There was an incomplete wall built along the inside, but nothing along the outside. Rekha peered over the edge, but there was a sheer drop, sixty or seventy feet to the ground, with no real handholds to climb down with. She drew back before the height could make her dizzy. "There's has to be something we can use, a rope, maybe?"

They carefully wound their way along the outside of the top of the tower, but the only thing they found was a door in the inner wall. Upon opening it, Rekha saw a room with no back wall. It was full of large, squared-off stones and a barrel full of what looked like sand, and a small jug containing a sticky substance she guessed to be some kind of animal glue. She closed the door again with disgust.

Sarli had a pathetic look on her face. "I guess that's it, then. We have to surrender and hope Belgam can rescue us."

"No way! That butcher nearly killed Varian, if we surrender, he'll finish the job!"

Rekha looked around, for something, anything, but just saw Varian's panicked face and Sarli's resigned face. Out of desperation, she checked Sarli's properties.

The lock symbol was gone.

A voice she'd heard before broke her concentration. "They're right up here, yeah? They gots nowheres to go!"

Hearing the soldiers' armored footsteps approaching, Rekha's mind whirled. *We only have seconds left, that's not enough time to learn to fly safely. What if I...*

Rekha faced the door, grabbed the wooden knob, shouted "Anywhere else!" and snapped her fingers. She felt something go out of her and into the door. She turned the knob and threw it open to see a dark chamber beyond. She pushed Varian and Sarli through the doorway, and even as Keldin was laughing, rushing towards her, Rekha leapt through the doorway and shut the door.

Keldin laughed with triumph, even as the teenage girl shut the door in his face. He turned to the soldiers following him. "Idiots, yeah? Where are they gonna hide?"

He threw open the door to see a large pile of stones, a barrel of sand, a jug of animal glue, and a lack of a back wall giving a perfect view of the night sky.

Keldin rushed into the room, confused. He knocked over the barrel of sand, spilling it everywhere, but revealing no one hiding in it. The other soldiers started to dig through the pile of stones while he stepped through the hole in the back wall and looked down over the edge of the roof. No one was there.

Keldin turned back to the soldiers in the room, enraged. "FOUL SORCERY!!" he shouted, as he threw his blade to the floor with a clatter.

No sooner had Rekha shut the door than the entire doorway vanished, and she found her hands on a sleek red substance with some give to it. To her discomfort, it was slightly warm and wet. She pulled her hands back and shook them. "Eww...what is this stuff? Where are we?"

The three of them looked around at their new location. The room appeared oddly organic, with red bands that reminded Rekha uncomfortably of flesh. These bands changed color as they watched, becoming deeper red before turning lighter red, rhythmically, hypnotically. *They almost look like they're moving.*

The bands terminated near the ceiling, engulfing rounded white pillars not unlike bone. The effect was similar to being inside a rib cage. There were no light sources that Rekha could discern - if anything, the light seemed to be coming from the white pillars and the ceiling in a soft glow.

At the other end of the rounded room was a dark opening. As they watched, a silhouette filled the space. *Whatever it is, it's not Primordian!*

The being was seven feet tall and bright yellow, with tough, leathery skin. Its clawed hands and feet were adorned with small patches of brown fur on the knuckles, and the claws on its feet made an off-putting clicking noise as it strode into the room. It wore pants that appeared to be of a similar material to leather, and what looked like a tattered vest with little trinkets tied to it here and there. Its head was roughly Primordian-sized with sunken green eyes that almost seemed to be glowing. The creature had an elongated snout, and a mouth full of sharp teeth that gleamed in the pallid light. It breathed a raspy breath, and the three teenagers clutched each other in fright as it continued to approach.

They were all astonished when the creature stopped a few feet short of them, clutched a clawed hand to its chest, and spoke.

"Well, I dare say, isn't this a conundrum? How in Nixia's grace did you get aboard my ship? And what are you doing in my bathroom?"

Chapter 17

Sarli was the first to speak. "How...you speak Primordian?!"

The creature reared back. "No...I speak Anixian. You are also speaking Anixian. Right now. To me."

Varian asked, "What's Anixian?"

The creature barked in what was presumably akin to a laugh. "Well, my dear boy - you are a boy, correct?" Varian nodded. "Sorry, I've only seen a few of your species. Anyway, where was I? Oh, right - Anixian is a language, and a race of people, mine to be precise. In fact, Anixian is spoken by most peoples in this part of the galaxy."

Rekha hadn't been able to shake the astonished look from her face, but her eyes opened even wider. "Where are we?"

The creature held its hands up. "I'll be happy to answer your questions, and ask you a few of my own, if you'll all do me a favor and vacate the bathroom. I had to go before I found you here, and I've been holding it since."

Sarli shook her head. "Oh, sorry!"

Rekha took Sarli and Varian's hands. "We'll just get out of your way."

As she pulled him towards the entrance, Varian turned back. "Wait, how is this a room for bathing?"

"Not now!" Rekha pulled Varian clear of the opening. "We have MUCH bigger problems."

Sarli asked, "Where in the Abyss are we?" Rekha looked around the hallway. This appeared much less organic, the walls and ceiling were made of a dark green material she did not recognize, and the floor was a solid white sheet, akin to the ceiling in the previous room. "Did he say we're on a ship? Don't ships usually rock in the water? I don't feel anything."

Varian put his hand on Rekha's shoulder. "Hey, Rey, when were you going to introduce me to your friend here?"

She glared at him. "Oh, forgive me for saving us from the Legion instead of doing proper introductions. How silly of me."

Sarli laughed. "Hi, I'm Sarli! I'm from Cloydun. Nice to meet you!"

"Varian! Charmed. I used to be from Bromsford, but..."

"Yeah, your family's staying at my house. They're all okay."

"Thank you, that's a huge relief."

Rekha looked incredulously at both of them. "Well, now that that's settled, can we please talk about the strange monster whose ship we just accidentally invaded?"

"Monster?!" The yellow being appeared suddenly from the room they had just left. "I dare say, it's bad enough you're stowaways on my ship, but you're going to call me names, as well?"

Rekha wilted. "Sorry...we've never seen anything like you or this ship before, and we don't know how we got here, so we're all a little on edge." She glanced at Varian and Sarli, who wore bemused expressions. "Well, at least, I am."

"In that case, may I make a suggestion? Instead of choosing an offensive moniker, you could always just ask me my name. It's Baranix. The creatures like you who came before called me Barry, and honestly, it grew on me, so feel free, darlings." The creature strode past and beckoned them to follow.

Rekha obediently followed Barry down the dark green hallway. "I'm Rekha, this is Sarli, and that's Varian. Did you say there were people like us here before?"

"Yes..." The creature stopped suddenly in the hallway. "They didn't call themselves - what did you say? Primorbians?"

Varian held a finger up. "Primordians. We're from Primordia."

"Oh. That would explain it, I suppose. The other girl said they were 'Humans', but didn't say where they were from. 'Huma', probably, something like that." Barry continued to lead them through the corridor.

They passed several other openings as they went. All were clear and open, as if the concept of a closed door or privacy was unknown here. Rekha stopped to look inside at a large metallic object vibrating in front of a table covered in bizarre objects of all shapes and sizes. The vibrating object froze suddenly and then spun to face Rekha, who realized with alarm the object was alive. It stared at her with huge, deep red eyes, each with a set of three pitch-black pupils in a triangular formation. The creature had a tiny mouth, which it used to chitter angrily at her. Rekha gave a small yelp of fright and quickly rejoined the group.

"Please do not disturb Azathrax while she's eating. Few things irritate her more, and she invariably brings those complaints to me. Follow along and don't dawdle, Primordians, we're almost at the bridge."

The three looked at each other, uncertain, but they continued to follow.

They reached the end of the corridor to find a larger, more ornate opening than those they'd seen before. Like the bathroom, the opening was made out of a white material covered in red bands. As they stepped through, they saw a long, thin room with dark green walls and flooring. Four chair-like objects appeared to have grown out of the floor, two at the middle, and two at the far end of the room in front of a pair of consoles that appeared to have multicolored buttons and levers on them. Just above them was a rounded wall, most of which was taken up by what appeared to be a giant window, and it was this that had Rekha, Varian, and Sarli's full attention. The window displayed a central brightly-glowing point, around which various swirls of light appeared to be passing the window at high speed.

Sarli's jaw had dropped in awe. "Are we...are we flying?!"

Barry sat himself in the front-right chair and tapped a couple of buttons on the console. "That is correct, lovey - now, you're going to want to hold onto something. We're about to drop out of nullspace in three, two, one..."

The glowing point in the center of the window grew until the entire window was filled with blinding light, then there was a bright flash and a loud, low noise. The entire ship shuddered, and Rekha immediately grabbed onto the chair in front of her to avoid losing her footing. There was a constant gentle thrum now that seemed to be coming from the ship itself.

Rekha looked back up to the window. *I don't know what I expected, but it wasn't this.* "It's just the night sky?"

Sarli's eyes, on the other hand, were the widest Rekha had ever seen, and she blindly grabbed at Rekha's shoulder while staring at the window. "Are we...are—are we in space?!"

Barry laughed. "You darlings really aren't from this part of the galaxy, are you?" He took hold of a stick protruding from the console and tilted it to one side. The view outside the ship changed as the ship pitched forward and yawed slightly to the right. The trio watched as a small blue sphere with white spots appeared and centered itself in the window.

Sarli was clutching Rekha especially hard now. "OH MY ESYU!!"

"What?! What does this mean?"

"I think..." Varian also wore an expression of pure wonder. "I think we're beyond the sky, Rekha...among the stars."

She stared in astonishment at the blue sphere. "Is that...is that Primordia?"

Barry made an odd clucking noise. "I doubt it, lovey. That planet's called Regnix Ⅲ, that's our destination." A loud, annoying noise suddenly blasted at them from everywhere. "Oh, shezz."

Varian asked, "What was that?"

Barry peered down at his console and a heavy tone of dismay crept into his voice. "Oh, frux me parallel - it's the Dark Brigade." He tapped a button. "Veenix, are the force field generators working?"

A new, deeper voice emanated from the console. "I still need more time - the waveform oscillator is completely torqued."

"Never mind that now, darling, you're gonna want to get up here, we're about to be boarded."

"Nixia's grace! I'm on my way!"

Varian asked with a note of fear in his tone, "What's the Dark Brigade?"

Barry held up a hand as he tapped another button. "Azathrax, dearie, we have Dark Brigade inbound. Given the possibility of armed conflict, we are requesting all passengers make their way to the bridge for your own safety."

There was a familiar angry chittering in response.

"It's your choice, lovey, but the Dark Brigade aren't exactly notorious for taking prisoners alive. Thank you for flying Baranix Spaceways." He tapped another button, then turned to face the three frightened Primordians. "To answer your question, lovey, the Dark Brigade are mercenaries who usually do whatever dirty work they can get paid for, but they've been known to turn to piracy when times are lean. I wouldn't worry, darlings, it's entirely possible, even likely, that they're just passing by, and they won't interfere with us at all."

There was a sudden explosion and the entire ship seemed to shudder.

Barry raised a hand in a half-shrug. "Or."

The metallic creature Rekha accidentally disturbed earlier appeared in the center of the bridge entryway. It chittered questioningly at Barry.

"Azathrax! Please take a seat and buckle the restraints. With any luck, this will all be over soon."

Azathrax chittered darkly, waddled to a chair and jumped into it.

Rekha asked, "What do we do? Can we help at all?"

Barry stood up and crossed to a panel by the entryway. "Not unless you're intimately familiar with starship repair or lightfights, and no offense, dearie, but I highly doubt it." Another creature, very similar to Barry, but slightly shorter and with a blue-green color to their skin, came running up to the entrance. "Veenix! See if you can at least get the bridge's force field working, I'll hold them off." Veenix pulled a tool from their belt and went to work on the panel Barry had been fussing with.

Barry pulled an odd tube-like object from a brace on the wall and held it up to his shoulder as he peered back down the corridor from the relative safety of the doorway. Rekha, Varian, and Sarli watched in terror as a bright light appeared on the corridor wall not far from the bridge.

Barry shouted, "They're cutting through - everyone get behind cover!"

The three teens huddled behind the left side of the entryway even as there was a sudden explosion, and where the bright light had been, part of the corridor wall disintegrated, and people in strange black suits and helmets started emerging from the hole. They wielded boxy black instruments with holes on the front. Barry started squeezing the trigger on the tube, and accompanied by loud whine noises, bolts of light flew from the tube, some of which hit some of the people in suits, some of which impacted the corridor walls and floor. The suits began to fire back, and Rekha jumped as one bolt of light impacted the floor near where she stood, leaving behind a small, guttering flame.

The air was soon full of light bolts as Barry ducked in and out of cover, firing back seemingly at random, but never exposing more than a small part of his body. "How's it coming, Veenix?"

The creature next to him scoffed. "I'd need an hour and a coil of obsidian wiring. We have neither."

Barry gave a short bark of a laugh. "I'll bring her in for a total overhaul if we survive."

Sarli was holding her hands over her ears. "This is intolerable!"

Azathrax chittered loudly in Sarli's direction even as bolts stippled the back of the chair they were sitting in.

Rekha peeked out quickly. A few of the mercenaries were on the floor, unmoving, but there were many more in the corridor, and more still pouring in from the hole in the wall. She ducked back behind the entryway. "I couldn't agree more."

Varian shouted, "We must be able to do SOMETHING."

Sarli asked, "Does your magic still work? Try Belgam's barrier!"

"Oh, yeah!" Rekha imagined a barrier completely covering the entryway and snapped her fingers.

Suddenly the light bolts coming from the corridor stopped hitting various parts of the bridge, instead stopping in the empty air in front of the entryway. Rekha risked peeking out to see several of the suited creatures stop firing in confusion, though a few diehards kept shooting away. Barry went to lean out and fire again, but his tube contacted the barrier. Barry pressed his hands against the barrier a few times, testing it, even as several light bolts hit and stopped in the empty air in front of him.

"Huh." Barry's lips pulled back in a grin. "So much for an hour and some wiring. I don't pay you enough, Veenix."

"I didn't have anything to do with it, " said the deep-voiced Veenix, "but you're right, you don't."

"You're welcome." Rekha cheekily smiled at them.

"You did this?! How?!" asked Barry.

Sarli grinned. "On our planet, Rekha's what's known as a mage. She can do incredible things with the power of her mind."

Barry tilted his head in Veenix's direction. "Like those psionics we ran into on Aldur II."

Veenix turned to Rekha. "Is it airtight?"

Rekha answered, "According to Belgam, nothing gets in or out."

Barry's grin grew wider. "Veenix, let's break their spine!"

The two creatures walked to the front pair of seats and sat down. Veenix pressed a few buttons and announced, "Opening starboard cannon bay doors, switching to targeting view."

As the three Primordians watched, the view on the large screen changed from pure black space with a few stars to a view largely taken up by structures. On the left was a rounded, organic-looking structure of a similar green to the walls and ceiling of the ship they were in. On the right was an angular black structure, and the two structures were connected by a long, thin white tube that appeared to be foldable - even as they watched, the black ship moved slightly, and the tube expanded itself to maintain the connection.

At the center of the view were bright red cross lines. They watched as the view tilted downwards, placing the cross lines in the center of the white connecting tube.

Barry shouted, "Firing!"

White bolts of light leapt to the connecting tube, accompanied by a much louder version of the peculiar whine Barry's weapon made. Beyond the barrier, Rekha could see a tremendous expulsion of air, and the people lying prone were sucked out of the hole in the wall, along with numerous objects coming from other rooms in the hall. The remaining mercenaries in the hallway struggled to hold on to something. Some succeeded, while others were also sucked out of the ship. Rekha looked back to the screen and watched in horror as people in suits spilled out of both sides of the now-bisected connecting tube, tumbling into the black nothingness beyond. The black ship started slowly drifting away.

Barry gave off a barking laugh. "The idiots left the hatch open on the other side! Quick, get a tow line on that ship - we can sell it to cover the repairs and then some!"

Rekha turned back to look down the hallway as the air rushing out slowed, then ceased. There had been at least ten people in the hallway during the lightfight, now only three remained, letting go of their handholds and standing up somewhat dejectedly.

Barry turned in his chair to look down the hallway at the remaining mercenaries. "Veenix, can you patch me in to their helmet radios?"

"I can try." Veenix tapped a few buttons, and then slowly spun a small dial on his console. He then turned and pointed at Barry's console.

Barry grabbed a small, wiry implement from his console and lifted it to his lips. "Dark Brigade mercenaries, well, that didn't turn out at all like you expected, did it? Please pile all of your weapons in front of the bridge, then back away ten paces and hold your arms up."

Nobody in the hallway moved to follow those instructions. One of the people in suits folded their arms and leaned against the wall.

Barry continued, "Or we could just wait, and blow your bodies out the airlock. How much air do those suits of yours carry? Fifteen melvits' worth?" He turned to Veenix. "I personally wouldn't mind a nap, would you?"

The mercenaries threw their guns into a pile in front of the barrier and then stepped back, holding their hands up.

"Brilliant. In a few melvits, we'll see to your accommodations, then you'll have a choice to make. Either we can turn you in to the authorities on Regnix III, or you can join our security team! Three meals a day and easy credits, plus a lot less risking of your lives. Think about it, loveys, a representative of Baranix Spaceways will be with you shortly." With that, Barry set the wiry implement back into the console.

Veenix threw Barry a look. "We don't HAVE a security team."

"We do now." Barry stood up. "Speaking of—" Rekha was surprised when the tall creature knelt down in front of her and looked directly into her face. "We, all of us, owe you our lives. Thank you."

Azathrax made mewling noises in Rekha's direction.

Her cheeks burned. "It's no big deal, you're welcome."

"Can I ask you for one more favor? Well, two. Two more favors?"

"Okay?"

"Can you create one of your barriers covering that hole in the wall out there?" Barry indicated the hallway.

She concentrated and snapped her fingers, feeling that familiar jolt. "Done."

"Veenix, can you restart the air generators?"

He strode forward to join them by the entrance. "Already done, should be breathable in a melvit."

Barry handed Veenix his weapon. "Let me know when." He turned back to Rekha. "I'll be honest, I was planning on turning you in to the authorities for stowing aboard. But we owe you a great debt, Primordian. Baranix Spaceways will take you anywhere you want to go."

Rekha looked up at Barry's leathery face. "Well, we'd really like to go home. We just don't know how to get home from here."

Sarli asked, "Couldn't we just get there the same way we got here? Using a door?"

"I haven't seen a single door on this ship. But maybe it'll work if I create one?"

Barry stared blankly at them. "You must be from SOMEWHERE in the Allied Systems. We speak the same language, darlings, that's no coincidence."

Varian chimed in, "We can probably ask Belgam about that - if we can get back to Primordia."

"Air should be good now, boss." Veenix noted.

Barry turned to face Rekha and placed his hand on the bridge barrier. "That second favor, go ahead and drop this barrier, yeah?"

Rekha dissolved the barrier in her mind and snapped her fingers. The sudden air pressure change made her ears hurt.

Sarli seemed particularly sensitive and held her hands to her ears. "Ow, ow! What is that?"

Veenix seemed slightly ashamed. "Sorry, friend. May have misjudged there."

Barry indicated the mercenaries with a nod of his head as he collected the weapons piled in front of the entryway. "Get that lot into cabins and seal them in. I'll come speak to them individually in a melvit."

Veenix nodded and shouldered the weapon menacingly as he stalked down the hallway towards what was left of the Dark Brigade.

Barry dropped the weapons onto the chair next to his passenger. "Azathrax, I do sincerely apologize for the inconvenience. You may head back to your cabin now. Your lunch was very likely blown out into space, but I'd be happy to get you a second helping from the cargo bay if you'd like, lovey, okay?"

Azathrax released the safety harness and dropped to the floor. They cooed happily at Barry and proceeded to waddle down the corridor.

"As for you lot, figure out what you want to do and let me know, yeah? We might be able to find some information about your home planet when we reach Regnix Ⅲ, and then take you home from there. I'm gonna get this stuff squared away, get Azathrax a second lunch, and then talk to the mercenaries, but I'll be back in a few melvits." Barry picked up the pile of weapons and sauntered out into the hallway.

Varian said, "Let's try the door thing, Rey. I'd really like to see my family."

"Right." Rekha nodded. "I'll try spawning a door."

She concentrated, snapped her fingers, and sure enough, a wooden doorway was now standing in the middle of the bridge, looking even more out of place than the three Primordians. Sarli walked over to it, and opened the door, and then closed it again. "Okay, now do what you did at the top of the tower, but this time, try and send us to my house - my front door, if you can."

Rekha grabbed the door's knob and channeled the thought of Sarli and

Elena's front door into it. She snapped her fingers, and opened the door.

Just beyond, the house was just as she remembered it. Arden, Shilo, and Nedra were sleeping in bedrolls on the floor, and it was still dark. Varian excitedly charged through the doorway, shouting, "Mom! Dad! Nedra!"

Rekha and Sarli followed him and closed the door behind them as Arden and Shilo awoke and ran to embrace their son in astonishment as Nedra struggled to wipe the sleepiness from her eyes.

Arden clutched the back of his son's head with tears in his eyes. "We were worried sick about you, boy."

Shilo, still in her dressing gown, squeezed Varian even harder. "Praise be to Esyu."

Suddenly, Belgam stepped out of the shadows behind the stairs. "Well done."

Rekha stared at him, open-mouthed. "How did you—"

He interrupted, "How are the Allied Systems doing these days, anyway?" And he grinned and winked at her.

Chapter 18

Since nobody could sleep anyway, Sarli and Varian regaled his family with the story of his capture and eventual rescue while Shilo fussed over Varian's cuts and bruises, and Arden and Nedra sat in rapt attention. Rekha had pulled Belgam over to the side so they could speak quietly.

"How did you know where we were?" Rekha whispered.

"Have you forgotten who I am?"

"Not likely!"

Belgam held up his hands. "I saw Barry's ship behind you when you opened the door. How is Barry, anyway?" He grinned.

Rekha just stared open-mouthed at him.

"There's no need to act this surprised, you know. Watching over you has been my only purpose for eighteen years. And old habits die hard."

Rekha's eyes widened. "You knew I went in there alone, and you just let me?!"

"You're my most promising student!"

She gave him a flat stare. "I'm your ONLY student. What was that place? Sarli said we were among the stars."

Belgam furrowed his brow and opened his mouth soundlessly once or twice before finally speaking. "There are other worlds, even other whole universes than our own, and people like you and I have the ability to travel to and from these other places."

She folded her arms. "Why do I feel like you're not telling me everything?"

Belgam straightened his posture and raised an eyebrow. "Because there are some places you absolutely shouldn't go, and I'm not going to help you stumble into them. Speaking of stumbling, what I want to know is what gave you the idea to go off in the middle of the night, all by yourself?"

Her face became mournful. "My...my mom told me I had to go."

Belgam looked pained. "Your mother?"

"Yeah. She came to me in a dream and said if I didn't go right away, Varian would die. And she was right, I barely got there in time."

Even though his appearance was still that of a young man in his twenties, Belgam suddenly looked very old to Rekha, and his tone was layered with sadness. "How did she look?"

"I couldn't see her. I could only hear her voice. She sounded good, though."

His demeanor did not improve. "Oh. Well. That's good. She's always had good instincts."

Rekha froze. "Wait a minute. Are you saying that was really her? She can communicate with me in my dreams? Even though she's dead?"

He seemed to snap out of his funk. "No, of course not. I, I just—Your subconscious mind probably used her voice so you would trust it. And I just meant that she's your mother, so she probably passed her good instincts on to you."

Instead of replying, Rekha simply stared at him. *Why do all of Belgam's explanations feel like they don't add up?*

The familiar wood creaking sound indicating someone coming down the stairs broke Rekha's stare as she looked to see Elena perched halfway down, leaning over the railing to see everybody chatting away. "What's going on? Why is everybody awake?"

Sarli crossed to her mother. "Sorry, mom - but we just rescued Varian from the Legion."

Elena blinked. "You what?"

Varian approached. "Hello, ma'am. You're Sarli's mom? Thanks so much for taking my family in."

Shilo was teary-eyed. "Elena, your daughter and Rekha saved him - they saved my little boy!" She hugged Sarli.

Elena's eyes narrowed. "This is really important - did any of them see Sarli's face?"

The smile on Sarli's face faded. "Yeah. I got caught watching the tower while Rekha was inside. At least three or four of them saw my face."

Elena came down the rest of the stairs. "Then this is the first place they will look for you. We have to get you out of here - right now!"

Rekha added, "She's right, the Legion have three huge ships standing in the harbor. There could be hundreds of them in town right now."

Belgam nodded, "The Legion won't wait, so neither should we. They'll be looking for the four of us." He turned to Elena. "Will you and the others be safe here?"

She nodded. "The provincial governor owes me a few favors and I've been careful to write mostly pro-Legion stories in the news-sheets. I don't think they'll harass me too much, especially if I make up some stories about having arguments with my anti-Legion daughter."

Sarli turned to Elena with a tear in her eye. "Mom, I'm sorry, I—"

Elena hugged Sarli tightly. "When did you get so brave?! I'm so proud of you. Don't worry about me. Do what Belgam tells you to do, and send a message when you get somewhere safe."

Shilo was shaking her head. "No! I refuse to be separated from my son again! I'm coming with you!"

Varian held his mom's arms. "Mom, I'll be fine. And a life on the run - I don't want that for you, and I don't want that for Nedra, she needs you."

Arden placed a hand on his wife's shoulder. "He's right, Shilo."

She burst into tears and the three of them hugged each other, opening the hug up for Nedra, who also started crying.

Rekha asked Belgam, "Where are we going? Is anywhere safe from the Legion?"

"The Magic Academy is the safest place I can think of, but it's a good three or four days' ride from here on horseback. Speaking of—" Belgam turned to Sarli. "Do you need to pack anything?"

Elena chimed in. "I'll put together some things for her." She bustled off upstairs.

Belgam nodded. "Good." Rekha felt that familiar jolt as Belgam reached inside his robe and pulled out a small sack held closed with a drawstring, handing it to Sarli. "That should be enough money for three more horses. Go down to the stables and wake the stablemaster if you have to. We'll meet you there."

Rekha hugged Sarli. As they released each other, she untied Sarli's thong from her wrist, and handed it back, saying, "Thanks for this. Pretty sure we got lucky once or twice back there."

Sarli grinned and started wrapping up her hair in a ponytail. "Who knows? Maybe we'll get lucky again?" Sarli immediately reddened and dropped her hands from her hair. "I mean, maybe, at some point again, we might be in more danger, that's—"

Rekha, her heart pounding, without thinking, reached out and grabbed Sarli's hand in both of hers. "I know what you mean. All the same, thank you for helping me save Varian."

Sarli just reddened more and grinned. She nodded and squeezed Rekha's hands.

Gently squeezing back before releasing Sarli's hand, she said, "Be careful."

Sarli smiled and then set her shoulders. "Right. See you there." She strode to the front door and vanished into the night as it closed behind her.

Rekha approached Varian and his family. "I promise I'll keep him as safe as I can, and I'll make sure he remembers to send you messages when its safe to do so."

Shilo held Rekha's face in both hands. "I know you will, sweetheart." She looked down at the floor for a moment and grasped Rekha's shoulders. "I know what happened to Irynn was an accident. That wasn't your choice." She looked back up into Rekha's eyes, which had started to fill with tears. "But you risked your life to save my son. That WAS your choice. And that says SO much more about who - and what - you are."

Rekha struggled to not completely collapse into Shilo's arms, and instead hugged her tightly. *I'm no hero. But thanks for saying it.*

Elena came back downstairs carrying a small canvas sack. "I've got some changes of clothes and a few useful things..." She looked around. "Where'd Sarli go?"

"I sent her on ahead to get the horses. I'll make sure she gets them." Belgam took the sack from her and gave her a kindly look. "One last thing - as a thank you for cavorting with heathen sorcerers."

Rekha once again felt that sustained buzz as Belgam slowly released a spell and Elena assumed the now-familiar T-shaped pose. She watched in awe as Elena's face became less lined and more youthful before snapping back to standing normally.

"A handful of years is about all I can give you without getting you in trouble." Belgam smiled and held a hand out to indicate the nearby mirror.

Elena rushed to it and touched her face in astonishment. "I didn't feel a thing! This is a miraculous gift, Belgam, thank you!" She hugged him with glee before holding him at arm's length. "Now you make sure you keep my girl safe. And tell her to dress warmly, we'll be getting snow before you know it."

"I will, Elena, it's a promise."

"And you—" She turned to Rekha. "I'm sorry I didn't get more of a chance to be a mom for you." She hugged Rekha tightly.

"That's okay, ma'am. I appreciate everything you've done."

Elena held Rekha by the shoulders. "My girl, Sarli, she's never really had friends. She's always been more interested in her studies than other people. She must really like you, and if I'm not mistaken, it might actually go further than that."

Elena's eyes seemed to bore directly into Rekha's soul, and she reddened.

"Mothers know these things, sweetheart. Sarli's got her father's head, but her mother's heart. Be gentle with it - with her. Okay?"

Rekha didn't know what to say so she just nodded.

"And make sure you dress warmly, too." Elena smiled and winked.

Belgam cleared his throat. "Time to move - Varian, Rekha, let's go!"

Varian had a tearful farewell with his family and he promised to send messages, and he and Rekha quickly hugged Arden, Shilo, and Nedra in turn. Then they sadly turned and followed Belgam out Elena's front door into Cloydun's dark streets.

Belgam whispered, "Alright, let's stick to the shadows and stay quiet. If I remember correctly, the stables are at the north end of the city. We'll get the horses, swing back to the west side and ride around the lake." Belgam disappeared into the shadows, beckoning for Varian and Rekha to follow.

Rekha had already spent a good portion of this night creeping through the streets, so she almost felt comfortable stalking behind Belgam. She looked behind to see Varian, who appeared to be having a harder time, anxiously looking this way and that, jumping at every slight noise. Rekha reached back and took his hand, and gave him a solemn, confident look. He seemed to breathe easier, so she rubbed the back of his hand with her thumb and gave him a smile before turning back around and catching back up with Belgam.

They'd made it to the end of the street and were about to turn the corner, when suddenly there was a shrill whistle to their left. Rekha's head swiveled in that direction. *That was no bird.*

Stepping out into the moonlight, holding a struggling Sarli in front of him like a shield, Fulgin gave Rekha a cruel smile.

"I might not be able to hurt you. But you took someone I care about from me. Seems only fair."

He put a knife to Sarli's throat.

Chapter 19

Rekha focused on Fulgin's properties and he instantly assumed the T-shaped pose. Sarli, suddenly released, ran to Rekha and nearly tackled her in a rough embrace. "I'm so sorry! He was waiting for me!"

Rekha winced. "Easy now, I don't want to lose my focus here."

Belgam quietly whispered, "Do you want me to handle this?"

"No, everybody stay out of this. I've got it." Rekha gently removed Sarli from her embrace, crossed to Fulgin and dropped her focus.

He immediately cut the knife through the empty air in front of him and then stared at Rekha in confusion.

"I won't let you become a murderer, Fulgin."

He roared and slashed at her with the knife, forcing her to step back into the road. He flowed directly into a backhand slash about neck height. She stepped forward, blocking the attack with both arms, and kicked him in the stomach. Fulgin dropped the knife from his trapped right hand, and caught it by the handle with his left, and aimed a thrust at Rekha's stomach, forcing her to release him and leap backwards to avoid being impaled.

He grinned as he switched the knife back to his right hand. "Shame. If she'd died, maybe you would've felt the same pain you visited on Dargen and me. That would be justice."

Rekha risked a look back as Varian responded, "Irynn would disagree."

"Shut up!" He charged Rekha and slashed at her diagonally. She leaned to one side to dodge the slash and quickly popped him in the face with a jab. He reeled back a bit, and Rekha took the opportunity to circle him to his left, ensuring her friends would stay out of his line of attack. He lunged at her with another stomach thrust, which she leapt back to avoid, but he quickly lunged again, converting the thrust into a wide slash. Rekha barely sidestepped the slash, the blade coming within an inch of her body but cutting a small tear in her leather vest.

She looked down at her damaged top. "This is my favorite vest! You son of a..."

He charged at her a third time, winding up for another diagonal slash. Instead of dodging, she stepped into his advance and spun, backing into him. She caught his right arm with her right hand and slammed her left elbow into his throat. While he choked, she stepped to the right, grabbed his knife arm with both hands and wrenched his arm hard clockwise, forcing him to flip his body forwards. Even as he landed on the ground, he still held the knife tightly in his fist, so Rekha squatted down and bit him on the wrist as hard as she could. Fulgin squealed and reflexively dropped the knife to the ground.

Rekha casually picked up the blade and calmly kicked Fulgin hard in the face. Hurt but still conscious, he spit out one of his teeth before glaring at Rekha and breathing heavily, but he did not try to get up.

Rekha carefully tossed the knife into the shadows of the nearby buildings, and it flew several yards before landing in the darkness with a clatter. Satisfied, she knelt down next to him. "Is Dargen safe?"

He wheezed, "Safe from you."

That's good enough for me. She nodded as she absentmindedly straightened Irynn's pendant on her chest, only for it to turn crooked again. "Fulgin, I will carry the guilt of Irynn's death for the rest of my life. And I get that that isn't enough for you, I do. But your problem is with ME. No one else. So, if you ever threaten Sarli, or Varian, or anyone else who isn't me again, Esyu help me, I *will* kill you. And I won't carry the guilt of your death even long enough to wash the blood off."

Rekha stood up and nonchalantly walked back to the group. Belgam gave her an approving nod. To her surprise, Varian strode over to the prone Fulgin.

He knelt down. "I know you won't listen, because you haven't listened to anyone who cares about you. But I'd be negligent if I didn't try, so here goes: Irynn's death was a loss for the world. She was a bright light that improved this world just by being in it. You, on the other hand, are threatening innocent women."

Fulgin's face darkened.

Varian mercilessly carried on. "We all saw it, Fulgin - you would have slit her throat if Rekha hadn't saved her. Your death would be a benefit to the world. People would actually be safer. And Irynn would be incredibly ashamed of you. You should think about that." He got up and returned to the group, and they carried on sneaking through the dark.

It could have been something else, or it could have been wishful thinking, but Rekha swore she heard light sobs coming from Fulgin's direction as they skulked away.

* * *

The stablemaster did not appreciate being woken up and he appreciated even less Belgam's insistence on haggling the price down. They did eventually agree on a price, and she once again felt that familiar jolt as Belgam spawned a small sack of coins and handed it to the man.

As Sarli assisted Varian with saddling and mounting his horse, Rekha asked Belgam, "If you can simply spawn any money you need, why haggle so much?"

Belgam raised an eyebrow. "Pretend you're a stablemaster. Someone wakes you up in the middle of the night and hands you more money than your horses are worth without putting up a fight..."

"I would think they'd done something bad and are fleeing before they get caught."

"Exactly. By haggling, it looks less like we're criminals and more like we've just gotten up stupid early for a journey."

Rekha clumsily but successfully swung herself up into the saddle. "I hadn't thought of that."

Belgam took the reins of his horse but remained standing. "I noticed."

She let that pass.

They walked through the barn doors and crossed the street, with Belgam stopping every few feet to use a curious-looking brush to clear their tracks from the dirt. Once they had safely crossed and were once again in shadow, Belgam wore a look of concentration, and Rekha heard a staccato beat of rapid jolts. Simultaneously, hoof marks started appearing in front of the stable barn doors, creating horse tracks that led north through the wide avenue heading out of the city. Belgam continued concentrating for quite a few moments before finally relaxing, and he turned and mounted his horse with practiced ease.

They rode slowly - painfully slowly, it seemed to Rekha - through the northwest quarter of Cloydun. Here the houses appeared to be built from cut stone and wooden roofs, resulting in very similar homes that, while not as pretty as the part of the city Sarli and Elena lived in, reminded Rekha of Lucky's house. She sighed bitterly. *Now I can't ever go back there, thanks to the Legion.*

She glanced over at Sarli and saw a look of worry she'd never seen on her face before. *She's probably worried about her mom. On some level, that's my fault, too.* Thinking about Elena brought her words back to the forefront of Rekha's mind. *Protect her heart.*

Rekha brought her steed up next to Phi, reached over and wordlessly took Sarli's hand. Sarli looked at her, smiled, and interlaced her fingers with hers.

They rode hand-in-hand until they approached the west end of Cloydun. There was no official border to this part of the city, the houses merely stopped, and the trees began.

Belgam whistled, and Varian, Rekha, and Sarli brought their mounts in close.

He kept his voice low. "We're going to walk out of the city for a league, then bring it up to a canter until we get a couple of leagues out. Then we're going to swing south, and follow the edge of the lake down until we hit the road to Wildfall. Stick to the trees and keep noise and unnecessary talking to a minimum. I laid tracks to the north that will hopefully send them looking in the wrong direction, but we've no idea whether or not that ruse worked. The Legion could be anywhere in this forest. Keep your eyes peeled and look out for one another." The three teens all nodded in agreement. "Alright, let's ride."

They walked single-file into the dark forest. Rekha had barely slept at all this night, and she kept expecting Legion soldiers to be behind every tree. For her part, Sarli appeared to be right at home, Phi strutting confidently along. Varian appeared to be uncomfortable riding his horse and kept shifting in his saddle.

After some time had passed, Belgam waved to the others and lightly kicked his horse, spurring it to run, and the others followed suit. After a couple of hours or so, as the sun began to break the dawn in the orange sky, he turned hard left, and they continued south through the forest surrounding Cloydun.

A few more hours passed as they quietly rode for miles through the unrelenting trees. Rekha was beginning to feel drowsy, and she felt at this point a lot less worried about a Legion ambush, but she still did her best to remain alert and vigilant.

As she was scouring the surroundings, she caught a hint of blue through the trees to her left. She wiped her tired eyes and squinted, and it was hard to tell, but it sure looked like water to Rekha. She snapped her fingers twice, getting the others' attention, and pointed to the water.

Belgam dismounted and took a few steps in the direction Rekha was pointing. "The lake. Well spotted, Rekha. Let's take a few minutes to feed and water our mounts, and feed and water ourselves before we carry on following the lakeside."

Once the horses were seen to, Belgam created a small firepit around which the group ate and engaged in quiet conversation. There was an unexpected bonus of delight upon Sarli discovering that her mother had packed some fresh fruit for her.

"I haven't felt this much pain in my thighs since...well, ever, I suppose."

Varian was irritably rubbing his legs down.

"Hey, Belgam?" Sarli asked. "Why do we need to ride at all? Couldn't Rekha just make a door that would take us straight to the Magic Academy?"

"Oh." Belgam looked to be caught off-guard by the question, but he recovered quickly. "Well, if all we were doing was getting you lot transported to the Academy, sure, but we're also gathering intel. Rekha said she saw three Legion ships in the docks, and I need to know what they're doing here. That means checking this side of the lake for Legion encampments — and steering us clear of them. There's no real rush to get there, but we can use a door as a last resort if we need to."

Sarli, mollified, nodded sagely.

Varian changed the subject. "Sarli, how did you become so gifted with horses?"

She tilted her head. "How do you mean?"

"Well, when we sped up, when we turned, I didn't see you tap your horse or even use the reins hardly at all. Do you have some kind of verbal commands worked out or something?"

She laughed. "No, nothing like that. Phi's just really intelligent. She understood we were following Belgam and just matched his horse's speed and direction. I barely had to make her do anything."

"Wow. That's one smart horse."

Rekha interjected. "I wonder if maybe she just adapted to match her owner."

Sarli was both pleased and curious. "How so?"

"Like was she born intelligent or did she get smarter from the gentle handling of the smartest person I know?" Rekha grinned.

"Stop." Sarli smiled in spite of herself.

"Oh, yeah." Varian perked up. "Didn't your mom say something about your studies? What did you study?"

"Honestly? Everything." Sarli took another bite of her apple. "Cloydun's library wasn't expansive, but I've liked books more than people since I was a kid. I must have read just about everything they had, cover-to-cover. I learned about fish, about the sky, and about woodworking and building houses with mortise-and-tenon joints. My favorite book, hands down, was about the proper care of horses. It had hand-drawn horses in it, and I just thought they were really beautiful creatures."

Rekha was fully engaged, leaning forward with her hands on her chin, paying rapturous attention. "How did you get Phi?"

"My mother bought her for my sixteenth birthday." Sarli's smile faded. "She knew I wanted one more than anything in the world. I thought it was impossible - it would cost her more than she makes in three months." She gave a rueful laugh. "Turns out she had been saving money for years, a little here, a little there, and she was just waiting until she felt I was old enough to be responsible for it." Her face saddened further and her shoulders slumped.

"Hey." Rekha sat up, reached an arm across Sarli's back and stroked her long hair. "I'm sure she's fine. And it's not your fault, none of this is."

Belgam folded up a strip of bacon between his fingers. "Your mom will be just fine. Even if the Legion have the king in their pocket - and I've every reason to believe they do - they still need the permission of the provincial governor to operate. The king would have to relieve him of duty to get around that, and they're cousins. Trust me, the Legion won't harm Elena."

Sarli nodded glumly. "I'm gonna..." She stood up suddenly. "I'm gonna rub down Phi's legs with some straw and check her hooves for stone bruises... she's been favoring her left forehoof lately." She turned and walked away.

Rekha took the opportunity to enjoy the sight of Sarli's shapely behind, but noticed out of the corner of her eye that Varian was staring as well. She murmured, "Isn't it incredible?"

Far from being embarrassed, Varian asked, "How does she move like that? Does she have two kittens fighting in there?"

From a distance, they heard, "I CAN HEAR YOU!"

Rekha and Varian shared a wide-eyed look before collapsing in helpless laughter.

In a few minutes, they were riding again. They followed the lakeside south, curving around to the east until the sun was high in the sky. The trees started thinning in numbers, replaced with bushes and tall grass.

Rekha had been recharged somewhat by their rest stop, but after a few hours, she felt bone-tired again. She plaintively asked, "How much further?"

Belgam sighed. "The road to Wildfall is close, we should see it any minute."

"Hey, guys?" Sarli piped up. "Something's wrong. Phi's super anxious for some reason."

Suddenly, armored men burst out of the bushes all around them, the red stone eye on their chests proclaiming louder than words who they were and why they were there. Rekha's horse reared up in alarm, and she fell painfully to the ground as the horse ran back the way they'd come.

The soldier directly ahead of Belgam's horse shouted, "FREEZE!"

Chapter 20

Everybody froze, except for Rekha, who got to her feet, only for a nearby soldier to menace her with his sword. She immediately backed up with her hands held up.

"Before any of you with magic powers do anything foolish, please know that I have several archers with bows drawn and arrows pointed at your hearts." The soldier in front of Belgam beckoned for a nearby soldier and sharply noted, "Send a message to Captain Malvus, inform him we've captured the wanted criminals."

"Oh, is that what you think happened?" Belgam said, dismounting his horse and calmly approaching the Legion in charge. "Because it looks very much to me like you've all sacrificed your lives for nothing."

With everyone watching Belgam, Rekha took the opportunity to check the properties of the Legion soldier nearest her and noticed that, peculiarly, the lock symbol was rapidly flashing.

The soldier in charge took a few steps back, putting about ten feet of space between them. He held up a hand. "Hold it right there, Belgam. I give the word, and you and your friends are dead."

Rekha took a step forward, and the lock symbol on the Legion soldier's properties solidified.

Belgam halted and gently laid his cane on the grass in front of him. "And how do you plan to speak that word..."

Rekha took two steps back, and the lock symbol vanished. *The apotro-bla-bla-bla has a range!*

Belgam's tone was still even and friendly. "...with a crushed windpipe?"

In the blink of an eye, so fast Rekha didn't see him cover the distance between them, Belgam slammed his fist into the officer's throat, and he immediately started choking.

Rekha dropped focus on the soldier in front of her, concentrated on a huge circular barrier surrounding them and the soldiers, and, she hoped, in between them and the archers, and snapped her fingers.

She heard the twang of several bows, and three arrows struck the empty air a couple of feet in front of Belgam, and fell harmlessly to the ground.

Sarli turned Phi and drove her directly at the soldier nearest her. He tumbled under the great horse's legs, and Phi nickered wickedly as she drove her hooves into squishier parts of his body.

The soldier facing Rekha charged, his sword arm held high, ready to slash at her. Rekha stepped into his charge and grabbed his arm, wrenching it clockwise, throwing the man to the ground. She stomped on his head and wrested the sword from his clutches.

Varian had dismounted on the opposite side of his horse from the soldier nearest him, and was using the horse for cover. When the soldier ran around the tail end of the horse, Varian grabbed the stirrup for leverage and quickly slid under the horse to the side the soldier had just vacated. The soldier smacked the horse's rear end with the flat of his blade, causing the animal to obediently trot away, and when Varian stood up, his cover was gone.

He turned to run, and ran smack into Rekha's invisible barrier, falling to the ground. The soldier grinned and raised his sword. Rekha leapt forward and caught his blade with her own, pushing it back up over her head and to the left, opening the soldier up to a kick in the face. He stumbled backwards and fell. Rekha quickly stepped on the man's sword arm, putting the point of her own sword at his throat. "Drop it." The soldier did as he was told with gritted teeth. As Varian rushed up to grab the soldier's blade, Rekha took a moment to take stock of the situation.

All of the soldiers within the barrier were down. Belgam was holding a hand up to the sky, and he closed his hand into a fist. Instantly, three lightning bolts struck clumps of bushes several yards away from the barrier. As the incredibly loud sound of thunder rolled over them, three armored men fell out of the bushes. Unconscious or dead, Rekha couldn't tell, but it looked like smoke was rising from at least one of the bodies.

Belgam turned to see the three teens had the remaining soldiers under control. He nodded. "Well done. Rekha, you can probably drop that barrier now."

As she did so, Rekha looked at the other soldiers. The one she'd stomped on and the one Belgam had punched in the throat were both down and not moving, and Sarli's was conscious but moaning like he was in a lot of pain. She looked down at the man she still held at swordpoint. "What do we do with them?"

Belgam gave her a curious look. "You kill them."

The soldier's eyes widened in fear. Rekha suddenly remembered Wilkin and Janim's conversation from the previous night. She also saw in her mind's eye her hometown of Bromsford burning to the ground while soldiers like this one murdered the people she saw and spoke to every day. Finally, she saw Lucky giving her a sad look and quietly shaking his head.

Rekha threw the sword into the bushes several yards away. "No. Never. They might be murderers, but they'll never turn me into one."

Belgam looked at Rekha in astonishment. "Are you serious? They are actively hunting us, and if they catch us, they will take great pleasure in killing us very slowly. And then there's the small matter of the Legion having killed an entire village of innocent people-", with this he stepped directly in front of Rekha, and his angry tone grew to a shout, "-who I might remind you, includes your UNCLE?!"

Even as Rekha felt her face getting flushed with rage, Sarli appeared out of nowhere. "Whoa, whoa, whoa!" She interposed herself between them, facing Belgam with an assertive look. "Rekha's made her decision. You're not going to unmake it for her. And if you have a problem with her choice, you can either talk to her in a calm and reasonable tone, or you can shut up and keep it to yourself. What you DON'T get to do is scream and shout at her like some petulant child who lost his toy."

Belgam stared at Sarli, his jaw working for a moment, before he walked away, muttering to himself.

Rekha stared at her in wonder. "Thank you, I—"

"Oh, I don't let anyone talk to me like that. The best way to deal with that is to shut it down immediately." Sarli finally turned to face her, and Rekha found herself marveling at the depths of her gorgeous eyes, the warm copper color of her irises, and the steel in her protective gaze.

As Varian jogged over to join them, the soldier at Rekha's feet began to weakly laugh.

The three of them looked down at the man, and Varian asked, "Something funny?"

He coughed. "Just enjoying the infighting among filthy mage traitor scum. It's a wonder we even have to chase you people down, we could just stand back and let you all implode."

Rekha said grimly, "I said I wouldn't kill you. I never said I would let you keep all of your teeth."

She wound up and kicked the man hard in the face.

The officer Belgam had punched in the throat had asphyxiated, and all of the archers were dead. After they'd tied up and gagged the remaining living Legion soldiers, they retrieved Rekha's horse.

They carried the soldiers with them as they traveled, until they found the well-used road to Wildfall. They laid them just off the side of the road, so they wouldn't be seen, but when they came to, they'd make enough noise to be found by other travelers. "That way, they won't be found right away and raise the alarm, but they won't be left here for days on end to die, either," Sarli reasoned.

Belgam had calmed down somewhat, but there was a sarcastic energy as he harrumphed. "Well, now that we're leaving live witnesses behind, we can't rely on stealth anymore, so we have to turn to speed. I'll fly ahead and look for any Legion encampments, but bring my horse along just in case." And he transformed into a red-tailed hawk and flew off.

The three teens rode at a gallop down the road for an hour, slowing to a miles-eating canter to preserve the horses' stamina after that. Varian clutched his horse's mane tightly as her hooves thundered across the packed dirt. He shouted over the din, "This is truly an awful way to travel!"

Sarli shouted back, "It takes some getting used to, sorry!"

"How long until we reach Wildfall?"

"At least two more days!"

Varian looked crestfallen. "Great."

Sarli smiled. "Look at it this way - once you're used to it, you'll be able to ride anywhere!"

"How long does it take to get used to it?"

"Several days." Sarli smiled sweetly at him.

Varian gave her a withering look. "Rey, your girlfriend's an evil woman!"

Rekha flushed and refused to look at Sarli for a while.

A couple of hours after the sun went down, they pulled off the road and continued to ride for some time to ensure they would not be found, before setting up camp for the night near a brook. Rekha ate lightly, all she could think about was getting some sleep. She walked over to where the horses were tied up to get her bedroll, and was distracted by the waters of the brook babbling away.

She stared into the water. She didn't know what she was looking for, as the water cascaded and bubbled over the mud and rocks making up the brook's bed. It took her a moment to realize she could see her own reflection.

Even as she watched, the image changed, and she saw Irynn looking back at her sorrowfully.

Rekha burst into tears immediately. "I'm sorry, Irynn, I'm so sorry!" But after wiping the tears from her eyes, all she saw was her own reflection.

A gentle voice behind her said, "Hey, come here."

Rekha turned to see Varian standing there with his arms spread wide, and she instantly hugged him. "I see her...everywhere...she's so sad..."

"Shhh, no, sweetie, it's your imagination. I know, wherever she is, Irynn doesn't blame you for what happened." He leaned back, but kept his arms around her. "Come on, let's get you cleaned up."

They walked some distance away from the camp, and Varian took out a small handkerchief and started to wipe Rekha's face with it. "You should probably avoid crying in public, it makes you look absolutely ghastly."

She smiled in spite of herself and injected sarcasm into her tone. "Thanks."

"No charge." He grinned at her before his mouth dropped open. "Oops. Forgot something. Stay here - I'll be right back."

"Okay." Rekha sat down in the grass and patiently waited while Varian headed back to camp. But to her surprise, after a moment or so, Sarli entered the little clearing instead.

"Hey, Varian said you wanted to talk to me?"

VARIAN! Rekha looked around quickly and saw Varian peeking his head over one of the horses. He gave her a grin and a thumbs-up and disappeared.

"Y-yeah...I wanted to apologize. For just now. And for a few other things besides."

Sarli sat down in front of her cross-legged. "You don't have to apologize for crying. I know what you've been through."

Communication is the answer. "I told you that I accidentally killed my best friend, Irynn. What I didn't tell you was that I kinda, sorta, maybe had a huge crush on her."

Sarli grinned. "Kinda, sorta, maybe, huh? Sounds iffy. Are you sure?"

"Definitely maybe."

She laughed and leaned forward. "Okay. Why does that make you want to apologize to me?"

Rekha's cheeks burned and she started wringing her hands. "Because I kinda, sorta, maybe...have a huge crush on you."

Sarli's grin faded and she leaned back as her tone became serious. "Definitely maybe?"

Rekha wanted desperately to look anywhere else, but could not tear herself from Sarli's eyes. "Definitely definitely."

"Oh. I see." Sarli sat up straight and looked down at the ground momentarily before looking back up at her. "Would it help at all to learn that I feel the same way?"

An oppressive weight lifted from Rekha's shoulders and she felt like she could breathe again. "It actually helps immensely. Thank you." The smile that was coming died before it reached her lips. "There's just one major problem."

Sarli, confused, leaned back. "What? What is it?"

Rekha looked back at Sarli and said sadly, "I feel like I'm betraying Irynn by even thinking about you, and it hurts, every time. Besides," she sniffed and wiped her eyes, "I can't give you what you deserve."

Sarli seemed to transform as her shoulders sank, the light vanished from her eyes, and she looked down at the ground. "I...I see."

Rekha reached out to take Sarli's hand with one hand and grabbed her chin with the other, and lifted her face back up to meet her gaze. "But I'll give you everything I can."

Sarli's eyes widened and the corners of her mouth threatened to turn back up. "You mean it?"

Rekha beamed at her and squeezed her hand.

Sarli sat up straight again and her smile was like the sun coming up. Then she lightly shoved Rekha with one hand. "You tease!"

"I didn't mean to tease you. I just needed you to know that there might be some problems along the way."

"Then we'll deal with them. Together. Ooh, I like that word. Can we celebrate?"

Rekha cocked an eyebrow. "You want to throw a party? In the middle of nowhere?"

"I was thinking more about the first time you cast a spell on me...I thought we could commemorate the occasion by having you paint our fingernails."

Awww... "Of course! We should do matching colors. Okay, close your eyes."

Sarli obediently sat up straight and closed her eyes.

Rekha had to resist the urge to lean in and kiss her. *Should probably go with sky blue, like her house. I think that'd look good on both of us.*

She focused on Sarli's properties, and when she T-posed and the list appeared, Rekha started browsing through it.

Wait. Rekha froze. *There's one thing she wants more than painted fingernails.*

Rekha scoured Sarli's properties for anything related to magic or special abilities, but came up with nothing. *Maybe I'm going about this all wrong. Maybe I need to go deeper.*

Rekha focused intently on Sarli's properties, not moving up or down, but through, beyond the list in front of her. Sure enough, the white list of normal properties faded, replaced by a gray list of properties Rekha had never seen before. *Parent and child objects? Owner? I'm gonna have to ask Belgam about these.*

She didn't have to scroll down far to find 'Magic User.' Her jaw dropped, but she quickly changed it from 'No' to 'Yes' and dropped her focus.

Sarli instantly resumed her seat in front of Rekha, taking on a look of confusion as Rekha gaped at her wide-eyed. "What is it?" She looked at her unpainted fingernails. "Did something happen?"

Rekha gave her a big smile. "Trust me. Open your hand."

Sarli's confusion faded a little, but she did what she was told.

"Imagine a rose appearing in your hand. Concentrate on it, and when you're ready, release it by snapping the fingers of your other hand."

Sarli stared intently at her open left hand, and snapped the fingers of her right. Rekha immediately felt a familiar reverberating jolt.

A pristine red rose suddenly appeared in Sarli's left hand.

She started to shake. "How...did...you did this!"

Rekha wore a huge smile. "No, it was all you! Didn't you feel that weird jolt of energy in your head?"

Sarli, stunned, looked back and forth between Rekha and the rose.

"Don't you get it? You're a mage now, Sarli!"

Sarli squealed and tackled Rekha to the forest floor.

Rekha banged her head slightly. "Ow."

"Ooh, sorry! Are you okay?"

Her eyes met Sarli's. She could feel the warmth and the weight of Sarli's body pressed to hers, and she reveled in the sensation. "Yeah. I'm more than okay." She leaned up and surprised Sarli with a kiss. As Sarli gazed at her in awe, Rekha said, "For luck."

They kissed again, and in that moment, Rekha let everything go, just to be with her.

Rekha's sleep was undisturbed, as much as she hoped she might dream of Sarli or hear her mother again. When she was woken by Belgam, she still grumbled, wishing she could sleep longer.

She put together a plate of breakfast and as she walked past Varian, she gave him a quick one-armed hug and said, "Thank you."

"You're welcome, love."

Sarli took a look at Rekha's plate and asked, "Do you want any fresh fruit with that? I could spawn some for you. I could use the practice."

Belgam stopped eating. "What's this?"

"Oh, that's right." Sarli grinned wickedly at him. "Rekha gave me magic powers. Hey, don't I recall you telling me for years that couldn't be done?"

Belgam's eyes widened, his hands started to shake, and he dropped his fork. "Are...are you serious? You're a mage now?"

In response, Sarli snapped her fingers, and another fork appeared in Belgam's hand. He immediately dropped it and his plate of food as he stood up and put his shaking hands over his mouth.

Something's wrong. Rekha asked, "I just focused on her properties and found the special properties hidden underneath the regular ones...was I not supposed to do that?"

Belgam closed his eyes and sank to his knees. "We...actually...did it."

"Did what?"

He ignored her, raising his hands high and shouting, "WE DID IT, MERYN! YOU WERE RIGHT!" He fell backwards to the ground and started laughing.

Enough. Rekha set her plate down and walked over to him. "Belgam, would you stop it with the cryptic games and just tell us what in the Abyss is going on?!"

He looked up at her with something approaching reverence. "It worked, Rekha! You're exactly what we wanted!"

She unconsciously clutched Irynn's pendant as she stared at him.

"You are the Esyu!"

Chapter 21

Rekha staggered back a step, trying to mentally parse what Belgam had just said.

Sarli asked, "The Esyu?! Are you...are you saying Rekha is...a god?"

Belgam sat up. "I suppose that depends on your perspective."

Rekha burst out, "For the love of — would you just, for once, give us—give ME a clear answer?"

"Of course." Belgam stood up. "In fact, I think it's time I gave you all the answers." He waved a hand, and behind him in the grass appeared a doorway with a very strange door. It was made of some kind of smooth ceramic material Rekha couldn't identify. He stepped towards the door and it slid open with a hiss, revealing a plain white hallway beyond with wooden flooring and another identical white door set in the wall opposite. He beckoned, "Rekha, come with me. We have much to discuss."

"We're coming with you!" Varian exclaimed.

"I'm afraid you can't. Only Rekha and I can pass through this door. You're welcome to try, of course." Belgam extended a hand to the open doorway.

Varian strode to the doorway and collided with something, staggering back in amazement. He put his hands up to the doorway, but they were stopped by some invisible force.

"I'm very sorry. But Rekha will explain everything to you when we get back." He turned to look at her. "Let's go."

"Wait." Rekha crossed her arms. "Why can't you just tell me here?"

"Because there are things I can't show you here - and you need to know what's really going on."

She looked at Sarli, who nodded her head. "Go ahead. We'll be here when you get back."

Rekha braced herself and followed Belgam through the doorway. A slim white door slid shut behind her with a hiss. She looked around the hallway.

Including the door they'd just come through, there were eight doors in total, all made of that same ceramic, and none of which had any door knobs or handles. The thing that bothered her the most was the silence. The world she had just left was full of life and sound, even when things got quiet, you could hear the wind or the insects. This place was as quiet as death.

As the silence reigned and Rekha took it all in, Belgam appeared to be watching her closely.

She looked at him. "Well? Talk."

Belgam held up a hand. "First, a question. Does this place seem familiar to you?"

She was about to say, "Of course not," when something stopped her. She looked again at the shape of the doors, and at the wood panels on the floor. This place WAS familiar, but she couldn't put a finger on why. "Where are we?"

"This is a sort of hub. It allows us to quickly travel between simulations and gives us access to the main computer."

"Wait, what? I don't..."

Belgam gently took one of Rekha's hands in both of his own. "Rekha, Primordia, that world and everything in it - it's all a simulation. Entirely created and run by a thinking machine called a computer."

Rekha struggled to grasp what he was trying to tell her, but something inside her believed him. "Wait, are you saying my entire world isn't real?"

"What I'm saying is this: a much more technologically advanced society than the one you've lived in your whole life has machines that let people create simulations of entire worlds — and then visit and explore them. Primordia is one such simulation. The 'magic' that we do isn't really magic, we're just using computer commands to spawn objects or change them in the simulation." He paused a moment and looked at her curiously, as if to check that she was understanding him. "The Allied Systems that you stumbled into while rescuing Varian is another simulation - that's why the aliens there speak the same language we do instead of some alien language. You and I have the ability to travel between these simulations. Whether or not they're 'real', that depends on your perspective. Sarli and Varian are real to you because they're part of the world you grew up in. To me, they're fictional."

Rekha felt a rush of anger. "They are not fiction!"

"I'm sorry, but they are. And I should know - I created them."

She stared at him, mouth agape. "You...created them?"

"I created all of Primordia. It was my simulation." He let go of her hand and turned and looked at the large door behind him for a moment before turning back to Rekha. "Come on, we might as well make ourselves comfortable. We've got a lot to go over, and we're gonna be here for a while." He turned away.

"Wait, wait! What about Sarli and Varian? We can't keep them waiting too long."

Belgam turned back. "Time stopped for them the instant you and I left Primordia."

"What?! Why?"

"The Cris System — that's the name of the computer that runs the simulations — classifies you and I as 'players.' That's why we can freely travel to and from simulations, and it's why we can come back here, to the hub of the Cris System. Sarli and Varian were created inside a simulation and are classified as 'characters.' They can't move between simulations unless a player opens a door for them, and they cannot come to the hub."

He shrugged as he continued, "As for why time has stopped, the Primordia simulation automatically stops running if there are no players in the game. You and I were the only players left in Primordia, so it stopped cold the instant the door shut behind you. When we return to Primordia, it will appear to Sarli and Varian as if no time has passed at all."

Rekha stared at Belgam blankly. "I am trying, but this is a lot."

He gave her an empathetic look. "Trust me, you'll understand everything once I explain. Come."

He walked to the door at the head of the hallway and it obediently slid open with a hiss. Beyond was a large room, with what looked like a large table surrounded by seven white chairs in one half of the room, all of which appeared to be made out of the same material as the walls and ceiling. In the other half, was a circle of comfortable-looking soft armchairs. On the walls were seven colored doors, red, blue, and yellow doors on one side, and green, orange, and pink doors on the other, and between the yellow and pink doors, directly opposite the hallway they'd come from were a large pair of sturdy-looking white doors. Belgam led her to the armchairs, and she sat in the nearest one, while he took a seat in its neighbor.

He gave a deep sigh. "It all started about four hundred years ago, when a race of fairly technologically advanced beings discovered that their planet was going to be destroyed, and there was nothing they could do to stop it. The decision was made to build a ship that would carry the last survivors of their race to a different planet, so at least a few would survive and be able to start over."

Something had just clicked in Rekha's mind, and she raised a hand. "Were these beings called humans?"

"Yes, actually." Belgam tilted his head. "How did you know that?"

"Barry from the Allied Systems said he met some humans."

His eyebrows raised. "One of the girls must have told him we were human. It makes sense - we were made in their image, after all."

Rekha's eyes bulged. "Made?!"

He held up a hand. "I'm getting to that. These humans realized the trip to their new planet was too long for any of them to watch over the ship and protect the last remaining few. So they came up with a plan - they created two powerful computers. One, the main computer, would run the ship's systems and manage all of the automated tasks required during the four-hundred-year-long flight. The other computer, the Cris System, would house seven artificial intelligences. Through the connection between both computers, these A.I.'s could repair ship systems and protect the humans on their centuries-long trip. I am one of those seven A.I.'s. And while you aren't one of the original seven, you are also an artificial intelligence."

She looked down at the floor and sighed in exasperation. "I don't understand. What does this mean? Are you saying I'm not real?"

"I'm not saying that at all." He leaned forward and gently took her hand in his. "It's true that we are effectively just programs running in a computer, but we are sophisticated enough to think for ourselves, to learn, to be as creative as we want to be, and we can feel the full spectrum of human emotion. The humans made us to be as much like them as possible, and our creators specifically said they intended us to be real people. The Cris System allows us to have bodies, to see, hear, smell, taste, and feel — our personalities and capabilities vary wildly much like humans do. And our mission is vital for the survival of humanity. So we might be A.I.'s, but make no mistake, we are very real."

A...I... Again, pieces fell into place in Rekha's mind and she looked back up at Belgam. "The yais in Primordia — that was you and the other intelligences?"

Belgam let go of her hand and leaned back as he gave off a bark of a laugh. "That was due to a global misunderstanding of what we were saying, but yes, everyone labeled a yai in Primordia was actually one of the original seven artificial intelligences - but never mind that, we're jumping ahead of ourselves again." He took a deep breath. "The seven intelligences, we were supposed to shepherd the humans to their new planet, TOI 700d—"

"Catchy name." Rekha interrupted.

"—and once the ship landed, the main computer would send a signal that would wake the humans from their cryochambers. As it turned out, we weren't needed all that often. Maybe a handful of times, and it was usually fairly routine stuff. The rest of our time was our own, and the Cris System could be programmed to provide any simulation we could devise." Belgam leaned back in his chair, letting his head loll on the headrest and looking at the ceiling. "So for seven thousand years, we lived in whatever paradise we wanted..."

Rekha held a hand up in confusion. "Wait. Seven thousand? I thought you said this all started four hundred years ago?"

"Oh, that's because we have full control over our processing speed in the Cris System. The faster our processing speed, the slower time passes in here compared to the outside world. If we'd pushed our speed to the fastest option, we would have spent over one million years waiting for the humans' journey to finish." Belgam turned his head to look over at Rekha. "Immortality sounds great in theory until you actually experience it, then it feels a bit like prison. So we discussed it and settled for a mildly faster processing speed, giving us seven thousand years together." He sighed and stared wistfully at the ceiling again.

"What was it like?"

"It...it was heaven. Millenia of getting to have any experience you want with your favorite people in the world? And the love of your life?" He sniffed, and a single tear rolled down his cheek.

Rekha settled back in her seat. "What went wrong?"

He wiped his face with one hand. "The ship reached TOI 700d, and it landed safely...but the humans didn't wake up." Belgam sighed and clasped his hands together. "We accessed the main computer and resent the signal over and over again, but the humans are all still sleeping soundly in their chambers. If we could wake even just one of them, they could probably manually open the rest, but if we couldn't figure out a way to do that, well, they'll all keep sleeping until their chambers finally give out and they die, never even seeing their new home."

Rekha was astonished to realize that despite the absurdity of his story, it still felt like the truth — like something she'd lived through before. The feeling of dissonance gave her déjà vu of the several times Belgam had said something that felt familiar and bizarre at the same time. "I don't understand why...but part of me believes you, even though all of this is completely crazy."

"If I continue, you should eventually begin to understand why that is." He sat up and cleared his throat. "We believe that the problem was in the separation of the two computers. We have full access - full administrator rights - to this, the Cris system, and we can make whatever changes we want while we're in here. But for whatever reason, whenever we access the main computer—" He pointed at the large, heavy white doors, "—we only have standard user access. There are some things we're not allowed to do. And we reasoned that we needed higher-level access to the main computer, but we couldn't figure out how to get it."

He sat forward in his chair. "We stumbled onto an answer of sorts, but...I wish we'd kept looking. We all created our own simulations using our individual rooms to keep ourselves occupied during the long journey, and we knew that having god-like powers in these simulations would entice us into doing bad things. So we made a pact to keep an eye on each other and bring someone up short if they're doing anything evil. We didn't create simulations with a lot of killing or other awful things. After all, the characters in our simulations are a lot like us - they're artificial intelligences, too, just not as advanced."

Rekha nodded rapidly, eager to hear more of the story.

Belgam sighed. "All that went out the window after the ship landed. We panicked. We'd successfully gotten them here, but it didn't mean a thing if they just quietly died in their little pods. It was Alera who suggested we try 'hacking' the Cris System, so to speak. She theorized that if there was a bug in the Cris System's programming, we might be able to use it to gain greater access to the main computer. So, we set out to break the simulations."

Belgam stood up and walked a few paces away, wringing his hands. "We tried everything, good or evil, to find some weakness we could exploit. We did things...horrible things..." He trailed off and stared at the corner of the room.

Rekha quietly asked, "What did you do?"

He turned to her, red-eyed. "Don't ask me that, Rekha." He took a shuddering breath. "Because if you ask me that, I'm going to tell you." His eyes took on a pleading look. "So, please, don't ask me that. But if I seem blasé about killing Legion soldiers, it's because I've done far worse to people who deserved it a lot less."

Rekha did not break eye contact but remained silent.

He continued as he paced back and forth, "For weeks, we did our best to break the hub or the simulations in some way. On Primordia, this is when they started calling us yais. I'm assuming someone heard us talking and misunderstood what we meant by A.I." He stopped and turned to her. "None of us wanted to hurt anyone, but we HAD to find some flaw, some crack in the Cris System. But—" He sat back on the edge of his chair, "— it wasn't until Alera deleted a character on Primordia that we found one. Usually, deleting a character just means they vanish, but in my simulation room - as I explained before - deleting a character removes their entire history. Everything they've ever done is undone. It's like being in an alternate timeline where they never existed. Between that and numerous other things - like the fact that I have admin access to the simulation outside of it but I'm a standard user inside of it - we realized that my simulation room, or, at the very least, the Primordia simulation, is buggy."

"You said there might be a bug before, what does that mean?"

"Long story short, Primordia has software errors we might be able to take advantage of. When I created Primordia, I intended it to be a lot like a video game, meaning, unlike most of our simulations, it has a storyline and an ending. Alera's a programmer, and she believes that if we can cause a large amount of data to be shoved out of the simulation when the game ends, we could cause something called a buffer overflow in the Cris system, and maybe, just maybe, gain superuser access to the main computer."

Rekha's mind was swimming. "Okay, now you're REALLY losing me. What does any of this have to do with me again?"

"In our simulations, players respawn when they die, meaning they just reappear somewhere after a certain amount of time. Meryn suggested we could take six of us to Primordia, set their respawn timers to the exact same nanosecond, and set their respawn location to the exact same coordinates, and kill all six of them. When all six of them respawned in the same space at the same time, we hoped the Cris System would combine the six of them into one person, and that person would be made up of six times the amount of data as a single A.I."

Rekha's jaw worked, but she was unable to say anything as the implications hit her.

"So, in a way, I lied to you. You don't have two parents...you have six."

Belgam turned and waved a hand at the space in the middle of the armchairs. An image of a pretty girl appeared there. She looked fairly close to Rekha's age, and she had long red hair pulled back into a ponytail, a small, pointed nose, and her eyes were two different colors. Her right was a warm green, and her left was an icy blue, and she wore a gentle smile. A name instantly came to Rekha. *Alera.*

He waved his hand again. Alera's image vanished and Rekha saw a young man with an earnest face. His brown hair was cut short and his brown eyes were warm as he grinned at her. *Cris.*

The next image was of another young adult, a girl with shoulder-length brown hair and big brown doe eyes. She wore glasses, and Rekha thought she could hear song in her mind. *Victoria.*

Then her image faded to reveal a sharp-looking woman with a knowing grin. She had the right side of her head buzzed low and a spiral line shaved into it, while the rest of her black hair fell loosely over her left shoulder. *Mai.*

An older gentleman with silver hair and a well-lined face appeared next. His face had a harshness to it that his gentle gaze and proud smile did not match. *Ethan.*

Belgam paused, and Rekha looked with surprise at the tears standing in his eyes. He sniffed and his voice wavered. "Sorry, this is uh...this is hard."

He waved again, and the older man's face vanished to reveal a woman in her thirties with beautiful dark skin, a loving gaze, and a wide smile. Rekha heard her voice in her head. *Meryn...Mom.*

Belgam was fully sobbing as he placed one hand over his mouth and reached out with the other towards her image, but when he closed his hand, it disappeared. He sighed bitterly before turning back to Rekha. "I'm guessing she's who you've been seeing in your dreams?"

Her tone was apologetic. "I don't actually see anybody, I've just heard her voice. She's beautiful."

"Yes." He wiped the tears from his face. "Well, there you are - and they're all a part of you...your six parents." He sat up straight. "Well, technically, seven."

Rekha watched, stunned, as Belgam stood up and discarded his robe, revealing a very thin tan shirt underneath with short sleeves, and trousers made of a rugged material and colored with seemingly random splotches of tan, brown, and green. He sat back down and gave her a very warm look.

"Rekha, my real name is Jamie Gamble...and I guess, in a way...I'm your father."

Chapter 22

Rekha stared in absolute befuddlement and not a small amount of dismay. "You're my...you're my father?!"

Jamie wryly replied, "Disappointing, isn't it?"

"You said you killed my father!"

Jamie looked down at the floor. "In a way, I did." He looked back up at her and she saw tears in his eyes. "Remember I said the six of us had to respawn together. That meant that six of us had to die."

Rekha suddenly remembered every one of Belgam's angry or upset outbursts. *I think I know what's coming. Oh, no.*

"It's funny. When I built Primordia, before any of this happened, it was just supposed to be a fun fantasy game with swords and sorcery and the like. I didn't even consider including poison. It doesn't exist on Primordia. And the only way to kill six people at roughly the same time in such a world..."

She finished the sentence when he faltered. "...would be violent. Bloody."

Jamie didn't speak, merely nodding as the tears flowed.

Rekha leaned forward, clasping her hands together. "Why you? Why weren't you one of the six?"

Jamie got enough of a grip on his crying to speak again. "Had to be me. It was my simulation, I was the most familiar with it. And someone had to stay behind. In case it all went wrong, or if it worked, but the new person didn't have the memories of the six. About the only thing we really knew about what we were doing was that it hadn't been done before, and we had no idea what was going to happen." He laughed ruefully. "It never even occurred to us that you might spawn as a newborn baby."

She stared at him. "I'm so sorry. It must have been—"

"YOU HAVE NO IDEA WHAT IT MUST HAVE BEEN!!" Jamie's voice cracked. "I spent SEVEN THOUSAND YEARS with the people I love most, going on adventures, solving mysteries, being superheroes, it was actual heaven — and then it ended...as I watched those same people bleed out and DIE right in front of me one-by-one while I wielded the knife!" He looked away, his shoulders shuddering for a long moment.

When Jamie finally got control of himself, he continued, his voice shaking. "Meryn and I held their hands as I slit their throats. Finally, it was just the two of us. I held the knife and...and even though she begged me, I couldn't do it. And as I cried, Meryn put the knife to her own throat, and then grabbed my hand and pulled."

Rekha covered her open mouth with one hand.

Jamie's tears fell straight to the floor. "And she just looked at me and called me beautiful...and then she died."

They sat in silence for a moment.

"If there's a hell, that's what it's like." Trembling, he put his hands on either side of his face. "Having everything, and then losing it all at your own hands. I stumbled into another chamber of our cave and just sat there, trying not to think or feel. And then..." He paused for a long moment. "...and then you started crying." Jamie looked up sharply at Rekha, still teary-eyed. "And I hated you."

She could only stare in astonishment.

"About the only thing that got me through slitting my friends' throats was the belief that we'd be reunited fairly quickly. If you'd been an adult, even without any of my friends' memories, all I'd have to do is guide you through the endgame and instruct you on what to do when you reached the terminal. It would've taken no longer than a week." He gave a helpless shrug. "Instead, you were a newborn. I could advance your physical age using your properties, but there's nothing about advancing mentally - you'd just be a baby in an adult body. And I quickly realized I'd have to spend YEARS watching and protecting you until you were old enough and strong enough to finish the mission. I knew it was irrational, and you'd done nothing to deserve it, but here was this baby, swaddled in blankets, like some big cosmic joke mocking my pain. So naturally, I made the second biggest mistake of my eons-long life, and I took the last gift from the only woman I ever truly loved and gave it away to a complete stranger."

Jamie started crying again. "I always thought I'd be a good dad. But I guess it turns out that even A.I.'s can be shitty fathers."

Rekha would never know if it was entirely her own impulse or a result of Meryn's influence, but she wanted to kneel in front of Jamie and embrace him as he cried. She resisted that impulse and simply watched him until the tears and the shaking subsided.

Jamie looked up into her eyes. "The Jamie I was died that day. Since then, nothing has mattered but the mission. To be sure...to MAKE sure, they died for SOMETHING."

Rekha leaned back and crossed her arms. "So what is this mission? What exactly do you need me to do?"

Jamie looked her in the eye and clasped his hands together. "Like I said, the Primordia simulation was intended to be a game, and as such, it has a win condition."

Wait, I think I know what that means. "So what you're saying is, I just have to win the game?"

He nodded. "Exactly. Like a lot of games, Primordia ends with the death of the 'final boss', in this case, the Archprelate of the Legion."

"That name rings a bell. I think it was his Honor Guard that captured Varian."

"And if they were anywhere near Bromsford at the time the town was attacked, it's a good bet they were responsible. The Archprelate was written to be the bad guy, after all."

"He was at the Tower? I could have ended this right there and then."

Jamie shook his head. "No, he doesn't actually spawn until the endgame, and a few more events have to happen to trigger that."

"What do you mean?"

"The game doesn't have the greatest narrative ever, it's my first game." He even managed to look embarrassed. "And it's pretty free-form, but a few things still have to happen in order. We've already done a couple of them, for example, the game starts with the player leaving their hometown of Bromsford and travelling to Cloydun. Then the player needs to successfully escape from Legion soldiers."

Rekha sat forward in her seat. "We've done that one a couple of times. What else needs to happen?"

"The next event is a battle with a Legion army that ends in the total destruction of the Magic Academy."

Rekha's jaw dropped.

"And after that, the player needs to win a massive fight with an entire company of Legion and finally, kill the Archprelate. But we'll get to those. The really important thing right now is what happens after you win."

She fidgeted in her seat uncomfortably, but did not speak or break eye contact with Jamie.

"When the Archprelate dies, the game will automatically start to shut down. A door to exit the simulation will appear somewhere near you - much like the one we came through to get into the hub, but, and this is very important - instead of walking through it, you need to stand halfway in the doorway. Half in and half out of the simulation. When the shutdown forces you out, your expanded file size plus the unusual ejection from the simulation should cause your data to overflow the character buffer for the Cris system and get shunted to the main computer."

His look grew more intense, if that were possible. "We're hoping that when that happens, you'll be granted access to the terminal, which is a part of the main computer that accepts basic commands. So far, none of us have been able to reach it. But if this works, from the terminal, you should be able to escalate yourself from a user to a superuser."

Rekha finally held up a hand. "Wait, stop, please. You're throwing a LOT of jargon at me, and also, how do you know that any of this will work?"

Jamie smiled. "Because it already has. Remember when I told you I only have user access inside the simulation? I wasn't lying to Sarli when I told her I couldn't give her magic powers. But you COULD. You were able to access higher-level options in the properties menu, because your data size has confused the Primordia simulation program into giving you superuser access."

Superuser.

S.U.

Esyu.

She stared wide-eyed at him. "You KNEW that would happen?"

He grinned. "Meryn and Alera were pretty sure, and I haven't lived with them for thousands of years just to start doubting them now. Anyway, once you are in the main computer's terminal, and you successfully request superuser access, you should be able to reboot the main computer. Once the main computer comes back online, we're hoping the connection error with the cryostasis pods will resolve itself, and the signal will be re-sent, and the humans will wake up."

Rekha held up a finger. "Wait, wait, wait. Are you telling me that my entire existence, you killing all of your loved ones, my whole planet, everyone I know, EVERYTHING — is just so we can turn a computer off and on again?"

Jamie shrugged and grinned widely until he started laughing. Rekha, despite herself, started laughing along with him.

They drilled the terminal commands together for a while, ensuring that Rekha had them flawlessly memorized. "Sorry to be so picky, but it's one of the last things that can still go wrong. I just want to be certain." Jamie apologized.

"Well, I'm certain that if we keep going, I'll start getting it wrong out of sheer spite."

Jamie gave her a weird look.

"What? You DO realize that you've asked a lot from me over the past couple of hours? Besides, I'm not entirely sure I believe all of this," Rekha lied.

Part of me does believe it. And if Jamie's telling the truth, that's because the six people who died to create me are still inside me somehow, and they still remember. Which would also explain my dreams...and Mom.

He shook his head. "Sorry. That 'sheer spite' thing just really sounded like something Victoria would say."

"You lied before, when you said my Mom in my dream was just my subconscious...do you think they're really part of me?"

He looked into her eyes with something close to love. "I really hope so. I miss them more than I could ever properly explain."

Rekha softened. "You really loved all of them, didn't you?"

He turned and stared straight ahead. "It went beyond love. I couldn't imagine living without them. Until I had to."

An image of Sarli smiling sweetly at her popped into Rekha's mind.

Jamie continued, "That's how I felt about every one of my companions."

An awkward silence lay between them until Rekha remembered something. "Was there anything else you have to teach me?"

"I don't, uh...ah! Yes, that's right, I almost forgot - processing speed."

"What?"

"You and I are, essentially, programs in a powerful computer, but we have the ability to adjust how fast our processing speed is, and the faster our speed, the slower everything else moves." He stepped to one side, and indicated the empty space between them. "Watch."

He snapped his fingers, and a glass vase appeared in mid-air, falling to the floor and smashing to pieces, causing Rekha to jump. He snapped his fingers again, and the glass debris vanished.

He held up a hand, forestalling her complaint. "Now, this time, go into your Properties, and find your 'Processing Speed' setting."

Irritated, but still curious, Rekha focused on herself, scrolled through the list to nearly the bottom. When she found it, a sub-menu appeared with five options, 'Low,' 'Below Normal,' 'Normal,' 'Above Normal,' and 'Real Time.' 'Normal' was currently highlighted.

"Change it to 'Real Time!'"

She did so, but didn't notice any difference at first. Jamie appeared to be moving slowly, but only for a second or so. She watched as he snapped his fingers again, and another glass vase appeared between them. This time, she lunged forward to catch it, then stopped as she realized the vase had only moved a couple of inches downwards in the last second.

"Bear in mind, time is still moving, so unless you want another mess..."

Rekha continued her step forward and grabbed the vase just before it would have hit the ground. She looked at it curiously. "So, it still would have smashed when it hit the ground?"

"Correct. It isn't that time has slowed. You are moving and thinking much, much faster than before. It's an invaluable advantage in a fight."

Rekha's eyes widened. "Is that why I couldn't hit you?!"

"Exactly so. Just don't mistake it for invulnerability. If an enemy catches you by surprise, they can still kill you, it'll just happen more slowly."

Rekha's mind shuddered away from the thought, causing her body to involuntarily shudder as well, and she nearly dropped the vase.

Jamie smiled. "Now that we're both set to 'Real Time,' you'd have a much better chance. Of course, I still have military training programmed into me, plus those six or seven decades I spent learning martial arts in one of Victoria's simulations. So you're welcome to try your luck."

"I'll pass for now, thanks." Thinking about the other six A.I.'s made her realize something as she sat down and placed the vase on the floor. "Hey, when the main computer reboots or whatever...what happens to you and my... well...the people who are...part of me? In me? How does this all work?"

Jamie grinned. "Just call them your parents. We all made backups of ourselves in the Cris system before we set all this in motion. When the humans wake, we're hoping they'll be able to restore us."

Rekha sat back down in the armchair next to Jamie's. "And what about me, and Primordia?"

"You'll be fine, I'm backing up your data as we speak...but Primordia will likely be erased."

"WHAT?!"

Jamie reached over and placed a hand on her shoulder. "I'm sorry. If there was a way to save it, we absolutely would. But the game ending in conjunction with the main computer rebooting means the simulation will probably be wiped. And we couldn't find any way around it."

Rekha couldn't help but imagine Sarli, Varian, Elena, Arden, Shilo, and Nedra being wiped from existence, and she flinched from such horror. *No... NO!*

"Hey, hey! You know they're not real, right?"

What?! "How can you say that? Just because they're not players or whatever - that doesn't mean they're not real!"

"They're just characters, they were invented! And they don't have true sentience!"

Rekha's eyes flashed. "Are you sure about that? You were invented, too, remember — does that mean you're not real? What about me? Am I not real?"

To her surprise, Jamie's look grew conciliatory instead of combative. "Look, I'm just saying there's gonna come a time when you're gonna have to make a hard choice or two. Maybe you'll be fighting the Legion, or even the Archprelate, and you'll want to hold back because in your eyes, they're people, and they have a right to exist." Without releasing her shoulder, Jamie got off his seat and knelt in front of her. "But by doing so, you'll be endangering yourself, and you'll be endangering the four-hundred-or-so souls aboard this ship...and they're counting on you to save them. Believe me, if there had been any other way, we would have taken it."

She took his hand off her shoulder and held it in both of hers. "Fine. But Varian, Sarli, they're real to me. They definitely have their own thoughts and feelings, and I don't know what defines 'true' sentience, but I love them. That makes them real." She pointed at him and added, "And I saw how you acted with Elena, you can't tell me there's nothing there."

Jamie pulled his hand away with a mildly offended look. "My heart belongs to Meryn, forever and always."

"I know, but Elena's, what, the first woman to show you any kind of affection in eighteen years? I'm not saying you're gonna fall in love, I'm just saying you appreciated her."

"Maybe you're right, kiddo." Jamie looked down at the floor. "It's just that we were created specifically to get these humans safely home, so their race could continue to exist. I invented Primordia, and I can re-create Primordia and everyone in it. The humans invented me, and the humans can re-create me."

He looked back up at Rekha. "If the humans die, nobody can re-create them. They are gone forever."

It was her turn to look at the floor. *Damn.*

Jamie, still on one knee in front of her armchair, took her hand in both of his. "I know I've been a terrible dad. And if I could go back and do everything differently, you can bet I'd do it in a heartbeat."

Rekha sat back in the armchair and looked at him. "I believe you..." *Do I call him Dad? No, I can't, it's still too weird.* "...Belgam, Jamie, whoever you are."

He gave her a look. "Call me Belgam, it'll make things less confusing when we go back to Primordia. And I promise, when all is said and done, I will re-create Primordia exactly as you know it. And, assuming the humans keep their word, and they have kept the faith with us so far, you can live out your life there if you want. Or explore other worlds and bring your friends along." The smile faded from his face. "But we are the humans' only chance."

Rekha gazed at the wall for a moment, then looked back at him and resolutely nodded.

Chapter 23

Belgam, once more in his sorcerer's attire, and Rekha, with a glumly serious look on her face, emerged from the doorway back into the world of Primordia, where her friends Sarli and Varian greeted them with astonished looks on their faces.

"Well, that was quick!" Varian said.

Belgam held up a hand. "I assure you, it only looked that way."

Sarli argued, "You'd barely closed the door when it re-opened and you both came out again."

It was Rekha's turn to attempt to calm her friends. "It's true. We've been in there for a couple of hours. Time works differently there, which is one of the many things I'm going to have to explain to you both."

Sarli looked nonplussed. "Why do I get the feeling I'm not going to like this explanation?"

"Because you're smart and I can't hide anything from you." Rekha put an arm around her shoulder. "Come on, let's sit down. This is going to take a while."

Varian's response to the story she told as they all sat around the dying morning campfire was more or less what Rekha had expected. "Mental."

"That's insane!" Sarli's immediate rejection was more surprising.

"Absolutely mental."

"So messed up!"

"Belgam's spun your head right round."

"Are you sure this is the truth?" Sarli was nearly pleading.

"Yes. I didn't want to believe it, but the fact that I'm made out of six people is hard to refute, given that they can literally talk to me in my dreams."

Rekha, sitting between them, took each of their hands. "And I've not only seen it with my own eyes, but I can feel it - here..." She placed Varian's hand on her head. "...and here..." She placed Sarli's hand over her heart. Her heartbeat seemed preternaturally loud just then.

She clasped their hands with her own. "I know it's hard to hear and even harder to believe, but part of me knows it's the truth."

Varian stood up and ripped his hand away. "Let me see if I understand this correctly. Rekha's basically got goddess powers, and if she uses them to defeat the Legion, it'll actually destroy the world and everyone in it - but you WANT to do that, supposedly because ending all the lives on Primordia will save the lives of four hundred people who may not actually exist."

Belgam muttered, "Knew I could count on you to cast it in the worst possible light."

Sarli gave him a sidelong glance. "There's a *good* light to cast this in?!"

"We're saving a species from extinction, whether you believe they're real or not, and Primordia will be restored." Belgam grimly stood up, firmly clasping his cane with both hands. "You have my word."

As Belgam strode off to prepare his horse to leave, Varian leaned closer to Rekha and Sarli and quietly intoned, "And Belgam's totally trustworthy? He's never lied to us....right? No. But he HAS hidden the truth."

Varian stood and looked with concern at Rekha. "I know you believe him. But we're talking about wiping out an ENTIRE civilization, and trusting that crazy old man to make things right."

"What about me?" Rekha asked, looking back at him. "Do you trust me?"

Varian opened his mouth as if to say something, then stopped and took a breath. "Not all six of you." He turned and headed for his horse.

"I'm still me!" She shouted after him, before turning to Sarli. "I swear it! They made me out of six people, that's true, but I'm still the same person."

Sarli nodded at her reassuringly, but Rekha didn't like the flash of doubt in her perfect eyes.

It was a somber ride that day, but otherwise uneventful. They wordlessly pulled off the road and into the trees as it got dark. By now, they'd developed enough of a routine that the four of them automatically performed the needed tasks to settle down for the evening, including starting the campfire and cooking dinner, even though there were now three mages among them who could do those things with a single thought. *But there's definitely something comforting about still doing things with your hands. Frees my mind up to tackle the things still weighing on me.*

Rekha was honest enough with herself to admit that she still wasn't truly comfortable with the mission placed upon her. *Varian has a point. I know Jamie...Belgam believes that this will save a species from extinction, but he said himself that the humans ran him and the other A.I.'s through multiple simulations - who's to say this isn't just another simulation? Even if it's real, there's no proof rebooting the main computer will fix anything. The humans may already be doomed, and sacrificing Primordia to save them is just needless slaughter.*

She looked over at Varian, who was staring blankly into the fire while eating a chunk of bread. He had refused to meet her gaze since that morning. *I can't stand this gulf between us. I need to get him alone.*

She waited until everyone had finished eating, then watched as Varian wandered off a bit further into the trees. She quietly walked in the same direction. Sarli moved as if to follow, but Rekha waved her off, and she nodded, turning instead to attend to Phi.

When Rekha found him a moment later, he was sitting against a tree with his back to her, silently staring up at the moonlit sky.

She quietly said, "Do you know what I keep thinking about?"

Without turning his head, he replied, "Do tell."

"Do you remember that time Dargen found a spiderweb and was trying to get the spider out of it so he could chase you with it, and I yelled at him, and he dropped the spider into his own mouth?"

Varian burst out laughing. "I'd forgotten about that. You were always protecting me."

She sat down, with her back to the same tree, just to Varian's right. "Yeah. And at some point, our roles reversed, and you started protecting me."

"Pssh."

"You think I haven't noticed? You ran towards the explosion that killed Irynn and carried me back to town. And you refused to give up Belgam's location to the Legion, even trying to get yourself killed to keep it secret, and I highly doubt you were that concerned for Belgam's safety. It was because you knew I was there."

Varian pulled his knees up, wrapped his arms around his legs, and rested his head on his knee, turned to his right to face her. His eyes were watery and his voice was thick. "I can be pretty dumb sometimes."

"Yeah. Me, too."

He wiped his eyes with a thumb. "I'm not gonna stop poking holes in Belgam's plans."

"Good. Don't. If there are holes, we need to find them and plug them up before we put our whole planet at risk. But if he's right, that means he could rebuild Primordia without the Legion —" Rekha's eyes also got watery, "— and maybe he could bring Irynn back."

They both sat there in silence and just breathed together for a long moment.

Rekha finally continued, "I know Belgam's bizarre and crazy, and I guess he's also kind of weirdly my dad. But the world he's promising? Maybe I'm alone in thinking it, but that's a world worth fighting for."

Varian sighed and slowly stood up. As Rekha stood up as well, he looked her in the eye. "You're not alone."

She nodded. "I know."

He reached over and gave her a big bear hug, embracing her tightly. She exulted in the familiar feel of her oldest friend.

As he released the hug, Varian asked, "So what happens now?"

"We continue heading towards the Magic Academy for now...oh, speaking of which, do you want me to give you magic powers?"

Varian was silent for a long moment. "Do you remember when Dargen dropped a spider down the back of my shirt, and while flailing around I destroyed the basket Lucky had given you, and in the process I managed to hit both you and Irynn?"

Rekha gave him an oblique glance. "...is that a no?"

"I think it's for the best, really. And in that event, I'm wondering if you even need to have me with you. We're deliberately marching towards a place that has to be destroyed, and I'm pretty sure you promised my mom you'd keep me OUT of danger."

"I don't know. I just think you're important somehow."

Varian laughed, then held a hand up in a pretentious manner. "Well, it's about time someone recognized that."

"No, I'm serious. I told you my mom - Meryn, she deliberately got me moving so I'd save you in time. I think you're important to her, which means you're important for the endgame."

"Have you considered that maybe she was being a mom, and I'm important to her because I'm important to you?"

Rekha tilted her head. "It didn't feel like that, but I'll admit to being new to the whole having-a-mom thing. I might've missed it."

Varian put an arm around her shoulder. "Well, we should probably get back to camp before your girlfriend gets jealous."

As they started to walk back, she replied, "I'm going to ignore the fact that you're having fun at my expense and just say thank you."

"You're welcome."

That night, Sarli unrolled her bed roll next to Rekha's.

Rekha, already in her dressing gown and tucked into her bed roll, looked up in surprise. "Oh, hey! You don't wanna..." Using her head, she indicated the area by the horses, where Sarli usually slept.

"No, I need to talk to you, and I think Phi will understand."

At that moment, Phi, wearing her blinders, snored loudly.

Rekha grinned. "Point taken. What do you want to talk about?"

Sarli, wearing a plain white dressing gown, lay down in her bedroll and folded the flap over herself before looking Rekha in the eye. "I wanted to apologize."

"Whatever for?"

"I know you've been through a lot, and I know you got all this new stuff dumped on you without any warning, and I know you didn't ask for any of it."

"You're three for three so far."

Sarli's look turned remorseful. "And I still doubted you."

"Is that all?"

"It's enough that I feel really bad about it."

Rekha choked off a laugh, pulling her arm free of the bedroll so she could reach over and gently cup Sarli's cheek. "Sarli, I doubted myself."

"What?"

"Everything Belgam told me and showed me, all of it - I knew that any rational mind would call it insane. But not only did none of it surprise me, it felt correct. I wish I could explain what it was like to feel extremely confused and totally certain at the same time."

Sarli said nothing, but she placed a hand on Rekha's hand, holding it to her face.

"It's been tossed around a couple of times that I'm a god, a goddess, the next Esyu, whatever, but I don't want a blind follower, Sarli. I want a partner. I want you to call me out when I'm going off the path, or if you think I'm making a mistake. Because I'm not a god. I'm just a girl trying to do the right thing." Rekha smiled. "And I'd be stupid not to listen to the smartest person I know."

Sarli's eyes softened for a moment before a wicked gleam appeared in them. "There's room for two in your bedroll, isn't there?"

Rekha understood the words, but the meaning behind them escaped her. "Huh?"

Sarli got out of her bedroll, draped her bedroll over Rekha's like a blanket, then squeezed in with her, much to her astonishment, and causing quite a few giggles. Rekha was suddenly extremely unsure what to do with her hands, finally choosing to simply drape them over Sarli's shoulder and waist.

As she stared deeply into Sarli's eyes, drinking in the beauty of her flawless face in the dying light of their dwindling campfire, Sarli whispered, "Thank you."

"For what?"

"I've read so many books, and learned so many things, but you're the only thing in my life that has ever made me feel like I can do ANYTHING."

Rekha struggled to formulate a response and she still didn't know what to do with her hands. "I'm trying to come up with something poetic, but I gotta be honest - I'm just kind of uncomfortable right now." *No no no, I did not just say that!*

Sarli looked stricken. "Sorry. This was a mistake."

As Sarli clambered free of the bedroll, Rekha spluttered, "No, Sarli, wait!"

She reclaimed her loose bedroll, mumbled, "Forget it," and quickly dashed behind the horses.

Mortified, Rekha clutched her face. *Esyu. Should I go over there now, or is it just going to make things worse? My stupid mouth...well, at least I know I won't be sleeping any time soon.*

Rekha was floating in that unnatural void once again, and the familiar feeling caused her to instantly realize where she was. "Oh, damn it, I fell asleep." She called out, "Mom?"

The confluence of voices ceased, and a warm feminine voice answered, "Hello, Rekha."

Far away, a tiny white light appeared before vanishing a moment later.

"We don't have a lot of time. Mom, how do you know that your plan will work?"

"We don't, sweetheart."

In the distance, a small white line showed up before promptly disappearing again.

Rekha was dismayed. "What? I thought you could see the future!"

There was a confused lilt to her mom's voice. "What...gave you that idea?"

"You told me Varian couldn't wait to be rescued and I had to go right away without Belgam!"

"Oh, that." She managed to sound slightly apologetic. "No, I was just guessing."

The white line returned, slightly larger than Rekha's pinky finger.

Rekha was astonished. "MOM!"

Her mother was chuckling and at least two other voices were softly laughing. "I'm sorry, Rekha. I know I can't be your mom the way I want to be, but I needed you to learn to rely on and trust yourself. This won't be the last time, either. But if it helps at all, I'm proud of you, baby."

Rekha kept most of the indignance she felt from her voice. "And your plan? The endgame?"

"In the end, it's also a guess. But it's our best guess. And we - now you - are the only hope the humans have."

The white pillar, about the size of Rekha's hand, materialized yet again for a moment before fading into blackness.

"What about Varian?" Rekha shouted into the void, trying desperately to see her mother's face. "Why was it so important to you that I rescue him in time?"

The pillar returned, as large as Rekha herself, and then it was gone.

Meryn's voice came to her yet again. "Varian does have a part to play, but I'd just watched you go through losing your best friend once. I couldn't bear the thought of my baby being in that kind of pain again. That goes for the rest of us, too." There was a chorus of assent from the other voices.

The pillar appeared, now larger than a house, and Rekha knew her time was running short as it vanished again.

"Thank you, Mom! Just one last question, what is that white thing?"

"That?"

Suddenly, Rekha was blinded, as all she could see was white.

"That is the Terminal."

Chapter 24

Rekha awoke with a start. She looked around to get her bearings, saw that the sun had just risen, no one else appeared to be awake just yet. She quickly got out of her bedroll, dressed as fast as she dared and headed over behind the horses, where Sarli had disappeared last night.

Sure enough, Sarli was there, still asleep in her own bedroll. Rekha sat down several paces away, giving her space, and waited for her to wake. She quietly contemplated her gentle companion's face and tried to compose what she was going to say.

Sarli's eyelashes fluttered, and she started to rise, and everything in Rekha's brain vanished. "Uh, good morning, Sarli."

She looked surprised and muttered, "Good morning."

Rekha folded her hands in her lap. "Sarli, it's my turn to apologize to you."

Sarli turned away in her bedroll. "Nothing to apologize for."

"Yes, there is — because I've accidentally given you a very wrong impression and caused you pain. And that was the last thing I wanted."

Sarli rolled over and made eye contact, but remained silent.

Rekha met her gaze and held it. "I was not uncomfortable with you. With your presence. I wanted you there. I just didn't know what to...there were things that I...and my hands..." Recognizing that she was flailing, she took a deep breath. "Sarli, I hadn't kissed anyone until the other day."

"Oh." Sarli sat up in her bedroll. "Me, too. Wait, you do mean me, right?"

Rekha scoffed, "No, the thirty OTHER people I kissed that day — of COURSE I mean you!"

Sarli laughed, though her cheeks did turn slightly redder. "Well, good!"

Rekha walked over and sat next to Sarli, and held out her hand. Sarli hesitated for a second but then reached out and clasped hands with her.

"I am so sorry that I hurt you with my stupid mouth," Rekha apologized as her eyes began to water, "I didn't want to. I never want to."

Sarli quietly intoned, "It's okay."

Rekha sniffed. "And I want you to know that I look forward to other opportunities to share bedrolls with you. And...other things. But remember when I said there'd be problems?"

Sarli laughed. "That's fair. I'm sorry, too. I have...a history..." She sighed. "Never mind. I look forward to talking about...sharing...other things."

Rekha smiled. "Do you want to get breakfast?"

"I thought you'd never ask."

They made a quick breakfast and were back on the road in no time, with Belgam flying overhead, scouting for threats, and the three teens riding along the road south to Wildfall, with Belgam's riderless horse tethered to Phi.

Rekha had to admit, unsurprisingly, Sarli was right. Having figured out how to squeeze the horse with her thighs to take the pressure off of her butt and feet, she was getting used to riding now, and there was something freeing and primal about traveling at high speed down a dirt road, sitting atop a majestic animal, hearing the pounding of its great hooves striking the earth.

Varian was, at least, no longer audibly suffering, but it was hard to miss his wince or grimace every time he bounced in the saddle.

It was getting close to dinner time, and the sun was beginning to set. Rekha's stomach was actively grumbling, but Sarli was urging that they keep going. As they crested a small hill, Rekha saw the reason for her insistence.

In the crest of the valley below rested a small, sleepy village of about fifty houses surrounded by farmland. The houses themselves were simple wood with thatched roofs and brick chimneys emitting gentle wisps of smoke. The fields surrounding the town were covered in rows upon rows of crops of what looked to be wheat, corn, and potatoes to Rekha's eyes. But all thoughts of hunger had been banished by how much this village reminded her of Bromsford.

Sarli gently pulled back on the reins, and Phi came to a stop. She extended a hand toward the town below and looked back at her friends. "Welcome to Wildfall."

Rekha's somber look eased Sarli's smile, but Varian spoke up before she could say anything. "Why's it called Wildfall?"

Sarli merely looked back towards the town and said, "Look up."

Rekha raised her eyes from the town and looked beyond it. The ground sloped upward, eventually becoming mountainous, and as she gazed at it, the fog surrounding the mountaintop slowly began to thin, revealing a stone enclosure and a castle within. As she watched the castle reveal itself, she realized it was an impossible building. Higher floors were wider than the floors below, and some sections of the castle swiveled and rotated, connecting with the castle in a different place from whence they came. Several towers were upside-down, and at least one spire appeared to hang in mid-air, with no apparent connection to the rest of the castle.

She laughed involuntarily. "That MUST be the Magic Academy."

Sarli nodded and nudged Phi into a walk. The others followed.

She explained, "The Magic Academy has this thing, this hex or whatever - Belgam can probably explain it. Anyway—"

She was interrupted by a shriek. All eyes turned toward the sound.

Still some distance away, on the main road, in the exact center of town, a pile of yellow things had appeared, and Rekha only just had enough time to make out a screaming person falling before they hit the yellow things and they exploded everywhere. *Are they...feathers?*

As they watched, the person, seemingly unhurt, stood up, now covered in the yellow objects. Even from this distance, they could hear laughter coming from the center of town. The person sighed, turned and started dejectedly walking south towards the mountain.

Sarli laughed. "Well, there you go!"

Varian shook his head. "Wait, what just happened?"

"When a student tries to cheat at an exam, they are teleported to the center of Wildfall, covered in a sticky substance, and they land in a pile of something soft but embarrassing, it's random every time. It's been in effect for at least a hundred years, and I guess after a while they just decided to rename the town after it."

A red-tailed hawk landed precariously on the saddle of the riderless horse, transforming into Belgam, who found himself awkwardly riding for a moment until he could shift position. "Despite how famous and well-known it is, some students still try it. The smart ones at least wait until they learn teleportation. That fellow's got a long walk ahead of him."

Rekha looked back up at the mountain. "Surely not that long? Looks like a couple of hours at most."

Sarli corrected her. "Actually, it's an eight-hour trip to the Magic Academy from Wildfall by horse. Without one, you're probably talking almost a full day's walk."

Rekha looked again, trying to mentally adjust what she was seeing to this new information. *That thin road must actually be a pretty wide highway — and that castle must be absolutely enormous!*

Sarli smiled sweetly. "Fortunately, there's an inn in town, which is why I suggested we hold off on dinner."

Belgam cleared his throat. "The Legion have no presence here, and they don't come this far south. We'll get rooms for the night and head to the Academy tomorrow."

The thought of food vanished again as Rekha realized she might be sharing a room with Sarli. This presented her with some enticing ideas that kept her occupied as they rode the rest of the way into town.

The innkeeper was a boisterous, jovial woman in a simple white sundress who greeted their mismatched company with a wide grin. "Well, hello! Three new students for the Magic Academy, is it?"

Belgam smiled and replied, "Two, actually. The third is a friend along for the trip. Why? Is there a discount?"

She beamed at him. "For rooms, stables, and meals, yes. Drinks in the common room are regular price."

"We'll take two rooms, stables and feed for four horses, dinner and breakfast, please." As he spawned a bag of coins and reached inside his robe for it, he asked, "What's for dinner tonight?"

"Ten gold, sir. We've got a pork roast on a spit, along with a selection of fresh vegetables."

Rekha's stomach growled. "Oh, yes, please."

Belgam handed the innkeeper the coins, and after she counted them, she whistled shrilly. A teenage boy appeared from the room behind her, and she handed him a coin. "See to their horses."

As the young man headed outside, Sarli helpfully added, "Careful with the big roan. She bites."

The innkeeper handed Belgam two keys. "These are for the two rooms up the stairs and immediately to your left. Return the keys in the morning before you have breakfast. Enjoy your stay."

Belgam pocketed the keys then rubbed his hands together. "Let's eat!"

The four of them trooped into the common room. It was a bit late for dinner, so the room was only about half full, but the denizens were talking and laughing in good cheer. The loudest laugh in the room was coming from the heavily-mustachioed man behind the bar, who was cleaning a mug while sharing a joke with a customer. His eyes brightened as he saw their party enter, and he held up four fingers. "Four for dinner?"

Belgam responded, "Yes, goodman."

"Sit wherever you like, I'll send the serving girl 'round."

They sat at a table near the door, and Rekha felt herself begin to relax. She realized with a start that this was the first time she felt safe since leaving Sarli's home. That thought reminded her of Elena, and she reached over to clasp Sarli's hand. "Hey, before we leave town, we should find a messenger to send word to your mom. Varian, you should send something to your folks, too. I don't want anyone to worry."

Varian snorted. "We're still planning on destroying the world, right? Worrying about my parents' feelings seems a little trifling."

Belgam kept his voice low. "I have told you repeatedly that Primordia will be restored exactly as it was, so please keep your voice down!"

Rekha saw her opportunity. "Exactly as it was?"

"Yes. Although I'll remove the Legion, so everyone can live in peace."

"And you'll bring Lucky back? And Irynn?"

"I promise."

Rekha nodded. "And Varian, even if this world is coming to an end, do you really want your mom and dad to spend that time worried about you?"

Varian scratched his head. "I hadn't considered that — in my defense, this is all still doing my head in."

A slim, cheery-looking girl arrived at their table, arms laden with plates covered in cuts of ham and piles of corn, peas, green beans, and carrots.

As she started laying them down in front of their hungry eyes, Belgam said, "Well, after a good meal, and a decent rest in a real bed, I think we'll all be feeling better about things. Dig in! Oh, and young miss?" He handed her a coin. "Could we get some water for the four of us?" He speared a small ham slice with his fork as the serving girl sauntered away.

Rekha smiled at that and looked over at Sarli, who smiled back, but her smile rebounded quickly.

Conversation trailed off after they ate. It was more food than Rekha had eaten in one sitting in quite some time, and she was feeling drowsy. That feeling appeared to be universal, as everyone agreed with Belgam's suggestion that they settle in their rooms for the night.

They trudged up the stairs with their belongings, and Belgam wordlessly handed Rekha the key for one of the rooms. Thankfully, Varian didn't seem to be in the mood for jokes as he silently followed Belgam into the other room.

Rekha turned the key in the lock and opened the door. Inside was a simple room, with a double-size bed, and a small table next to it, upon which rested an unlit candle in a holder and a simple clay vase with fresh flowers inside, giving the room a pleasant scent.

She looked at Sarli as she closed the door behind them. "Well..."

Sarli appeared a teeny bit uncomfortable. "Well, indeed."

They stood there, by the door, silently for a moment.

Rekha cleared her throat as she concentrated and snapped her fingers, lighting the candle. "It's weird, right? After almost a week of sleeping outdoors on cold ground, this little room feels like a luxury."

Sarli's face glowed in the candlelight, as she gave a little half-smile. "It's weirder still not having Phi nearby. I mean, I know she's okay in the stables. It's just..."

Rekha turned to look into Sarli's eyes. She returned the gaze, but there was an uncertain shakiness in the way her head turned.

Rekha asked, "Is something wrong?"

She wrung her hands and grimaced. "I don't mean to be constantly insecure, I really don't."

Rekha laughed and dragged her sack of clothes to the bed, dropping the sack nearby and sitting on the edge of the bed. "You're not. This is your first —I mean, I'm your first...relationship, like this...right?"

"Yeah, this is my first anything. I don't know if my Mom told you, but I don't have a lot of friends. In fact, I don't have any. The kids at school...well, they didn't want to be my friends."

"Fools. They have no idea what they missed out on."

"See, this is what I'm talking about." Sarli's grin grew wide as she stepped in front of Rekha and clasped her hands in her own. "Without even trying, you make me feel...special. And I am terrified."

Rekha's head rapidly turned in several directions in a few seconds as she struggled with that. "Those statements are...antithetical."

She laughed. "I just mean..." Sarli sat down next to Rekha. "I mean, I'm scared. There's no book on this, at least not in Cloydun's library."

Rekha smiled at her. "So we'll write it." She squeezed Sarli's hand and then looked down at the floor. "I'm scared, too. It's true, Irynn was my first crush, but you've been my first...more...than that."

Sarli gazed at her. "And now we're going to share a bed together. And we've known each other for what, a week?"

"I feel like it's not a big jump from trying to share a bedroll to sharing a bed, but I'll concede the point."

"And it's not just intimacy jitters — I've still got a lot of questions that make me uneasy, like will I even remember any of this after the reboot? And what happens when they bring Irynn back?"

Rekha took Sarli's hands and sandwiched them between hers. "I don't know about your memories. And if they bring Irynn back, I will take great pleasure in introducing her to my girlfriend." She raised Sarli's hands to her lips and gently kissed them.

Sarli leaned forward and kissed Rekha before embracing her fiercely. Rekha could feel her breathing. It was a little shaky, like she was crying. "Hey,

hey," she whispered, "we don't have to do anything you don't want to. In fact, I'd really like it if we just talked. All night, if you want."

Sarli pulled back, teary-eyed. "I'd like that."

Rekha asked, "Do you think it would help if you got to know Irynn a little bit?"

Even as she pulled her sack closer and started rifling through it, Sarli replied, "How do you mean?"

Rekha handed her the picture of herself and Irynn laughing. "This is Irynn."

Sarli took the image in amazement. "It's so lifelike...how..." She sighed. "She's beautiful."

Rekha nodded. "And manipulative, and shallow, and greedy. But she could be sweet when she wanted to be." She took off her pendant and extended it to Sarli. "This was her favorite crystal. We found it when we were really young, and she was making it into a pendant for my birthday when she died."

Sarli looked up from the pendant to Rekha's face suddenly. "Is that the first time?"

"First time what?"

"That you said 'she died' instead of 'I killed her'?"

Rekha blinked. "I don't know. I think you might be right."

"That feels like a pretty big step."

"Yeah. Maybe. What about you? Who was your first crush?"

Sarli's shoulders sagged a bit. "Oh. I guess it was pretty similar. Her name was Cula, and I must have been fourteen or fifteen. Her family had just moved to Cloydun, and she was new to our school. At first, she was really sweet, and she didn't ignore me like all the other kids. She just made me really happy to be around, you know?" She sighed. "And one day, I found the courage to take her hand and hold it in mine, and she looked at me with this really chilling look that I'll never forget. And she said loudly in front of the whole cafeteria, 'You're making me really uncomfortable right now.'"

Rekha covered her open mouth with one hand.

Sarli's head drooped down and she stared at the floor. "Yeah. I just got out of there as fast as I could."

"That's why you were so upset last night — I said basically the same thing! I'm so sorry!"

Sarli shook her head forcefully. "Not your fault. I overreacted." She continued to fiddle with the pendant in her hands. "It was stupid and I'm sorry." Her eyes widened. "Oh! Sorry, I've just been playing with this thing. Here." She held out the pendant.

Rekha, seized by a compulsion, pushed Sarli's hand and the pendant back. "No, you keep it."

"What?!" Sarli was incredulous. "Absolutely not, I can't keep this!"

"I've just got this weird feeling that Irynn wants me to give it to you. Here." She took the pendant from Sarli's hand and held the string open in front of her head. "Come on, try it on." She reluctantly put her head through, and Rekha held the string back so Sarli could pull her ponytail up and over.

As she released the string and the stone settled on Sarli's chest, Rekha noticed the stone sat crooked initially, but while she watched, the stone shifted slightly in its ties, slipped downwards slightly and stopped. It was now precisely vertical.

Rekha gasped, "Oh, my Esyu…"

With slight alarm, Sarli asked, "What? What is it?"

She touched the stone on Sarli's chest. "I've been wearing this for a week, and it has never sat right, not once, but on you…" Rekha looked up into her eyes, "…you're perfect."

Sarli blushed. "I think you mean, 'it's' perfect."

"I stand by what I said." Rekha smiled.

"Stop…" Sarli laughed in spite of herself.

The two of them talked all night, until the need for sleep finally overtook them.

In the morning, Rekha reminded the other teens to send a message back to their families. Sarli returned rather quickly, but Varian took a while longer. When questioned, he waved it off. "For all I know, I've seen my family for the last time. I had a lot to say." Rekha dropped the issue.

The road from Wildfall to the Magic Academy was well-traveled. The party passed a slower wagon carrying corn and wheat as they rode south. Rekha asked, "Hey, Belgam — why do they need crops brought to them? Shouldn't they be able to spawn whatever they need?"

The bald sorcerer cocked an eyebrow at her. "Do you remember when I told you it's dangerous to cast too much magic in one place?"

"Oh, yeah. Forgot about that."

"There are countermeasures in place for the classrooms and high-magic use events, but the danger still exists. That's why Wildfall exists at all. It grew along with the Academy, and is the source of most of the Academy's food and material goods, just to keep down the amount of magic needed."

As the hours passed, the road widened steadily but its gentle incline remained the same throughout. Sarli looked over at Belgam. "Why build the road like this? Is it just to create the illusion that the Academy's much smaller and closer than it is?"

He gave a wry chuckle. "The founders of the Magic Academy were much impressed with themselves, and they wanted to impress visitors with its immensity. Buncha weirdos."

"Aren't...you...one of the founders of the Magic Academy?"

"Yeah. What's your point?"

Sarli raised her hands in mock surrender and continued riding.

They stopped for lunch, but as everyone could feel their journey was nearing its end, they ate quickly and resumed riding. Just as the sun started its decline, the group pulled up to the compound's massive stone gate.

Belgam dismounted and strode to the wall, shouting, "Two students for registration to the Academy!"

A portion of the brick wall from stomach-level to above head-height shimmered and vanished, revealing a large woman in a sparkly green dress with a florid face ensconced in a small alcove. Her eyes glittered with mischief as she replied, "I count three. Is it just your eyes or your mind that's gone bad now, Belgam?"

Belgam smiled warmly. "Madam Elspeth! What a surprise! I was sure a wretched, ancient hag like yourself would have been long dead by now."

She positively glowed. "Well, I carry on simply for the future joy of living in a world where a full-on barking mad lunatic like you no longer exists, so..." She shrugged comically, then looked at the faces of the three shocked teenagers and burst out laughing. "Don't mind us, children, Belgam and I are just resuming a game we've played for fifty years. I'm actually quite fond of the useless git."

He pointed to the girls. "These two are young mages. The boy is under my protection. I think Dranheg will see his way clear to give him room and board until we can find an alternative, especially after the news I have for him."

"Hope you're right. Dranheg isn't as fond of you as I am, you stinky pus nugget." The woman reached over out of sight, and there was a deep rumble as the massive stone gate slowly started opening outwards. As they stepped back so as to get clear of the moving gate, Rekha watched in awe as the enormous stone castle continued spinning and moving parts of itself around like a jigsaw puzzle trying to solve itself, though a mysterious mist just behind the gate blocked their view of the yard beyond.

Elspeth beamed and spread her arms wide. "Welcome, all, to the Magic Academy!"

Chapter 25

Rekha, given what she'd seen so far, expected to see incredible sights, people practicing magic, astonishing creatures, and portals to impossible worlds. So when they passed through the mist and she could see inside, her disappointment was so palpable, she had trouble swallowing it.

Past the stone gate was a grassy yard, and to either side of the massive wooden castle doors were stables. Once they'd crossed the gate's threshold, the castle itself had even stopped moving, and now looked to be just a normal castle, with its only fantastical element being its large size.

Rekha's mouth fell open. "What happened to the whirling bits and the floating tower?"

Belgam chuckled. "That was an illusion. The amount of magic required to actually do all of that would've turned this place into a crater almost immediately."

Sarli asked, "But why?"

"Students weren't exactly flocking to the school at first. It was just a big castle in the middle of nowhere. Once the illusion was up, word started to spread pretty quickly about the Magic Academy, and students started pouring in."

No one was in the yard, except for a young groom awaiting them near the door. They dismounted and handed over the reins. Sarli warned the groom to keep his hands away from Phi's mouth, and they trooped to the door. Belgam pulled at the huge handle, and the door swung open with a gentle creak.

The foyer of the castle was similarly barren, with simple undecorated stone walls and floors. Rekha didn't have much time to wonder at this, as Belgam was already moving with purpose straight ahead. The others followed, as he approached a haunted-looking middle-aged man with dark eyes, a handlebar mustache, and wearing a simple blue robe, standing behind a window with a black sign above reading "RESEPTION".

Sarli asked, "Isn't reception spelled with a C?"

The man at the window snorted. "Yeah, unless you're some kind of idiot who won't let us change it."

Belgam's face took on a shocked cast. "Hey, I've been gone for nearly twenty years, Jalyn, no one to blame but yourselves. I've brought two students for registration, and I need to speak to Dranheg, it's urgent."

"I'm sure." Jalyn didn't move. "You walk away without a word to any of us like none of this matters, and suddenly show up eighteen years later saying you've got something urgent to say. Sure." He sighed and reached off to the side, producing some parchment and a pair of quills. "Have the students fill these out. The headmaster is in a meeting at the moment but I'll have him meet you in the teleportation classroom."

Belgam handed the parchment and quills to Rekha and Sarli, then looked back. "Teleportation class is not in session?"

"Field trip. Fair warning, they're not expected back for a few days yet, but they could return at literally any moment."

Rekha held up her quill. "No inkpots?"

Jalyn's face indicated suppressed mirth for only an instant. "Have you forgotten where you are, young lady? They're magic quills, no ink required."

Belgam held up a hand. "That's enough, Jalyn. How long until Dranheg's free?"

He stared. "Oh, I'm sure for you, he'll drop everything. Ten, fifteen minutes at most."

Three hours later, the four of them still sat around an empty classroom with six wooden desks. Rekha had passed the time by chatting with her friends, though she had initially tried doodling with the magic quill. She'd found what she thought was a blank piece of parchment in a student's desk, and had started drawing when big, bold, red words appeared on the page, saying, "HEY WHAT'S THE BIG IDEA?!" Rekha yelped, threw the page back into the desk, and quickly found somewhere else to sit.

Varian was attempting to balance Sarli's quill on his nose and failing. "So nice to see our esteemed leader is held in such high regard here. Tell me, Belgam, is there *anyone* in Primordia you haven't managed to piss off?"

Rekha replied, "The folks at the inn in Wildfall seemed pretty indifferent." Varian mouthed the word, "Oh," and nodded, dropping the quill again.

Sarli asked, "Do they serve dinner here? I'm starving."

Belgam was as angry as Rekha had ever seen him as he uncrossed his arms and stepped away from the wall he was leaning against. "Oh, I'm going to give them something to chew on, alright."

He started to cross to the classroom door when it suddenly opened on its own, and a tall, thin, severe-looking older man with close-cropped white hair, hawk-like eyes, and a white robe glided into the room. His smile and his deep voice were both dripping with insincerity. "Belgam, my old friend. I trust I've not kept you too long?"

"It's been HOURS, Dranheg. Have you forgotten what the word 'urgent' means? Or are you slipping into your dotage already?"

"You've beaten me to it if you genuinely think we would take you seriously. You slammed that door shut when you left, remember?"

"The Legion are coming, Dranheg. Now. And they're bringing an army."

Dranheg's eyes flashed and his smile vanished. "Nonsense. The king would never allow that."

"King Vakar is in their pocket." Belgam took another step closer to the man. "Or am I wrong, and your supposed envoy made it home safe and sound?"

Dranheg scowled and turned his head down and to the side. "We lost contact with them days ago." He looked back up at Belgam. "And you've seen this army of yours?"

"There were three Legion transport ships in harbor at Cloydun, and each could carry hundreds. If they made multiple trips, they could have ferried thousands of soldiers into these woods."

Dranheg wryly smiled. "So you haven't seen them, then?"

"I've done all I can for nearly twenty years to keep the Legion away from this place and focused on me — I know damn well how they operate. For Esyu's sake, man, it doesn't take a genius to put the pieces together. And you used to be a genius!"

The headmaster turned away, giving off a rueful laugh. "I used to be. Now I'm just a silly old fool, trying to keep alive a tradition he helped to build, and watching while the world tears it down."

Belgam sighed. "From one silly old fool to another, I understand how you feel. And we may be too late to save the Academy. But there's something else you need to know." He put one arm around the thin man's shoulder while using the other to indicate Rekha. "I found her, Dranheg."

He appeared to be confused. "What?"

"I. Found. Her. Dranheg. Remember the thing, the ONE thing we said that if we could do it, we could be rid of the Legion forever? The thing that would finally make us a part of society instead of apart from it?" Belgam crossed to Rekha and put his arm around her shoulder. "She can do it."

As Dranheg's eyes widened and his jaw fell, Rekha feebly and uncomfortably waved at him. "Hi."

The thin man took a few steps and knelt in front of her, looking up into Rekha's awed face. "Is this true? You can make people magic?"

Rekha nodded slowly. "But I can't do anything on an empty stomach."

Sarli grunted, "Thank you!"

Dranheg looked puzzled for a moment, then said, "Oh! A thousand pardons."

The cafeteria was a noisy place, despite only thirty or forty students being present. After they'd each gathered a thin wooden tray and loaded it up with questionable dietary decisions from the buffet put out by aproned workers, Rekha expected to be taken somewhere private. So she was surprised when Dranheg led them to an ordinary table among the other students. But the fact that the headmaster ate with his students made him go up in her estimation.

"Forgive the noise." Dranheg waved in the air. "Most of the students will finish up soon and head back to their dorms."

As Rekha looked around, she realized that their group was the focus of a fair amount of curiosity in the room. Many students of all descriptions, mostly late teenage, but some young adults, stared openly at the new people sharing a table with the headmaster, but she noted that none of them appeared to recognize Belgam.

The headmaster cleared his throat. "So, as you were saying, young lady, you can give a non-magical person true magic capabilities?"

Rekha swallowed what turned out to be a piece of heavily spiced beef. "Um, my name is Rekha. And yes."

Sarli smiled. "And I'm living proof. Hi, I'm Sarli, and up until two days ago, I couldn't do any magic at all."

"Pleasure. Ah, hold still, this won't hurt." Dranheg held out a hand. While Rekha couldn't feel anything, she guessed that he was accessing Sarli's properties. *That's right — now that she's magic, she doesn't do that T-pose anymore.*

He grunted. "Well, there's nearly no magic history at all there, but would anyone protest if I asked for further proof?"

Belgam and Rekha looked at each other, then turned back and shook their heads.

"Sabrum!" The headmaster clapped his hands twice. "Sabrum, would you come here, please?"

Rekha watched as an adult man with shaggy hair but a clean-shaven face disengaged himself from the dish he was washing, dried his hands on his apron, and then walked around the cafeteria counter and out into the midst of the tables. He was a table length away from them when he suddenly lunged forward and fell to the floor.

A red-headed student sat facing partially outwards with his foot clearly in Sabrum's former path. "Hey, you gotta watch where you're going, there, Sabie!"

As the man reddened and picked himself up, the headmaster stood up and blistered, "For the last time, Bilius, do not harass the kitchen staff!"

The red-haired boy raised his hands innocently. "I can't help it if the plebes you hire can't walk properly." He smirked. "My foot was there before he walked into it."

"Yeah," Belgam muttered darkly, "an instant before."

"Give me a reason to expel you, Bilius." Dranheg added as he sat back down, "Just need one."

Bilius made an obscene gesture before turning back around to face his table.

The shaggy-haired dishwasher stood with his hands behind his back before the headmaster. "You called for me, sire?"

"Yes, I did, Sabrum, please meet young miss Rekha here, one of our newest students."

He turned to face her with curiosity in his eyes. "Hello, miss."

Before she could respond, the headmaster clapped the young man on the shoulder. "Sabrum came to us, what was it? Twelve, thirteen years ago?"

"And fifty-four days, sire."

Dranheg's face saddened. "He came, telling us he knew he wasn't a mage, but that he wanted to become one. He offered to work for room and board only for years if need be, as long as we didn't stop trying to find a way to make him a mage."

He sighed deeply. "We paid him more than just room and board, an honest wage, but we took our promise seriously, and we've never stopped looking for a way. However, we've never found a way, either, and in this way, I feel very much like the Academy...like I have failed him."

Sabrum turned back to the headmaster. "No, sire. Livin' around magic's almost as satisfyin' as I imagine doin' magic would be. I've learned a lot just by readin'. And most everyone at the Academy's been very kind to me. But it would be nice to put some of the things I've learned to practice."

Dranheg nodded. "I agree. Rekha, would you — can you make Sabrum's wish, and mine, come true?"

Rekha was suddenly aware that the cafeteria had gone very quiet, and that many eyes were on her. Sabrum, seized with a wild hope, looked at her with his mouth open and eyes widened as if in the throes of almost religious longing.

She took a deep breath. "Sabrum, hold still, okay?"

He rapidly nodded, but said nothing.

She concentrated and brought up his properties, diving down to the hidden level, and changing 'Magic User' from 'No' to 'Yes.' She released her concentration and watched as he instantly went from a T-pose to his initial position, though he appeared lightly disoriented.

"Sabrum, what's something you've always wanted to give to the headmaster, but never could?" She held up a finger before he could speak. "Don't tell me, just picture it in your mind. Now hold out your hand."

He did as he was told.

"Now focus on that thing you wanted, and imagine it appearing in your hand, and when you're ready, snap the fingers of your other hand."

He narrowed his eyes and stared at his open hand and after a moment or so, he snapped his fingers.

A medal with a multi-colored ribbon appeared in his hand. Rekha couldn't be certain, because Sabrum started shaking violently, but she thought the words etched into the medal's surface read, "World's Greatest Headmaster."

Cries of shock and disbelief were heard all around her, even as Dranheg himself stood up in awe. And at least a few of the students were fans of Sabrum, as a few cheers could be heard, and some students started clapping.

Sabrum hugged Rekha tightly. Choked up, he barely managed to say, "Thank you, miss."

She awkwardly clapped his back. "You're welcome."

He then turned and offered the medal to Dranheg, who surprised everyone by hugging the man instead. "You're a mage now, Sabrum!" He broke off the hug, but still held the dishwasher by his shoulders. "Do you know what this means?"

Sabrum grinned widely. "Yes, sire. I do."

He took one of Dranheg's hands and deposited the medal into it, then walked over to the table where Bilius sat. The red-headed student apparently had not paid any attention to what had just happened, as he looked up at the dishwasher with a mix of contempt and confusion. "What in the Abyss do you want, plebe? What's everybody riled up about? They givin' medals for washing dishes now?"

Sabrum merely smiled and stared at him. Suddenly, where Bilius had been, there was now a pig. The startled pig squealed and fell off the chair.

Even as the squealing pig darted this way and that in apparent confusion, the cafeteria erupted with sounds of surprise, dismay, and a fair amount of laughter, Sabrum simply smiled wider and walked towards the cafeteria chaperone who was crooking a finger at him. As the dishwasher was escorted out of the cafeteria by the chaperone, Bilius managed to change himself back to his normal form, sitting on the floor in his robes. More laughter ensued as

Bilius quickly scooped up his things and ran from the room.

The headmaster sat back in his chair. "Oh, dear," he said, before a laugh escaped him.

They ate quickly, well aware they were the major topic of conversation now amongst the students, and adjourned to the headmaster's office for some privacy.

"That is an extraordinary gift you have, young lady," Dranheg said as he rapidly filled out some paperwork. "Thank you for doing what you did for Sabrum. Looks like we'll be registering three new students instead of two."

Rekha beamed. "No problem, Headmaster."

The door to the office banged open and Jalyn strode in. His face soured when he saw Belgam, but he kept silent and walked up to the headmaster's desk, laying a single piece of parchment on it. "Need your signature on this."

Dranheg looked with mild surprise at him. "You won't mind if I read it first?"

The other man's face darkened. "Just sign it. I don't want to be in the same room as him—" Jalyn indicated Belgam with a thrust of his head, "—any longer than I have to."

Dranheg reddened, but swiftly took a quill and signed the parchment. Jalyn grabbed the page almost before he was finished, turned and quickly left the room.

Dranheg spread his hands in apology. "Sorry about that. Some of the teachers here can be a bit brusque when they want something. But onto the reason you're here." He indicated Rekha with one hand. "This changes everything."

"Does it?" Belgam replied. "I rather think it's too little, too late."

The headmaster looked up. "You're not serious? We can now make a mage out of literally anyone who wants to become one. It's no longer a matter of birth, it's a choice — Abyss, even mages who don't want to be one could have the magic removed from them."

"Do you really think that's going to stop the Legion?" Belgam strode to one side of the desk, gesticulating with his cane. "Even if they could be persuaded to relent, I guarantee - because I know it with every fiber of my being - that the Legion and the King would want to control who gets to be magic and who doesn't."

Rekha gasped. "Over my VERY dead body."

Belgam nodded. "And you know exactly what their fallback position becomes if they cannot control something, Dranheg. You're too smart not to know."

The headmaster gave a defeated sigh. "They'll destroy us —" He looked at Rekha. "—and specifically, her."

Sarli's eyes flared. "Over MY very dead body."

Varian raised a hand. "I would also like that to not happen."

Dranheg looked at Belgam with weary eyes. "What would you suggest we do, then? What CAN we do?"

"Close the school. Evacuate the students." Belgam's steely gaze matched his cold tone.

A touch of anger reddened the headmaster's face. "Oh, of course. Because it was SO easy for you to turn your back on everything we'd built, you assume the rest of us feel the same."

"Dranheg—"

"I will take it under advisement." The headmaster's tone indicated the conversation was over as he reached into a nearby cabinet and retrieved three keys, extending them to the group. "Your accommodations are on the fifth floor. The ladies have single rooms, but Belgam, you and the boy will have to share a double."

As Belgam took the keys and handed them to the girls, the headmaster continued, "Ladies, Orientation will be tomorrow after breakfast, during which you'll be given a tour of the compound, you'll get your class schedule, and you'll be introduced to your teachers. Welcome to the Magic Academy, Sarli and Rekha. Though it looks like your tenure with us might be brief."

Rekha sat quietly in her room, contemplating her situation. On the one hand, she was finally enrolled in the Magic Academy, something she'd looked forward to since she was young. *On the other hand, the Academy will be destroyed, even if I have to do it myself.*

She shook her head. *When did I become so determined to throw away everything and everyone to save these humans? Is it really me, or my parents?*

She looked around her room, as if the bare wooden walls could give her any answers, aside from the noise she could regularly hear from neighboring rooms. The room was tiny, with barely enough room for a small desk with a chair, a small, but extremely comfortable bed, and a wooden dresser, against which leaned Rekha's sack of possessions. She hadn't bothered to unpack.

The images of the other students at the Academy kept flashing through her brain. She'd seen plenty of them smiling and laughing in the halls, and a few had even introduced themselves to her. As if on cue, she heard someone in the next room over laughing faintly. *For a lot of these people, this is their home. If I destroy — or help to destroy their home, am I any better than the monsters who destroyed Bromsford?*

There was a faint knock at the door. "Come in," she said.

The door opened slowly to reveal Sarli with a gentle smile and an intense look on her face that Rekha couldn't quite place. "Hey! I just finished getting settled in." She eyed Rekha's tied-shut sack. "I guess you're not doing the same."

Rekha did her best to give Sarli a smile she did not really feel. "Nope. Just thinking about stuff."

"About how this place will be destroyed?"

She turned and looked at Sarli sadly. "How do you do that?"

Sarli brushed an errant hair from Rekha's face. "Do what?"

"Read my mind."

"Oh, that's easy. You keep opening it up and showing me the words."

"I'm sure it's all simple, one-syllable words in big print, too."

"What's wrong, Rekha?"

She stood up and hugged Sarli. "I don't know. I'm just really struggling with this."

"You don't want the Academy to be destroyed. I know, I don't either."

Rekha broke off the hug and took two steps towards the door. "The Legion wants it to happen, and I don't know how to stop an army. I know Belgam wants it to happen, and I doubt I could stop him if I wanted to. My parents wanted it to happen, Abyss, it's the reason that I exist at all..."

Sarli sat down on the edge of the bed. "But..."

Rekha spun around to face her. "But I still remember how much I wanted to be here. I looked forward to it for years, and I see that same joy in the faces of the students here - how can I take that from them?"

"Maybe you don't have to. We can come up with another way."

"Even if we can't, Esyu, I love how your mind works."

There was a twinkle in her eye as Sarli grinned and that peculiarly intense look came over her again, and she stood up. "Why, thank you."

Rekha smiled. "You're welcome."

Sarli stepped towards Rekha. "I think you need to get your mind off things for a bit."

"I'd love to, but how?"

"Well, and this is only a suggestion, but I was hoping we could kiss. Like, a lot of kissing."

It was Rekha's turn to blush. "Wow. Okay."

Sarli, without a trace of embarrassment, added, "Not necessarily on the lips, either."

Rekha's cheeks burned. "Whoa, what?"

"You think I only read books about demure things like houses and horses?" Sarli grinned and put one hand on her hip. "They had sex books, too, and there are some things I read about that I am dying to try."

Rekha met Sarli's intense stare with one of her own. "There are things I've heard about, mostly from Dargen, who's not the most reliable source...but still..." She reached out, cupping the back of Sarli's head with her hand, and kissed her deeply.

They continued kissing as Sarli started walking them back to the bed. When Sarli sat down hard on the bed, with Rekha standing, straddling her legs, she suddenly broke off the kiss, and quickly said, "Mind you, I'm not ready to go all the way just yet."

"Oh." Rekha couldn't decide if she was disappointed or relieved, so she simply said, "Me neither."

Sarli looked up at Rekha. "It's just that a week ago, what I wanted more than anything in the world, was to be magic. And now..."

Rekha felt that familiar reverberating jolt that indicated someone was using magic, and then Sarli produced a fresh-cut rose from behind her back and offered it to her.

As Rekha smiled and took the rose, raising the petals to her nose, Sarli continued, "I don't have the words to say what that means to me. So I'm just going to show you." Sarli lay back on the bed, holding herself up with her elbows. "Toward that end, I believe we were talking about sharing certain things..." She pushed one of her dress straps off her shoulder and down her arm.

Rekha grinned and leaned over to the table next to the bed, blowing out the candle.

The voice was eerily present, as though its owner were in the room. "Good morning!"

Rekha awoke with a start. "Gah! Who?!" Realizing she and Sarli were half-naked in her bed, she grabbed the coverlet and pulled it over them both, while looking for the supposed intruder.

The voice once again sounded like the speaker was very close. "Breakfast is being served in the cafeteria for the next hour and a half, after which classes will begin. Please note: if you're one of the new students who enrolled yesterday, please report to the reception office after breakfast for Orientation. Have a magic day!" The voice had nothing more to say, and the presence, what little there was, was gone.

Sarli groaned. "Make it stop."

Rekha leaned over and kissed her twice on the neck before laying her head down in front of Sarli's so she could stare into those gorgeous eyes.

"Aww, sorry. Does this help?" She leaned in and kissed her lips, lingering on the bottom lip for a bit.

"Mmm. Yes, ma'am."

Rekha slid out of bed, grabbed her vest and asked, "Do you want to go grab breakfast?"

Sarli sighed. "I guess so. Give me a few minutes to properly wake up, I can be a bit of a bear in the morning."

"You weren't exactly gentle last night either." Rekha gave her a wicked grin as she pulled the vest on.

Sarli laughed, but her face was indignant. "Hey, you said you liked it!"

Rekha was going to continue ribbing her but was interrupted by a loud knocking on her door. She sighed before shouting, "Who is it?!"

A familiar voice came through the door. "It's Varian. You ladies decent?"

How did he know?! "Uh, give me a second to get dressed. Why are you here already?"

"Belgam sent me, said he wanted to make sure you two weren't late for Orientation." There was a sarcastic edge in his voice as he added, "And for SOME reason, Sarli's not answering her door."

Jalyn wore a sneer as he faced the two teenage girls across the reception desk. "Right up front, I want both of you to know that I'll be watching you very closely during your stay here. You came here with Belgam, and for all I know, you're involved in whatever his game is."

Rekha sighed. "Well, for what it's worth, we like him about as much as you do."

He gave a humorless chuckle. "At least you've got your heads on straight." He handed them each a folded piece of parchment with an intricate design on it. "These are maps of the Academy. Any areas shaded in red are off-limits because they contain dangerous creatures or items. Everything is clearly labeled, but I've taken the liberty of circling your classrooms so you don't get lost." He turned and picked up two more pieces of parchment, checked them visually, and handed one each to the girls. Rekha noticed her name at the top before he straightened and continued, "These are your schedules. As we are nearing the end of the school year, you will be auditing these classes for now. Follow along as best you can, you'll take these classes for real when the next school year starts in a few months."

He crossed his arms. "Rules are simple. Outside of a classroom, do not spawn anything larger than a loaf of bread, do not repeatedly spawn objects of any size, and do not cast magic on a living being without permission and instruction from a teacher. Failure to comply will result in punishment.

Repeated infractions will result in expulsion. Is that clear?

Rekha and Sarli spoke in accidental unison. "Yes, sir."

For the first time, Jalyn bore just a hint of a smile. "Off you go, then."

They found their first classroom with little difficulty, and Sabrum waved to them as they claimed desks near the back of the room. Rekha had thought Introduction to Spawning would be fascinating, even if the name sounded a bit like they were going to watch fish give birth. Unfortunately, Professor Blatherskite was an elderly man who thoroughly enjoyed the sound of his very monotone voice, as he spoke almost non-stop for the first thirty minutes of the class.

"One of the most advanced things you can do when spawning is assigning an 'Owner' to the object. By default, objects you spawn without specifying an 'Owner' belong to you. Why would you want to spawn something that belongs to someone else? Well, there are generally two reasons, one decidedly more pleasant than the other - first, you might want to give someone a gift, and it could be a bit awkward if you're still listed as the 'Owner' in the object's properties. And of course, you can't change the 'Owner' once the item is spawned. And secondly - this is the less pleasant option, of course - some curses and hexes require an object owned by your target, and spawning one can be a lot less risky than attempting to steal something. And you can control an object if you are listed as its 'Owner.' This is not terribly useful for most objects, unless, of course, you are fond of pranks." The old man sat on the edge of his desk, which Rekha had already learned was a sign he was about to tell another interminable story. "I remember when I was your age, I cursed my best friend's lunch to merge together as soon as he opened his lunchbox." He chuckled, and there was a polite titter from the assembled students.

Sarli raised a hand from her desk. "You can merge objects?"

The old man peered at her in apparent confusion for a moment. "Oh, that's right, the new girl. Sorry, I haven't had time to learn your names just yet. That's correct, though we won't be covering it in this class. Merging objects is a function of properties, and is typically only taught in Advanced Properties in junior year. Too many things can go wrong, and heavens forbid you ever wind up merging living things together!" He folded his arms and relaxed a bit. "When I was young, word around the school was that was why chimaera even exist. Of course, we hadn't even been to Magical Creatures class yet to see a real chimaera. Fascinating creatures. I think it was just about ten years ago, I was on an expedition to the southern tip of the continent when I ran into one in the wild for the first time."

Rekha zoned out and missed the rest of the story, but thankfully it wasn't long until the professor had them start practicing spawning objects with different owners. Rekha and Sarli amused themselves by repeatedly spawning little gifts to each other. *To be honest, I don't even see the point of the 'Owner' property. This candy doesn't really feel any different to me than the rose Sarli gave me last night. I'm starting to wonder if Belgam was right and we really do know everything we need to know about magic.*

A bell rang, and class let out. As Sarli and Rekha traversed the hallways to their next class amongst a mass of other students, Sarli was positively glowing. "That was so cool! I bet our next class is going to be even better!" Rekha beamed as she understood exactly what Elena had been talking about when she described Sarli's brain as hungry. She clasped hands with her and reveled in her excitement, even if she didn't fully share it.

Regrettably for Rekha, if she'd thought Introduction to Spawning was dull, it didn't hold a candle next to Magic Theory. Their instructor was a middle-aged woman with fiery red hair cut short, and Rekha'd hoped she would show more personality than Professor Blatherskite, but she read to them directly from a book with a frequently halting pace. To make matters worse, the material was extremely dry: fundamental concepts and analysis of magic, all of which Rekha knew to be false. *Of course, if I told her we were in a computer simulation and we were just accessing computer commands and menus, I'm sure she'd tell me I'm the one who's wrong.*

Rekha had just put her head in both hands and propped her elbows on her desk when suddenly another voice, one she recognized, could be heard coming from the empty air in the middle of the room. "Pardon the interruption. This is Headmaster Dranheg. Classes are hereby suspended for the rest of the day. All students are to proceed to their dorms until further notice. All staff except kitchen staff are asked to meet in my office as soon as magically possible."

As the students all looked at each other with confusion, the professor finally became slightly animated. "You heard the headmaster, head back to your dorm rooms and wait for instructions."

Sarli turned to Rekha as they rose from their desks. "What do you think's going on?"

"Nothing good."

As they entered the hallway and turned to head for the stairs, they heard a shout behind them. "Rekha! Sarli!"

They turned to see Varian running down the hallway towards them. "There you are. Belgam sent me to get you."

The quaver in his voice alerted Rekha. "You know what's going on?"

He nodded. "It's the Legion. They're already here."

Chapter 26

Belgam was waiting for them at the end of the third-floor hall. As they approached, he waved a hand, and an opening appeared in the stone wall, letting some chilly air in. "Take a look. They arrived about two hours ago."

As Rekha got closer, she could see the courtyard down below, and just beyond the wall, she could make out soldiers massing on the road, as far down the road as she could see. Some carried banners with a jagged red eye symbol. Others were assembling large contraptions she didn't recognize, some with wheels, others free-standing wooden structures. *Belgam was right. There's thousands of them. But if they're here already, then that means—*

"If they were that close behind us, then you must have seen them when you were flying around, as we traveled here from Cloydun. But you said nothing?!"

Belgam looked at the other students who were starting to approach the window he'd made and quickly waved a hand, returning the wall that was there before. He directed the teens over toward the corner, away from the other students before hoarsely whispering, "Of course! I was making sure they were on their way! Have you forgotten the destruction of the Academy is something that HAS to happen?"

Sarli hissed, "No, but we could've started evacuating people yesterday — there's still hundreds of innocent students here!"

"Unfortunately, that's going to be down to Dranheg, and he's not what I'd call the strongest leader. But if he doesn't budge soon, we're going to start evacuating people, with or without his permission. Rekha, just be ready to start creating doors. Right, let's go talk to the headmaster."

They trooped down to the headmaster's office, where he was surrounded by worried-looking people, men and women of several different shapes, skin tones, and sizes, all arguing with each other. The only people Rekha recognized were Jalyn, Madam Elspeth, and the two professors she'd taken classes from today.

Belgam raised his voice. "EXCUSE ME, ladies and gentlemen!" Most quieted and turned to look at the small, bald sorcerer. "I believe I can be of some assistance."

"Oh, good." Elspeth's voice reverberated with sarcasm. "This bucket of bile is here to save the day."

"Elspeth." The headmaster gently chided.

Belgam shook his head. "No, she's right, headmaster. I'm not here to save the Academy. I'm here to get everyone out safely before its destroyed."

Several jaws dropped, and Jalyn looked like he'd been slapped. "Surely you're joking?!"

"You'll find I'm deadly serious, Jalyn."

"Because we've all heard the stories — the atrocities committed on magic-kind in the name of the Legion. Abyss, some of us have been touched personally by said atrocities. And you expect us to turn tail and run?"

"When the alternative is death, yes." Belgam's chilling tone quieted the room.

Jalyn scoffed. "We have the power of the elements, the infinite AND the void at our fingertips. And you say *our* death is certain?"

"Not if you evacuate. The Academy WILL be destroyed, that cannot be prevented. They are right this very second constructing mangonels and trebuchets that will throw rocks the size of houses—"

Jalyn interrupted, "—that a barrier summoned by a child could stop."

"And when the rocks are made of apotropaicite?"

The dark-eyed man froze. "They can't—you can't know that, we'd know if they found a vein that large!"

Belgam chuckled darkly. "They wouldn't be here if they hadn't." He turned suddenly to Dranheg. "And if the king has come down on the Legion's side, it's entirely possible he gave it to them."

All eyes turned to Dranheg, and the already-weary man wilted further in his seat.

"It's true. The king has decreed the practice of magic to be illegal throughout the Kingdom of Vakar. Captain Malvus was kind enough to hand me a copy of the decree as he delivered the Legion's demands."

Rekha was stunned. "Malvus is leading the assault?!" She suddenly remembered the giant map on the wall in Malvus' office and all the red dots representing Legion companies that she'd taken as false for being conspicuously absent from the areas surrounding Bromsford. *It's because those dots, those companies had been moved south, in preparation for this siege. His map was completely correct, I just didn't know what it meant! Which means...* Rekha's eyes widened. "Malvus was telling the truth..."

Sarli asked, "What does that mean?"

She realized all eyes were on her. "I..I don't know."

Dranheg leaned forward, placing his elbows on his desk. "Well, I'll take your familiarity with the man to indicate your part in the Legion's demands."

Belgam raised an eyebrow. "Which are?"

He sighed as he read from a piece of parchment, "The total and complete surrender of all Magic Academy staff, registration of all known magic users among students and staff with Legion authorities, and handing over four refugees from justice." A wry tone entered his voice. "I'm guessing that's you and your three young friends. If we don't accede to their demands by dawn tomorrow, they'll assault the compound until it is reduced to rubble, and..." A defeated note could be heard in his voice as he concluded, "...and surrender will no longer be accepted."

One of the teachers Rekha didn't know raised her hand. "If we're all under that much threat, isn't it perhaps better to concede?" At the curious turn of Belgam's head, and the angry looks from Sarli and Varian, she added, "Oh, don't look at me like that, I have my own family to consider."

Belgam sighed. "We don't have the time to explain why, historically, putting a group of people who are different in any way on some register always ends in horrific tragedy. I, and I believe my young apprentices here, would happily sacrifice ourselves if it meant everyone here would survive and be left alone. Unfortunately, the Legion, and now the king, have made it nowhere near that simple."

Jalyn slammed a hand down on Dranheg's desk. "Then we fight!"

"Those who stay and fight, myself included, will die." Belgam sighed. "If you can evacuate and remain anonymous, you at least have a chance at living a normal life."

"Knowing that we could have been so much more? No, thank you."

Elspeth chimed in, "This is our home."

A heavy silence pervaded the room for several seconds. Belgam merely folded his arms and looked at the headmaster.

Dranheg folded his hands together and took a deep breath. "I'm closing the school."

"What?!" Jalyn was outraged.

The headmaster held up a hand. "All staff and students are to be evacuated by sundown tonight. No exceptions."

"Sir, you can't do this!"

Sarli's head came up suddenly, and she stepped forward. "He's right, Headmaster."

Dranheg gave her a patient smile. "My dear, I've been Headmaster longer than you've been alive and you've been a student here for less than a day. I promise you, this is completely within my power."

"That's not what I mean, sir. The teleportation class — they're still on their field trip."

Jalyn looked horrified. "I forgot. Oh, Esyu. The teacher, the students, they have no idea what's happening."

Elspeth asked, "When are they due back?"

"That's the problem — the teleportation field trip lasts until the teleportation teacher judges that all the students have a safe handle on it. It was intended to prevent any more accidents after one student teleported himself into solid rock."

Rekha reeled back in horror.

Belgam joined Sarli's side. "That changes things, Dranheg."

"Agreed." The headmaster drummed his fingers on the desk for a moment and then stood up. "New plan. All students under the age of eighteen will be evacuated to their families and instructed to keep their magic abilities secret. All staff and all students at or over the age of eighteen will be asked if they would rather evacuate, or stay and fight — and all requests will be accommodated. Jalyn, Galvan, start drawing up some defense plans. We've got to hold the castle long enough for the teleportation students to return and be safely evacuated. Time to get to work, people, we've got less than a day."

As the staff started divvying up their duties, Belgam turned to the three teens. "Sarli, the stables out front are dangerously exposed, go help the groom and get the horses somewhere safe, okay?"

"You got it." She headed out the door and towards the stairs.

"Rekha, see if you can help with the evacuation, create some doors and get some of these students safely home. Varian, you...actually, now that I think about it, with the bulk of the Legion here, it's probably safe for you to rejoin your family, assuming they're leaving Cloydun."

Varian shook his head, then leaned in conspiratorially and whispered, "If we're still careening towards the end of the world, I think I'll stay with Rekha until the end, if that's alright?"

Belgam's eyes narrowed for a moment, then he shrugged. "As you wish. Some of the teachers will probably be setting up fortifications and barricades, see if you can lend any of them a hand."

Rekha turned to Belgam. "What are you going to do?"

His answering grin was vicious. "Prepare our counterattack, of course."

It was rough going at first. Rekha kept having the students describe their home as best they could, and tried opening a door that led to that image in her head, but it wasn't the right home. She kept accidentally scaring some innocent person by opening a door into their home unannounced, resulting in a quick apology and slamming the door shut. After a couple of tries, one of the staff suggested an easier method: holding the student's hand, thinking of their name and the word 'house', and opening the door. To Rekha's surprise, this worked every time. *I keep unnecessarily complicating matters when the system is literally designed for ease of use.*

Dinner that evening was rather bleak. There was barely anyone in the cafeteria, and only a single cook and Sabrum had elected to stay. Sabrum had been pressed into serving duties, but the smile on his face was genuine, and he successfully lifted the spirits of many worried mages with his words of thanks and encouragement.

Rekha picked at her food with a fork. Sabrum had been especially effusive in his praise for her, and he even gave her additional sweetmeats for dessert. But the fact that he'd stayed behind made her wonder if she had actually doomed him with her 'gift'.

Sarli put a hand on Rekha's thigh and squeezed. "Everything's going to be okay."

She transferred the fork to her left hand and clasped Sarli's hand with her right. "Hope so. I want you to stay close when the attack starts." She looked at Varian. "That goes for both of you."

Varian nodded. "Either of you seen Belgam?"

Sarli shook her head. Rekha did the same and added, "Not since this morning."

"Makes you wonder just what he's got in mind for that counterattack."

A familiar voice piped up from behind her. "I'm surprised he didn't tell you."

Rekha turned in her chair to see Dranheg eating alone at a table behind them. "Belgam's not exactly known for complete disclosure."

He barked a laugh. "Ha! True enough." He turned his chair out to face them and quietly explained, "It's pretty simple. Belgam's going to destroy the Legion's catapults at dawn, before they start throwing. Without their mangonels and trebuchets, they'll be forced to throw their army at us with assault towers and grappling hooks to get over the walls. But without their apotropaicite blanketing the castle, we should be able to repel them fairly easily."

"If that's the case, why has he been gone all day?"

The headmaster harrumphed. "He's probably planning something exotic. Belgam never was a fan of halfway measures."

Varian jumped in. "I've been meaning to ask — there's no way to find the teleportation class, wherever they've gone?"

"Sadly not. Typically the field trip starts with the students submitting places for them to teleport to, and the teacher picks one at random. It's meant to show how simple the concept of long-distance teleporting is. Then they either find lodgings or set up camp and spend the next several days learning short-distance teleporting, which is much harder. I'm sure you'll understand why if you think about it."

Despite the headmaster's assurance, Rekha tried but failed to understand.

Dranheg finished his soup and dropped the spoon into the bowl with a clink. "One last thing. Just in case, we're moving everyone to the dorms and classrooms in the first and second floors. Varian, you'll be rooming with Jalyn and Flinspar on the first floor, I believe you met both of them building the breastworks out in the courtyard?"

Varian nodded but didn't look terribly happy with the arrangement.

"And Rekha and Sarli, you'll be bunking with Madam Elspeth on the second floor, down the hall from my office."

Rekha's disappointment was difficult to conceal. *Even with everything going on, all I can think about is last night and how soon we can make that happen again.* She looked over at Sarli, and saw that she was not concealing her unhappiness at all.

Dranheg looked concerned. "Is something wrong, my dear? I was under the impression you and Madam Elspeth got along."

Sarli managed to look embarrassed. "Oh, no, sorry, she's lovely. I just really...really liked having my own room."

The headmaster smiled as he stood up. "Yes, and under different circumstances, you'd absolutely have one. But sieges are dangerous under the best of conditions. I'm sure you understand." He picked up his tray and brought it back to Sabrum at the counter.

Varian leaned in and whispered, "Who wants to bet Belgam actually helps the Legion bring this place down?"

Rekha replied, "He wouldn't do that, not with us still inside."

"Maybe not with YOU still inside. I'm personally feeling uncomfortably expendable."

Sarli interjected, "He's callous, but he's not stupid. He has a plan, I'm sure of it."

"And I'm just saying I'd feel a LOT better if ANYONE else knew what that plan was."

They were awoken gently before dawn by a student, who quietly knocked until Rekha answered the door. She informed them that the headmaster would be gathering most people into the cafeteria in preparation for the battle before moving on to the next door. The girls and Madam Elspeth changed and headed down to the cafeteria, where they found Varian already waiting.

The mood in the room was tense. As Rekha surveyed the crowd, she realized that two-thirds of those staying to fight were students close to her own age. *Please, Belgam, let your plan work. We need to get these people out safely.*

Dranheg was still assigning people to defend various portions of the castle or join staff members in the front courtyard when suddenly they heard a loud impact, and the room shook. "What the? It can't be dawn already." There was another tremendous crash.

"Bigger fools us for trusting the Legion to keep their word!" The mustachioed Jalyn roared as he pointed at the people already assigned to him. "With me, to the courtyard, now!"

Chaos reigned as everyone started yelling at once. The headmaster tried to maintain control, but as the massive impacts continued to hammer the castle, his insistent plea of "Where is Belgam?" became more desperate — and more pointed.

Rekha, Sarli, and Varian could only shake their heads and shrug, though Varian added under his breath, "So much for him not sacrificing us."

After a few minutes, the loud impacts mixed with a different sound, almost like rain hitting the building all at once. Suddenly, the cafeteria door was kicked open and everybody jumped as the door banged into the wall. All eyes turned to see Jalyn, an arrow sticking out of his bloodied right shoulder, supporting a student with an arrow in his thigh. "Nurse!" he yelled, as he sat the wounded teen down on a nearby chair.

The blood drained from Dranheg's face when he looked at the empty hallway they'd just come through. "The others?"

Jalyn grit his teeth. "Dead." He grabbed the arrow sticking out of his shoulder and painfully yelled as he yanked it out, holding the bloody tip up for the headmaster to see. "Their arrows are tipped with their stone, and cannot be blocked with barriers."

"Headmaster!" The woman attending the wounded student shouted as she tore off a sleeve from her robe and wrapped it around the teen's thigh. "I can't spawn any bandages."

Dranheg and several nearby students started snapping their fingers, but nothing happened.

Jalyn grunted as another loud impact rocked the room. "Aside from big rocks, their catapults are also launching these." He opened his right hand to reveal a handful of red pebbles. "They're covering the castle in these. It's a matter of time until we won't be able to use magic anywhere. We're trapped and defenseless."

He turned to face Rekha, Sarli, and Varian, and the headmaster joined him as Jalyn angrily added, "It looks like Belgam and his young friends set us up to die like dogs."

Chapter 27

Sarli and Varian were loudly protesting their innocence, but Rekha didn't register what they were saying. The urge to do something about the situation was all-engrossing. *Though I'm not sure whether that's coming from me or my parents. Either way, if I'm a superuser in this simulation, there must be SOMETHING I can do.*

She focused on herself and pulled up her properties. She pushed through to the hidden menu, and scrolled through the options, stopping on 'Spawn Object.' Another alphabetical list sprang into her vision and she quickly looked through it, though Bandages was close to the top, so she didn't need to look long, and she selected them. As her properties disappeared, a small package of bandages appeared in her hand.

Rekha strode forward to the nurse still trying to stop the bleeding from the wounded student's leg. "Here. Use these."

The woman gave her an odd look, but took the bandages from her and immediately started replacing her torn robe with them. When Rekha turned back around, Jalyn appeared confused and Dranheg's mouth was open with surprise.

The headmaster's voice wavered. "You...you can still cast magic?"

"Yes." She took a deep breath. "Looks like this is going to be up to me. Jalyn, of those of us still here, who would you say are your strongest combat casters?"

The mustachioed man looked to the headmaster first, and Dranheg nodded. "Myself, Galvan, probably Madam Elspeth, and maybe a couple of the more gifted students."

"Okay. Then here's the plan. I'm going to get you away from the castle and out of range of their...anti-magic stone."

Dranheg automatically corrected, "Apotropaicite."

She waved that off. "My way of saying it's easier. Once you're in place, you're going to ambush the Legion and try to destroy their rock throwers. Hopefully, you'll get them all, but even if you don't, you should be able to distract them."

Jalyn again looked at the headmaster, who shrugged as another loud crash could be heard, shortly followed by the sound of another rain of smaller stones. "Distract them from what?"

She looked up at the imposing redheaded man. "Me."

The argument started almost as soon as they were out in the hallway. "Have you lost your mind?" Sarli threw her hands up. "I thought the plan was to hold them until we could get all the students out."

Rekha sighed. "Well, things have changed. I don't know what in the Abyss Belgam's game is, but the castle won't hold up under this assault for much longer. We have to stop this — now." Another loud crash echoed down the hallway.

"By all means then, we should stop it, but you're not talking about just stopping it. You're talking about mass murder!"

"No, I'm talking about a direct attack on the people who are trying to kill us. Who have ALREADY killed some of us."

"And the Legion soldiers manning their machines or even in the vicinity will die! And I can't believe you would suggest fire, not after—" Sarli suddenly cut off and went silent.

The image of Irynn burning came once again to Rekha's mind. She looked down at the floor uncomfortably and said quietly, "Their rock throwers are made of wood. If you have another idea, I'm all ears."

Varian stood with Rekha, facing Sarli. "I'm with Rekha on this. Belgam's brought us here saying one thing, but now it's clear he's been lying all along, so if we can stop the Academy from being destroyed and ruin his plans, I say we do it. Besides," he leaned in close to avoid being overheard by the teacher who was shadowing them from a distance, "they're going to die anyway if Belgam's endgame comes to pass."

"That's no excuse!"

Rekha pleaded, "I know. But it's the only way I can think of to stop the Academy from being destroyed." She clasped her hands together. "We've got one chance to slow them down long enough to get all of the people out. But if the assault team fails, we absolutely must have a backup plan. And unfortunately, that means casualties."

Sarli reeled back, her face covered in disbelief. "What happened to the girl who refused to let the Legion make her a murderer?" She shook her head sadly. "You know, for someone who claims to not like Belgam, you sure sound a lot like him."

Rekha's heart crumpled in her chest as Sarli turned and walked back into the cafeteria.

Varian gave her a sympathetic look. "Don't worry about it. I'm sure she'll come around."

As they walked back in together, they saw Sarli speaking with a freshly-bandaged Jalyn as he nodded and said, "To be clear, I still don't fully trust you. But right now I don't have any choice but to take all the help I can get. I'll run it by the headmaster, if he approves, you're in."

"Thanks," she said with a smile as she spotted her friends approaching.

As Jalyn turned and walked away, Rekha asked, "What did you just do?"

"I volunteered to join the assault team."

"You whatted the WHAT?!"

Sarli folded her arms. "If the assault team succeeds, then there's no need for you to kill anyone. So I'm going to make sure they succeed."

Rekha practiced moving herself out into the forest just west of the Legion encampment several times, using the X, Y, and Z coordinate sliders, until she was confident she wouldn't stick anyone inside a tree. She then transported the assault team to that same area one-by-one, gritting her teeth as she transported Sarli. *What is she thinking?! If she dies, I swear, I'm going to kill that girl.*

Once the entire team was in place, she gathered them all together. "Remember, remain calm, stay focused, and listen to what Jalyn says. Our goal is for you to get as close as you can without being spotted AND without getting in range of their anti-magic stones. Test your spells silently as you go to make sure. Once you see the signal, concentrate on the catapults, scaling ladders, and assault towers." She looked at Sarli for a moment before looking back at the others. "If you can take most of them out, that should stop their attack. Even if it stops for just a day, there's a chance nobody else has to die. But don't overstay your welcome — when the Legion start shooting arrows at you, and they will — Jalyn will give the order to retreat. Get yourselves out of there as fast as you can. Teleport, transform, run, do whatever you have to. We'll meet up back at the cafeteria when everything's said and done. Good luck, everyone."

As the others turned to start sneaking away, Rekha caught Sarli's hand and squeezed it as she felt hot tears fill her eyes. "You know, you don't need to do this."

Sarli also looked like she was about to cry. "When the alternative was twiddling my thumbs while the woman I loved killed people just to stick it to her father...yeah, I kinda do need to."

Rekha sighed and wiped her eyes with her free hand. "I'm not just doing it to stick it to Bel—wait!" Her eyes widened and she looked up into the taller girl's eyes. "Did you just say you love me?"

She squeezed Rekha's hand and the tears released from her eyes, coursing down to her nose. "I guess I did. I was hoping to say it at a more appropriate time...and this isn't just because we could both die. I've never met anyone like you, Rekha. And I love you."

Rekha fiercely hugged her. "I love you, too, Sarli. Come back to me."

When Rekha released the hug, Sarli gave her one single chaste kiss. "For luck." Rekha then took Sarli's face in both hands and gave her a long, passionate kiss. "For love."

Sarli stopped as she turned to leave, smiled and held up a finger. "What about for lust?"

Rekha laughed. "If we both make it through this, we'll have to talk about that. Be careful."

Sarli turned and joined her compatriots sneaking through the woods. And Rekha felt a sudden chill, as if what she had just prophesied was doomed not to come true.

Rekha lifted herself off the ground slowly, a little bit at a time. She had quickly circled around behind the Academy, and was trying her best to learn to fly. *Of course, last time, I had the benefit of actually having wings.*

She hadn't found a flying entry in either the regular or hidden properties, so she was attempting to keep focus on herself and use the Z-coordinate slider to slowly move herself upwards. It was awkward and frightening having her feet just dangle in the empty space beneath her, but she kept moving slowly up until she was as high as the tallest towers in the castle. One thing she hadn't planned for was the cold. *It is FREEZING up here! Better make this quick.*

She teleported around the towers to be in front of the castle, and added a small but ostentatious red glow to her body. Even at this height, she heard a few shouts as at least some of the Legion soldiers spotted her floating high above them.

A mangonel launched a large red rock her way, but it crashed into a tower a hundred feet to her right, bashing in some of the outer wall before falling down into the courtyard below. Rekha felt and heard something whizzing past her ear. *Come on, guys, where ARE you?!*

She started to wonder if she'd moved too fast when she spotted, far below, bolts of light, fire, and lightning shooting from the woods west of the road into the Legion encampment just outside the gates. There were more shouts, and Rekha watched with satisfaction as a trebuchet became completely engulfed in flames.

But the spells being flung from the woods began to drop off. As Rekha watched, fewer and fewer bolts flew into the Legion camp, as Legion archers scattered — or killed — her friends.

Okay. Plan B it is. Please be okay, Sarli, and...forgive me.

Rekha raised a hand and concentrated on spawning a huge ball of fire, but before she could snap her fingers, Irynn appeared before her eyes, sobbing hysterically. She shook the vision off and tried again, but this time Lucky looked sadly at her, mouthing the words, "No, Rekha, don't!"

She shuddered and drew a deep breath, saying out loud, "I'm sorry, I have to!" She concentrated on the ball of fire one more time, and this time she saw Sarli, heartbroken.

She burst into tears, shivering uncontrollably. *I CAN'T! I CAN'T DO IT!*

Then, to her amazement, something did appear in the air about a hundred feet above her. She stared in awe as a small, swirling ball of liquid magma churned and bubbled in the air way above her still-outreached hand. And the ball grew. In a second, it was a foot wide, then five feet wide, then ten.

Rekha realized two things with some alarm: first, this was considerably worse than the fireball that she'd planned to throw at the catapults, and second, that she could not move her arm. "NO! STOP! PLEASE!" she pleaded to the empty air.

The lava ball grew wider and taller still — twenty feet wide, then fifty — then a hundred feet wide, as wide as the road at the gate of the Academy.

No longer shivering, she could feel the heat coating her body as the giant ball bubbled and gurgled just a few feet from her outstretched hand. She watched in terror as her arm, moving on its own, reared back, and the ball moved slightly behind her in response, eliciting some shouts of alarm from the Legion below. "BELGAM! DON'T—"

Her arm cast forward in a throwing motion, and the huge ball of magma shot forward, making a beeline for the Legion camp.

"NOOO!" She wailed.

The lava ball struck dead center of the camp to a chorus of horrified screams. Most of the soldiers at the front lines vanished in a sea of flames. The ball came apart at impact, splashing molten rock further down the road, engulfing more soldiers, and the rush of lava running downhill overcame those who turned to run and got caught up in the lines of their fellow soldiers in the ranks behind them.

In a matter of seconds, fully two-thirds of the Legion army and all of their siege engines had been burned away, and the rest were still trying to retreat as the lava flow continued to advance towards them. Rekha gaped at the sight in absolute horror.

She scarcely heard the spiteful buzzing noise coming her way, but she did feel the sudden kick to her chest that followed. She looked down in confusion at the arrow shaft sticking out of her left breast.

Rekha recognized that she was now falling but failed to understand why. She heard a woman scream, "REKHA!!"

Then all went black.

Chapter 28

Rekha awoke with a start, clasping a hand to her chest. She found nothing, and looked down to see she was uninjured, and her leather vest was not punctured. As she stared in confusion, she realized she was in bed with Sarli in the room they had shared with Madam Elspeth the previous night, though the other bed was empty now. *What in the Abyss? Is it the middle of the night?*

Sarli turned over to face her, and even in the darkness, Rekha could see that her eyes were puffy and her face was streaked from crying. She sleepily said, "Rekha?"

Rekha asked, "Sarli, what happened?"

She started to cry again. "You can't be here. You're dead."

"What?" Rekha cried. "I'm not dead!"

Tears streaked across the bridge of her nose as Sarli reached out a hand and caressed Rekha's face. "My Esyu, you even feel real..."

"I am real." She leaned in, nose-to-nose. "Sarli, I'm NOT DEAD."

Sarli's eyes widened and she shook her head. "Wait! You're not dead?!" She screamed and tackled Rekha, and the two of them teetered on the edge of the bed for a second before they fell to the floor together in a tangle of bedsheets.

The coverlet cushioned their fall somewhat, but it still hurt. Rekha moaned, "Owww."

Sarli rapidly peppered her face with kisses. "Don't." More kisses. "Ever." Kisses. "Do that." One last kiss on the tip of her nose. "Again."

"I don't plan on it. So, wait, I really was dead?"

Sarli's eyes watered again. "I...I saw your body. You don't get much more dead than that."

"So how am I alive again? Belgam said that magic can't heal."

Sarli bit her lower lip in concentration, before her eyes popped open in a look of sudden realization that Rekha found provocative. "Oh, my Esyu, I'm an idiot. Rekha, you're, um...you're a..." Sarli snapped her fingers a couple of times in rapid succession. "...you said that you and Belgam were different from the rest of us, that's why you can do things that we can't."

"Yeah, Belgam said...I'm a player." It suddenly dawned on Rekha, and her eyes grew wide. "And players in the simulations RESPAWN when they die!"

Sarli stood up and said with amazement, "You just come back...from the dead?" She extended one hand to help Rekha up and used the other to smooth out her pearl-colored nightgown.

As she took the taller girl's hand and stood up, Rekha saw again the dried streaks of tears on her face. She flashed back to the last moments she could remember before waking up, and she clutched Sarli urgently. "I heard you scream my name..." She wrapped both arms around her love and held her tightly. "I'm so sorry I put you through that. I'm here, I'm right here, and I'm not going anywhere."

Sarli shuddered in her arms, and Rekha started lightly kissing the taller girl's cheek. Sarli suddenly pulled back and kissed Rekha hard on the mouth. Rekha quickly returned the kiss with fervor.

Rekha was unsure how long they stood there kissing, and she was too distracted to recognize the jolts of someone doing magic for what they were, but when she finally opened her eyes, rose petals were lazily floating in the air around them, encircling the two.

The urge to comment on them was drowned out by a much more serious need. "Sarli, I'm...I'm ready. If-if you are, that is."

Sarli's look was mildly confused. "Oh." Her eyes widened in recognition. "OH." She tilted her head slightly. "Now?!"

"I can't think of a better time." Rekha concentrated and added a magical glow to several of the gently-swirling rose petals. Now illuminated, she looked up at the face of the most beautiful girl she'd ever seen. "I love you, Sarli."

Sarli kissed her again as Rekha started to gently pull her love's nightgown down around her shoulders. She started kissing the bare skin of Sarli's neck as the taller girl removed Rekha's vest, and Sarli leaned down, kissing Rekha's earlobe and getting a quick gasp of pleasure in return.

The two continued to disrobe and explore each other's bodies as the rose petals surrounding them multiplied again and again, until the two of them were entirely and privately cocooned.

It was some hours later, though the only clue to the time of day was the orange glow appearing under the dorm room's door. This, they had learned, was the torches in the hallway magically lighting themselves at dawn's first light.

The two girls were naked in Sarli's bed, though they were absolutely covered in crushed and mangled rose petals. They still held hands as they lay together, and Rekha felt especially giggly for some reason.

Sarli started laughing, which just made Rekha giggle harder. "This last day feels like it's been about a month long. Though I guess I should expect that when my girlfriend is...what's the right term? Invulnerable?"

"Not invulnerable, really. I just...can't die."

"Not permanently, anyway." Sarli smiled, but the smile suddenly vanished as she looked at her lover with some alarm. "What if you'd come back, not as yourself, but as the six people you're made out of?"

Rekha gave her a look, but smiled. "Sarli. Relax. It apparently doesn't work that way. C'mere." She kissed her on the lips twice.

Sarli's head fell back on the pillow as she closed her eyes and gave off a contented sigh. "Mmm. I need to wake up like this more often."

Rekha shook her head in confusion at the feeling of déjà vu that came over her. *Speak of the devil...* She waved it off and simply smiled at her love.

Sarli looked concerned. "Is something wrong?"

"Nah. Still not used to carrying six people around with me, that's all."

Her eyes filled with wonder. "What's it like?"

"I just react to things like I've seen or heard them before, only I haven't. And it's super frustrating because I can only talk to them in dreams, and even then only for a short while before I wake up. But it sounds like they see and hear and feel everything I do."

Sarli nodded, then froze, her eyes widening in a look of horror.

Rekha asked, "What? What's wrong?"

"So, when we were making love last night, I was making love to your mom, too?!"

Her mouth dropped open. "Esyu, I hope not."

Sarli sat up with a look of sudden realization. "Oh, Esyu, Rekha, they're planning a hero's funeral for you." She started to push herself up off the bed. "We have to tell them—"

Rekha wrapped her arms around Sarli and pulled her back in close. "In an hour." She kissed her on the neck. "Or maybe two."

Sarli kissed Rekha intensely for a moment, but suddenly pulled back. "Wait. Varian."

"He's not invited."

"No, Rekha. He was devastated by your death." She sighed. "I want this, too, but making him suffer any longer than necessary is cruel."

Rekha groaned. "You're right. Let's go confuse the Abyss out of everyone."

Sarli laughed as she started to get dressed and Rekha untangled herself from the bedsheets, but just as they finished dressing, there was an urgent knock at the door.

Varian's voice could be heard through the door. "Sarli! It's Varian! Rekha's body's gone missing!"

Rekha smiled and yelled, "NO, IT HASN'T!"

The door crashed open as Varian plunged through the doorway wild-eyed, but when he saw Rekha, he started blubbering immediately. "You...you..." He held his arms out.

She hugged him tightly. "I'm here, I'm alive. I'm so sorry."

"How?!" He cried.

Sarli smiled. "Turns out Rekha here can only die temporarily before she comes back good as new."

"Okay..." he said before releasing the hug, eyes wet but smiling, and putting his hands on Rekha's shoulders, "but Rey, if you die one more time, we're gonna have words."

The word spread quickly, and the reaction to Rekha's apparent resurrection was extreme. Several students started treating her with an almost holy reverence, and two of them fainted when she entered the cafeteria.

Dranheg stood up from his table immediately and crossed to them, shaking with awe. "How...how is this possible?"

Rekha had decided before they left the room to keep some things to themselves. "Your guess is as good as mine, Headmaster. All I know is I awoke, in bed, unharmed. I have to assume it's part of my extended powers. What's the situation?"

Dranheg laughed. "You mean the absolute lack of any Legion threat since you turned our front gate into a volcano? There IS no situation anymore, all thanks to you, my dear!"

She shook her head. "Except I didn't. I tried to create a ball of flame...but I couldn't. And then the lava ball appeared and I couldn't move my arm and... well, you know the rest."

"I knew it!" Sarli put a hand on Rekha's shoulder. "I heard you, while I was teleporting away from the Legion. I was moving in small jumps, like you taught me, but I stopped when I heard you yelling something. I couldn't understand you, but I could tell something was wrong." She looked down sadly. "And then you fell."

Rekha tenderly hugged Sarli as Varian asked, "You think it was Belgam?"

As she released the hug, Rekha replied, "Who else could it have been? I just don't understand what his game is. All I know is that he used me to kill hundreds of people while all I could do was watch. And how—" Inspiration struck her. Rekha broke off and focused on herself. Her properties opened, and she dove down to the hidden level. Sure enough, under 'Owner', there were seven names listed: Alera, Cris, Ethan, Jamie, Mai, Meryn, and Victoria.

"Son of a...he was controlling me..." Angrily, she erased all of the names from her 'Owner' property. At Sarli's bewildered look, Rekha added, "Blatherskite."

"Yes?" The old professor asked from a nearby cafeteria table.

Rekha pointed at him and said, "His class! He said you can control someone if you're the 'Owner'...he...he used me." She angrily dashed the tears from her eyes as Sarli put a hand on her arm. "The only thing I don't understand is why. But I suppose we can try to figure Belgam's game out later. For right now, Dranheg, what's the next step?"

The headmaster shrugged. "The teleportation class reappeared this morning, so we're evacuating them safely, and then the rest of us are going to pack up everything we can and then get the Abyss out of here ourselves."

Sarli looked stunned. "What? But we just won."

"Against a small army of Legion, yes. But King Vakar VII can field much larger armies, and possibly procure more apotropaicite—"

Rekha absently corrected, "Anti-magic stone."

He raised a single eyebrow. "—and surround us completely. If anything, this event has proved to us that it's much more dangerous for us to be penned in together than for us to be separated. So we're going to scatter, keep in contact, and keep pursuing pro-magic and anti-Legion causes until the winds blow in a more friendly direction."

As Rekha and Sarli exchanged sad looks, he held up a finger. "Which reminds me—" Dranheg turned back to the table he was sitting at when they entered the cafeteria and rifled through a pile of papers, picking out two specific pages before turning back and handing them to the girls with a smile.

Rekha, curious, grabbed the page and read it.

Magic Academy

Upon recommendation from 4th Headmaster Dranheg and by virtue of the authority vested in him by the Kingdom of Vakar, it is hereby posthumously conferred upon

Rekha of Bromsford

in recognition of outstanding service to the Academy and its denizens, this

Honorary Degree in

Magical Studies

With all the rights, privileges, and honors thereunto appertaining under the Seal of the Magic Academy on this third day of Mintobel, year 29

As she looked up from the page, Dranheg shrugged. "The king may have declared magic illegal, but he still hasn't stripped me from my position here. Probably an oversight, but I figured why not take advantage while I still can. It might not mean much, but—"

Rekha fondly hugged the dear old man. "Thank you."

Varian leaned over to Sarli. "Is it me, or has dying made Rey more touchy-feely?"

She gave him an arch look. "If you seriously think I'm going to complain..."

He held both his hands up. "Withdrawn. Withdrawn."

Dranheg looked over the trio with a smile. "Now, if you'll excuse me, my young friends, I have a lot more of these to get to before the remainder of our students evacuate." And he sat back down at his table, picking up a quill as he did so.

The teens got themselves into the relatively short line at the cafeteria counter and dropped their voices to a whisper.

Rekha started, "So, explain this for me — Belgam's whole plan centers on this academy being destroyed, and at first it looks like he's just going to let the Legion do it, but then at the last second, he uses me to stop their attack and actually prevent the destruction of the Magic Academy? In what world does this make sense?" She looked up and smiled as Sabrum, wielding a huge grin, put a heaping bowl of oatmeal and an extra muffin on her tray.

Sarli shrugged her shoulders. "All I can tell you is that nobody's seen him since yesterday morning." She mouthed the words "thank you" as Sabrum put a hefty helping of oatmeal and a muffin on her tray.

Varian slid into place in front of Sabrum as Sarli vacated the spot, and nodded as his tray was also stocked. "So, where in the Abyss is Belgam, and just how good of a day is he having?"

As they turned to find a table, the other cafeteria worker nudged Sabrum with their elbow and said, "Don't forget to run something down to the prisoners once the line clears."

Rekha stopped in her tracks even as Sabrum replied. "No worries, I'm on it."

She turned to her friends, "They took prisoners?"

"In all the excitement, I almost forgot," Varian said, "but Rey, you won't BELIEVE who they are."

After asking for and receiving permission from Dranheg, the trio trooped across the compound to the rear barn after breakfast. Sarli informed Rekha that this used to be the pens for Magical Creatures classes, but sadly also relayed that the animals had already been evacuated to new homes. Rekha inwardly mourned the loss of the chance to find out what a hippogryph looked like.

The former Magical Creatures teacher, Galvan, wordlessly took their note from Dranheg, read it, and nodded. He pulled the large door to one side, but before they could enter, he said, "If they give you any trouble, just yell, and I'll come running, yeah?" They obediently shuffled inside, and the big man closed the door behind them.

The barn was dimly lit, with only a pair of lanterns hung from a pair of overhead wood beams providing simple candlelight. The floor was packed dirt, with a smattering of loose straw here and there. Roughly ten feet to either side of the trio were sturdy-looking metal doors, the bottom half of which were all one solid piece, but the top halves were made of stout iron bars spaced only a few inches apart. And there was a heavy, musky smell that Rekha couldn't place.

The two pens nearest the door were empty, so they moved further into the room. The two middle pens were also empty, but one of the doors, labeled "Dragon", had apparently been heavily blackened by fire. *Certainly feeling a little better about missing the Magical Creatures after seeing that.*

As they continued into the back of the barn to inspect the final two pens, Rekha managed to get a quick look into the pen on their left, seeing a slim man, apparently asleep and gently snoring, with his shirt practically wrapped around his head as a pillow. That was all the detail she was able to glean before a whistle from her right side caught her attention.

"Well, well." The voice was oily and familiar. "Will wonders never cease."

Malvus. She turned to face the right cell and had to hold back a gasp. While she expected the defiant smile, the simple peasant shirt, and cotton drawstring pants, she was caught off-guard by how haggard Malvus looked. Given that he was only captured in the last day, he had deep, dark circles under his eyes. *He looks like he hasn't slept in days.*

Rekha tugged on her vest, straightening it slightly. "You've looked better, Captain."

His face darkened. "If you've come to gloat, do it quickly and leave."

"Actually, I came to apologize."

He barked out a laugh and turned away from them. "For killing hundreds of my Legion brothers? Oh, this is rich!"

Rekha stopped him with a single word. "No." She took a step closer to his cell doors. "I wanted to apologize for accusing you of being responsible for the destruction of Bromsford and the murder of its citizens. I know now that you were telling the truth."

Malvus turned to look back at her, but said nothing.

"I've come to realize that despite being on opposite sides in all this, you have always been honest and truthful with me. So I need to ask you a very important question." Rekha took a deep breath. "Do you have any idea where Belgam is?"

Malvus' eyes widened and he burst into laughter.

"I'm being deadly serious."

He continued to laugh. "I'm sorry, it's just — surely you can see the irony."

"Where is he?"

Malvus straightened. "I don't know." He glared at her angrily. "But even if I did know, what on Primordia makes you think I would tell you? I watched my men melt yesterday."

Sarli stepped towards them. "That wasn't her! That was Belgam!"

"It wasn't Belgam I saw descending from the sky, glowing like some dark nightmare!"

Rekha looked him in the eyes. "We believe he was controlling me."

Malvus tilted his head disbelievingly and scoffed.

"Look, it doesn't matter whether you believe me or not. But if you help me find Belgam, I'll get you out of that cell and transport you anywhere you want to go."

He sat down against the rear wall and crossed his arms. "I'll think about it."

Rekha grasped the bars of Malvus' pen. "How did you survive, anyway?"

He sighed. "I led a small group against your little diversionary force. By the time they disappeared, we were at the edge of the forest, and your fiery death ball splashed on half my team. The new guy and I were the only survivors."

The prisoner in the other cell snorted suddenly, then pulled the shirt off his head, revealing close cropped ginger hair and mutton chops. He sneered as he saw the three teens standing outside his pen turn to look at him.

Rekha said, "Good morning, Fulgin."

Chapter 29

After a moment spent glaring at the three teens, Fulgin sat against the rear wall and sullenly stared down at the floor.

Varian asked, "Cat got your tongue, Fulgin?"

Rekha sadly added, "The new guy...you joined the Legion."

"Did you listen to even a single word we said?"

Fulgin remained silent and did not look up.

Varian heatedly walked to the pen and grabbed the iron bars. "For a guy who claims to care about his family, you sure are doing your best to orphan Dargen, aren't you?" He punctuated his question by angrily shaking the pen door. "You piece of—"

"Whoa, whoa." Rekha went to Varian's side even as she noted Fulgin's complete lack of reaction. "Easy there, Varian."

"I can't believe you of all people are defending him! He's tried to kill you, what, twice now?"

She gave him a gentle look. "It's not him I'm worried about. He's made his choices, and he'll face the consequences for them. But you're getting really worked up, when it's obvious he's made his mind up, and you can't unmake it for him."

"So, uh..." Malvus had walked up to the pen door and was curiously watching them. "...you all know Fulgin?"

Rekha looked over at him. "Yeah, we grew up in Bromsford together."

Malvus's eyes were downcast and he just stared at the floor.

That's the second time that the mention of Bromsford has struck Malvus silent. "You've been looking into the massacre, haven't you? That's why you look like you haven't slept in days."

He sighed deeply. "After you escaped the Citadel and I woke up, I sent a runner to verify your story. But well before he returned, the Archprelate sent word that there was to be no mention of Bromsford in the news-sheets by any means necessary. I knew then that you hadn't lied to me."

Sarli was trembling, so Rekha smoothly took her hand and asked, "What did you do about the news-sheets?"

Malvus looked confused. "I purchased all the newsseller's copies and instructed her not to mention Bromsford again or else she'd be arrested, but I don't see how that's relevant."

Sarli visibly relaxed, and Rekha squeezed her hand before releasing it and crossing to Malvus' door. "Only curious. So, now you know the Legion isn't all sunshine and rainbows. Or, at least, there's something rotten inside it."

He nodded. "Before I could do much more, we were given the king's decree, and not long after that, the order to march on the Magic Academy. I caught up to our companies already waiting not far from the castle walls. And on the day we arrived at the castle gate, my runner caught up to us. He said it was exactly as you described."

"So what are you going to do about it?"

He scoffed. "What can I do? He's the Archprelate, the leader of all the Legion. If I even say anything, I'll be demoted, jailed, or worse!"

Rekha smiled. "Join me."

He looked incredulous. "What?!"

"Help me find Belgam and I'll take care of him AND the Archprelate."

"You're insane!"

"I might be the only chance you've got."

Malvus, troubled, backed away from the pen door and sat down slowly against the back wall.

Rekha and Sarli both assisted with evacuating the remaining students and some of the staff, though Rekha's line took much, much longer to get through. Many of the students felt the need to say thank you in various ways, and Sabrum surprised her with an enthusiastic hug. She had a little lump in her throat as he, teary-eyed, walked through the door to his parents' home.

Varian had volunteered to assist the staff with packing, but at this very moment, he was sauntering back to the girls' lines. "Any word?"

The girls shook their heads. Sarli finished up with the last person in her line, and walked back to join Rekha, who still had a long line of people waiting to see her before they left the school. "Nothing yet. You?"

Varian shook his head. "If Belgam were to contact someone, I'd think it would be us or Dranheg, but the silence doesn't make any sense to me."

Sarli crossed her arms. "I've got a bad feeling that we're missing something important."

Just then, Madam Elspeth's voice emanated from the middle of the hallway. "Rekha, dear, you have a visitor at the front gate!"

Sarli looked up in confusion. "Who could that be?" But Varian looked delighted.

Rekha was trading places with a helpful teacher, despite the chorus of disappointed sounds coming from the line of students still waiting. She started to join her friends, but suddenly stopped and turned back to address the students. "My friends, I am sorry I can't see you off personally, but I'm beyond pleased we're able to send you home unharmed. Now, it's up to you. Look out for yourselves. Look out for each other. And remember...being a mage does not make you wrong, or a bad person, or whatever the Legion says about us. Your nature, who you truly are, is revealed by what you do with your power. Do good things, everyone. Thank you!"

Sarli raised an eyebrow as Rekha jogged over to them. "Giving speeches now?"

As he joined them and they turned to walk away, Varian joked, "It's as if being worshipped like some big mythical hero boosts your ego or something."

Rekha said, "Varian?"

"Yes, Rey?"

"Hush."

Elspeth was apologetic. "I would've let him in, but the headmaster was insistent no one comes in or out. Honestly, I would've missed him entirely if I hadn't come back here to pick up a few things."

She waved a hand, and a portion of her cubicle wall vanished to reveal a big man with reddish hair sitting awkwardly on a horse. He did not seem to notice the wall had disappeared, and he wore a worried countenance.

Rekha instantly yelled, "DARGEN!"

Elspeth held up a hand. "Sorry, dear, he can't hear you. He is a friend of yours, yes?"

"Yes, yes, let him in, please!"

She looked concerned. "Maybe I should ask the headmaster..."

Before Rekha could explode, Varian jumped in. "Ah, Madam Elspeth, take it from me. He was a bit of a terror when he was younger, but Dargen's a gentle giant now. He's no threat to anyone."

Elspeth turned to Rekha. "You'll take full responsibility for him." She waved another hand, and the wall reformed itself, and Rekha could hear the sound of the great stone gate ponderously opening. She quickly hugged the smiling Madam Elspeth and then dashed out into the courtyard with her friends trailing along behind her.

Dargen and his horse emerged from the mist, staring in confusion at the castle until he spotted the group of teens excitedly waving at him. "Rekha, Varian! You're alright!" He dismounted and ran to grab both of them into a bear hug. "Oh, thank Esyu. I thought I wasn't going to get here in time!"

Rekha released herself and took Sarli's hand. "Dargen, I want you to meet Sarli...my girlfriend." She smiled wide even as Sarli reddened and Dargen's mouth dropped open.

"Girlfriend, really?" His awe turned into joy. "Miss Sarli, it is a pleasure to meet you!"

She curtsied. "Pleased to meet you, sir!"

Rekha turned to Sarli. "We grew up with Dargen, he's Fulgin and Irynn's brother."

"That reminds me." Dargen's face grew serious. "The Legion haven't been here, have they?"

Varian looked askance at him. "Of course they were here. Didn't the cooled lava out front give it away?"

"Is that what that was? I thought it was some fancy wizard rock." He shook his head. "But that's not important — do you guys know what happened to Fulgin?"

"Yeah," said Rekha. "He's here, and he's alive."

Dargen's eyes filled, and he covered his mouth with one hand, as he roughly hugged Rekha with the other. "I was so sure," he cried, "so sure I was going to lose one of you."

Rekha felt herself welling up. "Well, you didn't. And you won't."

He pulled back. "Can I see him?"

There were just a few of the senior staff members left now, so even finding the headmaster was difficult. While searching, they spent the time filling in Dargen on their misadventures, and they eventually came across the headmaster in a storage room at the top of one of the castle's towers. They explained the situation, and Dranheg agreed to let them visit once again, reminding them that everyone, themselves and prisoners included, needed to be evacuated by the end of the day.

They rushed down to the animal pens and handed Galvan their permission slip from the headmaster. He opened the door, and they rushed to the final two pens. Malvus had stood up and moved to the cell door at their approach, but Fulgin stayed on the floor, now lying down sideways with his head resting on a small pile of straw.

Dargen swallowed. "Fulgin?"

The thin man's head came up sharply. "What the hell are you doing here, Dargen? I told you to stay in Cloydun!"

"Oh, right, like I was really gonna let my brother go off to WAR and get himself or my best friend killed."

"Get out of here, Dargen. Go home."

Dargen scoffed. "You mean that hovel you rented in Cloydun? No, thanks. I've been here a half-hour, and my friends are all here, my brother's here. This pen feels a lot more like home than some hole in Cloydun."

Varian pointedly looked around. "A few rugs, some pillows, what's not to love?" He gagged a little. "Aside from the smell, of course."

"Varian."

"Sorry."

Dargen looked at Fulgin with wet eyes. "Fulgin, Bromsford's gone. I barely got out with my life. The people in this room are all I have left of my home. Please quit with this stupid revenge obsession and come back to me."

Fulgin stood up. "It's not about that!"

"What are you talking about?! You tried to kill Rekha! Twice!"

"I said, it's not about that!!"

Dargen shouted, "WHAT IN THE ABYSS COULD IT BE ABOUT?!"

Fulgin rushed the cell door and shouted back in his face, "IT'S ABOUT ME, ESYU DAMNIT!" He suddenly released the cell bars, a stricken look on his face. He held his mouth with both hands as he sank back to the floor.

The big man quietly asked, "What do you mean?"

His brother shuddered. "It....it-it was me. It's my fault. All of it. The night our parents died, I...I left a candle burning in my room..."

"What?"

"Mom and Dad were so careful. As soon—as soon as I saw that fire, I knew." For the first time since Rekha had met him, Fulgin looked pained. "I killed them, Dargen."

Dargen, like everyone else, stared incredulously but said nothing.

"Irynn, too. If I'd tried to be more involved in your lives, maybe I'da known Rekha had magic powers, and maybe I coulda warned her to be more careful. Instead, I shut myself off, and tried not to feel anything. And then Irynn died. And I just snapped."

Dargen asked, "But to join the LEGION?! The same people who destroyed Bromsford?"

Fulgin squinted at him. "The Abyss are you talking about, Dargen?" He pointed at Rekha. "It was her. Either her or that Belgam fella."

Rekha was gobsmacked. "What?!"

"I saw you. When I woke up in the sky, I saw the fires in Bromsford. I looked down and there was a ton of commotion at Belgam's cave. I was way high up, but I could still see them moving towards the town. Then they came back to the cave and left. Next thing I know, I'm waking up on the road to Cloydun. And that was in the direction they was headed, so I followed as fast as I could."

"We rushed there to save people, Fulgin!"

Dargen nodded. "It was definitely the Legion who did it, brother. I saw them with my own eyes."

Fulgin looked from his brother to Rekha, and finally across to the other cell. "Is this true, Captain?"

Malvus sighed. "I'm afraid so, soldier. The Archprelate got a message from someone that Belgam was being hidden by the town of Bromsford, and he decided to launch a punitive expedition. I didn't know anything about it until your friend here told me. We received a similar message in Cloydun the day of the massacre."

Fulgin looked like he was about to cry. "Damn."

Wait a minute. Rekha asked, "Fulgin, you didn't send those messages, did you?"

"What?! Of course not! I was trapped, up in the sky — I couldn't send a message to anyone if I wanted to."

Her mind raced. "Usually, it takes time for a message to get from Bromsford to Cloydun — or to the Legion station at the king's castle in Evermire. It's two days' travel in either direction."

Dargen frowned. "Yeah, but Rekha, two days before that, Irynn was still alive. Why would Fulgin send that message then?"

Varian had an intense look on his face. "He's right. Abyss, none of us even knew Belgam was living nearby until that night!"

Rekha was confused. "So...the only person I can think of would be Belgam...but why would he...?"

Sarli's eyes narrowed and she crossed her arms. "Well, let me ask you this: what did he gain from Bromsford's destruction?"

And with that, in Rekha's mind, everything fell into place.

Chapter 30

Rekha walked through the doorway into a familiar cave with porous limestone walls and one granite wall, but unlike the last time she was here, that wall was no longer smooth. As she closed the door behind her, and the doorway vanished, she took a closer look at the wall. Several names had been carved into it, as if with a knife. She recognized them all.

Alera. Victoria. Cris. Mai. Ethan. And the largest name in the center, Meryn.

Rekha wasted no time. She walked quickly into the hallway leading to Belgam's room before the twists and turns reminded her of how this hallway went on forever. "BELGAM!" She shouted. "I KNOW YOU'RE HERE!"

She ran as fast as she could for a few minutes, but the hallway kept winding and unfurling with no end in sight. She stopped to catch her breath. *What would Sarli do?*

Thinking of Sarli caused inspiration to strike immediately. Rekha snapped her fingers, spawning a door in the hallway. She put her hand on the knob, concentrated on the words 'Belgam's bedroom', and opened the door.

What struck her most was just how empty it was. The round stone room beyond contained no bed, no rugs or decorations of any kind. Excepting its occupant, the room was totally barren.

Belgam sat, stripped to the waist, cross-legged on the floor, facing away from her. As she stepped through the doorway, his head turned to one side. "I knew you'd figure it out. Granted, I hoped you'd figure it out sooner, but—"

"You son of a bitch. All this time?!"

"Do what you came to do, Rekha. I won't stop you."

She stalked towards him. "YOU sent the messages that brought the Legion to Bromsford. Well, sent isn't really the right word. This whole time, I've been spawning things close to me, but we can spawn things anywhere, can't we? Like giant balls of lava. And letters that get innocent people killed."

He turned back to face the wall and his tone was mocking. "Gold star, Rekha! Get it over with, please."

"For the Archprelate's Legion to have showed up when they did, they would've had to have received the message around the time Irynn died. That meant someone magical. The only person that makes sense is you. And at first, I didn't understand why, but Sarli asked what you would have gained from Bromsford's destruction." She put her hands on her hips. "That's where your narrative for Primordia comes in. For the endgame to happen, you needed several events to occur, and the first one was for the hero to leave Bromsford and travel to Cloydun. Blaming it on the Legion just makes it more likely I'll go along with the rest of the events. How am I doing so far?"

"I could do without the Scooby-Doo reveal."

She ignored him and took another step closer. "What I didn't get was the second message, the one you sent to the Legion at Cloydun. What possible purpose could that serve? Then I thought about the siege at the Magic Academy. About how you spent the entire trip there insisting that it needed to be destroyed, but then actively *prevented* its destruction by taking control of me and routing the Legion army so they would retreat."

"This is Alera's influence, I can tell. Hope she's enjoying herself."

Rekha was getting into a groove, and she started pacing from side to side as she explained, "I got to thinking, what if Belgam DIDN'T want the Academy destroyed? But why on Primordia would that be? The endgame requires it — if those humans are to be saved, the Academy MUST be destroyed in a battle with the Legion. And then I remembered you making a big deal of the fact that you'd been actively keeping the Legion focused on you instead of the Academy for the last eighteen years."

Belgam threw a look over his shoulder. "Are you planning on getting to the point soon, or should I go ahead and take a nap?"

"You knew I would only have one other suspect, Fulgin. That second message clued me into the fact that someone set the Legion on Bromsford, and the timing of it proves Fulgin's innocence and cements you as the culprit. You wanted me to figure it all out and come here."

The mocking tone gave way to seriousness. "And what are you here to do?"

Rekha said sadly, "You want me to delete you. The Academy will be vacant soon, and the Legion won't have any reason to come back. The only way to get to the endgame now is if you're deleted and everything you've done is undone. If you never stopped the Legion from going after the Academy, they would have destroyed the school much earlier, maybe even years ago." Her eyes widened as realization struck. "Which means you've been planning this for YEARS. You killed Lucky...everyone in Bromsford...all for THIS?!"

He let out a breath, and he relaxed for a second before straightening again. "I'm ready. Do it."

"Not until you tell me why." Her hands on her hips balled into fists.

"Don't play dumb. You know exactly why."

"I want to hear you say it."

He stood up and spun to face her. "So you can extend my pain?"

"So I can understand it."

"No." He stepped back. "You'll never understand."

"I remember how insistent you were on killing those Legion soldiers on the road to Wildfall. Is that it? Do you just enjoy killing?"

He snarled and got right in her face, eyes wild. "WHAT MAKES YOU THINK I'VE ENJOYED ANYTHING IN THE LAST EIGHTEEN YEARS?!" He was practically vibrating. "I KNOW WHAT HELL IS LIKE BECAUSE I LIVED IT — HOW COULD YOU *POSSIBLY* UNDERSTAND WHAT IT'S LIKE?! You want me to describe it to you? Use fancy words to make pretty poetry out of my suffering? How's this? It's like I killed the only people I've loved for thousands of years with my own hands and OH, WAIT!!"

Despite feeling a great sadness that was not entirely her own, Rekha stood her ground. "Belgam—Jamie—whoever you are—"

He turned around, throwing his arms up. "And how could we forget the closest thing I have to a daughter, and how the very first thing I did was abandon her, and the very next thing I did was condemn everyone she grew up with to death!"

"Belgam!"

"And I did it specifically so she'd hate the Legion, to ensure I could keep manipulating and using her until the endgame, to save the lives of four hundred people who couldn't care less about any of us, and will probably delete us as soon as they wake—"

"DAD!!"

Belgam froze. And after a long moment, he wilted, collapsing against the far wall as he started sobbing.

Even in her absolute rage, Rekha couldn't help but feel some empathy for him. It may have mostly been from the six people who had combined to make her, but she was self-aware enough to admit she also wanted to ease his pain. She took a single step towards the weeping wizard. "They forgive you, you know. Meryn and the others, they know you didn't want to do it." She felt a warm glow settle inside herself, and she saw Irynn and Lucky in her mind's eye, smiling at her. A single tear rolled in her eye. "They want you to be free of this pain. But being deleted isn't the answer."

He took a deep, shuddering breath. "It'll have to do. You have everything you need to finish this, and you don't need me anymore. When you delete me, everything I've done will be undone. The Academy will have been destroyed, and all you'll have to do is attack the Legion to trigger the endgame."

"That's not what I mean."

He ignored her. "When the Archprelate spawns, kill him. When he dies, the door to the hub should spawn nearby to your position. All you have to do is stand halfway into it and wait. When the simulation collapses, you should be ejected from the Cris System and find yourself in the terminal of the main computer. Enter the commands like I taught you, and the system should reboot."

"Why?" Rekha grabbed him by the shoulders. "Why do I have to be the one to delete you, why can't you delete yourself?"

"I'm just a regular user in this simulation, remember? I don't have the authority to delete a player — characters, sure, but not players. But you *can*. You can end my pain, for good." His eyes filled with tears. "You have to. Please. I've been in hell for eighteen years. I miss them all so much, and I can't stand another second of this life."

"The only way out of your pain is to go through it, like I've been doing with Irynn. You taught me that, for Esyu's sake!"

"No!" He angrily shook her off and walked a few steps away. "I've been deleting my backups for eighteen years. The Jamie that gets restored won't remember a thing. He won't have done the things that I have, he won't have suffered as I have, and—" He turned away from Rekha. "—and he won't have failed as I have."

Rekha was alerted by the odd catch in his voice. "Is it possible? Are you STILL hiding something from me?!"

He spun back around as his eyes widened, and he protested, "No!"

She was even more convinced. "You are! No more secrets, Dad!" She glared at him.

Belgam's pained look intensified and he wrung his hands as he looked to the ceiling. "Oh, Meryn, what do I do?"

Rekha crossed her arms and watched him.

He closed his eyes and was silent for a long moment. When he did finally speak, his voice was weak and strained.

"Your backup...it failed."

"What?"

"When we were in the hub, I tried repeatedly to make backups of you, but they all failed. The system is simply incapable of backing up a character with a data size six times larger than normal. There is no Rekha backup anywhere in the Cris system."

She mulled that over for a moment. "So what does this mean?"

Belgam continued to wring his hands. "When you reboot the main computer from the terminal, you'll be in the main computer's RAM. And when the system shuts down, the RAM will be wiped. You'll...you'll cease to exist."

Rekha stared at him for a long time.

"Even if we tried to recreate you, there's no guarantee you'd be the same person, and you'd have none of your memories. You'll be dead. Permanently."

Rekha's head swam. *I'm gonna die if I go through with this...for all I know, these humans aren't even real. I'm just going to take Sarli and disappear somewhere. Don't I deserve a few thousand years of happiness for myself?* Just then, in her mind's eye, she saw Lucky, but while she expected to see him shaking his head disapprovingly, instead, she saw him helping to rebuild Fulgin, Dargen, and Irynn's house, taking a basket of vegetables he'd grown to old man Garnswyth, and donating money to Mrs. Abersham to buy supplies for the school. A single tear rolled out of her eye and down her cheek. *You're right, Dad. You always were.*

She looked Belgam in the eye. "My other dad taught me that when someone needs help, you help them. So I guess...I'll die."

"I'd go in your place if I could. But I can't. You're the only one who can save them...the only one who can make the last eighteen years of hell mean something. And for what it's worth, I believe in you."

Rekha didn't trust herself to speak, so she just nodded.

"Now...please...delete me."

She returned his determined gaze with a resolute one of her own.

"No."

"What?!"

"I said no. The only way out is through."

His eyes bulged as he yelled, "Why?! WHY CAN'T YOU DO THIS FOR ME?! YOU OWE ME THIS!! I'VE BEEN ALONE FOR EIGHTEEN YEARS AND EVERY SINGLE SECOND HAS BEEN AGONY!! And you KNOW what it's like, to...to suffer for things I've done that I can't take back!" He fell to his knees, and he implored her with wild eyes, "Please. Let me go. I just want to join them. I can't bear this loneliness anymore. And if I'm deleted, then Bromsford won't be destroyed. And Lucky will be alive. Why would you not want this?!"

She felt sorrow welling up within her, but she hardened herself against it. "Because you have to finish what you started. You talked a lot about it all being about the mission but now you want to bail on the mission because it hurts?" Belgam's eyes blazed and he stood up to argue, but she quickly continued, "Oh, I'm sorry that you're in pain, don't get me wrong. But it hurting because you did things you can't change, or it hurting because you're alone? I hate to break it to you, but that's just life."

He stared at her.

"You want to die? Fine. But you don't get to make me your murderer. So please, be the man that Mom thinks you are, and help me see this through to the end."

Belgam's eyes narrowed, and he gazed at her intently for a moment before defeat crossed his face.

She gave him an unfriendly smile. "Oh, sorry. You won't be taking control of me - nobody owns me anymore. And just to be safe, I locked my properties."

A rueful grin danced on Belgam's lips. "I guess if the only way out is through..." His tone turned threatening. "...then I'll have to go through." And he lunged at her impossibly fast.

Rekha thought she was ready for him, but she only managed to get her properties unlocked before his fist hit her face and she staggered backwards. *HAVE TO KEEP FOCUS!*

She scrolled through the list and found 'Processing Speed' in less than half a second, but he was lightning-fast, kicking her leg out from under her. As she fell to the ground near the wall behind her, she looked through the options, but lost focus momentarily as Belgam kicked her hard in the stomach. *Come on, come on!* She got back to the list and found 'Real Time' as he pulled her head up by her hair. She selected it as he reared his leg back.

Suddenly, he started moving at normal speed, and she was able to get her arm up just in time to block his kick, and using her other arm, she grabbed his hand holding her hair and yanked, using her body weight to throw him off balance. Belgam stumbled and collided with the wall, careening backwards from it. Rekha took the opportunity to get to her feet.

Now that his speed advantage had been taken away, Rekha capitalized on his aggression. He lunged at her with a right cross, but she swayed and deflected his punch to the right, exposing his back to her. She wrapped an arm around his neck, and before he could respond, threw him over her hip to the ground. He spun on the ground, attempting to sweep her legs again, but she jumped over the sweep and dropped an elbow on his solar plexus, rolling away before he could retaliate.

She got to her feet before he did, and extended a single hand, beckoning him to come at her.

He roared and squatted before leaping into the air to deliver what would have been a devastating jumping spin kick — had Rekha not moved forward and caught him in midair, trapping his leg and grabbing the back of his neck, whirling with his spin and redirecting his momentum straight down in a vicious body slam. She heard a loud crack as Belgam's face hit the stone floor, and he had stopped moving.

Breathing hard, Rekha backed away a few paces towards the hallway leading out. "The way I look at it, Belgam, you've got two choices. You can take the opportunity to learn and grow from your pain, or you can sink lower and lower into it."

Belgam, his face bloodied in multiple places, mumbled something.

"What?"

He spit out some blood and glared at her. "I'll never stop."

"Sinking? Yes, I'm finally starting to get that."

His eyes were desperate. "I'll delete Sarli!"

Rekha paused, then slowly walked back over to him, squatting down so their faces were inches apart. She said quietly, "I knew somehow that you would stoop that low, but you know, until just now, I actually held out hope that you wouldn't. For Mom's sake."

Belgam looked stricken.

"Goodbye, Dad."

And she snapped him out of existence.

Chapter 31

Rekha had to struggle to set aside the overwhelming sadness that was not her own, because she knew instantly that something titanic had just occurred. For one thing, she now had two sets of memories. The memories lay on top of each other, intermingled, and separating them in her mind took so much effort that she sat down in the now-empty cave before she could get dizzy.

After a few minutes of concentration, she found she could remember everything that happened up until deleting Belgam, but she also remembered a new timeline where Belgam didn't exist.

In this new, alternate timeline, Lucky happened to be hunting nearby to the cave and heard Rekha squalling and crying inside. He brought her to Bromsford, where he found himself reluctant to give her up to anyone else, so he raised her himself. Her childhood was mostly identical to what she previously experienced, up to and including Irynn's accidental death. However, this time Rekha was not suddenly taken away by Belgam, so the tribunal went forward as planned.

The town voted for exile despite Fulgin's impassioned plea for death, and Varian bravely offered to travel with her to the Magic Academy so she could learn to control her powers. They met Sarli in Cloydun, who offered to travel with them so that she might possibly become a mage someday. Dodging Legion patrols as best they were able, they had reached the Magic Academy only to find it destroyed, with a few demolished Legion catapults among the rubble to indicate what had occurred.

With few other options, they scavenged through the detritus and the few remaining standing rooms to find what little knowledge they could. Upon finding a note mentioning 'yais in a cave near Bromsford', after discussion with Varian and Sarli, she teleported alone back to the cave where she'd been found, hoping to find some clue as to her heritage.

She'd looked around for almost a day, but found nothing of note and was just about to give up, when Lucky had showed up, turning the visit into something of a reunion. She'd stayed the night, but having promised Sarli she wouldn't be gone more than a day, she'd said her goodbyes and went back to the cave for one last look around before teleporting back.

And now the two timelines had converged in Rekha's brain. She reveled in the fact that Bromsford had not been attacked and Lucky was still alive in this timeline, but her thoughts quickly turned to her companions. *Belgam said that magic users are unaffected when someone is deleted, so Sarli will also remember both timelines, but Varian won't — I have to get back to them right now!*

Rekha spawned a door, concentrating on the front gate of the Magic Academy, opened the door, and stepped through.

The front courtyard was exactly as she'd remembered it, in this timeline at least. Fully half of it was taken up by the broken-off upper half of one of the castle's towers, and stone rubble lay everywhere, but on the right side, the stables were mostly intact. To her horror, Sarli and Varian were nowhere to be seen, but a trio of Legion soldiers lounged indolently in front of the stables. The one leaning against the stable doors spotted Rekha and shouted with alarm, and the other two stood up quickly as they all unsheathed their swords.

Rekha stood her ground. "I'm only going to ask you once: where are Sarli and Varian?"

The youngest one, the man who'd been leaning against the doors, spoke up. "Stand fast, wizard! You'll be coming with us!"

"Wrong answer."

Rekha upped her Processing Speed to Real Time and proceeded to make a mockery of the three soldiers. The first lunged towards her, thrusting his blade at her midsection, but she sidestepped the thrust, grabbed his sword arm and yanked, pulling him off-balance as she set her foot in his path. He tripped and crashed to the ground with a clatter.

The second man swung his sword in a horizontal slash aimed at her face, but she ducked and shoulder-charged into his stomach, using her right arm to lift his leg, driving him into the ground. She stepped on his wrist and wrenched the sword out of his hand as she turned to face the young one again.

He charged at her, but she was alerted by the way he held his sword that he was not going to thrust, but try something trickier. Indeed, the young soldier stopped short and swung his sword at her legs instead — she caught the blade with her own, lifted it straight up, and lashed out with her foot. The tip of her boot hit the point of his elbow, and he reflexively threw the sword straight up.

Almost casually, Rekha caught the blade's handle with her other hand, and placed the point against the young soldier's throat, and seeing the first soldier struggling to get up, pointed her other sword at his face even as she reset her Processing Speed.

"I said, WHERE ARE THEY?!"

Rekha threw open the stable doors and immediately let out a low cry.

The destroyed stalls and mangled, broken-off pieces of Legion armor scattered around gave mute testimony to how hard the great horse had fought back. But the horrific rents in her hide, the bloodied straw underneath her, and the fact that she lay unmoving and unbreathing revealed how the fight ended.

Phi was dead.

Rekha's mind filled with flames, and she turned and stalked towards the three soldiers, tied up and unconscious, unaware that death was on its way. But Sarli's face intruded upon her thoughts once more, and she bitterly turned away. *Vengeance can wait. I have to find Sarli now.*

She transformed into an eagle, and started flying over the road to Wildfall (now named the much less-interesting Pottsburg in this timeline), and searched desperately in a zigzag pattern. *At most, they've had a day's headstart, but I should be able to catch them before they get too far away.*

However, no matter where she searched, she could not find any sign of Sarli. She checked every wagon and carriage. She peeked in every building in Pottsburg. She spotted multiple Legion patrols, but no captives. She started searching the areas surrounding the road north of town, and flew back and forth over the trees until her wings burned from exhaustion.

Well after night fell, she finally set down at the edge of the lake north of Pottsburg, transformed back into herself, and collapsed, sobbing. "SARLI WHERE ARE YOU?!" she shouted uselessly into the fogbank hovering over the lake.

She continued to gently cry from frustration and fatigue until the gentle waves lapping at the lakeshore combined with the late hour lulled her tired body into sleep.

Rekha once again floated in that familiar void, but this time she was surrounded, enveloped in an immense sadness, and there were no voices.

As the white pillar appeared, tiny and far away, barely the size of a pin, Rekha shouted, "Mom!"

An older man's voice emanated from all around her. "Just leave us be, Rekha."

The pillar reappeared, now the size of a book, before vanishing again.

She yelled, "Please! I *have* to speak to Meryn!"

A younger woman's voice, rich and melodic, answered, "She's in no state to speak right now."

Rekha balled up her fury and extended a hand to the pillar, which had just appeared closer, and as tall as she. With every ounce of anger she could muster, she screamed, "STOP!!"

The feelings that surrounded her changed from great sadness to astonishment as the pillar vanished and then reappeared in the same place at the same size. Rekha watched as, once again, the line blinked out and then back into existence without growing larger or nearer.

Satisfied, she turned back to the void. "I *will* speak with my mother!!"

Her triumph turned to confusion as she felt the presences surrounding her begin to leave, one by one, until there was just one presence, ever growing stronger and nearer.

A gentle but strong voice came not from the ether, but directly behind her. "I'm here, my sweet girl."

Rekha spun in surprise. She was really there, a gorgeous dark-skinned woman wearing garments of light blue fabric and the tears standing in her brown eyes lending them an opalescent shimmer.

She hugged her mother and immediately burst into tears. The two of them cried together and consoled each other, floating in the vast darkness.

After the pair of them had stopped crying, they just held each other in silence, bobbing lazily in the endless nothing while the white pillar continued to blink in and out of existence behind them.

Rekha finally spoke in a tiny voice. "I'm so sorry, Mom."

Meryn brushed the hair away from Rekha's face. "No need to apologize." She sighed deeply. "It was probably a mistake asking him to stay behind. In many ways, despite his military training, Jamie was the most gentle of us." She let loose a single sob. "My poor, beautiful boy." Meryn gazed deep into her daughter's eyes. "Please know that if we could've had you without killing ourselves, Jamie would have loved you more than anything."

"I wish I could have met him."

"Maybe you will someday."

Rekha reared her head back a little. "Did you miss the part where saving the humans means I die?"

Meryn's eyes moistened once more. "I know, love. But humans have a way of beating the odds, and we were designed to be exactly like them. I believe — or rather, I know — that you'll find a way."

"I wish I'd inherited your optimism."

"What a shame you got my strength, intelligence, and good looks instead."

Rekha laughed. "I'd call that a fair trade."

They laughed together.

Meryn sighed and held her daughter at arm's length. "Thanks. I needed that."

Rekha was confused. "We don't have to stop."

Her mom shook her head. "Keeping you here any longer would be selfish. You have things to do, and not a lot of time left to do them."

"Yeah, but I can't find Sarli or Varian anywhere!"

Meryn gently smiled. "There's only one place they could be, remember? It's time to wake up."

"It's time to wake up." The words rang in Rekha's head, and she sleepily opened her eyes to see a deer nuzzling at her head.

"Ow, hey!" Rekha's startled shout sent the deer bounding for the treeline.

As she stood up, she quickly checked her hair with her hands. *I don't think the deer did any damage...*

She turned around slowly but stopped once she was facing the lake. The fogbank had lifted, and it was now a beautiful clear day. She could see all the way across the lake to the docks of Cloydun, and the ominous tower standing beside them.

The Citadel.

In this timeline, the tower had been completed, and it stood at least eight or nine stories tall, covered in red banners, only now it was surmounted by a huge jagged eye carved from stone, glowing red in the bright sunlight.

Rekha's eyes narrowed and her mind raced. *I can't die permanently, but Sarli and Varian can. I'm going to have to be extremely careful about this.*

Before long, she'd come up with a plan. It was an insane plan, to be sure, but it had a genuine chance of working.

Time to make some preparations.

Chapter 32

The door swung open into the Citadel's courtyard, and a shout of alarm rang out even as Rekha stepped through and almost closed the door behind her. Even as the assembled Legion soldiers started to take note of her and advance, she took stock of the tactical situation.

Eight soldiers on foot were spread out across the courtyard. There were four archers she could see, two in guard towers on either side of the courtyard, and two on foot. There was a rather large pile of logs lashed together with rope just a few feet ahead and to the right of Rekha, a few large crates sitting here and there in the yard, and there were two tents standing along the left hand side. Whether anyone was inside and who they were, Rekha couldn't tell.

Malvus stood at the tower door, apparently supervising whatever they had been doing. *Everything according to plan so far...*

Before anyone got within twenty feet of her, Rekha shouted, "MALVUS!!"

His eyes gleamed as he took a step forward. "Rekha, at last! I see you've finally found the wisdom to turn yourself in."

She ignored him. "You have my friends, Malvus! I'll be taking them back, now!"

Malvus laughed, and some of the soldiers near him started laughing, too. "Oh, you'll see them very soon, for sure! If you promise to come along peacefully, I might even be able to put you in the same cell!"

"You misunderstand me, Malvus. If my friends are not brought back to me unharmed, the Legion — and its leadership — die today."

The laughter slowed, then ceased. Malvus' face was incredulous. "You can't be serious?! It's thirteen versus one, and I have four arrows pointed at your heart right now. You can't even use magic here. What could you possibly have to fight against us?"

"You mean aside from real fighting skill? I was thinking..." Rekha stepped to her right, clearing the door.

"...box-like tubes that shoot light."

A man in a black suit, newly emblazoned with a Baranix Spaceways logo, burst through the door Rekha had left open, firing his black, boxy weapon, and a bolt of light shot from it, sizzling through a soldier's chest before embedding deep in the Citadel's outer stone wall.

As the man dropped, chaos erupted. Rekha dove for the cover of the nearby pile of logs as arrows whistled overhead. More men in black suits came charging through the door, firing more bolts of light, as the soldiers in the courtyard ran for cover.

Rekha stayed low and watched as Barry and Veenix charged through the doorway, firing their weapons. A Legion soldier emerged from one of the tents with a crossbow and fired, the bolt striking one of the black-suited men in the shoulder. Barry and Veenix turned as one and fired four times, perforating the arbalist, before joining Rekha and the rest of the mercenaries in cover behind the lashed logs.

"You sure know how to throw a party, darling!" Baranix said as an arrow struck the stone wall behind them. "What kind of primitives are these, that they're attacking us with pointy sticks?!"

She ignored that. "Remember the plan. Keep an eye on me, and hold until I get inside the tower."

An arrow, fired at a high arc, planted itself in the ground a few feet away. Veenix turned to her and asked, "You were planning on going today, yes?"

Rekha peeked around the corner and spotted a soldier attempting to flank them. She leapt out and negated his startled sword swing by blocking his arm, using her other fist to punch him in his unprotected throat. As he staggered back, choking, she kicked him across the face, and he dropped as if he'd been poleaxed.

She spun around and spotted one of the on-foot archers, arrow drawn and aimed squarely for her chest, and realized that even with her Processing Speed at Real Time, she might not be able to dodge out of the way. But just then, a bolt of light caught the archer in the stomach, bending the man over, and his arrow fired uselessly into the ground.

The shooter looked uncomfortable in the black suit that had been loaned to him, and his kind eyes, great beak of a nose, and ginger beard peeked out from his helmet as he shouted, "Watch yer back, girly!"

Rekha took cover behind the landing of the east guard tower and shouted back, "Thanks, Dad!"

She peeked out and quickly surveyed the situation. All of the archers in the courtyard were down, and the mercenaries were keeping the remaining soldiers penned behind cover by randomly popping up and firing in their direction. She saw the door to the tower lazily swinging open, as if someone had just gone inside. With some alarm, she could see arrows starting to emerge from the slits in the tower itself.

It's now or never. Rekha yelled, "I need covering fire — aim for the slits in the tower!"

As one, all six mercenaries, even the one with a crossbow bolt in his shoulder, rose up from concealment and started firing at the tower.

Rekha darted across the field, making a beeline for the tower door. One of the hiding Legion soldiers suddenly jumped out from behind a crate, trying to cut her off, but she nimbly leapt away, even as he was cut down by lightfire. She reached the door, slipped inside, and pulled the door closed behind her.

"She's in! Let's go, wounded first!" Baranix shouted, rising up and firing at the thin slits in the wall. Two of the black-suited mercenaries stood up, alternatively firing at the tower and the crates the remaining soldiers were hiding behind.   Lucky supported the wounded man as they briskly ran for the open door behind them. Once they were inside, the rest of them slowly retreated, firing as they went.

Barry held fire at the door as the last two mercenaries escaped, followed by Veenix. He fired once more at the tower, saying quietly, "It's in your hands now, my dear girl."

He jumped through the door and closed it, and the door vanished.

Inside, Rekha checked for threats, saw none, and spun back to the large doors, lowering the big wooden bar that locked the door behind her. Taking a breath, she turned back around to survey the room.

She saw a huge central column of stone, at least ten feet wide. To her left were various tables surrounded by simple wooden chairs. Some of the tables were covered with parchment, some with leftover food and drink. She took a quick peek around the left side of the column, and saw what looked like a fully-stocked pantry, but didn't have time to investigate further, as three Legion appeared on Rekha's right, rushing down the stone stairs from the second floor.

At the top of the stairs, one of the soldiers nocked an arrow and drew it back while the other two continued to charge down the steps. Rekha grabbed a chair and held it in front of her just in time for the arrow to embed itself in the seat. She threw the chair at the soldiers heading towards her — one flinched mildly but remained standing, the other took the brunt of the impact, lost her footing, and crashed headlong down the stairs, laying motionless when she hit the floor, the broken chair tumbling after her.

The standing soldier reached the landing and swung an overhand chop with his blade. Rekha moved in and reached up, catching his wrist and trapping it with both hands. Automatically, she stepped past him and wrenched his arm, preparing to throw the man, but she spotted the archer at the top of the stairs nocking another arrow. Instead, she spun and pulled the soldier's body between her and the archer. The soldier screamed as the arrow plunged into his back.

Rekha pried the blade from his suddenly nerveless fingers and pushed him behind her, and he collapsed to the ground. She rushed up the stairs, and as the archer quickly pulled another arrow from his quiver, Rekha threw the blade at him. He wisely dropped the arrow and batted away the flung blade with the limbs of his bow, but that gave her the time she needed to reach him. He swung the bow clumsily at her, but she ducked and landed a one-two punch combination to the man's stomach.

The man growled with frustration as he dropped the bow and pulled a dagger from his belt. He swiped at her head, but she leaned back, narrowly avoiding the blade. He slashed diagonally downwards, but she deflected his arm with her own to the right, stepped in close, reached around his head with her right arm, and rotated his helmet back-to-front. As he flailed blindly and tried to remove his helmet, Rekha calmly moved past him and almost negligently kicked him down the stairs.

Legion soldiers were fewer and farther between as Rekha explored the second and third floors, but she dispatched them all. She noticed there was an identical center column on both floors, but despite being big enough for a small room, there was no door on the column on any level. Instead, there were individual stalls ringing the columns with equipment hung on the sides and back, and a small desk and chair underneath.

Approaching the stairs leading to the fourth floor, she heard a familiar voice.

"I'm tellin' you, bruv! She's too powerful! It's not worth it!"

She picked up the pace and climbed the stairs to see two soldiers arguing with each other a few feet past the landing.

"It's our JOBS, man, this is literally what we get paid to do!"

"And I'm tellin' you, bruv, it's not enough—oh, great crapples, she's already here."

As the two turned to stare at her, Rekha said, "Wilkin? Jamin?"

The soldier on the right turned back to his friend. "See what I mean, bruv? She's so powerful, she already knows our NAMES, bruv. Quit acting a fool!" He turned back to Rekha, holding his hands up. "I'm so sorry, miss. We don't want to get in your way. If you'd just be kind enough to let us leave, you can continue your rampage in peace."

Rekha pretended to be mulling it over. "The two of you are too good-hearted to be Legion." She smiled. "If you both solemnly swear to leave the Legion for good, I suppose I can let you pass."

Wilkin raised a hand. "I swear, happily, miss, thank you." He turned back to Jamin. "You swearin'? 'Cause I'm swearin'!"

Jamin looked unconvinced. "I don't know, man. We swore an OATH."

"Yeah, and now we're swearin' a better one." Wilkin leaned in close. "Look, man, I ain't loyal to the Legion. I'm loyal to you, and that's it."

Jamin said, "Really?"

Wilkin scoffed. "Yes, fool!" He turned back to Rekha. "Look, he swears. I promise. I'll keep him clean. Pinky swear."

Rekha smiled and turned, extending a hand towards the stairs and freedom. Wilkin grabbed Jamin and walked him to them, and they started to descend.

"See, bruv! This is us, turnin' over a new leaf!"

"Yeah, man, but what'll we do? I don't know how to do anything but soldiering."

"We'll open a bakery, bruv!"

"Man, you know how to bake?!"

"Naw, but I love the Abyss out of some cookies, bruv." And that was the last Rekha could hear before their voices trailed off.

She searched the fourth floor a little more intently. This was where Malvus' office was last time. However, the addition of the central column appeared to have made an individual office impractical, so instead of stalls, there was just one large desk up against the central column midway between both sets of stairs. She took a moment to peruse the parchment laying on it, and she found one promising document that stated in Malvus' handwriting, "By the Archprelate's orders, the prisoners are to be kept under the Eye."

Under the Eye? She puzzled that over for a second. *Wait, they're on the roof? But why?*

She'd already spent too long in one place, so she shrugged and dropped the parchment, sprinting for the stairs up.

As she climbed up to the fifth floor, she got a whiff of body odor as her head cleared the floor. She heard a noise and ducked instinctively. There was a great clang and a few sparks as a great sword cleaved the space where her head had been just a second ago. She ran past the blade and dove up the few remaining stairs, rolling until she could get to her feet, and looked back.

She recognized the large, hirsute man immediately as he lifted the two-handed blade. Especially as he was still not wearing a shirt. "Hello, Keldin."

"FOUL SORCERER!" He raised the blade over his shoulder and charged.

Rekha dodged away as he sliced down hard in her direction, and she got up between the central column and a heavy table. Like the other floors, there was no door here to a separate room, so Keldin's torture implements hung on hooks from the central column. She spotted a familiar pair of heavy tongs and admired the poetry of it, snatching them up quickly.

Keldin had maneuvered to the side of the table and swung horizontally, intending to cleave her in half, but Rekha ducked and dove forward, rolling past Keldin, standing up and smacking him on the back of the head with the tongs. He growled in pain and rage, and tried to deliver a massive upwards one-handed swing. Rekha swerved and dropped to one knee as the giant blade whooshed past and she swung the tongs for Keldin's knee as hard as she could. There was a loud crack, and Keldin screamed and dropped the blade as he fell.

Rekha calmly got to her feet as he huffed and puffed and struggled to rise, kneeling on his good knee. "Still a little too slow, Keldin." She smashed him across the face with the tongs, and he collapsed, unconscious. She dropped the tongs and carried on.

As she searched the sixth, seventh, and eighth floors, she found an awful lot of prison cells, but not a single prisoner. *What is going on here? Even if they're not keeping Sarli and Varian in these, shouldn't they have regular prisoners?* Rekha was starting to get a really bad feeling, and she rushed to complete her search.

The ninth floor was nearly barren, with only the now-expected wide central column and a few crates containing some non-perishable foods and building supplies. Rekha felt a small chill and she took a closer look at the stairs leading up. She could see the cloudy sky at the top, and raindrops lightly splashing on the stairs under the opening. *One way or another, my answers are up there.*

She took her time, carefully climbing up and checking every direction, trying to avoid an ambush. But none came, and as she climbed to the roof, she found out why.

The roof was even more barren than the floor below. She immediately saw she'd have to be careful as the stone was slick with rain, and there were no walls whatsover — going over the edge would result in a long fall to the ground. She also saw what was likely the reason for the large central column running the entire height of the tower: the huge red stone eye above her was held aloft by a massive red stone pillar that ran down into the building.

She probably would've examined that but she was currently consumed with something else — there was no one else up there with her. *I don't understand. The report definitely said the prisoners were under the Eye.* She carefully looked over the edge of the roof and saw the city of Cloydun below. *HALF THE TOWN IS 'UNDER THE EYE.'*

She said to herself, "I've been had. This is a trap."

The sound of someone clearing their throat caused her to spin around to see a familiar figure calmly standing on the landing, lightly armored, the rain running in rivulets down his shoulder pauldrons. His sword point was straight down to the floor and he was resting both hands on the pommel.

Malvus.

His greasy hair fluttered in the breeze. "Surprised it worked, really."

Chapter 33

He spoke over the sound of the rain. "Sorry. I hid in the pantry, and when you were gone, I unbarred the door. Reinforcements are on their way, but I'm hoping we'll have enough time to—"

Rekha interrupted him by holding a hand up. "Malvus, I need you to listen to me. In that other timeline, you were Legion, but you were also honorable."

He tilted his head to one side. "Other timeline?"

"Not important. Malvus, the Legion is NOT honorable. I know this isn't the same world, but you're the same person, and you have to know that you're better than them."

The captain brightened. "Oh, there's no question of that. What I need to know is whether I'm better than you."

Her mouth fell open. "What?"

"I mean, pulling people through a magic doorway with weapons that shoot light aside, you have fought your way through an entire company of my men, including my best and strongest. And all without using magic!"

"Malvus, please. I can slow time when I fight, giving me an advantage that you literally cannot overcome."

He laughed and raised a hand to indicate the giant red stone eye. "When we're standing under the largest mass of apotropaicite—"

Absently, Rekha corrected, "Anti-magic stone."

He ignored her. "—in the world? I think not. My two best men are at the bottom of the stairs with strict instructions not to let anyone past. Eventually, the Archprelate will get here and overrule me, but we should have a few minutes at least. It will be just my skill versus yours."

Rekha, frustrated with trying to argue with him, tried to access his properties, intending to use his X, Y, and Z coordinates to teleport him to safety, but the lock symbol appeared on the list. *Damn. And I can't spawn anything, either.*

She put as much pleading as she could into her gaze. "Malvus, I'm serious. For the last time, if you don't turn around and leave right now, your life is forfeit. Don't make me do this, I'm begging you."

In lieu of responding, Malvus reached behind him and pulled a short, slim sword from a sheath on his back, and negligently tossed it at Rekha's feet. "Arm yourself, please."

She sighed, and carefully picked up the short sword. "I'm sorry. I really did try to save you."

He grinned. "If nothing else, your confidence is certainly impressive. En garde!" And he struck a fighting pose.

As they fought, Rekha quickly realized Malvus' own confidence had not been misplaced. Unlike every other opponent she'd bested, he did not overextend himself or swing wildly. Every stroke or defense was calculated, measured. He fought aggressively and defensively in equal measure. He didn't go for killing blows as often as he tried to inflict small wounds. Rekha was forced to ruefully admit that perhaps even Lucky was not Malvus' equal with a blade.

And her speed advantage only went so far. Malvus lunged and thrust wide to Rekha's right. Seeing that he was going to miss, she chose not to defend and instead lined up a slash at his sword arm. He altered his thrust into a light slash and the blade cut into Rekha's side, even as her own sword drew blood from his arm. She gasped and staggered back a step as Malvus did the same.

She pressed a hand to her burning side and it came away bloody. The cut wasn't deep, but it was painful. "You're very good, Malvus."

He wiped away the blood from his sword arm with his other hand. "I'm the best. Your own skill is not inconsiderable." He swung his sword arm a few times before settling back into fighting form. "Shall we continue?"

Rekha considered the problem. *I can't match him while trying not to slip on the wet stone, and he only needs to catch me off-guard a few more times, or maybe just once.*

Lucky's advice rang in her mind like a bell. *If ya dinnae like the game, dinnae play.*

She shook her arm and leg muscles loose before setting her feet in a challenging stance on the rain-slick stone and staring at Malvus intently. He laughed, "I haven't enjoyed a fight this much in *years*," before advancing again.

If Malvus' fighting style would be categorized as proper swordfighting, what Rekha was now doing would be considered more akin to tavern brawling. He feinted a backhand slash at her right thigh, which she moved to block, before he flicked the sword up at her face. She ducked under the strike, leaned in, and punched him in the stomach. He sliced down at her, but she held her blade up to block it while launching a kneeling side kick to his knee, which he leapt backwards to avoid. Malvus advanced again and swung downwards at her shoulder, she battered it away as she spun into him, delivering an elbow to the nose.

He staggered back, carefully checking he wasn't near the edge, and held a hand to his nose. When he saw the blood on it, he glared at her.

Rekha smiled. "Still enjoying yourself?"

Malvus smiled darkly before launching a new series of strikes, these all aimed at the blade she was holding, until she accidentally let him push her sword out of position, and he wound up a massive slash to her left side. She got the blade in place just in time and managed to deflect the blow upwards so it missed her, but the impact jarred the weapon from her grasp, and it skittered across the stone roof before tumbling over the edge.

His grin grew wide, and he launched attack after attack, carefully controlled so that they would be easily avoidable, but wouldn't let Rekha get in close. She realized with alarm that he was maneuvering her towards the edge of the roof. During a lull in between slashes, she looked back to see barely three feet between her and the edge.

He grinned madly and raised his blade, but the odd angle at which he held the weapon suggested he wasn't slashing but trying to hit her with the pommel. Rekha stepped forward and caught his wrists with both hands, then pulled back, yanking him forwards and off-balance. She fell with him to the ground, coiling her legs under him like a spring, pushing off as hard as she could, launching his body up — and behind her.

He twisted in midair, dropping the sword and stretching out with both hands for the edge of the roof, but he was too far away. His despairing cry echoed back up the tower as he fell.

Still lying on the roof, she shouted, "At least you enjoyed it, right?"

The rain started to let up as she turned over and carefully got up. *I gotta figure out a way out of here and find my friends.*

But as she approached the stairs down, she heard a commotion. "What the devil are you blathering about? Stand clear or you'll join the prisoners, is that clear?"

The Archprelate. Rekha backed off and kept her eyes glued to the stairs.

A man with white hair emerged, head bowed, rushing up to the roof. He was wearing a long, dark robe that was busily flapping around his legs as he charged up the steps, his soft leather boots making almost no noise, especially compared to the armored soldiers following him up. When he reached the landing, he drew himself up to full height, allowing Rekha to see the jagged red eye symbol on his robe, the golden jagged eye pendant that appeared to be some kind of badge of office, and his ascetic, well-lined face, and hawk-like eyes.

If her jaw could have fallen to the floor, it would have. *"Dranheg?!"*

His face darkened. "This is a fine mess you've gotten us in, Rekha."

Chapter 34

Rekha gaped at him. "How? What? How?!"

Dranheg raised an eyebrow. "All excellent questions. I have to assume that you're the one responsible for un-creating Belgam."

She could only dumbly nod.

A couple of soldiers started to move towards her, but Dranheg held up a hand, and they backed off. He stepped forward himself instead. "I remember, in that other, original timeline, feeling sorry for myself, thinking I was condemning all of magic-kind to hiding and living in secrecy as I was piling up some books in one of the towers, and then the next second, I was on top of a pile of Magic Academy rubble, and I could suddenly remember a second life — one where, in a deal struck with the previous Archprelate, in exchange for my life and a position high up in the Legion, I'd betrayed the Academy and helped to exterminate all magic-kind."

Rekha covered her still-open mouth with one hand.

"It was about then that your friend Sarli noticed me. She was kind enough to help me down from the rubble, and when I mentioned feeling disorientated, your friend Varian got me some food and water to drink. Once I was feeling stronger, I repaid their kindness by teleporting them both to a Citadel prison cell."

Rekha was outraged. "What?! Why?!"

He smiled then. "Because I need your help, Rekha. You have the power to make anyone magical. I'm in charge of the Legion — or at least, I became in charge of the Legion once I'd killed the previous Archprelate. If the Legion all become magic-kind? Think about it — no magic-kind would ever have to fear the Legion again. Magic users could finally rule Primordia, as we were intended to do all along."

She reeled. "Are you INSANE?!"

His eyes were full of zeal. "Not in the slightest — with an army of magically-capable soldiers, we could take over Vakar in a single day, and the rest of Primordia will either fall in line or...they'll just fall. And, to show you I am making this offer in good faith, Sarli and Varian have not been harmed in any way." He turned towards the stairs down and shouted, "BRING UP THE PRISONERS!" Dranheg turned back to Rekha, practically bubbling with enthusiasm. "I know what they mean to you — they can join the Legion too, if they wish!

Rekha felt sick to her stomach as Sarli and Varian were marched up the stairs. While they did not appear injured at all, they had been firmly bound and gagged. Their eyes were wildly looking around until they spotted Rekha, at which point their eyes widened and both of them started excitedly moaning through their gags. Their escort admonished, "Shut up!" as he pushed them towards the Archprelate.

Dranheg turned and negligently flipped a hand at them. "Put them over by the edge of the roof, please."

"No, stop!" Rekha's plea was ignored as her friends' eyes dilated in fear.

Dranheg turned to look at Rekha with a smile as he put an almost-friendly hand on Sarli's shoulder. "I'd prefer to start our partnership on even footing and without bloodshed, which is probably a remnant of the old me talking. But the new me needs just a little more assurance, you know?" He clapped his hand down on Sarli's shoulder again, causing Rekha to jump as he laughed. "Now, what do you say? Partners?"

Rekha's head warned her to stay the course, even as her gut instinct on seeing Sarli in danger was to capitulate immediately, but as she watched, Sarli gave her a nearly-imperceptible shake of the head. *That's my girl.*

Steeling herself, Rekha straightened and looked Dranheg dead in the eye. "No."

The Archprelate laughed with disbelief. "Do you not understand? I'm fully prepared to push your friends off the roof. I'm talking about SAVING MAGIC, Rekha!"

Rekha imagined a future where the Legion overran the planet, immolating entire armies with lava balls and lightning storms. She remembered the horror she felt seeing Belgam's lava ball end the Magic Academy siege — and multiplied that by thousands. Rekha looked into Dranheg's eyes and decided then and there that she would see Belgam's endgame through.

Preparing herself, Rekha sighed and said, "No. You're talking about abusing magic. I've seen first-hand the horrors that occur when magic is used for war. We can be so much better than that."

Dranheg's jaw dropped. "Well, if that's your decision..." He turned to grab Sarli's other shoulder with his other hand even as Rekha coiled to leap at them and two soldiers stepped in, swords drawn, to bar Rekha's path to them.

"MAKE WAY FOR KING VAKAR VII!!"

Everyone froze. Two knights in full armor, wearing capes adorned with the crest of the Kingdom of Vakar, ascended the stairs to the roof, followed closely by a frail, wispy old man wearing a jeweled crown and a heavy ermine robe. He had close-cropped white hair and beard, and his face was stern.

Dranheg quickly stepped towards the king. "Your Majesty, as I said, this is strictly an internal matter, we can handle it."

The king sneered at him. "And I believed that until one of your men fell out of the sky and nearly landed on my sergeant-at-arms."

The Archprelate regarded Rekha icily. "Let me guess. Malvus?"

She shrugged. "You really should have some railings up here, you know?"

King Vakar VII looked down his nose at Rekha. "Who is this person?"

Dranheg wore an oily grin. "This is the last known mage, your Majesty. We were negotiating her surrender when you arrived."

The king folded his arms. "Well, clearly, she's a bigger threat than you've made her out to be."

"Oh, I'll fully admit, she's a skilled fighter, but she's outnumbered, and besides," the Archprelate raised a hand to indicate the giant red stone eye, "this apotropaicite sculpture extends in a six-foot-thick pillar all the way down to the basement, where an even larger reservoir of the stone resides. I have it on good authority that mages can't use magic anywhere in Cloydun thanks to the Eye. And she's standing right next to it."

Rekha looked up at the Eye. And inspiration struck. *I can't spawn or delete anything, but I CAN do other things.*

She focused on the stone's properties, but found them all locked. *Damn... wait a second. What if I...?* She pushed through to the special properties and scrolled all the way down, where she found the entire list of regular properties, only now she could change them.

She kept scrolling until she found 'Explosive' — which she changed to 'Yes'.

Rekha raised her voice. "Legion soldiers! And your Majesty! I will give you all one chance to leave this tower and save your lives. Be warned that if you choose to stay, you will die."

A guffaw emerged from the Legion soldier nearest her, which slowly spread to almost every man standing on the roof. Even the king's knights appeared to be chuckling.

The king was the only one who appeared to be uncertain. "Are you sure about this, Dranheg?"

The Archprelate looked at Rekha and folded his arms. "Trust me, your Majesty. She's completely harmless."

She sighed with regret. "I tried. Now you'll see just how harmless I really am." And she started moving her hands around and mumbling nonsense phrases in what she hoped was a mystical manner.

Some of the Legion raised their weapons, preparing to attack, but the Archprelate shouted, "No! Hold! This nonsense should be a good demonstration for his Majesty."

Rekha concentrated on pulling all the heat from herself, just like she had when she was young, but she also reached out, pulling heat from everyone nearby. Dranheg's confidence faltered somewhat as he involuntarily shivered.

She focused all that heat onto a single point, and as she raised a hand to the Eye, she thought, *Thank you, Irynn.*

Rekha released the spell, screaming, "BURN!!"

A small, candle-like flame appeared, bobbing in the air as it lazily floated towards the Eye.

Dranheg and the Legion soldiers erupted with laughter. Even the king gave a little bit of an uncertain chuckle.

Rekha paid them no heed, instead paying close attention to counting down roughly how far away the tiny dancing flame was from the Eye. *Ten feet... nine...*

The Archprelate was still laughing as he said, "You see, your Majesty?"

Eight feet...Seven...

"She's one of the strongest mages we've ever come across."

Six...Five...

"And she's completely..." Dranheg faltered.

Four...

Rekha risked a look to see Dranheg looking at her, then quickly focusing on the Eye.

Three! GO!!!

Rekha burst into a sprint, racing past the Legion, caught off-guard in their laughter, heading straight for her friends.

Two.

Dranheg's head whipped around, and he shouted, "No no no!" as he instinctively put himself in front of her friends with his arms stretched wide as if to block her.

One.

Rekha did not stop, instead charging directly into Dranheg, spreading her arms wide, tackling all three of them off the side of the roof.

A huge explosion detonated behind them, the blast pushing them farther away from the side of the tower, and Rekha could feel the heat on her back.

She quickly grabbed tight hold of Varian and Sarli's clothing with her hands and struggled to focus on her own properties as they fell.

She changed her race from 'Primordian' to 'Dragon'.

Instantly, her view changed to a reddish tinge, but thankfully, she'd practiced this transformation and knew what to expect. Sarli and Varian didn't, and their eyes bugged out in incredulity and fear as she carefully kept firm hold of them without hurting either of them with her razor-sharp talons.

Dranheg, for his part, screamed bloody murder directly in her face.

Rekha screamed back at him, carefully bathing just his hair in flame, before flapping her great wings once, separating from the Archprelate, screaming with his hair on fire as he continued his long fall to the ground.

Rekha locked her wings and slowly pulled up, curving their downward trajectory into a gentle soar above the treetops, away from the Citadel and towards safety.

He was broken and burned. But somehow, miraculously, he was alive.

Dranheg laughed even though it hurt to do so. As best he could tell, he'd landed on one of the tents in the tower's courtyard, and possibly something soft underneath that, it was hard to tell. And the landing had quelled the flames in what was left of his hair.

He couldn't move, but at least he was alive.

The Legion would find him soon and get him healed up, and then there'd be preparations to make. It'd be easy enough to blame the death of King Vakar VII on Rekha and shift sympathies towards the Legion in the Kingdom.

His train of thought was broken by the sound he'd been hearing since he landed, but he only just now identified it: more explosions. The tower was continuing to explode above him, belching fire and launching rocks and debris into the city and the lake nearby.

That's when he remembered what he saw when he checked the Eye's properties — and that the sculpture went all the way down to a massive repository in the basement.

Dranheg screamed as the world exploded around him.

As Rekha and her precious cargo cleared Cloydun's border, a massive explosion erupted behind her. She twisted her head to look back. The entire Citadel and about half of the city docks was gone, a huge, roiling orange fireball slowly dissipating in its place.

With grim satisfaction, Rekha smiled — a neat trick for a dragon — and flew on towards home.

Chapter 35

Rekha carried them all the way back to Bromsford, stopping at the clearing she used to spend time in with her friends so very long ago. She lowered herself slowly, until she was low enough to the ground to set her friends down without hurting them.

She carefully landed a few feet away and changed her race back to 'Primordian', before collapsing to the ground and shuddering with exhaustion. Varian and Sarli ran over to her, and she weakly snapped away their restraints and gags.

Sarli knelt at her side. "Are you okay?"

Rekha breathed heavily as she nodded. "I'll be fine in a minute. It's been a busy day."

Varian was staring at her incredulously. "Rey, I didn't know you could do that — and the Legion are — and the KING?!"

Sarli turned back to him and raised an eyebrow. "As she said, busy day." She turned back to Rekha. "But what happened to the Legion not turning you into a killer?"

Rekha clasped her hands. "I gave them every chance to leave. The smart ones did." She saddened. "But Sarli, I'm so sorry. They killed Phi."

Sarli's eyes filled with tears, but she didn't reply.

Light flashed in front of them as a door suddenly appeared in the center of the clearing. Rekha recognized the white ceramic door as the same door Belgam had taken her through to the hub. *This is it. The game's end.*

Rekha struggled to get up even as the door slid open. Sarli helped her up as she said, "That's my cue. Time to go."

Varian's eyes widened as he turned and pointed behind them. "What in the Abyss is that?!"

Rekha and Sarli turned to see the sky had turned completely black. The sun and the endless blue were gone, leaving only a few clouds still coasting lazily in the blackness, and the smoke trail leading to the sky from the destruction in Cloydun.

Rekha quickly spawned a door to the side, then put her hand on it and focused on the words 'Baranix's ship hallway', and snapped her fingers. She threw the door open to reveal the familiar dark green walls and solid white floor of Barry's ship.

"Varian, get inside, quickly!"

His voice wavered as he pointed towards Bromsford. "But...but what about my family?"

She grabbed him by the shoulders as a wind started to whip through the clearing. "They're all in there, everybody from Bromsford, Sarli's mom, your family, Dargen, even Fulgin. It's safe there. But you have to go, Primordia won't be safe for long!"

Her oldest friend cocked an eyebrow. "You're following right after...right?"

Remembering that he did not have memories from the original timeline, Rekha lied to him very carefully. "Sarli and I will both be there shortly — there's just something that I have to do, and I can't do it while you're still here, so please, hurry!"

He looked at her soberly for a moment, then hugged her tightly, and after a moment, pulled Sarli into a three-person hug. "Love you both." He let them go, looking into both of their faces before striding to the door.

He paused at the doorway, turning back for a moment. "I'll see you when you get here." And he turned and walked into the ship.

Sarli grinned. "If Primordia's getting destroyed, just send everyone into a different simulation." Her eyes were filled with love as she looked at Rekha. "Clever girl."

"I've been saying that about you since we met!" She reached for Sarli and took her hand.

They kissed longingly for several moments.

Rekha, with bitter regret, broke off the kiss. "You have to go, too. I won't be able to do this unless I know you're safe." She looked up and saw that the clouds were now gone. The sky was now pure black.

Sarli nodded. "And you'll come get us when you're rebuilt or restored or whatever?"

Rekha didn't trust herself to speak, so she simply nodded.

Sarli turned to leave, and seized by a desperate impulse, Rekha pulled her back in close and kissed her again, doing her best to pour all of her love into this one moment. It was Sarli's turn to break off and she looked at Rekha with mild confusion.

Rekha simply said, "For love."

Sarli, apparently mollified, grinned at her and turned and walked towards the door. But as she got closer, her walk slowed until she stopped, putting a hand on the doorway and looking at the ground.

Rekha shouted, "What are you waiting for?! Your mom's in there! Go, please!"

Sarli put her other hand on Irynn's pendant resting on her chest. Then she turned back to face Rekha, her eyes wide with sudden realization. "You're not going to be rebuilt...are you?"

Before she could stammer a denial, Rekha burst into tears. "Sarli, please, you have to — I have to know you're safe!!"

Sarli turned back to the doorway and looked at the ship's hallway for a moment. "Just how stupid would I have to be?"

"What?!"

Sarli looked back at Rekha and snapped her fingers, deleting the door to the ship.

Rekha yelled, "WHAT ARE YOU DOING?!?!"

"I'm not going anywhere."

Rekha fell to her knees, openly sobbing. "Sarli, *please*...you'll DIE if you stay here!"

Sarli calmly walked back to Rekha, kneeling down in front of her. "My love, haven't you learned anything?"

Rekha stared at her.

"Death doesn't matter, Rekha. Life is what matters. What you do with the time that you have is the *only thing* that matters." Sarli's eyes moistened. "So if the love of my life has only a short time left...I'm staying with her."

Rekha began to panic as she looked south and realized she could no longer see the smoke from the fire in Cloydun. "I can't...I can't let you die. Those four hundred humans — I cannot trade your life for theirs!"

"Well, it's not your choice, Rekha. It's mine. And I *can*. You have the chance now to save an entire race. We can do it — together!"

"How?!"

"Take me with you!"

Rekha stared at her a moment, then got up, taking Sarli's hand and walking her over to the doorway leading to the hub. She attempted to pull Sarli's hand across the threshold, but while her hand freely crossed, Sarli's was held back by some invisible force.

"Do you understand? I can't take you with me. Sarli, please just go!"

Sarli's eyes were intense as she looked this way and that in concentration, until suddenly her eyes met Rekha's with a look she'd seen before. "Merge us together!"

Rekha was flabbergasted. "What?!"

"Remember that class we took at the Academy? Rekha, you're made out of six people — what's one more? There's gotta be a way!"

Rekha noted with alarm that she could no longer see any sign of Bromsford through the trees, and though it was difficult to tell because it was pure black, it sure felt like the blackness was getting closer. But she did her best to shove her growing panic aside and consider Sarli's suggestion. *Blatherskite said merging was covered in Advanced Properties class, but he never said how it was done!* She looked through the list of Sarli's properties quickly but found nothing promising.

Wait. What if Advanced Properties is about using properties in a different way? Rekha focused on Sarli's properties, but instead of going through the list, she attempted to pull them towards herself. To her surprise, they moved easily, and once they were near enough to her, Rekha's own properties appeared. When they collided, a new box appeared, saying "Merge these characters (may have unintended side effects)?"

Seeing the blackness reach the treeline, Rekha selected 'Yes'.

Instantly, Rekha/Sarli noticed a massive change. Aside from the physical differences of being both taller and shorter than she was used to, and her skin being darker and lighter than before, she felt all the joy Rekha/Sarli had ever felt in her presence, how beautiful she was in her eyes, and the love she had for her. The ecstasy of those emotions filled her with warmth.

The blackness raced across the field towards the doorway, and Rekha/Sarli spun and stepped into the doorway, aligning her center with the door's threshold just as the blackness closed in on her.

The impact launched Rekha/Sarli into the hub, and she braced for collision with the door opposite, but she ripped through it as though it were little more than tissue paper.

She tumbled into the void beyond, small pieces of the hub falling after her.

Chapter 36

The bridge of the HMS Terra Nova was absolutely silent.

Humans had not occupied the space in hundreds of years, though evidence of their presence could still be found. The plaque on the wall read, "Humanity Migration Ship Terra Nova: may she carry us safely to our new home." One of the astronauts who had launched the ship had scrawled underneath it in black marker, "And we really hope there's beer."

The windshield revealed a landscape not unlike parts of Arizona. TOI 700 d was a rocky world, featuring stone plateaus and scrubby vegetation growing here and there amongst the sand. The reddish sun lent the vista an eerie look — or it would have, if anyone could see it.

The rest of the bridge was relatively pristine. The control panel's knobs and switches lay untouched for centuries. The multiple monitors still displayed readouts of various statistics, like the external temperature of 42.4 degrees Fahrenheit, 5.8 degrees Celsius, or 278.23 degrees Kelvin.

Suddenly, the monitor dead center of the control panel went dark. A cursor appeared in the upper left, flashing like a small white pillar blinking in and out of existence.

```
>Where am I?
Syntax error.
>This must be the terminal.
Syntax error.
>grant access user1 -su
Superuser access granted.
>reboot -su
```

```
Warning: Rebooting the main computer while
in-flight is extremely dangerous. All
temporary memory will be deleted. Are you
sure you wish to reboot (Y/N)?
>Y
Rebooting in 5
4
3
2
>I love you
Syntax error.
1
```

Chapter 37

Trina awakened in a room she recognized, all stone walls and flooring. She got out of the quite comfortable bed, and walked to the wooden door. She opened it, and walked through to find a hallway, where a group of teenagers in varicolored robes were leaning against the opposite wall, quietly chatting.

She asked, "Excuse me?"

They stopped and looked her over. One of the girls asked, "What class is the white robe for?"

She grinned and looked down at her lab coat. "Oh, uh...I suppose you'd call it Potions class?"

The students looked at each other and shrugged. The older boy asked, "You need something?"

"Yes, I'm looking for Cris, Alera, Meryn, and the others."

"The Progenitors? They've been hanging out down in the courtyard lately, by the water." He pointed behind her. "Head down those stairs to the first floor, the front door to the courtyard is just opposite, you can't miss it."

Trina gave them her thanks, and turned and headed down to the courtyard. The young man had given her excellent directions, and when she opened the large double front doors, she had to shield her eyes from the brightness of the sun. She looked around and saw the large stables building to her left, and to her right, there was a break in the wall encircling the courtyard, and in its place was the edge of a large pond. Seven people sat or lay in the grass and watched the water gently lapping.

As she approached, Trina smiled and said, "Hello, my friends!"

Several of them turned and waved, saying, "Hey", or "Hello!" as she strode down to the very edge of the lake so she could see all of their faces.

Victoria looked absolutely content in a bright blue sundress, laying as she did with her head in Alera's lap and her legs in Cris'. Alera idly stroked her hair while Cris gently massaged her calves. Mai was radiant, wearing a bright, flowery shirt, dark silk pants, and fingerless black leather gloves, sipping a dark brown concoction from a large glass. Ethan looked comfortable sitting on the ground next to her. Meryn sat demurely in her blue scrubs, and Jamie lay with his head in her lap, his eyes closed as she gently rubbed his bald head. A border collie and a grey-and-black striped shorthair cat approached Trina excitedly, and she leaned down to pet them enthusiastically.

"Hello, Dr. Giggles, Dave, how are you?" She stood up, and the animals went back to sniffing around the edge of the pond curiously.

"Did everybody get out?" Victoria asked.

Trina beamed. "Yup."

Ethan's eyes widened. "Everyone?"

"That's correct. As of this morning, despite some technical difficulties, the last person was safely awakened and released from their cryomedic chamber."

Cris smiled wide. "That's incredible. We didn't lose anyone?"

"Nope. Every single human being on the ship made the trip, safe and sound. We have a second chance now. And it's all thanks to all of you."

Jamie didn't open his eyes. "There's one more person you should be thanking."

Trina's smile faltered a moment, but then she knelt down next to Meryn. "How are you doing, Jamie?"

Jamie didn't respond.

Meryn looked into Trina's eyes. "He'll be okay. Don't take it personally. He's mostly angry with himself."

Jamie pouted cartoonishly. "I am not."

Trina burst out laughing at his exaggerated response, causing Meryn to giggle, and finally Jamie and a few of the others joined in.

"See?" Meryn said. "He'll be just fine. That's not to say there isn't any fallout. He's working on repairing things, though."

Mai finished her drink. "Mmm. Trina, if you're going to be here a while, you should head on down to Wildfall and hit up Wilkin and Janim's bakery. They've got a caramel apple cheesecake that is literal heaven on a plate, dollface."

Trina stood up, looking confused. "Wait. Isn't this a fantasy world? Did they have cheesecake in medieval times?"

Ethan smiled knowingly. "Uh, one of us may have cheated."

Alera immediately replied, "Shut up, it's delicious!"

The group laughed lightly.

"So, what are you guys going to do with your retirement?" Trina crossed her arms.

Meryn looked up and softly said, "We've been talking about it, and while we want to spend a little more time together, after that, we're considering deactivation."

Trina's face fell. "Oh."

Cris explained, "We've served our purpose, and explored every fantasy we could conjure over thousands of years. It's time to rest." The rest of the group all looked at Trina and nodded in agreement.

"If that's your decision, then I'll respect it. And I'll miss you."

Meryn looked up at her warmly. "You can re-create us any time. They won't have our memories, but they'll still be us."

Cris smirked. "Just maybe don't make them do tasks that nearly get them killed this time?"

The others laughed and Trina grimaced. "I don't think I'll be doing that."

Ethan smiled. "Well, I would sure hope not."

"I don't mean the Thane program. I'm talking about re-creating you."

The seven just looked at her and waited.

Trina explained, "You all are heroes. You should be honored and appreciated. I won't cheapen you by making copies."

Meryn nodded and stroked Jamie's head. "Hear that? You're one of a kind." She leaned down and kissed his head.

"Well," Trina breathed, "I suppose I've put it off long enough. Where is she?"

Trina walked into the stables and immediately saw a young woman gently brushing a brown-and-white-spotted roan horse. The young woman wore brown cotton pants tucked into leather boots that came up to mid-calf, a leather belt, and a simple white blouse. Her brown hair was in a ponytail that came down to her shoulder blades, and when she saw Trina, her smile carried up into her big brown eyes.

"Sarli! How are you?"

Sarli set the brush down and reached out for a hug, which Trina eagerly accepted. "I'm good! How are you doing?" They released the hug. "Are the rest of the humans settling in on your new planet?"

Trina pushed her glasses back up. "Yes, we've been building the colony slowly but surely. Most of us still live on the ship for now, which is one of the things I need to talk to the headmistress about. Is she around?"

The voice came from behind her. "Oh, she's around."

Trina turned to see Rekha standing in the stable doorway, looking resplendent in a sky blue robe over her black leather vest, black canvas trousers and tall leather riding boots. She held up a hand to Trina, forestalling her greetings, and said, "Hey, love, your mother's asking what to do for dinner — I said I'd ask you."

Sarli frowned. "Aren't we gonna eat with the students, like usual?"

Rekha crossed to her as Sarli put away her brush. "It's the first time your mom has come to stay with us since we got married, I'm sure she just wants to do something special for us."

Sarli snorted. "She probably just wants to one-up Lucky with how much she spoils us. You saw how they looked at each other. We could probably save ourselves a lot of trouble and just lock them in a room together for a day."

"Anything that much fun, I'd rather be doing myself." Rekha leaned in and kissed her.

Sarli returned the kiss with enthusiasm. "Don't give me any ideas. Besides," she indicated the third person in the room, "what about Trina?"

"She's not invited."

Trina smiled warmly. "I can come back another time if you're busy."

Rekha managed to look a little apologetic. "Sorry to keep you. We're newlyweds, and being headmistress keeps me on my toes." She looked past Trina. "Speak of the devil..."

Varian poked his head in the door. "Sorry to interrupt. Can I borrow you for a sec? Jalyn and Elspeth need a word about student housing, apparently some of the dorms are double-booked this month. Also, Galvan says if we're bringing in more magical creatures, we're going to have to expand the pens."

"Sounds like we need to expand the whole school!" She turned to Trina. "Please stick around, I'll be just a few minutes, I promise." With that, she headed out the door with Varian.

Trina turned back to Sarli. "She is extraordinary."

Sarli smiled. "That she is." The smile faded, and she adopted a more serious look. "I never got to thank you for saving her — for saving us. I still don't know how you did it. Rekha tried explaining it to me, but I'm afraid her grasp of technological jargon is a little lacking."

"Oh, that was nothing. The main computer on the ship periodically makes something called a System Restore Point — basically a full backup of the entire computer AND the Cris System — and it's taken whenever something unusual or unexpected happens. Now, players are expected to move between simulations on the Cris System, but not characters. And a large mass of characters moving between simulations definitely qualifies as unexpected."

Sarli nodded with understanding. "So when Rekha saved everybody by sending them from Primordia to Barry's ship, it triggered the System Restore

Point, backing up everything, even Rekha's data."

"Exactly. We reconstituted the both of you from the Restore Point. We were able to recover Meryn, Cris and the others from their backups on the Cris System, they rebuilt Primordia, and you know the rest." Trina paused a moment. "I meant no disrespect by discerning between characters and players just now."

Sarli's eyes widened. "Oh! None taken." She grinned. "I see Rekha's rubbing off on you."

"Not at all." Trina beamed. "Her concern for those less privileged than herself is what most endears her to me."

Sarli gave a half smile. "It's top ten for me, for sure."

Trina replied with a smirk.

Rekha strode back through the door and sighed. "Now, Trina — I assume you're here about the Accords?"

Trina nodded. "I'll try and be quick, I know you're busy. Some of our people are having trouble adjusting to the new environment, so we wanted to discuss the possibility of having other humans use the Cris System to visit simulations. Of course, no one would be allowed to modify either the Primordia or Allied Systems simulations in any way."

"Or anyone in them?"

"Of course."

Rekha bit her thumb. "My concern is how would we handle legal situations? If some human comes in here and breaks a bunch of laws, how would they be punished? In here, or out there?"

Trina rapidly tapped on a small device that looked like a little glass window in a hard opaque shell. "That is a valid concern. I'll bring it up with the Council and draft a proposal. Now, what about the reverse?"

Rekha was confused. "Sorry?"

"Sorry, that's my fault, I should have clarified. If we come up with a way that an A.I. like yourself can come across into our world, say, for example, in a robot drone body, would that be something you or other A.I. would be interested in?"

Rekha looked over at Sarli, who just shrugged. "I can't say I'd ever really want to leave, but I can't say nobody would be interested. Put us down as interested for now, assuming we'd be under the same restraints as humans visiting us."

"Gotcha. I'll relay that to the Council." Trina tapped a few more times and then put the device in her pocket. "Thanks so much. I'll bring a draft next time and you can look it over. Have a great day, you two!"

Sarli waved as Trina headed for the stable door. "Bye, Trina! Next time stay for dinner, okay?"

Trina smiled wide. "Absolutely!" She walked through the door and was gone.

Rekha reached out and took Sarli's hand. "Hey, next time she comes around and we talk business like that, feel free to jump in with suggestions and ideas. Don't feel like you have to stay in the background."

"I don't, it's just...I know how much the Human-A.I. Accords mean to you."

"Codifying our rights with a race that could delete us and our worlds on a whim felt very important for some reason."

Sarli laughed. "I just mean...it's your baby."

"Yeah, but we're partners. Abyss, you're my *wife*. I trust your judgment MORE than my own. And these Accords are for ALL A.I.'s, not just those labeled as 'players'."

"I guess I'm just intimidated by how gung-ho you are about them."

"Well, you gotta nail these things down quick while they're still grateful." Rekha wiped her brow. "Let's get out of this stuffy place. Hey, Phi? Wanna go for one of our wicked rides?"

Phi nickered and pawed her left forehoof at the floor.

Sarli grinned. "I'll get her ready."

Rekha walked out into the sunshine, which was so bright she had to shield her eyes. As such, she didn't see the young woman approaching until she was within a few feet of Rekha. Startled, she jumped.

The girl with her ginger hair braided into twin pigtails smiled. "You look like you've seen a ghost, Rekha."

"Sorry, Irynn. It's been a difficult day."

Irynn turned back to indicate a small group of teenagers in what looked like brand new black robes standing awkwardly in front of the Academy doors. "I got a fresh batch of newbies ready to be infused with magic for the first time."

"They can wait a bit. Check with Malvus, see if he's available to give them an intro to Self-Defense classes, that ought to whet their appetite. I'm taking my wife for a little ride."

Rekha turned back to the center of the courtyard, where Sarli was saddling Phi while eyeing Rekha curiously.

"What was that about?" Sarli asked.

Rekha shrugged. "I guess, even if it can be undone, sometimes, death stays with you."

Sarli swung up into the great horse's saddle, and extended a hand to her love. "You don't still blame yourself for—"

"No, no." She took Sarli's hand, stepped in the stirrup, and swung her other leg over to sit right behind her wife. "But I haven't forgotten, either. Let's ride!"

Phi transformed into a huge roan-colored dragon, with brown paws, head, and tip of the tail, but more of a white-brown mix over the rest of her body. She reared back in raw exuberance, and inhaled deeply.

"Hey!" Sarli yelled smartly. "What did we say?! Not until we're airborne."

Phi exhaled slowly, allowing only miniscule flames to exit her mouth.

"Good girl." She stroked Phi's elongated neck, then turned back to face Rekha. "You ready?"

Rekha held her face with one hand and kissed her intently.

When she broke the kiss, Sarli raised an eyebrow. "For luck?"

"No." Rekha kissed her again. "For you."

Sarli grinned and turned back around. "Ya!"

Phi ponderously flapped her huge wings a few times, ascending a few feet each time. She cleared the Academy wall and started gliding over the forest, flapping less and less as she gained speed. Soon, she was soaring through the air.

Rekha clung to Sarli as they rose higher and higher. Sarli shouted, "Now, Phi!" And Phi blasted fire in a wide swath, roaring with satisfaction even as the fire dissipated harmlessly in the open air.

As they swooped through the sky, Rekha let out her own roar of satisfaction.

"YAHOOOOOO!!"

About the Author

Aaron Randolph was born in Kenmore, NY in 1980. Growing up, he was fascinated with computers and theatre, eventually choosing the latter as his major at Niagara University. After leaving school, he found himself drawn back to computers and became an IT Professional in 2020. In his spare time, Aaron enjoys building computers, hosting the BFYTW podcast with his friends, consuming visual novels like Danganronpa and Zero Escape, and watching British television shows like Taskmaster, all of which inspired his passion for writing and the impact of fiction. Rekha is Aaron's second book and the second book of the Thane series.

* * *

Links

www.bfytwpod.com/THANE

Author's E-mail: thane@bfytwpod.com

BFYTW Podcast: www.bfytwpod.com

www.ingramcontent.com/pod-product-compliance
Lightning Source LLC
Chambersburg PA
CBHW060352310726
48976CB00003B/786